When the trials begin,
in soul-torn solitude despairing,
the hunter waits alone.
The companions emerge
from fast-bound ties of fate
uniting against a common foe.

When the shadows descend,
in Hell-sworn covenant unswerving
the blighted brothers hunt,
and the godborn appears,
in rose-blessed abbey reared,
arising to loose the godly spark.

When the harvest time comes,
in hate-fueled mission grim unbending,
the shadowed reapers search.
The adversary vies
with fiend-wrought enemies,
opposing the twisting schemes of Hell.

When the tempest is born,
as storm-tossed waters rise uncaring,
the promised hope still shines.
And the reaver beholds
the dawn-born chosen's gaze,
transforming the darkness into light.

When the battle is lost,
through quake-tossed battlefields unwitting
the seasoned legions march,
but the sentinel flees
with once-proud royalty,
protecting devotion's fragile heart.

When the ending draws near,
with ice-locked stars unmoving,
the threefold threats await,
and the herald proclaims,
in war-wrecked misery,
announcing the dying of an age.

—*As written by Elliandreth of Orishaar, c. −17,600 DR*

FORGOTTEN REALMS®

THE
SUNDERING

THE COMPANIONS
R.A. Salvatore

THE GODBORN
Paul S. Kemp

THE ADVERSARY
Erin M. Evans

THE REAVER
Richard Lee Byers
February 2014

THE SENTINEL
Troy Denning
April 2014

THE HERALD
Ed Greenwood
June 2014

FORGOTTEN REALMS

ERIN M. EVANS
THE ADVERSARY

FORGOTTEN REALMS

THE
SUNDERING

Book
III

THE ADVERSARY
©2014 Wizards of the Coast LLC.

Published by Wizards of the Coast LLC. Manufactured by: Hasbro SA, Rue Emile-Boéchat 31, 2800 Delémont, CH. Represented by Hasbro Europe, 2 Roundwood Ave, Stockley Park, Uxbridge, Middlesex, UB11 1AZ, UK.

Prophecy by: James Wyatt
Cartography by: Mike Schley
Cover art by: Tyler Jacobson
First Printing: May 2014

9 8 7 6 5 4 3 2 1

ISBN: 978-0-7869-6536-6
ISBN: 978-0-7869-6437-6 (ebook)
620A6852000001 EN

The Hardcover edition Cataloging-in-Publication data is on file
with the Library of Congress

Contact Us at Wizards.com/CustomerService
Wizards of the Coast LLC, PO Box 707, Renton, WA 98057-0707, USA
USA & Canada: (800) 324-6496 or (425) 204-8069
Europe: +32(0) 70 233 277

Visit our web site at **www.dungeonsanddragons.com**

This book is dedicated to the memory of Benjamin G. Goodier,
who came of age in the Santo Tomas Internment Camp
and survived to continue a whole chain of Benjamins,
including my favorites—Benjamin K. and Benjamin I.
His stories sparked the idea for this book.

PROLOGUE

Frost crusted the leaf curled a handspan from Farideh's face. But it shouldn't have.

She shut her eyes, a thousand half-formed thoughts buzzing in her skull. But only one took hold: it had been hot enough the day before that there was no way frost—

The *hyah, hyah, hyah* of a crow scattered her thoughts. She winced and turned her face to the ground. Hot the day before . . . or maybe it was the same day, or maybe it was a lifetime ago. She couldn't be sure of anything but the cold air, the hard ground, and the bare forest around her, vanishing into thick patches of fog.

Farideh pushed herself up. She brushed away bits of leaf and dirt, and hissed as the motion sent a tremor through her arm. Every muscle felt stiff and overdrawn. And her head—the tiefling blinked heavily as the throb behind her eyes surged to a state that couldn't be ignored. She pressed one hand to her eye, cupping the curve of her horn ridge as she did, trying to remember what had happened. Maybe she'd fallen ill. Maybe she'd drunk too much whiskey. Maybe Havilar . . .

Farideh looked around the clearing for her twin. The light through the tree branches was bleached as white as old bone and just as lifeless. She eyed the ragged edge of fog creeping over the

1

clearing, a season's worth of dead leaves, the bare sentinels of trees staring down at her. Their low creak of protest broke the silence as a sagging earthmote settled into the trees to her left.

Farideh jumped to her feet and scuttled back, away from the leaning trees. The floating island of earth was caught by the trunks like a rock clutched in a giant hand. It hung so low that she could make out the strange blue flowers flocking the meadows beneath its rocky spires. And it was slowly sinking lower.

Earthmotes don't do that, she thought, her panicked breath a cloud of vapor on the cold air. A taproot snapped and a tree crashed to the ground.

The faint and unmistakable smell of brimstone drifted on the air.

Hyah, the crow screamed. *Hyah.*

Farideh wet her mouth, not daring to look away from the earthmote. There was a nauseous feeling building in her stomach and the small of her back. Her tail started to lash the deadfall. Brimstone meant Hells-magic. Portals. Hands shaking, she checked her sleeve for the rod she carried, the rod that helped her channel the same dangerous, boiling magic. It was gone. Worse, the shirt was not hers.

Her heart squeezed. *Something's wrong,* she thought, looking for the devils between the trees. *Something worse than Havi's whiskey . . .*

Havilar. The cold sunk down to the core of her. Oh gods— where was her sister?

"Havilar!" she cried, though her voice was hoarse, as stiff and unwilling as her muscles. "Havi! Havi!" The fog smothered her shouts. "Havilar!"

Someone groaned behind Farideh, and her heart tripped over itself. She ran at the noise, stumbling as if her legs were relearning how to move. She crashed into the patch of ferns her twin sister rose weaving out of.

"Fari?" she said, in a voice just as broken as Farideh's.

"What…?" Farideh threw her arms around her sister and held her tight, watching the grove over her shoulder. The smell of brimstone pricked at her nose again.

"What happened?" Havilar said. She pushed Farideh back far enough to look around. "Where are we?" She frowned. "What happened to your face?"

Farideh shook her head, as the same question died on her lips. For all her young life, Havilar's face had been a mirror of her own—same horns, same cheekbones, same softly curved nose. The only difference was Farideh's silver left eye against Havilar's gold ones. If that was still so, then the same subtle but undeniable changes had been wrought on Farideh's own features.

Thinner, she thought studying Havilar. Maybe harder. The chin was firmer and the cheekbones sharper. Hollows under the eyes that hadn't been there before. Paler.

"Your hair," Farideh said. Havilar reached for her braid, grabbing instead a hank of purplish-black hair, smooth as silk.

Havilar looked around at the deadfall. "Where's my glaive?" she asked muzzily. She pressed a hand to her head and winced.

The earthmote crept nearer to earth, and another tree moaned and cracked. Havilar jumped. "*Karshoj*." She looked around the clearing. "What happened? It's all . . . different. Isn't it?"

It's different—Lorcan's words echoed in her memory. *You're different. I chose you over her back there. I was ready to let her attack me so you could get away. Doesn't that mean anything?*

Lorcan.

Farideh's pulse sped. It stirred up her pact magic and sent a surge of shadowy smoke wafting off her skin, through the strange shirt: Lorcan, the cambion she drew her powers through, should have been there.

But *all* of their things were missing, and so were their traveling companions. And while the half-devil might have vanished without saying a word if he found the means—

3

In the same moment, Havilar's thoughts seemed to clear. "Brin." She lurched out of Farideh's arms and out of the ferns, shouting for the young man she fancied who would never have left her behind. "Brin! *Brin*!"

No one answered but the crow, hopping from tree to tree like a loose shadow, flapping noisily.

"We must have . . . ," Farideh started, but she had no answer. "He must be . . ." No weapons, no gear, no armor, no Brin. No Lorcan. Brimstone on the air. Cold. She wet her mouth again. Something was wrong. She had to remember what. The crow stopped, bobbing on the branch directly ahead of her.

Here, the crow was shouting. *Here, here, here.*

Only it wasn't a crow. A tiny devil with black wings and a cruel, clever face hopped down to a lower branch, and grinned at the twins with red, jagged teeth. Farideh heard Havilar gasp.

Rod or not, Farideh drew on the Hellish powers her warlock pact granted her, pulling Havilar behind her as they poured into her veins. The devil bobbed and smirked at her. "Bad idea," it said. "Very bad. Here, here, here!"

"Oh do shut up," a new voice called. "I heard you the first *hundred* times." Farideh spun, flames surging into her hands. Opposite the earthmote, a woman—a half-devil, a cambion—strode toward them. Small-boned and red-skinned, Lorcan's sister, Sairché, rustled through the dead leaves in no apparent hurry, her wings held back like those of a hawk about to take flight. Her armor gleamed as silver as the needle-sharp eyelashes framing her gold eyes and the tattoos tracing her clean-shaven scalp.

"Wretched imp," Sairché spat.

"*Adaestuo,*" Farideh said. The ball of burning energy collected between her fingers, swirled together and streaked across the distance, aimed straight at Sairché's face.

It shattered an arm's reach from the cambion, broken on a magical shield that flashed red and disappeared. Sairché clucked her tongue.

"Now, now," she said. "That wasn't part of our agreement."

"What does she mean?" Havilar asked. "What agreement?"

Farideh didn't answer, all her swirling half thoughts colliding, landing together in a swarm. *What other choice do you have?* Sairché had said.

Cold horror poured down Farideh's core.

"Fari?" Havilar demanded. "What does she mean? Fari, what have you done?"

CHAPTER ONE

27 Eleasias, the Year of the Dark Circle (1478 DR)
Proskur

FARIDEH HAD BEEN PREPARED FOR MANY THINGS WHEN Havilar asked to speak to her alone, just after they'd arrived in Proskur: Another appeal they take on a bounty on their own, without their absent foster father. An admission Havilar had been the one to start the tavern brawl that had chased them from the last waystation. Devils in the nighttime, urging Havilar to make a pact. Zhentarim. Cultists of the king of the Hells, out for revenge. There were so many possibilities, so many dangers to keep track of, that Farideh had stopped guessing by the time they sat down at the inn. She was ready for Havilar to say almost anything.

But not for Havilar to ask to switch bedrooms.

"You see Brin all day," Farideh said, aware even as she did that she sounded childish.

Havilar pursed her lips a moment, her golden eyes locked on the heavily waxed surface of the table between them. "There's things," she said delicately, "you can't do walking in the market or at a campsite with your sister."

Farideh drew a breath, trying to slow the flush of blood creeping up her neck. "Right. I mean, I understand, how . . . why you're asking. I just . . . Is it the best idea?"

Havilar wrinkled her nose. "Well, I think so. Obviously." She scratched at the wax. "You're making this sound like I'm asking if I can fight a pile of owlbears with my bare hands. It's not a big deal. I'm not asking your permission, anyway." She looked up at Farideh. "I don't *need* permission."

"Right," Farideh replied, because she had no idea what to say. For the last two months, Havilar had been encouraging Brin, a young man they'd crossed paths with while they pursued a bounty to the city of Neverwinter. A young man, as it turned out, with a lot more to him than first appearances suggested.

"You know this isn't going to last," Farideh blurted.

"Of course I do," Havilar said huffily.

"Because you seem like you're getting awfully attached, and once we get to Suzail and rescue Mehen—"

"We can be attached, in the meantime. And when it's over . . ." She scraped more at the thick wax coating the table. "Anyway, it might not go all dire and pointed. You don't know."

"Brin's in line to be the king of Cormyr," Farideh said dropping her voice. "It doesn't matter how much you love him, no one is going to let a tiefling be queen."

"Too bad," Havilar said with a grin. "I bet I'd look fantastic with a crown."

"I'm serious. If we get to Cormyr and he sees everything he's giving up—"

"He doesn't want to be king," Havilar said. "Or almost-king, or almost-almost-king . . . or however you call it. So stop worrying about it until he does. Anyway, *you're* one to talk. What am I always telling you but to get away from Lorcan before he corrupts you or snatches your soul or gets you hurt? And what do you say?" She shifted her voice, a mockery of her sister, " 'It's fine. Nothing like that's happened.' And Brin isn't remotely interested in my soul."

Farideh pointedly did not glance across the room to where Lorcan—looking like nothing but a striking human

man—lounged at another table. Watching. Waiting for Farideh to finish. The lines of the protective spell linking the two of them tugged on the nerves along her right side—the half-devil had made a point of sitting at the very edge of its range. At the point where she couldn't quite ignore him.

"We are not talking about Lorcan," Farideh said. "But it brings up a good point—where's he supposed to sleep?"

"You can take him."

A blush forced itself up Farideh's neck, into her cheeks. "*No.*"

"Fine," Havilar said. "Tell him to come down and sit in the taproom. You've made the spell stretch far enough, right? It's not important where Lorcan stays." She bit her lip. "It *is* important that you . . . Look, I don't care what you think about me and Brin." She focused on the table again. "It's just . . ." She bit her lip again and added a little softer, "We've never slept apart, you and I, and I don't want you to be angry about it."

Farideh tried to imagine falling asleep, alone, without the sound of Havilar's soft wheezing, without the weight of her sister beside her. One way or another, that night would come.

Better than having it happen because she tried to fight a pile of owlbears, Farideh thought. Or because some devil snatched her.

"It's all right," she said finally.

"Promise?"

"Yes. But you promise you'll be careful. And *promise* you're not going to tell me about it."

Havilar looked crestfallen. "Not even a little?"

"I want to be able to look Brin in the face. So a *very* little."

"All right," Havilar sighed. "You have to promise not to tell Mehen, though. He'd probably get his lightning breath going for this."

Farideh doubted she'd have to tell their adoptive father a thing—Havi and Brin were so *obvious* it was hard to be in the same space as them. And then Mehen would blame Farideh for not stopping Havilar from being infatuated with Brin in the first place. "As far as I'm concerned you and I were never once apart."

Havilar grinned. "Perfect."

Lorcan tipped his chair back, and the spell's lines yanked again, hard enough Farideh drew a sharp breath. She glared across the room at him, and he scowled back. *Stop it,* she mouthed. Lorcan stood and started toward them.

Havilar was looking past her, up at the stairs, the way Brin had gone when they'd returned from their errands. "Is it harder to be good at, do you think, than, say, killing orcs and things?"

Farideh's blood rose in her cheeks. "I suspect it's different."

"The first time I killed someone I threw up," Havilar admitted. She looked back at her sister. "*Four* times."

"I don't think you'll throw up."

"If I do, I'm going to tell you whether you want to hear it or not," Havilar cautioned, as she stood. "You deserve the warning."

Havilar glared at Lorcan as he came to stand beside the table. He smiled back at her, pleasant as could be, but in those black, black eyes was something sharp as razors.

"Well met," he said. "What have you two been talking about?"

Havilar gave Farideh a look that said Farideh ought to be just as careful—if not more so—turned on her heel, and headed up the stairs. Lorcan chuckled watching her go. He looked down at Farideh.

"Well," he said, appraising her face and no doubt the high color of her cheeks. "I have to assume it was something . . . interesting. What did she want?"

Farideh hesitated. "Your half of Brin's room."

Lorcan gave a low throaty laugh. "Well that *is* interesting. What is she going to trade me?"

She looked past him at the tavernkeeper, who was eyeing them both. Or maybe, Farideh thought, she was just watching Lorcan. Out walking through Faerûn, Lorcan took precautions and made his appearance shift, taking on the skin of a human

man. Gone were the horns, the red skin, the wings that would have stretched halfway across the taproom. His eyes were still black as nightmares, but they were ringed in white. His dark curls lightened several shades, and his skin was a shade brighter than Farideh's. But he was still hard not to look at.

Farideh took a deep breath. "I presume she'll pay you back your half of the room fee. What did you pay for it again?"

Lorcan smirked. "Where am I to sleep?"

"You don't sleep."

"I sleep a little. This plane is *wearisome*. And why not, if I have nothing else to do?" His eyes didn't leave her face, but still Farideh had the sense he was appraising every inch of her in his head.

What would you do if he asked to sleep with you? she wondered to herself. If he didn't try to make you say it first? She quashed that thought as well—it didn't matter. It didn't matter because Lorcan wouldn't ask, Lorcan had no interest in sharing a bed with her and every interest in keeping her off-balance. After a month, the sureness of it had been hammered down into her bones. All she had to do was keep herself focused and sensible and not get pulled into Lorcan's manipulations.

"But," he went on, "more importantly, I need a chance to let this disguise drop. You don't want me to tire of holding it up."

Farideh let out a breath. She'd forgotten about his spell's limits. "Well, Havilar will have to think of something." She stood. "Shouldn't we go?" Without waiting for him, she crossed the taproom—pointedly *not* looking at the staring tavern-keeper—and out the door. The protection spell that had hidden Farideh from the Hells now hid Lorcan as well, and meant he had to follow wherever she went.

That didn't help matters between them either.

The sun was setting as they made their way through the winding streets of Proskur. Lorcan threaded his arm through hers. As they passed graying clapboard houses and window-less shops, he held her close and it was strange how right and normal *that* had begun to seem. Even though too many people were watching her walk past—even though they were headed to meet another of Lorcan's warlocks—she relaxed and held him too. Just a little.

A tiefling wasn't an everyday occurrence, and most people were circumspect about the descendants of humans and fiends—even if that past transgression was too many generations back to count. Despite the heat of the day, Farideh wished she'd worn her cloak and hood.

Lorcan hung on her arm, distracting them. A real fiend, Farideh thought bitterly. A wolf in sheep's clothing.

It had been eight months since she'd accepted the infernal pact of a warlock, since she first learned to channel the dark and blistering energies of the Nine Hells. Eight months since she'd been banished from the mountain village she'd grown up in, eight months of hunting bounties for coin—all the way west to the Sword Coast, and far north as Neverwinter, down into the heart of the Nether Mountains, and everywhere in between. Eight months of little comfort, little sense of the future. Eight months of Lorcan, for better or worse.

"What's she like," Farideh asked, "this warlock?"

Lorcan's hold on her arm eased. "You won't like her. But then, you don't need to talk to her."

"Is she wicked?"

"She won't do anything to you."

They walked a little farther down a narrow, dirty street. Lorcan's grip on her loosened as he searched the doors on either side.

"But she can get you back home?" Farideh knew it was the reason for this errand. Lorcan had only escaped his sister's clutches a month or so prior. Bound under the same protection spell as Farideh, Sairché couldn't scry him, but Lorcan couldn't return to the Hells either. Farideh wasn't sure he should. "Is she a very powerful warlock?"

"Powerful enough to call someone who can answer some

questions for me." He eyed a man passing them by, all bundled up and hidden. "Find out if it's safe. Temerity's clever that way."

Temerity. He hadn't said her name before.

Farideh had always known Lorcan had pacts with other warlocks, other descendants of the Toril Thirteen. She'd been certain most of them were more talented than her, better suited to the pact. But hearing it—Farideh's stomach twisted. She pressed the feeling down. He moved ahead of her, letting her go completely. She folded her hands together instead of trying to catch his.

"Who was her ancestor?" she asked.

Lorcan frowned at her over his shoulder. "What?"

"Like Bryseis Kakistos," she explained. "What was the name of the warlock Temerity descends from?"

"Why do you care?"

"It's only a name," Farideh said, falling into step beside him.

Lorcan turned back to scanning the shops they passed. "You of all people should know better than to be indiscriminately curious. Ah," he said, eyes falling on a dark green door. A sign with a picture of a mortar and pestle hung over the entrance. As they drew nearer, the thick scent of spices and perfumes curled around them, beckoning them in. Lorcan considered the door for a moment. The street had widened, edging back into something bordering on respectable.

"Wait out here," he said finally. "I won't be long." With that, he swept into the shop without so much as a glance at Farideh.

She sighed. There was a bench in front of the shop beside Temerity's and she settled herself there to wait, trying not to wonder too hard about Temerity and the warlocks of the Toril Thirteen.

Almost a hundred years ago, thirteen tiefling warlocks had come together to work magic that helped the king of the Hells, Asmodeus, rise up and claim the mantle of a god—transforming all the tieflings on the plane of Toril into the descendants of Asmodeus, cursed to wear that blood plain on their skin, no matter what they seemed before. At the coven's head had been Bryseis Kakistos, the Brimstone Angel. Farideh and Havilar's ancestor. By those lines of descent, devils like Lorcan sought out sets of warlocks to reflect the Toril Thirteen.

So like Farideh, Temerity had been chosen for some long ago ancestor's sin. Perhaps she'd been pursued by many devils—some of the heirs, she had come to understand, were rare, though none so rare as those of the Brimstone Angel.

Perhaps Temerity had known her blood's story from the cradle and sought the devils out. Perhaps she, too, had merely been in the right place at the right time for Lorcan to say all the right words and snare her in a pact that changed everything.

Farideh picked at the fraying edge of her sleeve and thought of Lorcan standing in the little stone house she'd grown up in, summoned accidentally by her sister. She thought of his hot breath on her cheek still cold from the snowy wind outside. She thought of him whispering, "Say you're mine."

A shiver ran up Farideh's spine. She might not be able to return to a normal life, but she could surely find her way out of the tangle of emotion Lorcan had trapped her in and into something simpler. More sensible.

A woman stood in the doorway opposite the bench, watching Farideh with a wary eye, no subtlety in her distaste. Farideh shifted uncomfortably.

"You waiting for someone?" the woman said after an interminable time.

"My friend," Farideh said. "He won't be long."

"Buying spices from another devilborn." She sniffed. "Your kind do like to stick together."

Farideh's tail flicked nervously. She pulled it closer to lie along her thigh. "My friend's human, many thanks."

"Is he now?" Farideh met the woman's skeptical gaze. Without the ring of white humans were used to, Farideh's eyes were unreadable. Emotionless. Inhuman. The shopkeeper could stare as long as she liked and Farideh knew she wouldn't see anything there, not without practice.

"Do you want me to have him show you?" Farideh said. "Or do you want to say what it is you're getting at?"

Farideh knew perfectly well what the shopkeeper was getting at: she didn't belong here. Whatever clientele the shopkeeper was used to dealing with, a seventeen-year-old tiefling trying to rein in the tendrils of shadow that curled and coiled around the edges of her frame was not a part of it. The woman's eyes moved from the swell of the horns along Farideh's brow, to the flat color of her eyes, to the sharp points of her eyeteeth when she spoke, as if hunting for a sign of what, exactly, she was up to.

"You a friend of the Dragon Lords'?" the woman demanded.

"Do I look like someone your lord would employ?"

The woman's eyes lingered a little longer on Farideh's heavy horns. "Of course not," she said. "But then, that's the sort they'd like to have, innit? Skims beneath your notice, and catches you all unawares when the wrong someone happens by your shop. All 'cause you thought sure the Lords on high wouldn't give a ragged tiefling two coppers together." She smiled nastily. "No offense."

The powers of the Hells surged up in her veins, forcing their way down into her hands, throbbing behind the beds of her nails as if they were trying to force their way out in a torrent of fire that would show the shopkeeper just how careful she ought to be about offending the heir of the Brimstone Angel.

"None taken," Farideh lied.

"But if you're not with the Lords'," the woman went on, "then I'm thinking I ought to report you to the city watch. Ought to be conscientious. Since there's such a fear of criminals." Farideh could almost hear the old saying about tieflings, running through the woman's thoughts: *one's a curiosity, two's a conspiracy, three's a curse.*

Farideh drew a slow breath, trying to calm her pulse and push the powers back down. "He'll only be a moment," she said.

"So will the watch," the woman said.

They couldn't afford to bribe the watch, Farideh knew, nor pay a trumped-up fine. They couldn't afford to wait for some jailor to let her out of a cell or some magistrate to say she'd done nothing wrong. Farideh stood, glanced up and down the street.

"That's what I thought," the woman muttered.

But Farideh couldn't leave, not with the spell still tethering Lorcan, and if she went the twenty steps the spell would stretch, she'd still be well in the woman's sight. The engines of Malbolge churned more slick magic into her and she seemed to pulse from the soles of her feet up to her ears. Her veins were darkening with the unspent power. She had to go. She could not go. The woman narrowed her eyes.

There was nowhere to flee but Temerity's shop.

An army of scents assaulted Lorcan once he crossed the threshold—arispeg, bitter marka, myrrh, and juniper—crawling so deep into his nose, they lay across his tongue. Long ropes of drying garlic hung from the rafters like garlands, and bins of seeds and blossoms and teas lined the walls, making the space feel much closer and narrower than it was.

Lorcan never understood why Temerity had such a banal cover for her powers—perhaps the smell covered the stronger components of her rituals, perhaps she liked being the one who came by such rare and precious commodities, perhaps she just enjoyed having a supplier for her personal perfumes—but the little shop seemed to satisfy her, which was good enough for him. He had everything he needed from Temerity.

Almost, he amended, crossing the shop. Which step triggered the magical tinkling of a bell, he couldn't have said, but Lorcan was ready when an auburn-haired tiefling woman with the angry tips of a pact-brand reaching up from under her low, wide collar came around the shelves behind the counting table. He leaned against the table with the sort of smile that usually made her forget he was such a bad person to trust. "Temerity," he said. "Well met."

She stopped dead. "Well met," she said, a smile of her own creeping across her lovely features. "Didn't expect to see you coming in by the door."

"All these years, I can still surprise you—I like that," he said. That sounded right. He was out of practice with her—with any of them, really, aside from Farideh. "I was in the city, and how could I pass through without checking on you?"

She held his gaze, eyes like silver pieces. Eyes empty of the sort of warmth and interest Temerity usually had for him. Lorcan tensed. Reconsidered.

"How long *has* it been?" she asked, coming right up to the edge of the counting table. "Do you remember?"

He didn't, which was sloppy and he knew it. He'd been distracted by other things—the plots of his mother and sister, the complicated machinations of the Lords of the Nine. Farideh.

"Too long," he settled on, with a tone of regret.

Temerity's smile didn't waver. "Indeed," she said. "Ten months. And another two before that."

"And you didn't call," Lorcan said. He took her hand in his. "I assumed you didn't need me. I hate to be a nuisance. I do hope," he added, lower, drawing a small circle on the skin of her wrist, "that I'm not being a nuisance."

A little warmth stirred in Temerity's features. She was simple—much simpler than some other warlocks he could name. Make her feel special. Make her feel wise. Make her think that she's making the best possible decisions, even when she isn't. Make her think there's something there, under the surface, between them.

"Too long," she agreed, brushing her curls away from the side of her face. Then, "Long enough your rivals have come calling."

"Oh?" Lorcan said, as if it didn't concern him. "I'm glad I can still count you mine."

"For now," she said, but she relaxed.

"Well," he said smoothly, still toying with her hand, "you'll at least give me the chance to make a counteroffer. I'd hate to lose you because other people's mistakes kept me away." He brought her hand to his lips and she exhaled unevenly. What sort of idiots were those other collectors if they couldn't sway Temerity? "Haven't I given you everything you want?"

"Not everything," she said.

"Well we'll have to see about remedying that, won't we?" he murmured, even though he knew what she was asking for and he wouldn't dare try to get it. It didn't matter—not now. She was listening, and that was enough. "But in order to do that I do need a small favor. A little ritual—no," he cut himself off and leaned a little nearer, close enough to kiss her just below the ear. "We can get to that later, of course, darling." Temerity raised an eyebrow and smiled. He drew another slow circle across her wrist.

The bells chimed again, and Lorcan glanced back over his shoulder, careful to hold tight to Temerity as he did. Things weren't nearly far enough along that he could risk her getting distracted by some customer.

But it wasn't some customer. Farideh stared back at him, frozen.

No, not at him. At Temerity's hand in his.

Lords of the shitting Nine, he thought.

"Well met," Temerity said, the picture of a sweet-tempered shopkeeper. But Lorcan knew better and heard the sudden venom in her voice. She yanked her hand free and moved around the table. "Can I help you?"

"I . . . um . . . ," Farideh trailed off and she looked away at a chain of seedpods hanging down from one of the heavy shelves. Shit and ashes, Lorcan thought, already sorting through all the things he was going to have to say to soothe her. Every option would turn into something far more complicated than he wanted to handle. Why couldn't she be like Temerity, wanting to be soothed?

If she were like Temerity, Lorcan thought, you'd have a much bigger problem on your hands. For now, he needed space and quickly, before anybody got any more ideas.

"You're interrupting," he said.

When Farideh looked up at him, her expression was guarded—nothing for Temerity to see there. There at least was that. "Clearly." She looked to Temerity and held out a hand. "You must be Temerity."

Shut up, he thought. Shut up, shut up. There were too many things still hanging hidden in this conversation. Too many risks. And as much as he wanted to intervene, that might make things worse.

Temerity glanced at him, then crossed to take Farideh's hand. "I should have guessed. Were you just going to leave her out there in the dark?" she asked Lorcan.

"She can handle herself."

"But can she handle Proskur?" Temerity considered Farideh. Looking for all the world as if she and the younger tiefling were about to be dear friends. Lorcan edged nearer.

Temerity turned Farideh's arm up, revealing the fading streaks of dark magic tinting her veins. "A warlock," she said, rubbing a hand over her forearm. "And so young."

"Not that young," Lorcan pointed out. "No younger than you were." But the jab didn't shift her attention, her growing ire back to him.

"Well," Temerity said to Farideh, "then you still have time to grow wiser." Still holding Farideh's arm, Temerity looked over at Lorcan. "Whose heir is she?"

Shit. *Shit.* Lorcan sighed dramatically. "Can't you guess? I feel as if every time I replace my Greybeard heir, they can hardly don their own clothes without instruction." Lorcan shook his head, as if exasperated—not a lie, but the careful placement of truth by truth, and he prided himself on the difference. It was, after all, the sort of thing that separated devils from the cacophony of fiends howling throughout the planes.

"What part of 'sit outside and wait' did you misunderstand?" he asked Farideh.

Farideh kept her blank expression, but her cheeks reddened and she wouldn't look at him. Good enough, he thought. Fix it later. You'll think of something.

Temerity held his gaze for a long time, as if she were trying to decide whether there was something to tease out of his comment.

"Don't you have a little side room or something she could wait in?" he asked. "I seem to recall you do."

Temerity rolled Farideh's sleeve down over her wrist, any trace of her previous tractability gone. "Ten months is a long time," she said. "I've had offers. Several. I won't tell you it's not tempting. But none of them said they could get me what I really want, so what was the point?"

"It's hard to reclaim that sort of thing," Lorcan admitted. This was going all the wrong ways. Four steps to Farideh. Twelve steps to the door.

"But not impossible," Temerity said. "It sounds to me like there are plenty in the Hells who'll consider a trade," she said. "A soul for a soul."

"Not many gods look kindly on that sort of trade," Lorcan reminded her, shifting closer to Farideh, who was still watching Temerity cautiously. Good, he thought—she knew something bad was happening here. "You send another to the Hells, you might well end up unclaimed when your time comes. End up in the Hells anyway."

"Better odds than I have now." She stared at Farideh again. "Whose heir are you?"

Farideh glanced at Lorcan. "The Greybeard. Didn't he say that?"

"It's *Titus* Greybeard, dear. You'd know that if you descended from him." Temerity shook her head. "You're the Brimstone Angel, aren't you? The heir of Bryseis Kakistos."

"Would I walk the streets with such a valuable heir?" Lorcan scoffed. He slipped between the two women, pushing Farideh away from Temerity. Prod her, he thought, provoke her. Get her mad at *him*. "You knew I had more than one warlock. Just because she's younger and—"

Temerity shoved him into Farideh. "Don't play me. You don't walk the streets with any of your warlocks. Not like this."

"Necessity makes us all change paths eventually," Lorcan said. He reached back to push Farideh toward the door, taking careful stock of Temerity's expression. She'd likely try to scratch his eyes out—she'd tried it before. "You're wiser than this. Or you *were*. Temerity, tell me you—"

Temerity pulled the rod from her apron so quickly he couldn't react. But in the same moment as he spied the spell surging up the implement, Farideh kicked his knees in so that he fell under the bolt. He felt the magic sizzle across the edge of the spell that disguised him.

Before he could stand, Farideh grabbed his shoulder and pulled him back, with a soft gasp of Infernal, through a vent in the world. One moment he was looking up at Temerity, at the rod pointed at his throat, the next there was a fold of darkness and brimstone closing over him, and when it passed, they were at the door. Farideh stepped in front of him, her own rod out and aimed at Temerity. Lorcan scrambled to his feet.

"If you don't believe I'm no one," Farideh said quietly, the faintest tremor in her voice, "then I think you know this isn't a fight you want a part of."

The dark powers of Malbolge crept up Temerity's brand, clawing at her throat. "Little girl," she said coolly, "don't defend him. He'll bring you to ruin in the end."

"So will you, by the sound of it, and a lot quicker," Farideh said, not lowering the rod. "Lorcan seems to have some fond feelings for you, but I don't know you. I don't like you. And your neighbors already seem to think I'm a criminal, so don't think there is a *thing* stopping me. If I see you set one foot out into the street after us . . ." She hesitated, no doubt sorting through suitable threats. "I'll show you what it means to be the heir of Bryseis Kakistos," she said.

Perfect, he thought.

Temerity didn't falter, but neither did she come after them as they backed from the shop. The neighbors Farideh had mentioned were watching, and Farideh needed no prodding to hurry away from the shop, Temerity, and any rival Temerity might call down out of the Hells.

I should have cut her loose ages ago, Lorcan thought, glancing back at Temerity's shop. She'd been easy to catch, young and disaffected and *wanting* so badly to rise above her grubby upbringing—and pretty enough to make it a pleasure to help her do so. And when the pact hadn't done that to her liking, it had been a simple thing to trade her soul for a constant trickle of gold and the sorts of spells that kept the watch out of her hair. She'd thought him more a faerie story prince there to rescue her than a devil with his own desires. Age had made her wiser, but not enough to recognize that in her wanting, she was the author of her own fall. Lorcan was only the tool she'd used to make it happen.

And now she was looking for more powerful tools.

The streets were dark and poorly lit as they wound back through Proskur. From the shadows, cold, appraising eyes watched them pass. He kept Farideh pulled close. Try it, he thought at the sharpjaws lingering there. Oh, give me an excuse.

As they walked, Farideh didn't say a word, and the longer she didn't talk, the more Lorcan worried. The longer she was silent, the more she was deciding things for herself, not letting Lorcan explain and nudge her conclusions somewhere more palatable.

"You sounded ridiculous, back there," he said. "Thundering around like some chapbook Chosen. Where did you get that nonsense?"

"One of us had to do something," she said tightly.

"Darling, that wasn't what it looked like."

"Yes it was," she said, still not looking at him. "I'm not an

idiot. That's how you talk to us. How you keep us in check."
She'd gotten much better at not wearing all her feelings on her
sleeve, but not enough to hide the quiet shame and anger from
the likes of Lorcan.

"That's how I talk to *Temerity*. It's different." She said
nothing. "*You're* different," he started.

She stopped in her tracks and pulled free of him. "Don't.
You owe me better than that."

"I've *given* you better," he said sharply. "I chose you over
her back there. I was ready to let her attack me so you could
get away. Doesn't that mean anything?"

She looked away, at the lights of the streetlamps flickering
in the gloom. "Not really. You *have* to choose me. I have the
protection spell. Besides, which of us is the rarer heir?" Now she
looked at him like she was making herself face all the ugly, sharp
edges of their pact. Like she was daring him—or maybe daring
herself—to tear away the veils of artifice and careful words.

I would choose you anyway, he thought and hated himself
for it. There was no one else on any plane Lorcan would have
counted on the way he did Farideh. Allies were dangerous,
more ways for the hierarchy of the Hells to manipulate your
actions and force your hand. This alliance . . . he didn't have
any sense of how to manage it anymore. But he knew down
in the core of himself that he'd take Farideh over every other
warlock in his retinue.

And that he would never, never tell her that.

"Margarites," he said.

Farideh blinked at him. "What?"

"You asked for the name of the warlock Temerity is
descended from," he said. "She was called Margarites."

"Oh." Farideh was quiet a moment, as if she were turning
that bit of information over in her head. "Was she like
Temerity?" she asked finally, though what she was thinking
of, Lorcan couldn't imagine.

"She was reluctant," he settled on. "They say Margarites

was one of the warlocks Bryseis Kakistos coerced. You ought to watch out for those heirs," he added, as they approached the inn. "Some of them aren't too happy with their lot."

"How did she know who I was?"

Lorcan didn't answer. He could hope it was an accident—a rumor gone 'round the ranks of his sister's erinyes, the assumption of a rival that Lorcan would stick close to his most valuable heir, a simple guess born of Temerity's envy and rage.

But there was one person in the Hells who knew for certain Lorcan was traveling with Farideh, and Sairché was not someone it paid to stand around wondering about.

Temerity stood watching the door to her shop, the air clotted with spices and brimstone and unspent magic. The sound of her breath, angry and flustered, was a roar in the room's quiet.

Sairché stood in the doorway to the rear of the shop, several paces ahead of the portal's opening, and flanked by two monstrous erinyes, female devils all armor and teeth atop shining hooves. She watched Temerity for several moments, noticing the rage shimmering through the tiefling. Lorcan had surely been here, just as surely as he'd gone.

When the erinyes began to fidget, Sairché sighed. Temerity startled and turned, rod high.

"Well met," Sairché said. "I gather that didn't go as we'd discussed. It's quite all right," she added when Temerity scowled. "I know he distracts you."

"He didn't distract me," Temerity snapped. "*She* was with him. She tried to kill me—you didn't mention that."

"I didn't think I had to."

"She wasn't just a girl," Temerity said, as if Sairché hadn't spoken. "You made it sound as if she were a novice, a nothing, and she tried to kill me."

"I can all but guarantee whatever she threatened you with

was a bluff. Every word." Behind her, Sairché could hear her half sisters shifting, their hooves dragging on the floorboards as they restlessly reconsidered their stances. Not time to draw things out, she thought.

"Nevertheless," Sairché said, "you've done far better than any of his other warlocks. We can consider our deal complete."

Sairché pulled a scroll from out of a pocket and handed it over to Temerity. "Your agreement. You're released from the Pact Certain."

Temerity unrolled the parchment. "It's real?"

Sairché smiled. "Of course. I keep my word."

The tiefling regarded her warily. "*He* doesn't. Why should I trust you?"

The erinyes' building annoyance was palpable now—annoyance at Lorcan, at Temerity, at their little sister playing dress-up with their once exalted mother's mantle. Sairché was well used to skirting the edges of the hierarchy of the Hells, to plucking secrets and turning them into treasures. Excellent practice for parts of her new status, terrible for others—she had gained some measure of respect from her warrior half sisters, but these sorts of meetings, mortals who didn't know their places, concessions that seemed out of proportion . . . the erinyes talked.

Sairché gave Temerity a thin smile. "That isn't my problem."

"It *will* be your problem if you're lying."

"Well, it hardly matters. You're going to give it up again."

"I will not lose it," Temerity snapped.

"Please. You'll shift your pact now—you must if you want to keep your powers. You'll find a new devil, a new patron, a new set of sweet words and promises—don't deny it. We all have a type. What exactly do you think will go differently?" Sairché moved closer to Temerity and ran a friendly hand down her arm, feeling the tension of her biceps. "Accept it. Only this way, Lorcan doesn't get the credit, so we can all be pleased by that."

High spots of color marred Temerity's creamy cheeks. "You cannot speak to me that way."

"Have I upset you?" Sairché said, all too aware of the watching erinyes. "Here, let me make it up to you. I'll give you a safeguard. A way to be sure no devil tricks you out of your soul. All right?"

The muscle of Temerity's arm softened and her silver glare became wary. "How will you do that?"

Sairché drew the long stiletto blade from her belt and held it up, showing Temerity the gem-studded hilt, the delicate chasing. The tiefling bent a little nearer to see. "It's a simple thing," Sairché said. "Hardly takes a moment."

In one smooth motion, she flipped the blade into a stabbing grip and plunged it between the tiefling's ribs, forcing it past muscle and organ and deep into her heart. Temerity's eyes widened, her mouth wide in shock as Sairché twisted the blade, locking it against the bone. Temerity clutched at the gushing wound, gaping up at the cambion.

Sairché turned to her guards, pleased at the faint look of approval they both wore. "When she's done bleeding," she said crisply, "do something about the body and get back to the Hells." She turned back to the door and cast a simple spell to remove the spatter of blood marring her armor, before drawing her wings down and pulling her cloak over them. "I have to attend to our brother."

If Farideh *had* asked for details, Havilar thought, lying tangled in the rough sheets and Brin's arms, she didn't know what she could possibly say to give it any justice.

Much like kissing, it wasn't how Havilar had expected—it was stranger and worse and also far, far better. She sighed and settled her head on Brin's shoulder, careful to avoid butting his jaw with her horns.

"I feel," she said, "like I passed through another plane. But no one told me."

Brin chuckled and kissed her forehead. "I like that."

"And tired," she added. "I don't know if I've ever been this tired. I don't even want to move."

"I'm going to pretend that's a compliment."

And, she thought to herself, I didn't throw up. I have a lover, and I didn't throw up. A faint breeze stirred the dirty curtains over the open window, cool on their sticky skin. She wondered if anyone outside heard them, knew what they'd done. She sighed again, content.

"Don't laugh, all right?" she said. "I thought it would take longer. All night maybe."

He didn't chuckle that time; he ran his fingers up and down her shoulder. "But . . . it was all right?" he asked. "I mean, it would go better with practice—"

"Shush. It was perfect. The best."

It hadn't been like in chapbooks. At least not quite for her. Maybe for Brin—it seemed more like chapbooks for him. But Havilar figured that the fact he'd known a *little* of what to do after, when it became clear she hadn't had the same experience—even if there was plenty of fumbling and giggling and not much serious romantic gazing—meant that their first efforts could be considered very good overall. She'd rather, she thought, laugh than be serious about something so messy and ungainly and *personal* anyway.

Brin rubbed his thumb over her knuckles, his skin so pale next to hers. "Was it how you imagined?" he asked. "Am I . . . how you imagined?"

She pushed up on one elbow so she could look at him. "I really don't know. It's been so long, it feels like, since I wasn't thinking about you anyway. I forget."

"Two months," he said, holding up his fingers.

"I *can* count," she said and pinched him. He pinched her back, and this time she grabbed his hand and pulled it close. "It's not as if I'm what you imagined."

"No," he agreed. He traced the edge of her horn over her

forehead. "Not outside anyway. Inside . . ." Brin smiled and shook his head. "No, you're better. Inside and out."

Havilar snorted, but didn't tease him about the accidental wordplay. It was too nice a compliment to spoil. He could have a princess, she thought, and he likes you better.

Brin glanced past her at the open window. "Ye gods, it's still hot as blazes." But he didn't push away from her.

Havilar smiled. "Is it this hot where you're from?"

"In Suzail, it's not so bad," he said. "The water keeps the city cooler. As long as you don't go too far inland, it stays pretty pleasant." He brushed a strand of hair over her shoulder. "The Citadel's cooler still, but it's up in the mountains, so it would be."

"Does it snow?"

"Lots. I used to have to shovel it off the courtyards. It was supposed to build character." He chuckled to himself. "Aunt Helindra would have dueled the holy champions herself and won by sheer temper if she'd known. It's unprincely, shoveling. Anyway, it would always just snow another load the next day. So all winter, I was in the courtyard. Shush," he said, before she could tease him like usual. "I can shovel snow."

Havilar smiled—she wouldn't have teased him, not anymore. Not when she'd seen for herself he was stronger than he looked. "It snows in Arush Vayem, too," she said. "Right up to your knees. And then the winds come and blow it all around. No one tries to move it—you just stomp it down again and again until spring finally comes."

"Well I suppose there are other ways to build character," he said cheekily. He looked her in the eyes for a long moment. "After this, we can go up into the Stormhorns," he offered. "I could show you the Citadel. Where I grew up. We could even stay the winter, if you like."

"Will they let me stay? Let us stay?" she amended.

Brin nodded. "I'll convince them and you convince Mehen. Then in the spring we can go to Tymanther and you can show me your mountains." He hesitated. "I mean, you and me. I know Farideh can't."

"No," Havilar said with a sigh. "I wouldn't be welcome either. I'm the one who called Lorcan after all."

"Summoned," Brin corrected, but he was still playing with her hair, so Havilar didn't pinch him for that. "Do they even know that, though? And anyway, you led him away. Surely they'll forgive you."

"That's not how Arush Vayem is. The rules we broke, they're the kind of rules too big to forget. We can't go back home."

He stopped. "That's so sad."

It was—the kind of sad Havilar spent a lot of effort not thinking about. She'd always thought of the future as a vast, uncertain mess, so why worry about it too hard? But Brin made her think ahead, think about the paths that were open to her and those she could never go back to again. It was strange to think of how much she'd planned without planning—she wouldn't grow old in the little stone house; wouldn't return from some adventure through the big, spiked gates; wouldn't see if any of the handful of boys near to her age turned out to be interesting.

Havilar sighed, as if she could exhale all those feelings right out in a vapor. "Yes," she agreed. "But maybe someday that will change. Or maybe our mountains aren't that different."

"And if you'd stayed," he said, "we wouldn't have met. So there's that?"

She grinned at that, but a second thought made the smile soften. "I always would have left," she told him. "I'll always choose Farideh."

"Don't worry. I know." And if there were anything she loved best about Brin it was probably that: he knew what she meant, even when she wasn't saying it right. She smiled at him, pleased at the realization. "I love you."

Brin went still as a rabbit, as if he were thinking she wouldn't see him if he didn't move. Even though Havilar couldn't remember imagining this moment, she was sure this wasn't how it was supposed to go.

"This is a court thing," Havilar said. "Isn't it?"

"No," he insisted, and Havilar knew he was lying, even if he didn't. "It's just . . . it's kind of sudden is all."

"When was I supposed to say it?" He didn't answer, so she added, trying for impudence, "Do you have a writ for this too in Cormyr?"

Brin didn't laugh. "No, I don't mean you weren't supposed to."

Havilar sat up. She hated this. She hated when he got snarled in old rules and expectations, and there was nothing for her to do but wait until he picked his way out. It happened now and again, and much as she didn't understand it, she was prepared. Still, she thought, pulling the covers up and trying to decide where she ought to look, she wished in this case *she* might win out over all the odd rules of Cormyr's court and Torm's citadel tumbling around in Brin's head.

He sat up too and reached for her arm. "Wait. This . . . It's not what I meant. Please come back."

"It's fine," she said, because she wanted it to be. "I just thought it, so I said it. You don't have to think any way about it."

He gave her a look, as if he knew exactly how much of that was a lie. "Havi, I'm sorry. I'm not trying to ruin things. Really, you just surprised—"

Farideh and Lorcan's muffled voices filtered through the wall, sharp and angry, and Havilar shushed Brin. "Do you think they heard us?"

"Heard us what?" he whispered. "Talking? They haven't been back that long."

"How long?"

"I don't know. The door shut earlier when we were lying about."

"Are you *sure*?" Havilar asked. "She doesn't want to know details. I promised."

"I'm sure," Brin said. He took her hand. "Look, can we just start over—"

Farideh's cry sliced through the wall as if it were tissue, followed by a strange pulse, as if a spell had been cast. Havilar leaped off the bed and yanked on her leathers. "Something's wrong."

"Havi, they're just arguing."

"Then I won't be long," she said, pulling on her blouse.

"No." Brin threw back the covers and groped at the floor for his own clothes. "If you're going, I'm going. And we're talking about this."

A crash. Another shout. Another voice, that wasn't Farideh, wasn't Lorcan. Havilar snatched her glaive from where she'd set it against the wall, blood thrumming. Here was something she could solve, she thought.

"Gods damn it," Brin cursed. "Where are my breeches?"

Farideh turned at the door to her room and held up a hand to stop Lorcan from following her. "Go down to the taproom," she said, wishing she didn't have to, wishing he'd known well enough that she couldn't be around him right now. "Just come up when your spell's running out. We can trade."

"Don't be ridiculous," Lorcan said, brushing past her and into the room. "Surely you can control yourself for a few hours."

Farideh stood, hand on the doorknob, remembering Temerity's hand in Lorcan's, him leaning close enough to kiss her. *We can get to that later of course, darling.* Her stomach was in knots. "Go down to the taproom. Please."

He looked at her as if she were making a terrible joke, and if possible, it made everything worse. "So I cool my heels and wait to see if Temerity's new friends come calling? I suppose the protection spell will let you know if I've been torn back to the Hells? Think it through, darling."

"Don't call me that," Farideh snapped. *Of course, darling.* She shut her eyes, embarrassed at how deeply that had wounded her. Lorcan was silent. She heard him cross the room, felt him reach past her to slip her hand off the knob, and for a moment was relieved.

"If you're going to shout," Lorcan said, "close the door."

Farideh looked away. "Do you call all of us 'darling'?"

For a moment, Farideh felt sure he was going to change the subject, twist their argument into something she'd done wrong. He stared at her for so long with those dark eyes that weren't really his. "No," he said finally. "It doesn't suit all of you."

"How many does it suit?"

"Four, now," he said. "Two of my warlocks are dead, two have thrown me over. Four of the remaining have no interest in me calling them any sort of endearment, and one thinks of herself as old enough to be my grandmother, so I'm the one she calls pet names. You, Temerity, my actual Greybeard heir, and the heir of Zeal Harper seem to enjoy it just fine." Stubbornly she held his gaze, and it was like pressing on a bruise.

It seemed to agitate Lorcan too, and he burst out, "And that is one of the many reasons I don't care for my warlocks to introduce themselves to each other. You build up these little versions of the pact that don't exist and get angry when you find that they're not real. Did you think it would make you *happy* to know?"

"No," she said quietly. "But I'd rather know the truth."

You are a piece in a collection, she thought. A little idiot he amuses himself with by keeping dancing.

Farideh drew a long slow breath and bit down on her tongue to shock the thoughts from her head. Don't wallow. Don't be a fool. You knew this was how it was. You knew there were others and you were only one of a set. You knew he was a devil. You were doing so well . . .

"Please go," she said, tears crowding her throat. She wasn't about to cry in front of him, not now.

Lorcan stayed where he was. A surge of magic rolled over him from the center of his chest outward and the illusion dissolved, leaving behind his natural form. Horns curled back from his brow, his skin turned red as live coals, and batlike wings erupted from his back, spreading wide enough to block Farideh from the door before curling closer.

"No," he said. "You don't get to chase me off because you refuse to have a little sense, darling."

"I told you not to call me that."

"You need to decide," he went on, "what you want from this pact. You push and you pull, you struggle like you're fighting every step of it but then you refuse any chance to get free of it. You turn around and make rules and get angry I haven't broken them for you. I'm not your lover. I'm not your champion. I'm the devil you made a deal with, and I've done more than enough for that. We don't have any other sort of agreement."

"I know that," she said, but the words came out soft and damaged.

"You haven't asked for any other sort of agreement," he said coming closer. Close enough to touch. She didn't want to be angry at him, didn't want him to go—

And then he added, nastily, "It certainly didn't occur to you before, when you were swanning around with that paladin."

She blew out a breath. Why did she think she could master this? "First, if we don't have an agreement, then you have no right to throw an acquaintance in my face. Dahl is not your business. And second"—she curled her nails into her palms— "No. I'm done. I'll go and sit downstairs. Come find me when you can disguise yourself again." She moved to slip around him, but he caught her by the arm.

"I meant what I said—Temerity learned about you from somewhere, and the gods only know who she contacted once we left her shop." He leaned nearer. "If you leave me, then we're both in danger."

"If I stay . . ." She looked up at him, her anger tangled in embarrassment, her embarrassment in lust. "Lorcan, I am two breaths from breaking this pact," she said, her throat a knot.

She swallowed hard. "Let me go, or I——"

"Or what?" he said, holding all the tighter to her arm. "You'll throw me to Sairché because of other warlocks that you have *always* known about?"

"I didn't say that."

"Because that's what happens if you break the protection spell," he went on. "She finds me, and I'm done for."

Her pulse sped—he was getting angry. "I don't want that——"

"You clearly want to punish me for some indiscretion that wasn't even——"

Farideh felt her cheeks warm. "This isn't about punishing you."

"Really? So it's about poor Temerity?"

"It's about *us*!" Farideh shouted. "It's about the fact that there is *nothing* under the sun that is ever going to make you stop being a devil. And I know that, and I've always known that, but this . . . This makes it abundantly clear how much I haven't believed it. You're right," she said softer. "I'm no one special. You're no one special. I don't know what I want from this and I should. So give me some gods-be-damned space to figure it out, because if you make me choose right here, right now, I choose to be done."

Lorcan was as quiet as a hunting cat watching her. "Because of Temerity?"

Farideh shook her head. "Because I know myself. And I know you a little better now."

"Whatever you think you know," Lorcan said, every word packed with rage, "whatever I call or do not call Temerity is a trifle only a stupid girl would fixate on when Sairché is extremely capable of tracking us right now."

Farideh's heart was still pounding, her head still light enough to float away. There was no changing Lorcan, and apparently, there was no changing herself. "Then break the pact," she said. "Sairché doesn't want you, she wants me."

"And that's better than accepting you don't get to tell me

what to do? Do you think my sister would have done half the things I've done for you?"

"I think your sister would know to give me a little space," Farideh said, "instead of insulting me until I want to run from her."

Lorcan started to retort when the door opened. He had no more than turned, reaching for the sword he wore on his belt but a burst of magic splashed over him, freezing him in place. Farideh leaped out of the way, back to the wall, and pulled her rod from its place in her sleeve.

Sairché stepped around her brother, a wand in her hand, and with a quick spell closed the door behind her.

"Well met," she said. "I do hope I'm not—"

Farideh pointed the rod at the cambion. "*Adaestuo!*" Sairché threw herself behind Lorcan's still form as a bolt of energy streaked past and obliterated a wooden chair pushed up against the wall, narrowly missing the curve of her batlike wing. Farideh ducked around Lorcan, another burst of Hellish magic ready, but Sairché had rolled to her feet, and as Farideh marked her position, the cambion took hold of a charm that made her shimmer and vanish.

Farideh kept the rod out, searching the empty room for some sign of where Lorcan's treacherous sister stood. "What have you done to him?"

"Nothing permanent," Sairché said from somewhere behind her. Farideh spun, but when Sairché spoke again, it was from off to the left. "Not yet. I wanted to talk to you, and let's face it, Lorcan's a terrible distraction."

Farideh cast another bolt but it smashed against the wall. How long before someone came to see what all the noise was about? How long before someone caught her casting magic with a frozen devil in the middle of her room?

"Put away the rod," Sairché's voice said. "I'm not here to hurt you."

"How did you find me?" Farideh asked, moving into the

curve of Lorcan's wing. If she was going to hit Sairché, she'd have to be careful. Keep her talking—that was the only way to find her.

"You mean the protection? I suppose Lorcan didn't think about the fact that there are more mundane ways around such things. Temerity was most helpful. Put the rod away, and give me a chance."

"What do you want?" Farideh asked, still holding tight to the implement.

"I'm here to offer you a deal," Sairché said.

"I don't want it. I told you that before." In Neverwinter, Sairché had laid out her offer to take Farideh's pact from Lorcan, telling Farideh she'd change her mind eventually. Or else.

Sairché clucked her tongue. "A lot of devils are looking for you, and make no mistake, they'll find you soon enough. If I can do it, a dedicated collector can too. Lorcan *ought* to have told you that much."

Farideh looked up at Lorcan's frozen face. He would have said she didn't need to know that. He would have said it was handled. But how could it be if Sairché was standing here, and he was trapped? She held the rod more tightly. "I'll manage."

The door swung open again, and Havilar, glaive leading, appeared. She looked from Lorcan to Farideh to Farideh's rod . . . then froze stiff as the same magic stopped her in her tracks.

"No!" Farideh rushed to stand in front of her twin, to block Sairché's reach.

"Ah, the infamous twin," Sairché's voice came. "She *is* a firecracker, isn't she?"

Panic sank its cold claws into Farideh's chest. "He said you didn't know about her."

Sairché stepped out of the air and gave Farideh a pitying look, as she sat down on the bed. "He says a lot of things, doesn't he? Obviously he lied."

Did he lie or did he underestimate Sairché? Did it matter?

If Lorcan couldn't protect them from the Hells, she had to do something.

If Sairché cast another spell, Farideh thought, she might be able to keep her from harming Havilar. Or Lorcan. Not both. And still whatever spell held them in place might last for moments or might last for eons.

"This is my offer," Sairché said. "Nothing nefarious—those collectors *will* come calling, make no mistake. I'll give you protection from such harm—I have resources now my brother could only dream of. You give me your sister, a Kakistos heir of my own."

"I'll fight them off myself before I give you Havilar." Farideh pointed the rod at Sairché's chest. "*Adae—*"

"Now wait!" Sairché interrupted. "Lords, did Lorcan never let you negotiate? Never mind. Of course he didn't. My second offer: my protection—Hells, let's extend it to your sister as well—for twenty years. A decent chance at life, wouldn't you say?"

"And what do you want?"

Sairché's smile grew sharper. "Just Lorcan. Reject your pact, break the protection, and I'll do the rest."

Farideh thought of Temerity, of the way Lorcan had smiled at the other warlock. *I'm not your lover. I'm not your champion.* She thought of all the times he'd lashed out at her or prodded her off-balance. All the times he'd hurt her.

But then there were all the times he'd saved her, all the times he'd been the only ally at her side. The times he'd been kind. It did matter, a little, that he'd chosen her. And she wasn't going to let him die because she couldn't sort him out.

"No," she said.

Sairché narrowed her eyes. "I don't think you understand what it is you're up against. My brother is soft-hearted and lazy and entirely self-absorbed. His schemes do not tend to reach beyond the tips of his fingers. Even for a collector, he is peculiar. The others will not be so careful with you. Or with your sister. Refuse me," Sairché added, "and *I* will not be so careful with you."

Farideh kept the rod pointed at Sairché, but found the trigger word wouldn't speak itself. The thought of armies of devils, pouring through a portal from the Hells, eager to make Havilar their tool, eager to kill Lorcan and tangle Farideh in some worse agreement—she couldn't let that happen either. She needed time to think. She needed Sairché to back off.

She wet her mouth. "What would it take to protect us for only a little while?"

Sairché paused and considered her brother's frozen form. Farideh wondered if he could hear what was happening, see what she was up against. She wondered if he was struggling to curse at her. She reached back with her free hand and squeezed Havilar's wrist. It was warm but still.

"A favor," Sairché said finally. "And I'll protect you and your sister from death and from devils, until you turn twenty-seven." She smiled at Farideh. "A pretty number, don't you think? And a very good deal."

Farideh hesitated. "What do you mean 'a favor'?"

"Just some little thing I can't do for myself," Sairché said. "But it won't be your soul or your sister. Or Lorcan, since you've laid those out."

"But it's anything else." Farideh pursed her lips a moment. "I won't get you another soul."

Sairché chuckled to herself. "Any soul *you* could get me was already half in the basket."

"I won't kill anyone," Farideh said.

"My, you're squeamish all of the sudden," Sairché said. "Sure you won't kill *anyone*?"

"You won't trick me like that," Farideh said. If she said yes, Sairché could easily turn her against someone good or dear or important. "The favor can't be killing someone."

"No killing," Sairché agreed. "To be honest, I wouldn't have wasted it on something like that. It's not as if I don't have erinyes for that sort of thing. Let's agree that the favor will end up harming a common enemy." She smiled at Farideh again, much like Temerity had. "You can't argue with that."

"Why would you do that?"

"Well, I'd like for us to be friends. Or at least for you to trust me a little—how else will I get anything worthwhile out of you? Even Lorcan knows better than to lead with a Pact Certain." She smiled at Farideh as if the tiefling were being impish. "Honestly."

Farideh swallowed. A common enemy—the favor would be an act against another devil, another wicked soul. Dangerous, but not, if she made the deal right, an evil act. Not something she couldn't do.

Maybe it would even be best for the world, she thought. Maybe by helping Sairché she could rid the world of something worse.

You can't trust her, Farideh thought. But did she have time not to, with collector devils at her heels and Sairché threatening Havilar and Lorcan?

"What about Lorcan?"

"I think his own rivals will sort him out," Sairché said. "He doesn't even realize how worn that spell has gotten—it was never meant to protect the both of you. And he's made an awful lot of devils angry."

"Protect him too," Farideh said. "That's what I want."

Sairché chuckled. "Oh, he won't like that."

Once Sairché had held her brother prisoner in the Hells. The nightmares that had plagued Farideh during that time flashed through her thoughts: Lorcan screaming, bleeding; eyeless, tongueless, pinned to the wall. If another devil wanted Lorcan out of the way, the same thing would happen. "Protect Lorcan, Havi, and me for all those years. I'll give you the favor—but no souls and no killing. And I don't want to hurt anyone . . . anyone who's innocent. Even if it's to stop someone I call an enemy."

Sairché raised her silver eyebrows. "That's quite a lot of caveats. I may need more for my efforts. Two favors."

"The same *sort* of favors," Farideh said.

Sairché seemed to weigh this. "Fine," she said, extending a hand. "Not my first choice, but I do love a favor."

"When does it start?" Farideh asked.

Sairché smiled and took hold of Farideh's hand. "Right now."

All in an instant the spells holding Lorcan and Havilar dissolved and both were shouting. Sairché spread her other hand wide, and tendrils of magic shot out, glowing red as hot steel to wrap around Lorcan and Havilar both. Brin kicked the door in, looking around wildly, and Farideh tried to shout, to tell him to get back, out of Sairché's reach.

A wind whipped out of the still, hot air, blew up from the floorboards and swirled around Farideh, around Sairché, around Lorcan and Havilar as the magic pulled them close. It caught her warning and tossed it away. It caught Brin's cry of protest and ground it into a wordless howl, as he grabbed Havilar and tried to pull her free of Sairché's spell.

Sairché released Farideh's hand. With a small, wicked smile she spread her fingers, sending out another set of glowing lines that plunged into Farideh, wrapping around her sternum, her heart, burning her from the inside out. She might have screamed. She might have tried to tell Sairché this wasn't what she wanted. She couldn't hear her own voice. There was only the whirlwind and the fire and the blackness that grew out of Sairché's spread hands to swallow them all up and smother any more words she might have spoken.

CHAPTER TWO

I N THE FROZEN WOODS BENEATH A CRASHING EARTHMOTE, Farideh remembered. Sairché smiled—the same sort of smile Sairché had given her as the blackness surrounded them—and horror bloomed in Farideh.

"What have you done?" she breathed. "*Karshoji tiamash*, what have you done?"

"I gave you what you wanted," Sairché said.

"When did I want to wake up in a forest?" Farideh demanded. "When did I ask you to lose my friends? Where's Lorcan? Where's Brin?"

Sairché pursed her lips briefly. "The forest," she said, "is immaterial. Lorcan is on his own. Whoever Brin is, I assume he's handling himself. I've held up my end. I've made you safe."

"You've made us *lost*," Farideh said. The powers of the Hells scaled Farideh's frame, wrapping around her nerves and pulling her bones down with heavy magic. "Where are we?" She looked around the chilly grove, the fog snaking eerily over the ground. "This isn't the Hells is it?"

"Please. You'd know it if you woke up in the Nine Hells." Sairché looked up at the earthmote and glared at it a moment, before taking a scroll from one of the cases on her hips. She opened it wide to display a map of Faerûn, shivering with faint magic. She muttered something vicious sounding under her breath, then sighed, as if it couldn't be helped.

"Here," she said, laying the map on the ground and pointing to a block of forest just outside of Waterdeep where a silver mote pulsed. "That's where we stand."

Farideh's blood stilled as she studied the twining lines of roads and rivers, the dots of cities, the swell of mountains. The distance between the little cluster of towers marked Waterdeep and the little cluster marked Proskur.

Havilar's arm threaded through hers, as she leaned over the map. "That's not right. That spot is *leagues* from Proskur."

Sairché gave her a cold look. "Clearly," she drawled, "there is a problem with my portal, many thanks for pointing it out. Yes, you are quite a ways from where you started." She rolled the map back up and stood, giving them both a wicked smile. "It's not as if you can't walk back there again. It hasn't moved."

"A portal?" Farideh said. "You weren't supposed to take us through any portal."

Even as she said it, Farideh realized while Sairché had not said anything about a portal, she hadn't said anything about *not* using a portal.

Sairché narrowed her eyes at Farideh. "Perhaps Lorcan was in the habit of explaining the finer details of his spells to you. I will not. You'll have to trust me."

Farideh swallowed. " 'Was'?"

That made Sairché's wicked smile return. "Do you really think you're still his warlock now?"

"You said . . ." Farideh's voice failed her. "You *said* you'd protect him, too." But there was no sign of Lorcan, no pull on the spell of protection they'd shared.

"I did," Sairché agreed. "And I have. But if you think he's pleased you came looking for my help . . . well, I would prefer a clever warlock, but it's not a necessity."

"I didn't pact with you."

"Not yet." She took one of the rings strung along a chain

around her neck and slipped it onto her finger. Sairché rubbed the sapphire in the center with her thumb until a patch of the ground shimmered and a pile of gear appeared beside one of the leaning trees. Sairché gathered up a sword and belt, a glaive with an enameled haft, and a small case.

"Rod," she said handing it to Farideh. "Sword. And glaive." She pulled out a pair of daggers next and new haversacks, new cloaks, new rations.

The sword was not Farideh's—it was far newer, far lighter, and the blade was sharp and freshly oiled. She opened the case and found a similarly unfamiliar rod: ivory shaft carved over in Infernal runes, rubies at the tips instead of the cracked and cloudy amethysts her last implement had borne. She took hold of it, and her powers surged forth as if the rod had cleared some impediment. It made her dizzy.

"The weight's wrong," Havilar said, pushing the unfamiliar glaive back at Sairché. "And the length."

"You'll adjust," Sairché assured her.

Havilar shoved the glaive into the ferns. "Give me back my glaive."

Sairché looked as if she were reconsidering the deal they'd made. As if she were deciding if it were worth the trouble to call up her erinyes and have them both killed. "You can certainly see about replacing them in Waterdeep but take these for the moment. It's several hours' walk to the city, and heavens know what you might find. I'm sure you're well acquainted with the sort of things one encounters in the wood."

Out of the litterfall, she picked up the last two items: a bottle and a small velvet bag.

Sairché handed the bottle to Havilar. "A restorative. The spell tends to sap your strength a bit. And I know *you* need it."

Havilar pried out the lead stopper and knocked back the amber liquid. "Havi, don't!" Farideh cried.

Havilar gagged. "*Pah!*" She swallowed and a shudder went through her. "It tastes," she said, "like old burnt meat and spoiled cream." She wiped her mouth. "And cinnamon. As if that would help."

"There is a reason one does not source cordials from the Hells," Sairché said. "Nevertheless, it works." She pushed the bag at Farideh. "This is for you—from Lorcan."

The velvet was thick and dark as night. Whatever was in it was surprisingly heavy.

"I thought you said he was done with me."

"Perhaps it's a parting gift? Perhaps it's something he felt he still owed you?" She pressed a finger to her lips. "Perhaps," she said. "It's a trap."

Farideh nudged the velvet open. At its heart lay a coiled necklace of rubies. The largest gem was the size of her eye, and it seemed to glow even in the pale light. Farideh stared at it, too stunned to say anything.

Havilar leaned over her shoulder, her breath still smelling of the foul potion. "*Karshoj*. How come you get *that*?"

Sairché frowned. "Excellent question." She held out her hand. "Let me see it."

Farideh folded the velvet over the gems. "No." Lorcan's gifts had always been spells or items for casting—the necklace was something different. Did it mean Sairché was right and he'd put her pact in Sairché's hands—a parting gift then? Or was it a reassurance, a promise?

"It *might* be a trap," Sairché said again.

Whatever it was, whatever it meant, if Sairché wanted it, Farideh wasn't about to give it to her. "You had plenty of time to look at it before." She slipped the bag into her pocket.

"Well," Sairché said, dropping her hand. "If you're going to be difficult." She pointed away from the falling earthmote. "Waterdeep is that way. Do try and make it alive."

With that she selected one of the rings she wore on a chain around her neck, held it up, and blew through the center. A whirlwind seemed to spin out of the silver circle, then gusted back and enveloped Sairché. The cambion blurred as the wind threw her through the fog and out of the plane of entirely.

"Brin will be wondering what happened to us." Havilar blew out a breath full of nervous energy. "Do you think he's still waiting at the inn?"

Farideh shook her head. "I don't know." Why had a portal been necessary? Why had it dropped them in the middle of nowhere?

And Lorcan—gods, Lorcan. Her deal with Sairché looked terrible, on the face of it. Especially when they'd been fighting. If he'd just give her a chance to explain, that there hadn't been time . . .

"We might never find him again," Havilar said, of Brin. "He might just go on to Suzail without us, and then what?"

Farideh looked at the bag in her hand. Lorcan gone, and Brin lost. And Havi—she didn't understand. She wouldn't understand until they'd figured out what to do about Brin, Farideh knew that much.

"We'll go to Waterdeep," she said. "Find Tam. Or Dahl. They can do that sending ritual and find out where Brin is. We can use the portal Mehen took. I'll sell the necklace to pay for it. We'll find him."

Havilar wrapped her arms around her chest. "I cannot *believe* you made a deal with another devil. What *karshoji* demon possessed you?"

A very good question, a part of Farideh thought. They were miles from where they'd started, missing gear, missing allies. And her breath kept freezing on the air—how high up the mountains were they?

"I did it to protect you," Farideh said. "Protect us."

"From *what*?" Havilar demanded. She picked up her own cloak and haversack, fastening the garment shut with shaking fingers. "Proskur? Brin?"

"Devils," Farideh said. She picked up the strange rod—the ivory that *wasn't* ivory—and her nausea surged again. "They wanted my pact."

"Well if you hadn't *made* a *karshoji* pact," Havilar said, "neither of us would need protecting and neither of us would be waking up on the other end of the *karshoji* continent!"

"No, it would have been worse!" Farideh drew a deep breath, trying to quell the sense of unease that she couldn't seem to push past. "I didn't tell you," she admitted. "I should have. But there's a reason Lorcan wanted me for a warlock."

Havilar bent to grab the inferior glaive. "I don't care how special he says you—"

"You *and* I are descended from one of the first Hellish warlocks," Farideh went on. "The worst of them, I think. She helped Asmodeus become a god. She . . . she did horrible things to make tieflings what they are. There aren't many people descended from her—just three, and me. And you."

Farideh had held the secret for so many months, but now it was no good to hide it. "You have the same spell of protection as me. They can't scry us, but then Sairché found you anyway. Found us. There are devils out there who would do almost anything to have an heir of Bryseis Kakistos. Sairché's going to protect us—it was that or let her have you. She said she would protect us until we turn twenty-seven, and I thought maybe . . . maybe I could find some way—"

"Stop," Havilar said, looking angrier than Farideh had ever seen. "You knew all that and you didn't tell me?"

Farideh looked away. "I was scared."

"Scared of what? Scared I'd do the same stupid thing and take a pact? Because you're the only one who can handle it? Because you think I'm scared of some bugaboo old tiefling? *Karshoj* and *tiamash*, who *cares* who our great-whatever-grandmother was? I'm not scared of nightmares!"

Farideh shook her head. "You should be. You *need* to be. Trust me, Havi, Lorcan is *good* for a devil. If you don't—"

"I'm not going to make a pact!" she snapped. "Besides, how safe is it if now we have *her* chasing us around?"

"She can't hurt us," Farideh said. "That was the deal; that was the most important part." She reached for her sister, but Havilar moved away. "She would have killed Lorcan back there. She would have taken you. I traded with her so she has to protect us instead. It was the only way I could stop her, I promise."

Havilar brushed her hair back behind one ear. "I just want to get out of this *pothac* forest, figure out where we are, and find Brin." She started tramping in the direction Sairché had indicated. "I cannot *believe* you got a necklace out of this, and I only got a *disgusting* potion."

Dahl Peredur lingered over the last swallow of ale in his flagon, dreading returning to the offices above the Harper-run tavern. He had been sitting scribe for status meetings since daybreak, bent over a scroll and keeping his thoughts to himself. He would be there until sunset, no doubt, the Harper spymaster Tam Zawad asking him periodically if he had anything to add, the other Harpers giving him the sort of looks that clearly said "You'd better not" or "Go ahead, try—you'll be wrong again" or "What are you even doing here?" Looks he didn't dare point out to Tam.

A petite Tuigan woman with a shock of short black hair and large eyes dropped into the chair across from him. "I have been sitting over there," she said, "well within sight, for the last three-quarters of a bell, and I know you noticed. So why are you sulking over here?"

Dahl swallowed a sigh. "Well met, Khochen. You had company." He nodded at the woman sitting at the table, wearing a carefully unremarkable dress, her blonde hair caught up in a scarf. Lady Hedare, the agent who carried messages for the Masked Lords of Waterdeep these days.

"Yes, I know. That's half the reason you should join us."

Dahl glanced at the noblewoman, who was very deliberately not looking at Khochen or him, and made a face. "I'm fine here."

"She hasn't got a brightbird," Khochen sang.

"One," he said, "I'm not interested in Lady Hedare, and I don't know why you'd think I was. Two, she does so have a brightbird. That bodyguard is doing more than guarding her body—*you're* the one who told me that."

"Did I?" Khochen looked back at Lady Hedare and waved her over. "Well you have to assume if it's secret, it can't be that serious." The noblewoman smiled at Khochen, but took one look at Dahl and declined with a polite gesture.

"Three," Dahl said, "she doesn't like me."

Khochen glared at him. "Well, if you're going to be sour at her."

Dahl tilted his glass, considering the dregs. "I've *never* been sour at her."

"Liar. She said something you didn't like, I'll wager. What was it?"

Dahl hesitated. "After Lord Nantar died and she came up . . . there was a misunderstanding. She thought I was Tam's *secretary,* for Oghma's sake." He folded his arms. "I may have snapped at her. Now she acts as though I need to be coddled."

"You *are* his secretary."

"Only because someone has to be. I'm still—" He let the protest fall. It was arguable that he really counted as a Harper any longer, and that wasn't an argument he felt like having. "Fine," he said. "I'm his secretary."

"I don't know why that bothers you. It doesn't mean you don't count," Khochen said, and not for the first time, Dahl wondered if the Westgate spymaster could pick through his thoughts. "You still have your itchy little tattoo to prove it. And while I'm sure it comes in terribly handy while you gather reports and make Tam's schedule, it seems to mean you're dedicated."

Dahl scowled. "You're going to have to have it done eventually."

"And ruin this flawless skin?"

"You can't see it once it's done," Dahl said, "unless you trigger it. And it only itches for a tenday."

"I'll hold out. I can hide a pin." Khochen took his flagon from him and finished the ale.

"You owe me another ale for that."

"For a sip? Hardly. Shall we go up?"

Dahl scowled at her again. "What do you mean 'we'? You're not due until this afternoon."

She shrugged. "Vescaras and I tied our missions together. We're to debrief as a team—didn't you know that, Goodman Secretary? Come on." Khochen stood, and though Dahl would much rather have stayed behind, he wasn't about to make Lord Vescaras Ammakyl comment on the time.

"By the way," Khochen said, as they slipped through the door that led to the more secretive areas of the Harper hall. "I found out why Vescaras dislikes you so."

"I don't care," Dahl said. "What mission did you help him on? You've been in Westgate."

"Shipping issues. And you care. Otherwise he wouldn't bother you."

"He *bothers* me because he's a self-important prig who can't see when he's turned the wrong direction." They headed up a flight of stairs, down a long hallway lined with rooms, and into an unassuming guest room that held another stairway. "His last reports were insisting that six earthmotes crashing on or in sight of the Trade Way means a conspiracy of wizards."

"He's cautious."

"He's idiotic," Dahl said. "The rituals needed to take down *one* earthmote would have to mean that a cadre of archwizards the likes of which Vescaras of all people would have noticed is running around Faerûn wasting their powers on making caravans detour."

"Did you tell him that?"

"No, and I wasn't intending to. Tam will give him some other mission, and it won't matter. Arguing will just set Vescaras against me more."

"Maybe Tam thinks he could be right. There are worse uses of magic."

"Yes, well, if you find Karsus, the Srinshee, and bloody Elminster gloating over a caravan they've just tipped, then I'll concede. Until then . . ." He opened the door to Tam Zawad's study and waved Khochen in. Vescaras was already there. Of course he was.

Vescaras hardly looked at Dahl, which was probably for the best. There was not another Harper in all of Faerûn who pushed Dahl so close to snapping. The black-skinned half-elf looked like nothing more than the wealthy, hardworking second son of a noble family—crisp linen and spotless silk, each row of his braided hair threaded decadently with gold. Posh and polished and like he'd never dirtied a finger in his life. If the mix of Turami ancestry and elven blood made him stand out among Waterdeep's old blood, Vescaras's impeccably cool manners reminded his peers of where they stood. Not even the Ammakyls suspected that their son's interest in the family wine trade masked the fact that he ran a network of Harper spies working along the merchant caravan routes. He was very good at what he did.

And—for a time—Dahl had been very good at finding where he could do better.

"Let's begin with your joint efforts," Tam said settling behind his scarred desk. "Then Lord Ammakyl—I know you have family business to attend to. And Khochen, you can sew things up." The older Calishite man still wore the plain gray garments of an itinerant priest of Selûne, despite having been made a High Harper five or six years prior. In any other setting, a person might have assumed he was petitioning Lord Ammakyl for tithes.

"Many thanks," Vescaras said, inclining his head. "I had word, you'll recall, from one of my agents of potential smuggling through Westgate. Additional smuggling," he added, as

Khochen started to speak. "We crossed networks and uncovered quite an operation."

"Gems out of Vaasa," Khochen said. "But also a great deal of weapons, some rarer ritual components. And people."

"Headed toward Sembia," Vescaras went on.

"Not all of it," Khochen said. "I asked around. Some of it's gone straight to Shade. Some of it—not the gems, obviously—were headed back north. Fortunately there are reputable shippers thereabouts as well. We found a serious mining operation in place. They're fully routed and all but one of the mines are in working order."

"There are four shafts in place," Vescaras said. "All still finding gems. We pointed the prospectors from Thentia over to them."

Which only made Dahl wonder. "And the fifth shaft?"

Khochen smiled, with a pause that lasted half-a-heartbeat. "Broke through to the Underdark," she said. "We sealed it back up."

"Shade did that?"

"No," Khochen said. "We did. We took out the miners in one of the farther locations. Some well placed explosives and there were more drow than even the Shadovar can handle." She smiled at Dahl. "Impressive?"

Impressive they'd pulled it off. "How did you keep the rest of the mining teams busy?" he asked.

Khochen's smile flattened, and beside her Vescaras's jaw tightened—ah gods, Dahl thought. His stomach dropped as Vescaras went on. "We had some help from the Dalelands Harpers. Slowed them down with stray sheep and other nonsense. Very minor."

Tam's eyes stayed on the scarred surface of his desk. "Were any killed?"

"Eight, by the drow," Khochen admitted. "One of ours, seven of the Dales'."

"Seven," Tam repeated.

"Not ideal," Vescaras agreed. "But they were willing and—"

"And that doesn't matter," Tam said sharply. He ran a hand through his silver hair. "They don't know what they're offering, shepherds and farmers and milkmaids."

Dahl dropped his eyes to the parchment and finished scribbling notes on Vescaras's reports. Even if the half-elf and he didn't get along, even if Vescaras clearly thought Dahl should have been thrown out of the Harpers' ranks, they agreed on this score: the Harpers not overseen by Tam were still a worthwhile resource, milkmaids, shepherds, and all.

Tam cursed under his breath for a moment. "What else?" he finally said. Khochen and Vescaras ran down the more mundane parts of the mission—coin spent, contacts made, resources lost. Dahl wrote every item down, all the while thinking it was not such a transgression to have let that question slip. Probably. He would have done the same thing in Vescaras and Khochen's position . . . which might well mean it was the wrong thing to do altogether.

Gods, he thought. You're a mess today.

Vescaras then gave a detailed accounting of more than a dozen missions the agents who reported to him were running along the caravan routes. He paused and gave Dahl a sidelong look. Perhaps Khochen was right. It might help to know why Vescaras disliked him so.

Because you say all the wrong things, a part of him seemed to say. Make all the wrong decisions.

Vescaras looked back to Tam and cleared his throat. "I've lost a village. A farmstead, really. Roarke's Crossing, east of Berdusk."

Tam cursed. "To the Shadovar? When did they capture it?"

"I'm not convinced they did. I received reports two tendays ago that it had been deserted. There are signs of struggle throughout, but not a single body, beyond a few animals. No goods taken—they weren't fleeing and they weren't killed. But they're gone."

"It happens," Tam said. "Maybe the raiders caught them at the right time."

Dahl thought of the farmstead he'd grown up on, some miles outside New Velar in Harrowdale. Of what it would look like if everyone had just vanished—cow unmilked, butter half-churned, his mother's bread burning in a dying fire. His brothers' and their wives' tools fallen. Only his father's grave watching over the empty farm . . .

The image brought with it the sick shadow of grief, and he glanced out the window. Well after highsun. And Khochen had drank half his ale—Nera couldn't fault him for one more.

"Did you check the state of their stores?" he asked. Vescaras and Tam both looked at him, as if surprised he was speaking. Khochen smiled between them.

"Low," Vescaras said. "And tidy. Exactly what you'd expect to find this time of year."

Dahl shook his head. "Right." He cleared his throat. "Anyone raiding a farmstead would have ransacked the stores. And if they fled, they would have taken supplies."

Tam frowned. "Did you have a wizard search it?"

"They didn't find much," Vescaras said. "The two I brought down there said it would be a feat to kill as many people who lived there with magic that destroyed the body so completely and left no trace. If there were portals involved, they sealed closed. If it was some other planar passage, it had been too long to find evidence of it.

"There's more," Vescaras said. "Possibly. A connection, perhaps. I've lost two agents as well. One scouting along the High Road, one working out of Athkatla. Again, out of the blue, no word, no sign."

"Still, not as odd as we'd like," Tam said sadly.

Vescaras shook his head again. "It doesn't feel right. They were good agents, careful agents. They weren't heading into anything difficult. Athkatla was recovering from fieldwork, watching donations to Waukeen's temple. She missed a report,

I went to see her. No one knew where she'd gone. The scout was in Daranna's territory, reporting to her as well. Nothing. She's covering a lot of empty wilderness," he admitted, "but it's *Daranna*."

That made eight lost agents in the last tenday. And a farmstead, Dahl thought, wiping his quill on a rag. And much as he thought Vescaras was over-cautious, he agreed: something felt wrong.

"What else?" Tam asked.

"There are Shadovar picking through the ruins of Sakkors," Lord Vescaras Ammakyl was saying. "I can't say what they were doing, precisely. I didn't want my people getting too near, but I would wager they're looking for artifacts."

Tam nodded at the dark-skinned half-elf over his steepled fingers, staring intently at the surface of his desk. Dahl kept writing and waited for the older Calishite man to say something—what else would the Shadovar be doing with the ruins of their floating city? Looking for survivors a year after the collapse?

"I still have no count of those who might have fled by arcane means," Vescaras went on. "One assumes there were some, but we haven't ascertained what exactly brought the city down yet. There mightn't have been time." Dahl dutifully added this to Vescaras's report as well.

"Why are you still looking?" Khochen interjected. "It's been ages."

"Clues," Vescaras said. "Sakkors falls, then the earthmotes start. It could be connected."

"You mean the Trade Way crashes?" Khochen asked. "Dahl thinks that's idiotic. I think he makes a convincing argument."

Dahl froze, his mind a swirl of doubt. Vescaras glared at him.

"Oh?" Tam said, turning to face his scribe.

Dahl laid his quill down, swallowed to wet his mouth, and gave Khochen a glare of his own. "Most likely."

"Then how do you explain it?" Vescaras asked.

"Bad luck? Odds? I'm not trying to be difficult, all right? It makes more sense."

"*Six* within sight of the Trade Way and that's the odds?" Vescaras demanded. "I'll not be dicing with you throwing anytime soon."

"If they were *dice*, you'd be right, but they're great hulking mountains of earth." Dahl shook his head, too far to stop now. "Moving an earthmote isn't as easy as people seem to think. They float, but they're enormously heavy and especially if they're moving, it takes an absurd amount of power to turn them. They're falling all across Faerûn, you know; it's not that odd to have six fall near a road that runs the entire length of the continent. Otherwise you'd find signs of the rituals long before you'd get up to six earthmotes.

"And," he added, "if you're going to poke around Sakkors, a much better question to be asking is where are they taking those artifacts, because there is absolutely nothing else to be looking for in those ruins, and who is looking for them, because it's almost certainly someone who expects to find something, and is possibly hoping that their fellows don't notice, since you *didn't* see a great bunch of Netherese soldiers. So yes: it's idiotic, there are better uses of your time."

Deliberately ignoring Khochen's smirk, Vescaras's glare, and Tam's raised brow, Dahl picked up his quill again and set his eyes on the parchment.

"Lord Ammakyl," Tam said, "Khochen. Would you give us a moment?" Dahl didn't dare look up as the other Harpers left, his face burning, and for a long moment, the older man said nothing.

"My apologies," Dahl said. "It just came out."

"To be honest, I'm glad it did," Tam said. "You almost sounded like your old self."

"My old self is not exactly in high demand."

"Oh for the gods' sakes." Tam stood and came around the desk to stand opposite Dahl. "What else haven't you been saying?"

"It's nothing important."

"Dahl."

Dahl blew out a breath. "Daranna's agents could cover the ground Everlund's leaving open, and instead, she shouldn't worry about the possible slavers crossing into Anauroch. Our Zhentarim agent requested 'reinforcements' be sent to help the Bedine near there, and they're going to walk straight into a moot of Bedine tribes, and you know exactly what they think of slavers. It will probably help Mira's case, really—get them all banded together against the slavers as a mass for once. Brin's reports are over-detailed—they boil down to two important facts: Crown Prince Irvel has the nobles in line for the moment and all our intelligence about the Dales and Sembia is correct. You could tell him to stop wasting parchment." He paused. "That's all I can recall. I expected to re-read reports tomorrow. No, wait—Vescaras's agents and farmstead. That comes to eight agents—plus the farmstead—reported missing, although I haven't gotten a report from Sembia or Many-Arrows, so it could be ten."

"Were you planning to bring any of this up?"

"Of course," Dahl said. Then added, "When I was sure."

Tam sighed and covered his face with one hand. "How long is this going to go on?"

"I don't know what you mean."

"Dahl you're not the first person to have a mission go sour," Tam said. "You aren't the first Harper to let a target slip by. You aren't the first one to find dead bodies that shouldn't have been there."

"Nor will I be the last," Dahl finished.

Tam gave him a stern look. "If you believed me, I wouldn't have to repeat myself. I pulled you off the field to give you time to collect yourself, to use your skills inside the house."

"And I've done that," Dahl protested.

"By deciding not to tell me things you don't think I want to hear."

"I just told you," Dahl said. "Do you want more? I think you need to see a barber, you're wrong about Storm Silverhand's Harpers—in this case, anyway—and I'm pretty sure your daughter's thinking about running off with that Bedine fellow or murdering him, maybe you should talk to her. Shall I keep going?"

Tam shook his head and chuckled softly. "You're impossible."

Dahl studied Vescaras's report, the blot of ink marring the runes that spelled *farmstead*. "You can always dismiss me."

"That would be easier wouldn't it? A pity, I dislike easy answers. Mira can take care of herself—which she'd be quick to remind me if I delved into her love life—so until she murders him or asks for my opinion I'll stay mum. I'm right about putting untrained bystanders with their heads full of myths and stories into harm's way, and you certainly don't put other people's safety in their hands—we have protocols for a reason."

"It's how they did it in the olden days," Dahl said.

"Yes, well how did that suit them once Shade returned? Storm Silverhand can certainly let her networks run how she wants, only I don't want my spies leaning on brethren who lack good sense and training. We ought to—"

"Forgive me, if you suggest you're going to track Storm Silverhand down and explain what a terrible idea—"

"That was once," Tam said, and he had the grace to look embarrassed. "I may be too old to blame wine as if I don't know what it does to a man's senses, but I'll do it anyway."

Dahl smiled. "I'll not hold it against you."

Tam regarded him. "Nera tells me that you've stacked up quite a lot of receipts in the taproom."

Dahl made himself still. "It's all paid for."

"That's not what I'm worried about. Anything troubling you?"

Dahl gave him an empty smile. "I've been a drunk, Tam. These days it's just thirst."

Tam nodded—as if he were waiting for Dahl to spill out

everything he wasn't saying. "War can make a man thirsty."

Life can make a man thirsty, Dahl thought. "Yes," he said. "Well."

"How sure are you about the Dales?"

Not sure, he thought. Not sure enough. "Fairly," Dahl said. "Brin seemed sure that Harrowdale was out of the worst of it at least. The elves won't let Sembia break through, and Sembia seems to have better things to do. Their armies should keep well out of the northern countryside for awhile yet, and we should have fair warning before that changes." He hoped. Gods above, he hoped.

He'd tried to get his mother to leave the farm. He'd tried to convince his brothers there were good reasons to come to Waterdeep before Sembia turned north. But without divulging his allegiances to the secretive Harpers, why would they believe him? Who was he but the runaway brother who had the gall to throw away the life he was offered for another, only to fail at it? Who was he but the son who'd left their father baffled and disappointed when he'd come home to admit he was just a secretary in Waterdeep? And then armies filled the heartlands, making Harrowdale an island of relative safety in a sea of war.

"I know you just took a break," Tam said. "But I'm giving you another one. Let Khochen keep you company. She's in town the rest of the tenday. We'll come back to her reports when you've sorted yourself. Is Lady Hedare in?" Dahl nodded, too embarrassed at the dispensation to speak. "Send her up, get that done with." Tam ran his fingers through his silvery hair. "You're probably right about the barber. Find me some time, would you?"

"Of course," Dahl said, like a good secretary would, and shut the door behind him.

In the parlor that marked the barrier between the inn's public areas and the Harpers' private floors, Khochen was waiting for him on a battered settee, tuning a lute. "If I apologize," she said, "will you at least admit that did you a little good?"

"What good?" Dahl demanded. "I told Tam something he surely already knew and Vescaras something he refused to believe. Then I got singled out like an errant schoolboy and gods above only know what Vescaras is telling people about me now."

"Nothing most likely," Khochen said. "He's not much of a gossip."

But Vescaras was thinking about it. Adding it to the list of things that proved Dahl wasn't cut out for the Harper life anymore, right below *bad temper, can't handle shock,* and *botched mission, let people die.*

And possibly *drunk* now that Nera was telling everyone he ordered an ale too often, he thought grimly.

"Yet you got him to tell you why he hates me?" Dahl said. "He must be a little bit of a gossip."

"No," Khochen said, with a smile that was only for herself. "I'm just that good."

Dahl sighed. "Are you going to tell me or not?"

Khochen set down the lute and leaned on her armrest. "It seems," she said, all drama, "many months ago, *someone* may have gone to a revel, had a bit to drink, and snubbed a certain someone else's sister."

"What? Jadzia Ammakyl thinks *I* snubbed her? I hardly spoke to her."

"That's what 'snubbed' means," Khochen said. "At least, she would have liked you to talk more, and she apparently made an invitation for you to come back the next day."

"To look at her library. Which I wouldn't bother with. It's a pokey little—" He colored at Khochen's smirk. "We only talked for a few minutes. About books."

"Girl has to make an inroad where she can."

And lovely Jadzia Ammakyl had absolutely no need to make inroads with a scruffy farmer's son, Dahl felt sure. "You're wrong. Vescaras is wrong."

"Vescaras is *right*," Khochen said, "although he's mad as the wizard under the mountain to still be carrying that around.

Jadzia's forgiven and forgotten, so far as I can tell. Swarmed with suitors."

"Of course she is," Dahl said. "She's rich as Waukeen's handmaid."

Khochen clucked her tongue and rose to stand beside him. "I have another guess," she said. "I think you *did* notice. Why else would you pick the right sister—he's got four, hasn't he? You noticed and you choked because you are utterly convinced no one of quality is interested in you."

"Why are you always picking at my love life like you can stir it up into something interesting?" Dahl demanded.

Khochen's wicked grin fell away and she regarded Dahl with utter seriousness. "Because it's the safest thing I can tease you about."

Dahl pointedly turned toward the taproom, knowing Khochen would follow but knowing it would give him a minute to compose himself. Gods, he needed a drink. *One* drink.

Khochen caught up to him. "Where you got the idea that *anyone* in Waterdeep gives two cracked nibs about where you grew up or what god left you behind or how you've erred—"

"You've made your point."

"My point," she added, gentler now, which made it all worse, "is that you needn't be so determined to make sure you're right that everyone dislikes you as much as you believe. Whether that's Jadzia or Lady Hedare or Vescaras."

"Vescaras *does* dislike me," he pointed out as they descended the stairs. "I don't need your pity, all right?" He paused at the foot of the stairs and looked back at Khochen. "By the way," he said more quietly, "are you missing any agents?"

"I lose some low-level recruits, street-eyes and such. Gangs pick them off, Zhentarim pick them up."

Dahl shook his head. "No, I mean agents dropping off your map. No word, no sign, no bodies. Strange things."

She frowned at him. "Not that I know of. But then that might be any of my lost ones."

"It's probably nothing," he admitted.

"I'll think about it. And," she added, coming to stand beside him again, "might I note, if you talked to Vescaras the same way as you do me, instead of being an absolute prat, he might listen too."

Dahl rolled his eyes and headed into the taproom. If he drank the ale quick, if he made it a small one, Nera might not notice, might not tell Tam. It wasn't as if the High Harper could tell if he'd had just one.

"You already said he's not a gossip," he said. "So how am I supposed to talk to Vescaras like I do to you?"

"You could tell him your sad stories about your father."

Dahl flushed. "Khochen, enough. I don't need—"

But the words evaporated out of his mouth, stolen by the sight of a ghost, standing thirty feet before him, in the middle of the Harpers' inn.

CHAPTER THREE

FARIDEH EYED THE DRINKERS SCATTERED THROUGH THE taproom, marking the heavy cloaks, heavy boots, the thick skirts and padded jackets. Things were far, far worse than she'd imagined.

The cold—she'd figured it was the early morning, the higher altitude, being farther north. Maybe she shivered because she was a little ill from Sairché's spell—she certainly didn't feel well. But as they came down the slopes and the sun rose higher behind the clouds, the chilly air didn't warm.

Maybe it's just a cold snap, she thought, a strange bit of weather here and then forgotten. She said as much to Havilar. But then they'd reached Waterdeep and she saw the old snow packed against the buildings, the bits of melting ice hanging from their eaves.

Havilar didn't seem to notice, her expression closed and her hands clinging tight to Farideh's arm. If her thoughts had moved away from Brin, from her missing glaive, from poor Mehen left in Cormyr, she gave no sign at all. She moved as if she just wanted Farideh to get her to Tam so they could right everything again.

But could they right anything, Farideh wondered, if Sairché's spell hadn't merely moved them? If perhaps, it had snatched away a season when it was cast?

She couldn't see another option, and it made her whole body jagged with fear and nerves. It was, inescapably, winter. Late winter. It was late winter and they were both frailer, thinner. And Sairché had cut their hair—to hide the loss of time? Five months, she thought, or six or seven or more? She had to find out before Havilar did, that was sure.

You will fix it, Farideh told herself. There is nothing so broken here you can't find a way to fix it.

"Come on," she said to Havilar, and pulled her up to the bar and the tavernkeeper. "Well met," Farideh said. She swallowed and dropped her voice. "We need to see Master Zawad."

The tavernkeeper's expression was puzzled. She shook her head. "Don't know him."

Terror poured down Farideh's bones. Calm, she told herself. They like their secrets. "He's a friend," Farideh said, "and it's urgent. Please."

"Can't help you," the tavernkeeper said. She cut her eyes to the left, to where a lean human with pale skin and freckles was watching without watching.

"Please we—"

"You going to order?" The tavernkeeper gave Farideh a pleasant smile, an empty smile.

"I need to talk to Tam, I need to talk to him right now."

"Because if you're not going to order," she went on, "I think you ought to be on your way."

"Gods damn it!" Farideh hissed. "I know he's here! He'll see us." Or maybe he won't, she thought, maybe he's given orders to keep us away. Maybe he died. Maybe the Harpers moved. "He will," she added softer, a plea. "He has to."

The woman shook her head. "Don't know who you mean," she said, sounding apologetic. "Maybe you should try the Rusted Anchor."

He wouldn't be at any Rusted Anchor. If he wasn't here, she had no idea where he *would* be, and they would have no one who might help them find Mehen, find Brin. She squeezed Havilar's hand. She reached for the necklace in the pouch at her belt—a bribe, maybe a bribe would do it. She said a silent apology to Lorcan.

"Farideh?"

She looked up to see a tall man with gray eyes and several days' worth of stubble on his chin. He looked tired—so tired it took her a moment to recognize him.

"Dahl," she said, almost a sigh of relief. The Harper agent had been assigned to Tam—he'd know where the priest was. If not, Dahl was the one who'd taught Farideh rituals. He knew the sending spells. He could help them. It would be all right.

But he was staring at her as if she were some terrible beast, risen up and asking politely about the weather. Her stomach clenched. They hadn't parted angrily—she and Dahl had had their share of clashes, but things were settled enough between them. He had no reason to be angry at her.

Unless word had gotten back that she'd made a deal with Sairché.

"Please," she said. "Whatever Tam thinks we've done—"

"Nera," Dahl said to the tavernkeeper, "I need a room. The griffon room. Send up . . ." He shook his head and looked the twins over. Farideh shifted uncomfortably. "Bread, cheese, and some tea? And whiskey. A pot of it. Come on," he said to Farideh, "I'll take you to Tam."

He led them to the stairs at the far end of the taproom, passing a petite woman with short dark hair. As they passed her, Farideh heard him whisper, "Go get Tam. This is the very next thing he needs to deal with."

Farideh's pulse was speeding. This was the next horrible step. They knew, they had to know. Her stomach churned, but she held tight to Havilar's hand and pressed forward. What had happened had happened, she told herself. Now you just hear it and fix it.

But a little part of her was starting to worry that this time, there was too much to fix.

Dahl led them into one of the rooms. As they entered, Farideh felt the faint itch of a spell cast over it. There was a bed, a table with four chairs, and a writing desk with a soot-smudged painting of a griffon tearing into a sahuagin over it. Dahl opened the heavy curtains wider to let in more of the cold, bleached light. He lit candles. He moved the table out of the way. He wouldn't look at Farideh again.

Farideh kept Havilar's hand in a firm grip. When she found out that they'd lost half a year, she would be frantic. Furious. She wouldn't understand the perils of the devils that could be after her, not right away. Farideh steeled herself for the inevitable fight.

Dahl finally ran out of things to fuss with and turned to the twins again.

"Do you want to sit?" he asked. "He'll be a moment."

Farideh would rather have stood, but Havilar dropped into a chair, and it was easier to land beside her, still holding her hand. She didn't like the way Dahl was watching them. They couldn't know about Sairché, she reasoned. Why would Brin tell the Harpers anything, after all?

"Thank you," she said.

Dahl nodded absently. "Where have you been?" he asked after another interminable pause.

Farideh swallowed against the pulse in her throat. "It's a long story."

"What do you mean?" Havilar asked. "Where should we have been?"

"Well," Dahl said carefully, "the last I heard . . . people seemed to believe that you had died. On the way to Cormyr."

Farideh drew a sharp breath. For Dahl to have heard would have taken time—time for Brin to give up, time for him to get to somewhere he could get a message to Waterdeep, time for that to filter down to Dahl.

She was right. Sairché had snatched them away. A whole summer, a whole winter just *gone*.

Havilar squeezed her hand tighter, and Farideh could not look at her. "Where did you hear that?" she asked. "*How* did you hear that? We've only been gone a month."

Dahl eyed her again with a puzzled expression. "It's longer, isn't it?" Farideh said.

Dahl seemed to struggle to answer. "Yes."

The door opened, and Tam entered, his irritation evident even beneath the patina of peace he exuded. Farideh's heart stopped cold as he smiled pleasantly at Dahl. "I hear there's something terribly important to—" Farideh stood up, and he stopped in his tracks.

When they'd left Waterdeep, the Calishite priest's dark hair and beard had been liberally scattered with threads of gray. Now every hair on his head shone silver as his goddess's emblem. *That doesn't happen in a few months,* Farideh thought, her head spinning. The world felt as if it were closing down on her. Even Havilar noticed—she tensed, pulling her sister nearer.

"Shar pass us over." Tam shut the door behind him, his eyes never leaving the twins. "You're alive."

"Why do you keep saying that?" Havilar asked, sounding as if she dreaded the answer. "How long have we been gone?"

"She thinks it's been a month," Dahl said.

A pretty number, don't you think? Sairché had said. *I'll protect you and your sister from death and from devils, until you turn twenty-seven.* Farideh couldn't catch her breath. Couldn't slow her pulse. She looked at Tam, at Dahl, at Havilar. They weren't just tired. They weren't just thinner. It hadn't been months. It can't be, she thought. It can't be.

"How long?" Havilar repeated, firmer.

"They turned up in the taproom," Dahl said. "Nera had given the signal to throw them out."

Tam shook his head. "Lucky timing."

"*How long,*" Havilar demanded, "have we been gone?"

"It's ten years," Farideh said, hardly more than a whisper. She looked up at Tam, at Dahl. "It's been ten years, hasn't it?"

"Seven," Dahl said, "and a half." Farideh sat back down, all the blood draining away. That wasn't better.

Havilar stared at Tam and Dahl, as if either might contradict Farideh, might say this was all a prank or a misunderstanding. They looked back, sadly.

She let out a breath, half a cry, and yanked her hand from Farideh's. "Seven years," she repeated. "*Seven. Karshoji. Years.*"

"I didn't know," Farideh said, shaking her head. She felt as if her whole body would turn itself inside out if she twisted wrong. "I didn't think—"

"Of course you didn't!" Havilar said. "You *never* think!"

There was a tap at the door—the tavernkeeper with the food. Dahl poured a few fingers of whiskey for each of the women, and some for himself. Farideh watched, feeling as if these things were happening on the other end of the world. When he handed her a glass, she took it with numb hands and only held it, cupped in her lap.

Every fiber of her being was coiled tight, vibrating with the knowledge of how badly she'd erred, how completely she'd destroyed so many lives, because Sairché was cleverer than she. Every bit of her *hurt*.

Only a tiny part of her mind clung screaming to the fact that seven and a half years meant her deal with Sairché wasn't done. That she'd see Sairché again.

"All right," Tam said, shaken. "All right. You'll stay here. That's easiest. We have healers. A wizard who can . . . Right."

Havilar drained her cup. "I want my own room."

That drove the last of the air from Farideh. "What?" Havilar did not look at her.

"Of course," Tam said. "You'll need to answer questions. Be checked. We need to be sure this isn't something bigger."

"It's not," Farideh said, but she could hardly get the words out. "It's only us."

Tam sat down in the desk's chair. "We need to make sure you're well enough, too. I'll stay with you." He turned to Dahl.

"Send for Mehen. Right now." He hesitated before adding, "Brin too."

Farideh clung to the cup as if it might be an anchor, and shut her eyes tight as the world started swimming. She had to fix this. She had to make Sairché fix what she'd wrought.

There were, Dahl thought, standing before the closed door, a hundred other things he could be doing. That sending to Everlund. Re-sorting the handler's reports. Attempting to contact Sembia again. Get Tam an hour or so to get his hair cut and his beard trimmed. He took a mouthful of whiskey from the flask in his pocket, rubbed a thumb nervously over the card case in his hand, and then knocked anyway.

Khochen had been on him the very breath the door to the guest room had closed, but Dahl had brushed her off, unable to form an appropriate answer to any of her questions: *Who are they? How do they know Tam? What's going on?* He couldn't fathom the full answer to that last one in particular, even as Tam repeated the wizards' and healers' findings, the twins' answers to the same questions.

"They're remarkably healthy," Tam said. "Aside from a little muscle weakness, a little slowness of the reflexes. Aside from losing seven and a half years of memories."

"They just volunteered that it was a deal with a devil?" Dahl asked.

Tam studied his desk. "Could be worse, I'm sorry to say. At least it *seems* to be an isolated event, not some harbinger of a new invasion. Another front to the wars."

Dahl held his response in—not wanting to disagree, not wanting to be wrong, not wanting to be right—until he was quite sure he might burst. "But why would a devil just set a person—set people aside for over seven years? There *has* to be more to it."

"That I won't doubt," Tam said. "But it's not either of their doing. Neither one has the sort of mark such evil leaves. Perhaps it was some kind of punishment."

"Or a small step in a greater plan?" Dahl suggested. "I'm *not* saying she's wicked, but you're not going to argue in Lorcan's favor." He thought of the devil Farideh had an agreement with, the smirking human face he'd worn the last time Dahl had seen him, the last time Dahl had left a gift for Farideh. If Dahl was a prat, that one was a straight bastard.

Tam sighed. "I would argue he has moments of goodness, and I suspect he's not the sort to lead an invasion of the mortal plane. But I wouldn't trust him to black my boots, no." He paused. "When will Mehen arrive?"

"The day after tomorrow. Earliest appointment for the portal."

"So you have that long to tease anything useful out of them then," Tam said. "Once Mehen's here, I doubt he'll let anyone near them for a time, and if you're right . . . well, it might be too late."

"I don't—" Dahl stopped himself and tried again. "Is that the wisest course? Surely there's someone else. Someone they're more likely to talk to."

"You and I are the only souls in this building—maybe even in this whole city—who they know," Tam had said, in a way that said he would hear no argument. "And as you are so fond of pointing out, I am terribly overextended. This is *your* task."

This is my next failure, Dahl thought, standing in front of the door to Farideh's room. His chest was a knot of guilt and fear and anger—a snarl of feelings all pulled up and pressed together into something new and unnameable and awful.

She hated me, he thought, considering the grain of the door. She convinced me to do things I still regret. Or did he have it all jumbled—did she try to save him and *he* scorned her? Was she more a herald bearing the god's message than a devil sent to vex him? He couldn't deny—not even in his worst moments—that he'd been the one to lead her into terrible dangers, that he'd had good reason to wonder if he bore a portion of the blame for her rumored death. But he thought surely he could remember Farideh laughing, smiling, talking in a serious but comradely way. So which way was he wrong?

After more than seven years, Dahl still wasn't sure.

He was sure, however, that if he couldn't get a little information out of someone he *knew* Tam would be right to throw him out of the Harpers. "Farideh?" Dahl called through the door. "Are you in?" There was no answer. She does remember, he thought. You were the worse one. He turned to go. Maybe Havilar was still awake.

The door cracked open, and Farideh peered out, her silver eye framed in the gap of the door. "Yes?"

A flood of fear rushed through him—without realizing, he'd been hoping she wouldn't open the door. "Well met," he said. She eased the door wider. Her face was red and swollen from crying—ah, gods. "I thought you should know. Mehen will be here the day after tomorrow."

Whatever sorrow she'd pushed down threatened to burst free for a moment, but she looked down, overcame it. "Oh."

Gods, don't make her cry, he thought. "He's well. If you're worried about that. Not . . . not a Harper. I think he thinks we're all making things harder than they have to be." He gave a nervous laugh. "I was surprised, when I first met him, you know? I didn't know your father was a dragonborn."

"Is he angry?" she asked, and in that moment, Dahl couldn't imagine why he'd ever cast her as a devil.

"No," he said gently. "Not at you, anyway." He hesitated. "I assume . . . he's going to be mad at Lorcan."

She gave him a strange look he couldn't read. "Lorcan didn't have anything to do with this."

"Oh. Well . . . whoever it was," Dahl said, "do you think they're likely to come after you?"

Farideh shook her head. "I don't know."

"Do you have any idea what . . . the devil wants? Why they took you? Why they brought you back?"

She swallowed hard. "I said before. I don't know."

Stop asking, he told himself. Just go. This is not the time.

He held the card case out instead. "Here. They're Wroth cards," he added as she took them from him. "I was trying to buy just a playing set. That's what they had. They're meant for fortune-telling, but you can divide the numbers and it will work."

"Thank you," she said, sounding reflexive.

"There's a reason. I mean, do you know Deadknight?" he asked. She shook her head. "It's a card game. You play it alone. When my father died . . . It's hard not to just sink into all that sadness. I was starved for things to distract me, to keep my hands occupied. I played a lot of Deadknight." He stared at the case, all too aware of that sick, sad feeling creeping up on him. Whiskey worked a lot better than Deadknight these days. "I wished someone had told me about that. Before."

"I don't think cards will fix this," she said, her voice catching.

"No," he said. "They just make it easier to sort through. Slow it down."

She blew out a heavy breath. "Give them to Havilar."

He took the second deck from his pocket. "I have one for her too."

She stared at him. "I don't know how to fix it."

"Maybe you can't," Dahl said and regretted it immediately. It might be what he wished someone had said to him, but it wasn't what she needed to hear.

"Thank you for the cards," she said after a moment, her voice softer, smaller. She turned the deck over in her hand. "Is there anything else? I'd . . ." She swallowed again. "I don't really want to talk."

"No," he said quickly. "Sorry. I'll check back another time. But can I say—"

She slammed the door before he could finish and a moment

later . . . a heart-wrenching wail, muffled so he wouldn't hear. Dahl shut his eyes and stood before the door, wanting so badly to be anywhere else, but finding a perverse penance in listening.

You didn't cause this, he told himself. You couldn't have. Whatever you regret, whatever you were afraid happened . . .

He shouldn't have stayed so long. He should have left her alone. At least, he thought, as he went to Havilar's room, he hadn't managed to apologize—that had been a foolish plan.

His life had gone on, snarled and frayed as it was, but hers had stopped. He tried to imagine what it felt like—if it was anything remotely like how it felt to have fallen.

Gods, he thought as he knocked on Havilar's door, either no more whiskey or enough to shut you up. Two makes you maudlin.

Havilar wasn't much happier to see him. She took the cards as if they were some sort of trap. "Brin is coming too. Isn't he?" she asked.

"I don't know," Dahl said. That might smooth things over and it might start everything up again. "Do you want to talk about what happened, before they—"

"My *pothac* sister made a deal with a devil," Havilar interrupted. "That's what happened."

"What did the devil have you do in exchange?"

Havilar scowled. "I didn't *do* anything but get sucked into her stupid decisions. This *aithyas* isn't my fault."

"I wasn't blaming you," Dahl said.

"Well, don't. Go bother Farideh. She's the one who has to fix this mess." Havilar slammed the door in his face.

Dahl sighed. You still have tomorrow, he told himself. He could show them each the rules to Deadknight, get them talking. He wandered back down the stairs, through the twisting corridors. He was already dreading it.

The sound of an off-key lute drifted through the hallway and he stopped beside a small alcove, where two battered chairs faced each other. Khochen had draped herself across one.

"Are you going to tell me?" Khochen asked, not looking up from her instrument.

"Tell you what?"

"The tiefling. The one with the odd eye." She plucked a string, frowning as she tweaked the pins to raise the pitch. "Although, I'm curious about the other one too. She just seems to be less interesting, when it comes to you."

"Oghma's bloody paper cuts, Khochen," Dahl said. "Stop trying to invent me a love life you can gossip about."

She raised her eyebrows as she adjusted another string. "I didn't say love life."

"But were you about to. Honestly—say no and I'll owe *you* an ale."

Khochen looked up at him and smiled. "What's her name?"

"Farideh," he said. "And Havilar. They're . . . they know Tam. And one of the Suzail agents."

"And you."

"And me," he agreed. "It's not that interesting, I promise."

"Don't tell *me* what's interesting," Khochen chided. "If she hadn't gotten into a shouting match with Nera, I would've guessed they were agents, maybe you were assigned together at some point. You and Tam both hopped-to, casting sendings and summoning the wizards, not even once suggesting this is a trick of Shade or Thay or Vaasa or who-in-the-Hells-can-even-predict-anymore, so she's—"

"*They're,*" Dahl said.

"—someone you trust and care a little about. If she weren't a tiefling, I'd guess old lover and be done."

Dahl rolled his eyes. "*There* we are. She's not. Not even close."

Khochen waggled her fingers at him. "You say that, but you're loitering around her room with gifts?"

"I got both of them gifts."

"I'll spare you the obvious ribbing about twins," Khochen said dryly, and Dahl scowled. "I've never heard of you going for anything more complicated than a half-elf, so it's not that."

"It's not that, because I *said* it's not that."

"So I'm left with two options," Khochen went on. "Either your mother had a tumble with a devil-child at some point and those are your misbegotten sisters, or you have a very good story you're not sharing with me. And I know you'll tell me your mother is practically Chauntea come to mortal flesh." Khochen patted the seat beside her. "So do you want to tell me, or shall I just keep guessing?"

Dahl stayed standing. "It's personal."

"*Everything* is personal with you, Dahl. That's part of your problem." When he didn't speak, Khochen rolled her eyes. "I figured out about Oghma and your fall," she said. "I'll figure this out too."

"Please don't," he said.

"You're upset," she said. "So you're feeling guilty, I suspect. Embarrassed. It's old, because you're not angry—and you, poppet, stay angry a long time. You've had time to cool off and realize this might actually have been your fault and not hers or the world's. Which means it's something rather bad, isn't it? Accidental though—you can be thoughtless but never cruel."

"Stop." But Dahl knew there would be no stopping Khochen, and his heart was too close to the surface to ignore. He dropped into the opposite seat. "Look, it's complicated. It's terribly complicated, and embarrassing, and it's not for gossip, all right?"

Khochen's brown eyes met his. "I'll trade you," she said solemnly. "I'll tell you something personal, and you tell me this."

Dahl snorted. "Be serious. You'll tell me some fancy full of shocking details that I can't verify—or won't dare to. Nothing's personal with you, Khochen." He sighed. "Which is probably quite wise of you."

"Poor Dahl," she said. She regarded him a long moment. "I've started sleeping with Vescaras."

Dahl waited for the jest, the sly mockery to come. But Khochen watched him, as if she'd done no more than remark on the possibility of finding currants in the market this time of year.

"You have not."

"Have so," she said. "You know how it is—you carry out a mission, you get to talking, one thing leads to the next. Naturally, we've agreed it's no one's business but ours—Tam would have opinions. Vescaras's family would rather he settle down. And I lose a certain amount of . . . effectiveness if my network gets word I take a man who wears silk smallclothes to my bed and he leaves keeping all his coin." She snickered as Dahl looked away. "But," she added, "now it's your business too. So trade me."

Dahl tried to tell her that wasn't fair, he hadn't agreed. He tried to tell her that wasn't such a terrible secret, not worth his own. He tried to ask her what in the world she saw in Vescaras.

"I'm sorry," he said eventually. "I didn't know. I should have kept my tongue about him."

Khochen waved him off. "Oh, why? *You're* not sleeping with him. Come on, out with it. Or I'll start telling you *more* personal things."

"Gods." Dahl rolled his eyes. "Shortly after I joined the Harpers," he said. "They assigned me to Tam, and . . . I don't think I ever got the full story, but he was watching out for the twins. Only I convinced Farideh to go to this revel. And the host—do you remember Adolican Rhand?"

Khochen frowned. "The mission that—" She bit off what she'd been about to say, a skip so quick and subtle anyone else might have missed it. But Dahl knew what she meant: *the mission that broke you.*

"—you were on before you were pulled into the house?" she finished. "What was the twist? Something unpleasant."

"Four bodies," Dahl said quietly. "Mutilated coin lasses. And an apprentice." He'd found the apprentice, the freshest victim, himself, and he never had shaken the memory. She'd been one of the sources Rhand was playing him through. If he'd been quicker, if he'd found out Rhand had been feeding him false information sooner, she, at least, might have survived.

"Right." Khochen shuddered. "You ever catch him?"

"No. He's still in Shade for all we know. Untouchable. Seven years ago, he held a revel," he said, "and he'd invited Farideh. He'd marked her, I suppose. She was afraid, and I *needed* to get into that revel. Tam was going to do something dangerous, and we were going to lose the artifacts we needed to get ahold of—I thought." He rubbed his forehead, the tension that rose there. "I convinced her it was safe, and then as soon as I walked away, Rhand drugged her. If I hadn't dragged her off . . ."

Khochen was quiet a moment. "He liked to take pieces unevenly, as I recall. A hand. A foot. Some fingers. Let them bleed out eventually."

It wasn't until they'd found those bodies years later, that he'd realized what a terrible set of cards he'd dealt her. And then there were the scraps of rumors about what had happened to the twins—and no one could say, only that they'd disappeared on the road to Suzail—well within reach of Adolican Rhand.

"I wasn't nice to her," he said, "even after, although she was just as bitter with me. I just sort of decided she was exactly what you'd expect a tiefling to be—wicked and sharp-tongued and not half as clever as they seem. She embarrassed me once, in front of Tam, and not on purpose and that was it, I—"

"You don't have to describe it," Khochen said mildly. "I've seen you with Vescaras."

But it was not the same as Vescaras. If Vescaras pointed out Dahl's shortcomings, it was to put him in his place. But when Farideh had called him out—told him he thought he was so smart but that every other word out of his mouth was another assumption that wasn't fair—she'd been right.

And it had made Dahl wonder if that was why he had fallen from Oghma's grace, if perhaps he hadn't failed at one of the many strictures of paladinhood but done something more fundamentally opposed to Oghma's doctrine. For the first time in the years since he'd lost his place as one of the

God of Knowledge's paladins, Dahl had an idea of what he could remedy.

But it hadn't been enough, and the world had yanked Dahl around like an errant hound as he tried to find the answer. He'd started to curse Farideh for even putting the thought in his head—wasn't it just like her to get under his skin like that?

He'd nearly given up, nearly decided that he'd wasted time and energy on utter nonsense that some tiefling girl out of the mountains had poured in his ear.

And then Oghma spoke to him.

But after that, it had been the Church of Oghma's turn to speak, and Dahl had lost his hope, his future, his father's respect, all in one awful year. And part of him still traced the thread of heartbreaks back to a mission in the Nether Mountains and to a tiefling girl whom he couldn't stop fighting with.

Who is she? Khochen had asked. A devil, an angel, an ally, an antagonist, a symbol, a nightmare? I don't know, Dahl thought. I don't know.

"So your secret shame," Khochen said, "is that you were a smug, reckless hardjack to someone and you feel bad about it?"

"More or less," Dahl said.

"Hmmph. That's less interesting than I expected. I don't think it's worth my secret."

She said it light and teasing, as if she meant to lighten his burden. But it wasn't so minor—through Farideh, Dahl had lost his last hope at returning to the Church of Oghma and his faith in his skills as a Harper. The urge to prove the Oghmanytes wrong, to find the answers and regain his standing, still rose up in him from time to time—but that was what ale was for, after all. His old mentor, Jedik, sent letters, now and again, and Dahl relegated them all to a box beneath his dresser, not sure enough to burn them, hurt enough to never read them.

If Khochen said a single, witty word about any of that, he would never speak to her again.

So Dahl only smiled. "You'll just embellish it to be more

interesting, anyway." He stood and headed toward the taproom.

"You don't think," Khochen called, starting another little tune on her lute, "that there's something odd here?"

Dahl turned. "What do you mean?"

"It's awfully convenient that this girl—these girls—that you and Tam cared about and grieved for have suddenly turned up, in the taproom of the Harper Hall, hale and whole but in need of care and comfort?"

"You think she's someone's agent?"

Khochen shrugged. "I think if she'd turned up looking for anyone else, you'd be the first to suggest it." She frowned and tweaked one of the tuning pins. "At least, you would've a few years ago."

Dahl hesitated. The thought had crossed his mind—he'd pushed it aside when he'd seen how sure Tam had been, when no one who'd examined the twins had noticed anything amiss. "It'd be a clever plan," he said. "But all you have is that."

"All I'm saying is you ought to keep an eye on them. Especially the warlock."

"I know that."

"Do you?" Khochen looked up at him, as serious as he'd ever seen her. "Because truly, I would have guessed that little gesture—if she's not some sweetheart you're trying to win back—was that of a man trying to absolve himself. Trying to walk away. Which does sound like you, right now."

Dahl gritted his teeth. Every urge to run from the overwhelming embarrassment that wrapped him like an invisible cloak at the sight of Farideh seemed to turn solid and unavoidable in his thoughts. "I know what I'm doing," he said tensely.

"Good," Khochen said, cheerful once more. "Did I hear you say 'Mehen' was coming? As in Lord Crownsilver's bodyguard?"

"They're his daughters," Dahl said, still smarting.

"Interesting," Khochen said. She strummed the lute. "You'll have to introduce me."

"Of course," Dahl said. " 'Meet Khochen, she's the one

who started a rumor about your daughter, the Shadovar spy.' "

" 'And her torrid affair with the Shepherd's secretary,' " Khochen finished cheekily. "If you're going to tell tales, tell good ones."

Dahl scowled at her. "Give my regards to Lord Ammakyl. And *never* tell me about his smallclothes again." He turned and went down to the taproom, trying hard to ignore Khochen's laughter.

Farideh had no sense of how long it took for the swell of grief to pass, only that it had wrung her dry. She sat up and wiped her eyes—hoping dearly no one had heard—and found Sairché standing on the other side of the small room.

"I see you discovered my little ruse," she said.

Farideh lunged at the cambion, all fury and instinct. She felt the surge of Sairché's shield go up, but it provided no more resistance than a stinging across her knuckles as she slammed a fist into the other woman's jaw. Sairché's head snapped back and Farideh's hand exploded with pain. She didn't care. She aimed another, more thoughtful strike at Sairché's throat, but before it connected the shield flared again. The magic pushed back, yanking her arm against the socket and throwing her off balance. Farideh fell backward to the floor.

Sairché pressed a hand to her bleeding and rapidly swelling lip. "You little bitch," she said, half-marveling.

"Seven years!" Farideh cried, tears streaming anew down her cheeks. "You stole seven *years* of my life, destroyed my sister, broke my father's heart. And then you sent us off, without a word of what you've done? You're lucky I only hit you, you miserable *tiamash*."

Sairché's golden eyes seemed to simmer. "Maybe next time you'll think about that before you throw around insults." Her cruel smile returned. "And really, if you think about it, it's closer to eight years."

Much as Farideh would have liked to tackle the devil again, to lash out and drive some of the anger out of her heart, the shield was still there, shimmering faintly. She clutched her bruised knuckles.

"Why?" she said softer.

Sairché picked Dahl's case of cards up off the floor. "Do you play cards, Farideh?" she asked, sliding the deck out. "You cannot lay just any old suit, any value down. You must think ahead, plan for what you will need." She fanned the painted cards out. "This fortunately is not a game of cards, and so I can keep my best plays in my pocket and take them out when they are needed. Much better than laying everything out at the start or waiting for someone else to force my hand."

"Havilar is not yours to play!"

"Not yet. But she and I haven't gotten to know each other yet."

"If you go near her, I swear, I'll—"

"What? Strike me? Throw more bolts at my shield? I've had all this time to prepare for your little tantrums. There is nothing you can do to me."

"Yet," Farideh said. "You haven't seen what I have to play."

Sairché laughed. "Do you want a *game*? Fine. The next move is yours—two days to yourself. Go ahead. Figure this out. Undo our deal."

"Then what?"

"Then it's my turn again." She gave Farideh a wicked smile. "And I'll collect on my favor."

"I owe you *nothing*," Farideh said. "You didn't keep your end—"

"I *always* keep my ends up," Sairché said. "Protect you until you're twenty-seven, isn't that what I said? And did any devil in the Hells give you the slightest trouble these last years? *Hmm*? No. Not a one. And I fully intend to hold to that until the Marpenoth after this. Full circle." She sneered. "You owe me a pair of favors, make no mistake. And I'll collect the first in two days."

Farideh swallowed. "And if I refuse?"

"Then your soul is mine," Sairché said.

"You said my soul wasn't on the table!"

"I said it wasn't the price," Sairché corrected. "And it's not: it's the forfeit. You don't carry out your end of our deal, I get your soul. That's standard practice—I shouldn't have to specify *that*."

Farideh's heart hung in her chest like a lead weight. If there were a way around Sairché's deal, a secret path through the phrasing she could exploit, Sairché had already had seven and a half years to find it. Seven and a half years, and a lifetime of the machinations of the Hells. She was born to this, Farideh thought. You were not.

But that didn't mean she could stop hunting for the answer.

"What if you fail to keep your end?"

Sairché's expression grew stony. "Then I have my own punishments. Trust me—I won't fail. And neither," she added, "will you."

She wouldn't. She couldn't. Not with her soul in the balance. Not with Havilar to protect. Unless . . .

"What would you take . . . What would I have to do to take it all back?" she asked. "To go back. Even . . . even just Havilar. If you could just put her in Proskur when—"

"I doubt even the gods would grant that deal," Sairché said. "Much as I'd love to strike a bargain. Time isn't to be toyed with."

Farideh looked down at her lap. "Tell me what you've done with Lorcan."

Sairché reached over and patted her cheek. "Poor girl. He has a lot of other warlocks to worry about. Maybe he's just washed his hands of you?" She chose a ring off the necklace and slipped it over her finger. A portal opened in the air behind her, leaking fumes of brimstone and ash. "Do cheer up," she said, before backing into the portal. "There are plenty of people in worse straits than you."

Is it the waters of the Fountains of Memory that make the air so cold? Or is it the magic that holds them? Farideh leans over the stone basin, watching her breath curl like the unearthly fog had that first day and asks the apprentices if they know. The wizards eye her and then each other, as if they can't decide whether it's their place to make her leave. The brown-bearded one finally offers that it's both—the source is frigid, the magic keeps it so. Farideh takes a pinch of the blue petals from the bowl beside the waters and crushes it into a powder that smells like heavy perfume and bitter roots as she watches the look his peers give him—they don't know what to do with her at all.

Let them think she's charmed by the Fountains of Memory. The fortress won't give up its secrets, its master hides away, and the guards only smirk as she searches—the apprentices might not be so cautious. Or maybe the waters *will* have the answers. But not this first time.

The first vision she summons is for her own satisfaction, her own penance. The crushed petals dissolve into the clear water, lending it a momentary murkiness before the waters reflect a dragonborn man sitting in a prison cell—her father, Clanless Mehen. He has been there for two months, most of the summer. They've taken his armor and the falchion he prizes for reasons Farideh knows he pretends are entirely practical. The Crownsilvers have imprisoned him for kidnapping their secret scion, even though nothing of the sort has happened.

A guard stands off to the left, beside a woman with a dark bob and a stiff back, her tabard marked with the symbols of her family and her god. Mehen glares at the knight of Torm, as if waiting for an answer.

"If he doesn't return," Constancia Crownsilver says, "then . . . we will have to decide what to do with you."

"Clever plan," Mehen says. "Are you going to keep me here? Feed and clothe me? Or are you going to get out the executioner's axe for a crime you know I didn't commit?"

"Do *I* know that?" Constancia asks coolly.

Mehen snorts. "Fine. You don't know it. But your god does. How about that?"

Constancia scowls at Mehen. "He'll come back. He's a good boy."

A commotion comes from where the waters don't show—both turn to look off to the left, Constancia's hand on her sword. Farideh hears the sound of the guard apologizing and apologizing. "Your aunt commanded it," he explains. Constancia's perfect brows raise and the relief on her face is clear.

"And I command you let him out," Brin says in a voice Farideh has only heard him use once or twice—something that will grow into imperiousness given proper exercise. "No one kidnapped me, you plinth-head." He steps into view. "Unlock this cell."

"Where are my girls?" Mehen says, unmoved by Brin's changed demeanor. The answer is in Brin's drawn expression, his ragged clothes. It hurts to look at him, but Farideh keeps watching.

"Hail and well met," Constancia says. "Where are your manners, Aubrin? You can't just countermand Helindra."

"You want me to stay here more than the next few breaths, yes I can." He looks up at his cousin. "I think Helindra will be pleased I remember I have something she wants. Open the stlarning cell."

"Where," Mehen says, almost a roar, "are my daughters?"

And every ounce of imperiousness is gone from Brin's face. He is young, painfully young, and Farideh's heart aches thinking of what he's done: he's bought Mehen's freedom with his own—shackling himself to his scheming family once more—not only because Mehen deserves to be free but because no one else in all the world can help him figure out what to do now.

"They're gone," he says, and Farideh shuts her eyes. She cannot watch the rest.

CHAPTER FOUR

17 Ches, the Year of the Nether Mountain Scrolls (1486 DR)
Waterdeep

Tʜᴇ ʟᴀsᴛ ᴛɪᴍᴇ Fᴀʀɪᴅᴇʜ ʜᴀᴅ sᴛᴏᴏᴅ ɪɴ ᴛʜᴇ ʜᴀʟʟ ᴏf ᴛʜᴇ portal to Suzail, she had marveled at how peaceful it seemed, how much like a temple. But now the frescos were all covered with heavy cloth to protect the paint, the wooden columns gouged by too-wide goods. The fine marble floors were covered with crates and bales and supplies meant for a distant war, and there were cracks where something too heavy had been pushed wrong over the tile. Farideh stared at the zigzag of broken stone and imagined what could have found the weakness in the rock and shattered it just by passing through.

The last time she had stood in the hall of the Cormyrean portal had been seven and a half years ago, and it had been the last time she'd seen Mehen.

"Leave Havi and me here," she'd said, when the portal had been too expensive to carry Mehen, the bounty and both girls to Suzail. He hadn't wanted to, but she'd convinced him. "What can happen in a few days?" she'd asked.

Everything, she thought, running her gaze up and down the crack in the marble. Days became tendays, became months. Became years.

She couldn't bear to watch the portal itself. Every flash and crackle that marked another successful traveler from the forest kingdom of Cormyr to Waterdeep made her heart jump. Seven and a half years ago, she'd already been nervous about finding Mehen again, about how angry he might have been that they'd taken too long to get to Cormyr. But seven and a half years later, she had no way to guess what his reaction would be when he stepped through the portal to see his daughters alive and well.

He'll be furious with you, Farideh thought, eyes still fixed on the crack. He'll be twice as angry as Havi. She felt as if a squall had blown through the core of her and left everything tumbled and nauseated. She folded her arms across her stomach to stop from shaking.

Tam squeezed her shoulder. "It will be all right."

Farideh said nothing. Beside them, Havilar stood, eyes locked on the screen that hid the portal. She had not so much as looked at Farideh since the moment they found out how much they had lost.

The portal flashed again in the corner of her eye, and Farideh heard Havilar's sharp intake of breath a moment later. Every drop of blood in her seemed to rush down to her feet, and she made herself look up.

Her father stood on the first of the three stairs that led down from the portal, unmoving. The scales of his face had grown paler around the edges, but Clanless Mehen still looked as if he could wrestle down a dire bear himself. His familiar well-worn armor was gone, replaced by violet-tinted scale armor with bright silvery tracings. There was a blazon on his arm as well, the mark of some foreign house. The sword at his back was the same, though, the one he had carried since even before he had found the twins left in swaddling at the gates of Arush Vayem.

For all her life, Farideh had known that reading her father's face was a skill she'd been fortunate to learn. A human who couldn't spot the shift of her eyes or Havilar's would certainly see only the indifference of a dragon in Clanless Mehen's face. But the shift of scales, the arch of a ridge, the set of his eyes, the gape of his teeth—her father's face spoke volumes.

But every scale of it, this time, seemed completely still—the indifference of a dragon, even to Farideh.

Farideh's breath stopped. In her mind's eye she replayed the last time they stood in the hall: Mehen putting his arm around her, hugging her close, the edge of his chin ridge rubbing against her hair. The sound of his heart where she had laid her head against his chest.

"When we get the bounty settled," Mehen had said, releasing her and mussing her dark hair with one massive hand, "first thing, we get you a new cloak." He'd reached over and tugged on Havilar's long braid, teasing. "And you need a haircut. Getting to be a damned axe man's handle."

Mehen's jaws parted, showing yellowed teeth. She saw the flutter of his tongue tapping the roof of his mouth, tasting the air for trouble. As if he suspected a trick. Far more likely, wasn't it, than his foster daughters returned from a grave seven and a half years cold?

She shook her head as if she could will it not to be so, maybe pass through the portal and come out again seven and a half years back, no matter what Sairché said. Her knees seemed miles away, and her lungs were useless, unable to draw air past the sob that exploded from her before she could clap a hand to her mouth.

"I'm sorry!" she managed around the gasps. "I'm sorry! I'm sorry—I thought it would be all right." Every eye in the hall was on her, and she pressed both hands to her mouth as if she could smother the thoughtless, stumbling words; the sobs that made her breath buck and hiccup. She couldn't. This was her fault. Even Mehen couldn't forgive—

Then he was there, his great arms around her and around Havilar, crushing her close enough to drive the uneven air right out of her. For a moment, Mehen, too, was wordless, and there was only the dragonborn's soft, shuddering sobs as he held his daughters close again.

"My girls," he whispered. Farideh buried her face in his shoulder. "My girls." And for the first time since they'd returned to Toril, Farideh thought there might be some things that weren't completely ruined. She wept and wept and wept.

Over Mehen's shoulder, Farideh saw a young blond man with a reddish beard, standing at the foot of the platform watching them, his expression guarded. For a moment, his intrusiveness embarrassed Farideh—was there nowhere else to look?

And then that closed expression slipped, just a bit, as Havilar lifted her head, noticed him. And Farideh realized it wasn't a stranger standing there. It was Brin.

His clothes fit much better—a suit made for a lord of Cormyr all in pale wools with a dark emerald cloak—and with the beard, he finally looked his age. But it was Brin all the same.

Havilar stood poised on the edge of motion. But Brin didn't move, didn't speak. Mehen held both his daughters tight, but he was watching the floor behind Havilar, tense with worry. As if, perhaps, he knew what was happening over his shoulder. As if he were doing his part to stand in the middle of it. To keep Havilar safe and apart.

For so long, none of them moved, none of them spoke, and the sick feeling in Farideh's stomach rose up like a maelstrom, threatening to overtake her again. She held Mehen tighter, wanting back that fragile moment of peace, unable to look away from the sad expression fighting through Brin's studied calm.

Sairché stood in front of the scrying mirror, watching Farideh hanging off the dragonborn, weeping her little heart out. Though rage boiled through Sairché at the mere sight of the tiefling, she smiled. Her revenge wasn't complete, but already it was going so well.

It had been Farideh—and Lorcan too—who had gotten

Sairché trapped in this unenviable mess. While Glasya, the Archduchess of the Sixth Layer, had seemed to favor Sairché by raising her up in the hierarchy and making her a powerful agent in executing Asmodeus's sprawling plans, it was an illusion. Sairché's life hung on a balance so finely weighted that the merest mistake would drop her into immeasurable torments.

If Lorcan had not flouted Sairché, if Farideh had not stolen him away from Sairché's clutches, Glasya would not have decided to make an example of Sairché. She would not have handed her the king of the Hells' orders and all but told her to fail at them, trapping Sairché between the two most dangerous powers she knew: the Risen God of Evil and his scheming daughter.

Eight years of careful planning, and still Sairché was not certain she could manage. To fail without seeming to fail. To undo the work while letting someone else shoulder the blame. The other devils in the hierarchy were just as determined, just as slippery. She couldn't give in to inconvenient emotions and let them win.

Sairché let the mirror relapse into darkness, still seething. She liked to imagine it was a gift of her mother's blood, the blessing and curse of being the cambion daughter of Glasya's most infamous erinyes. It certainly felt so—a nearly uncontrollable tide on her otherwise calculating nature. She wondered if Lorcan—Invadiah's other half-devil child—felt the same pull.

When the little bitch had struck her, it had taken all of Sairché's wherewithal not to return the favor. Not to make her gape and gasp over a dagger like Temerity had. She drew a slow breath, focused on the faint moan of the skull-palace of Osseia that filled the air around her. The fleshy walls twitched, and a thin line of bloody mucus dripped down a panel. Sairché clung to the calm.

Not for the first time, Sairché wondered what would have happened if—seven and a half years earlier—Farideh had taken the pact Sairché had offered her in Neverwinter. Would Sairché have come so quickly under the archduchess's wing? Would she have been able to broker the pact with the Brimstone Angel, selling her off to another devil quickly enough to make none of this her problem?

Would she have found out about the twin sooner?

Sairché thought of Havilar, of the familiar rage that flowed off the woman, the grief and sadness that seemed to choke her. Promising, Sairché thought, and *mine*. No collector devil would snatch up either Brimstone Angel, not while Asmodeus's edicts were in play. She would have time to wrap the other twin up in pacts and promises, to shape her into something useful.

And Farideh, as much as she needed her now, would make an excellent tool to do the shaping. Sairché smiled to herself as she left the scrying mirror's room and crossed her apartments. By the end of the tenday, Farideh wouldn't have a single ally left. By the end of this mission, there would be more than enough people determined to kill the warlock and end her treachery. And Sairché's hands would be clean enough for the archdevils.

The portal Glasya gave Sairché use of took the form of a gaping wound in the wall of Sairché's apartments. Seven and a half years of it and Sairché still loathed the gift.

"*Albaenoch,*" she said, and the wound widened, the wall emitting a slow, pained screech.

Sairché wrinkled her nose—all of Malbolge was formed of Glasya's predecessor's body, the palace her unfortunate skull. Day in and out the very presence of the devils of Malbolge tortured the lost leader, and Glasya made special efforts to ensure it kept going. The archduchess might have claimed the layer well over a century ago, but what was time to an immortal? What was mercy to an archdevil?

Where is her pity for the rest of us who have to listen to it? Sairché thought, stepping into the portal. The wound and world seemed to close in on her, collapsing Sairché into the space of a fist, and then scattering her in pieces on a burning wind.

When she opened her eyes, she stood in a hallway made of

glossy black stone, and Sairché cursed. The fortress had several powerful spells sheltering it, hiding it away. She had told the owner a thousand times to make specific allowances for her so that she went where she intended, but if he had, they didn't work. Not for the first time she wondered if the wizard was intractable or merely not as clever as he presented himself to be. Likely both. She took another deep breath—now wasn't the time to punish him.

Like Osseia, the fortress seemed less built than grown. The wizard had done that—acquiring potent scrolls, coaxing the rock out of the ground and shaping it to his liking. A waste of magic, Sairché thought, not the least because it had thrown her timeline into disarray—the time it had taken to raise the tower meant delays in mastering the spells she'd gathered for him, meant delays in finding the best methods to collect specimens, meant that she now had to pull out a piece she'd hoped to save. At least it would be unpleasant for Farideh.

She threw open the door to his study, still simmering. The wizard, a dark-haired man with pale skin and piercing blue eyes looked up, unruffled. If anything, it made Sairché madder.

"Well met, Lady Sairché," he said. He did not stand. "To what do I owe the pleasure?"

"I've got your tool," Sairché said. "I will need a few days to secure her transport. Make the most of them." He sat, considering her, waiting—no doubt—for an apology. Sairché narrowed her eyes. Seven and a half years of this, and Sairché would be damned if she uttered anything like an apology to the man.

"Better late than never," the man finally replied. "Though better never late."

Sairché's mother would have torn a hand right off the human's arm, plucked it free like a spring onion from the mud, for that insolence. Sairché ran her tongue deliberately over the sharp edges of her teeth to keep that erinyes blood from replying.

"Charming maxim," she said a moment later. "In the Hells, we prefer, 'Don't forget where you stand.' Don't forget, *goodsir*, that you're the one who advanced our timeline. You're the one who went ahead with the experiments I schooled you in. And without my assistance, you're the one whose superiors will overlook his good works for their lack of progress. So I suggest you reconsider your tone."

The Netherese wizard looked back at her. Seven and a half years of these visits and still the mortal's gaze made Sairché's temper flare—if he thought to cow her with that leer, that skin-piercing stare, she would *gladly* show him otherwise.

At least, she thought, Lorcan's blasted warlock will have to suffer it too.

"Your pardon," Adolican Rhand said. "I will be most happy to receive her."

There were words in Tymantheran Draconic that didn't exist in the common tongue. *Omin'iejirsjighen* meant the things you owed your clan because you were taught their importance, while *omin'iejirkkessh* meant the things you owed your clan that you shouldn't need to be taught. There was nothing in Common like *throtominarr*, the honor you showed your ancestors by improving on what they created, and Common had no use for the many words that described the nuanced markers of a dragonborn's mood—*asaurifyth*, *yuthom-turil*, *othrirenthish*.

But in neither tongue were the words Clanless Mehen needed: A feeling of relief so strong it overwhelmed any other feeling, including the anger Farideh seemed to fear. The sense of disorder, of upheaval in knowing that the horror that had defined his life for so long was only a nightmare, something that he had woken up from but found he couldn't quite shake. The knowledge of what could be lost and the hole it could leave in you.

If he could have bundled his daughters close and held them, like he had when he'd carried the foundling babies out of the snow and into the village of Arush Vayem, by every god he would have, and never let go. But the girls were not babes in swaddling. Not even girls anymore, Mehen thought.

For all he felt like drawing his blade against time itself, beating the years into submission like a vicious beast, Clanless Mehen had learned a little better. He would master this. He would savor what he had. He would give his daughters what they needed first.

"Up!" he barked, as if they'd never left. "Keep the line straight!"

The sun dropped low, setting the sky between Waterdeep's crowded buildings afire and casting long shadows over the Harper inn's open yard. He had certainly not wanted to set them practicing in the yard—not now—but while he could keep them near and quiet the first day, this afternoon Havilar had taken up her returned glaive with a single-mindedness that brooked no compromise. Mehen was so grateful Farideh had followed when he beckoned so they could all be together.

Even though Havilar clearly didn't want her there. Maybe didn't even want him there.

Seven and a half broken-hearted years had passed for Mehen, but his girls had lost only days. The relief that buoyed him up smothered any sort of anger he might have been able to muster at them—at Farideh—wasn't there for Havilar. Farideh kept herself tucked in the shadows of unneeded equipment, knowing better than to offer to spar with Havi.

Havilar's blade came up hard, the point striking the dummy and tearing through the batting, lodging in the grain of the wood beneath. She yanked at it. It wouldn't budge.

"Here," Mehen said gently, laying a hand on Havilar's back. This, too, he thought: there was no word for the pure, wordless joy of feeling her solid and live beside him. He jerked the weapon free of the dummy and handed it back to her. "Maybe we should—"

Havilar didn't wait for him. She sprang back and threw herself at the dummy again, striking out with the butt of the glaive, the shaft, the blade.

"Havi, you're going to hurt your—"

She screeched and the glaive struck the side of the dummy. The weapon jolted right out of her hands, the strike too hard for her weakened grip. She glowered at it, panting.

"You need to go slow," Mehen said.

"I don't need help!" she shouted. She glowered at Farideh. "And I *don't* need an audience." Her sister seemed to collapse further into herself.

"Enough!" Mehen roared. He held up a hand, but Havilar turned from him and his heart ached. "All right. How about you take some time for yourself? We'll go in, you vent some old breath. Just promise me," he said, setting a hand on her back once more, "you'll be careful. You'll get your skills back, I promise. But not today. No matter how hard you hit that dummy."

Havilar nodded, not looking up at him, and he fought the urge to hug her tight. She would be inflexible as steel and rage against every moment of it, and neither of them would be soothed. "Come in, in an hour or so," he said instead.

Mehen left then, though every part of him fought it. But he knew Havilar—and while seven and a half years ago her problems might have been minor enough for him to insist she listen, to roar at her until she obeyed, to send her to bed straightaway, now . . .

Havilar needed to be alone. He was sure of that, even if he was sure it would kill him to walk away from her.

Farideh stood as he approached and fell into step beside him, staring at her boots as she walked. His stubborn, challenging, resourceful Farideh, and all the steel had gone out of her as if someone had drawn it like a sword from a sheath.

Mehen wrapped an arm around her and held her close. "It will be all right. She's grieving."

Farideh leaned against him, but said nothing. Mehen walked with her, leading them to the little library the Harpers kept here. They sat together on a bench.

"Will you tell me what happened?" he asked quietly.

Farideh shut her eyes and pressed her mouth shut. "I told you to go to Cormyr," she said after a moment. "And then everything went wrong."

"Fari," he said, almost a sigh. "Please. There aren't words for how glad I am that you are alive." He pulled her close again, rubbed his chin ridge over the top of her head, before he choked up too. "There isn't room for anything else. Whatever came before doesn't matter," he said firmly.

She shook her head, buried against his neck. "It should."

"No," he said. "You matter. Your sister matters."

She made a broken little sound, half a sob, half a bitter laugh. "I almost wish you were angry," she said. "I was ready for angry."

Mehen shut his eyes and cursed to himself, held his daughter tighter.

"I made a deal with a devil," she said after a moment. "It was supposed to protect us. It didn't work."

"Oh, Fari." Would it have happened if Mehen had killed Lorcan in the first place? If he'd marched Farideh to the nearest priest and made her renounce the pact? He'd had reasons at the time—but they were so far away, he didn't trust them, not when his daughters were so broken. "I should have helped you get rid of him."

"Not him." Farideh pulled out of Mehen's embrace. "Not Lorcan." She swallowed and scrunched her eyes shut once more, as if flinching away from a swell of emotion. "Lorcan's gone. I think he's gone forever."

Well there's the dragon's hoard, Mehen thought, pulling her near again. If they had to tangle with such a terrible tragedy, at least that good came of it.

But at the same time, he felt his daughter's grief acutely, and he had to admit, the cambion deserved a *little* mourning. After all, he'd saved Mehen once too.

"It's all right," he said.

"No," she said, "it isn't. I made that *stupid* deal, and then she hid us for all that time, and I didn't even have time to find a way to keep Havi safe. I thought I had plenty of time to figure it out."

"Safe from what?"

Farideh laughed. "I found out who our birth parents were," she said, as if she were mocking her own efforts. "Or what they were. They were warlocks too—horrible, wicked ones. And their ancestor is one of the worst warlocks, one so bad that devils seek her descendants. They're going to come looking for Havilar, I know it." She buried her face against his shoulder again. "And all I've done is made it worse. I gave those devils a hundred things to offer her, and now they can find her just fine."

"And you told me," Mehen said, "and do you think I will let your sister do something so foolish?"

"Right," Farideh said dully. "I'm the foolish one when you get down to it."

Mehen hushed her, and stroked her hair. When he had found the girls by the gates of Arush Vayem, plenty of people had warned Clanless Mehen that he knew nothing of raising children, nothing of girls, and nothing at all about tieflings. But he'd been stubborn, even then, and sure that these were a gift, a reparation for what life had snatched away from him when he stood firm against his clan and was exiled. Day by day, month by month, year by year, he had struggled against the fact that they were right, every one of them—he had to learn every single thing about raising his girls.

It was, oddly, the village midwife who set him right. He clashed with Criella over the girls more often than not, and she'd been quiet while others told him to leave those babies in the snow before he let Beshaba herself walk in the gates. But when the girls were three and Mehen was certain he had made the wrongest choice he ever could have, Criella was the one who said, "You're not the first to think you have fallen into the mire. This has nothing at all to do with what they are, or what you are. Girls, boys, tieflings, dragonborn—no one knows what they're doing, raising children. You guess, you mimic, you listen to your gut, and you learn as you go. And you fix what you do wrong."

At the moment, there was no one to learn from, no one to ape. There was nothing Clanless Mehen had learned in all the years he'd raised his twins, or all the years he'd thought them lost, that would relieve the grief in either daughter's heart or close the gulf between them. There was nothing he could do to unmake the thousand choices that had led up to this, nor break the threads that tied his precious girls to a fate handed down by some ancient villain. There was no part of him that knew, it seemed, what to do. Listening to his gut would bring all the wrong results—and he couldn't bear to do anything that might drive the twins away or apart.

So there was only guessing left, only learning as he went. Only holding tight to his daughter as she wept.

CHAPTER FIVE

18 Ches, the Year of the Nether Mountain Scrolls (1486 DR)
Waterdeep

THE GLAIVE SLIPPED IN HAVILAR'S GRIP, THE BLADE TURNING aside as it hit the dummy. She stopped and patted her sweaty hands on her shirt. When she'd taken up her old weapon again, she'd felt the first faint stirrings of hope at its familiar weight. But after a long practice session, that hope felt as hard to hold onto as a greased string.

Lorcan's sister might have given her back some measure of her previous strength, her mind might still know how to direct her arms and legs, her wrists and hips and feet. But her muscles hardly listened and all the time the devils had stolen from her had let her calluses fall away. The skin of her hands was soft as a newborn's and every practiced chop and jab was accompanied by the screaming pain in her hands and the burst of blisters.

Havilar took up the weapon again, gritting her teeth.

In the back of her thoughts, Havilar was as frightened as she'd ever been, and wishing she'd gone with Mehen when he'd asked her to, instead of telling him to leave her be. She wished she'd stopped Brin by the portal and held him tight. She wished she could have just screamed at Farideh, and maybe let out some measure of this anger, this sense of betrayal. She wished she could curl up and cry for a bit.

But if Havilar knew she felt these things, they were buried deep behind a certainty that before anything could be made right, first she had to master the glaive again. Before anything could go back to being right, the one true thing about her life had to be so once more.

And to master the glaive, she had to keep drilling.

She aimed a chop at the dummy's neck. The glaive broke out of her slippery grip and flipped back over her shoulder to clatter to the ground.

"*Karshoj*!" Havilar shrieked, stamping her feet. It was wrong, *everything* was wrong. She lashed out at the wooden dummy's chest until the bones of her arms rattled and her breath came hard. She looked at her hands—not just sweat, but blood.

In the distance, the clock they called the Timehands chimed the hour. She counted the bells as she bent to retrieve the glaive. It had been three hours since she'd last noticed the time. No wonder she was so tired.

As she straightened, she saw him standing on the edge of the practice field, all garbed in fine clothes and carrying a battered wooden box.

"Brin." She held the glaive close, as if she could hide behind it. "I hope you weren't watching that."

His mouth quirked into a smile she knew well, even under that stranger's beard. "Only some of it," he said. "Mehen said you were out here. He's worried about you."

"I'm going in." She swallowed against the lump in her throat. "Just a moment."

"I'm worried too."

Havilar looked at her feet. What did that mean? He would have said, before. He would have told her what he was worried about and what made him say that—her sloppy jabs, her bleeding hands, the late hour, or maybe the fact she'd come back at all? He would have told her things were going to be all right, or if they weren't, what they would do differently.

Everything was wrong.

"Thank you for keeping my glaive," she said.

"Of course." He held up the wooden box. "I thought you might—" He cleared his throat. "That is, these are your things. Yours and Farideh's. From before." She crossed the field and took it from him, balancing the glaive against her hip. "Besides, you know, the weapons."

Havilar stared at the box, at once wanting to drop down on the ground and tear through it, and wanting to throw it away, so that it couldn't taunt her. She settled for cradling it in her arms, wondering what was inside. What Brin had thought important enough to save. What Brin had been so eager to return.

"Are you married?" she blurted.

He laughed, maybe nervously. "No."

Was that a stupid thing to ask? She didn't know. It seemed like every scrap of confidence she'd earned and gathered and prized was gone. She couldn't use her glaive, she couldn't talk to Brin, she couldn't do anything.

He looked so different and still so much like her Brin. She wanted so much to hold him tight again, to kiss him through that stupid beard. But he made no move to come any nearer to her. Too much had changed.

"Are you staying long?" she asked.

He shook his head. "No, I can't. I probably shouldn't have left Cormyr, only, well, I couldn't *not* come." He was quiet a moment, while she stared at the sand. "Havi, I'm really glad you're alive."

"I have to go," she said. It was too much. She wasn't going to be the silly girl who said all the wrong things, not with him. Glaive in hand, box on her hip, she hurried past him, tears rising in her eyes.

She passed the entrance to the cellar and grabbed one of the bottles of wine sitting there, waiting to be ordered. After all, she thought, heading up the stairs, it wasn't as if she were a child. It wasn't as if Mehen or anyone else could stop her.

She was nearly to her room, at the top of the stairs, when

she passed the little library the Harpers kept. The doors were open and Farideh sat on the floor, several books open around her. Reading, Havilar thought, as if nothing were wrong.

Farideh looked up and in her expression was all the fear and contrition Havilar didn't want to see. "Havi—"

"You were right," Havilar said, shaking, she was so angry. "It didn't last. It didn't even get a *chance,* because you had to get in the way, thinking you're the only one who knows how to fix a *karshoji* thing, and ruin my *entire* life just to stop something that you didn't even stop! Are you happy?"

Tears brimmed her sister's eyes, and Farideh looked away. "I'm sorry. Havi, I'm so—"

"Shut up," Havilar said. "Shut *up.* I was on your side when they kicked you out of the village, I was on your side when you decided to go racing around Neverwinter, I was even on your side when you wanted to go down in that crypt and nearly got us both killed, but I am *not* on your side now, and I'm *never* going to be on *your* side again."

Havilar didn't wait for Farideh to respond—there wasn't a thing she could say that Havilar wanted to hear. She turned on her heel and, toting her glaive and box and the bottle of wine, went up to her room.

Door shut firmly behind her, Havilar pulled the cork from the bottle with her teeth and considered the box thrown onto the bed. Give it to Farideh, she thought, make her sort it out. She took a heavy swig of the wine, flinching at its dryness. But she wasn't going back out—not for better wine and not for Farideh. She drank more, enough to warm her belly, and sat on the bed, the box in her lap.

"It's just a box," she told herself.

It was emptier than she'd expected. A stack of yellowed chapbooks. A stylus. A bottle of ink, long dried up. Stiff strips of leather for tying her braids. Farideh's little dagger, spotted with rust. A bright red feather she'd found and stuck in her braid for a day or two. Squares of cloth snipped off her old clothes—she rubbed a piece of her cloak between two fingers. It was softer than she'd remembered. She set them aside and found, pooled in the bottom, a chain of silver.

She drew it out—Farideh's amulet of Selûne. The one that bound devils.

Havilar took another gulp of wine, squeezing the chain hard enough to hurt her palm. A single word—that's all it would have taken and she could have stopped that Sairché. But Farideh wasn't wearing the amulet then, because Lorcan had told her not to. *Henish,* Havilar thought, and drank more wine.

She slipped the necklace on, over one horn and then the other. *Karshoj* to Farideh, if it had been Havilar that stupid Sairché wanted, she could have stopped all of it—with the amulet or with a spell or with her blade. She rubbed her thumb over the spiral carved into the back of the amulet, and imagined taking her glaive to Sairché the way she had the dummy.

Havilar took another gulp of wine, and considered the amulet again—it would make things even easier to fix, if Sairché came back again. Because if anyone was going to fix this, it would have to be Havilar, and it would have to wait for tomorrow.

Every tome and scroll in Tam's library that so much as hinted at referencing devils or the Nine Hells lay open on the floor around Farideh. She'd even pulled down what seemed to be a chapbook in a memoir's skin about traveling backward through time, just in case.

But all she could think about was Havilar saying, "I'm *never* going to be on *your* side again."

Footsteps made her look up, and there was Brin, staring down the hall where Havilar had disappeared, holding a book under one arm. Farideh shut her eyes—so that was what made Havilar finally talk to her again.

"Well met," she said. He looked over at her, surprised, but said nothing. "Or not," she added, wishing she'd said nothing at all. "That's all right." She cleared her throat. "I'm sorry, Brin. I didn't—"

"Of course you didn't," he interrupted. "You're not a monster." But he still wouldn't look her in the eye. He held the book out to her. "Here. It didn't fit in the box."

Farideh took it from him—a thick tome bound in dark blue silk, smudged with dirt and marks of damp. Her ritual book. She leafed through it, skipping the first few pages instinctively, turning to the spells she'd written in herself, sitting in the back of a cart lumbering along the path between the Nether Mountains and Everlund. Havi and Brin trailing the cart, hand in hand, heads together. Dahl explaining how the components of the ritual fit together, rambling on and on, caught up in his own love of the magic more than any love of teaching her. Human-shaped Lorcan, sitting on the back of the driver's box, close enough for Tam to bless him back into the Hells, and watching everything.

She closed the book and held it to her chest.

"You should have taken me too," Brin said quietly.

Farideh looked down at the book beside her, the grotesque woodcut of a grinning devil that leered up at her. "I would have. If I'd known what would happen. You have to believe that."

"So you say," he replied, his voice too full of pain and anger to bear. "But I don't." She watched him turn and go, wishing she knew what to say, what to do.

You can fix this, she told herself. You have to fix this. She set the ritual book beside her and went back to her studies, skimming pages full of advice it was too late to take.

A wind came from nowhere, rustling the pages of the book. A wind out of the Hells themselves.

"Are you ready?"

Farideh did not turn to look at Sairché, did not give her the satisfaction of seeing the fear that no doubt raced across her features.

"You ask that as if I have a choice in the matter," she said quietly. "If I say 'no,' will you give me time?"

"Don't sneer at my courtesy," Sairché said. "You might find you still need it." Sairché's robes swished as she circled around Farideh. "Have you found a way around our deal?"

"You know I haven't," Farideh said. "And I want *none* of your courtesy. Just tell me what I have to do and leave me alone."

Sairché's jaw clenched, but she didn't respond in kind. She held up a golden ring and looked through it at the tiefling. "A portal," she said, and pressed the ring into Farideh's palm. "I would accompany you, but since you have no need of my courtesy I shall let you figure things out on your own. Gather your belongings, make your excuses, and go. We'll see how well you manage things *alone*."

Farideh turned the ring over in her hand. It was warm to the touch. "You like rings for portals," she said. "You and Lorcan both."

Sairché narrowed her eyes. "Your new master isn't expecting you immediately, but get moving. If you aren't there by deep-night, I'll have to come find you." She smiled wickedly at Farideh and brushed the tiefling's hair off her face. "And you wouldn't want that."

Farideh ignored the threat. "No killing," she said. "You promised. No stealing souls."

Sairché shook her head, as if Farideh were an incorrigible child, and Farideh was suddenly aware of the thousands of things she hadn't marked out. But it was too late, too late for any of that. "No killing. No soul-stealing. But," Sairché added, "if you don't fulfill your promised services *your* soul is forfeit."

"As if I care," Farideh said.

Sairché leaned in to hiss in Farideh's ear, "You should. You should care very much. Because if I have to, I will kill you and put your sister in your place."

Farideh shut her eyes, but there was no stopping the fat line of tears that welled up at that. She rubbed her thumb over the ring—the link to whomever Sairché had promised her to, the only way to protect Havilar from Farideh's bad decisions.

"There, now," Sairché crooned, a perfect mockery of sympathy. "It will all be over in a trice. And then you can go back to dodging collectors and disappointing your family. Until I can redeem that second favor."

Farideh said nothing. As much as she would have liked to turn the storm of Hellish energies that thundered along her pulse against the cambion, she knew too well the sort of magic Sairché would have access to. If she couldn't kill her outright, it would be suicide to strike.

And worse, she thought: Havilar would bear the brunt of her failure. She closed her hand over the ring.

"A word of advice," Sairché drawled. "When you arrive, try to pretend you're not such an innocent. You'll get eaten alive otherwise." When Farideh looked back over her shoulder, the cambion was gone.

It was still three hours to deepnight, but with her nerves threatening to overtake her and ruin what resolve she'd managed, Farideh headed straight to her room and packed what little belongings she had into a haversack. Sairché hadn't said where the ring would take her, and Farideh hoped a rod, a sword, the ritual book, a whetstone, and a comb would be enough.

Dahl's deck of cards sat between the candles on the little table where she'd dropped it. She considered it a moment, then added it to the pack as well. She pulled her cloak closed, went down to the kitchens, and took the end of a loaf of bread and a few apples.

From the library, she'd snatched a bit of foolscap and a stylus, a little bit of ink.

I am so sorry, she wrote. *I hope this makes things easier.* She finished the letter and folded it up quickly, so that she wouldn't have to see the words.

Havilar was sleeping, curled tight on her cot, her lips stained purple from the mostly empty bottle of wine on the floor beside her. Farideh stood in the door a moment, her grief and guilt trapping her feet like a heavy mud. She thought of all the times they'd fought before, all the fights that had seemed vicious, world-ending, but always, eventually, settled out, eased off. They always came back to where they'd started, or near enough to it. They would always be sisters.

Until this, Farideh thought.

She left the note on the bedside table, and piled Lorcan's necklace atop it. As a peace offering, it lacked. But there was nothing Farideh could leave Havilar that would make much of a difference, and if Sairché wanted the thing, at least she knew Havilar would be stubborn about letting go of it. She kissed her sister's head, just above her horns, fighting the urge to shake Havilar awake, to tell her once more that she was sorry.

She left before she lost her composure or her nerve. Havilar would find the note after she woke and take it to Mehen. By then Farideh would be gone, and Sairché would leave the both of them alone. She hoped.

Heart pounding—head pounding—Farideh pulled her cloak closer around her and hurried through the Harpers' stronghold. There were still at least two hours before her deep-night deadline. She could make it out of the city, well away from anyone else who might track her.

Farideh made it as far as the middle of the crowded taproom before the sudden sensation of walking into a wire fence stopped her. Lines of power pulled her back toward the stairs. The protective spell, she realized, reminding her of its limits. Reminding her she was too far from Lorcan—who was gone.

Farideh took a step back, searching the faces of the tap-room's customers. A broad-shouldered half-orc nudged her out of the way, back into the sharp edges of the spell. When she tried to go back the way she came, she found it blocked by bodies pressed close to the bar. She edged her way around the tables and chairs, the searing pain of the protection's limits enough to make her hold her breath, enough to make her head pound. The edges of her vision started to crackle, stars flashing bright as she inched around the last of the tables.

It should have pulled Lorcan toward her. It should have eased for her, if not for him. But if he's not in the protection, she thought frantically, as the stars popped across her field of vision, a thousand swirling colors and shadows, if someone else has hold of it . . .

Farideh turned and stepped away from the edge of the protection, square into a person. Ale sloshed over her cloak, and she heard a man curse.

"I'm sorry," she said automatically. The lights bloomed over her vision and she couldn't make out how annoyed he was. "I didn't see—"

"Farideh?" Dahl said. She took a step back, and the lights dimmed a little. He didn't look annoyed so much as surprised, even with an empty flagon and ale down his shirt. "What are you doing down here?"

She shook her head—not now, not now. The lights were still popping in and out of her vision, so abrupt and bright that her ears imagined sounds for them. She glimpsed Dahl's face between flashes of blue and teal and silvery gray. Between the pops his expression hardened.

"Were you going somewhere?"

"Something's wrong," she said. "I don't know . . ."

"All right. You need to talk to Tam. Now." Dahl took her by the arm and guided her back through the crowd, but also toward where Lorcan must be.

Or toward whoever's captured an edge of your protection spell, she thought, weaving alongside Dahl, back through the bodies and the furniture and the exploding lights. There were more devils in the Hells than a person could count, and any one of them might be aligned against Sairché's success. Her and Lorcan's monstrous mother, any one of their half sisters, their terrible liege-lady, another collector devil—

"Is this . . . fit you're having to do with the devil?" Dahl asked as they ascended the stairs.

"I'm *not* having a fit," Farideh said. But was she? Maybe it wasn't Lorcan. Maybe this was some illness she'd caught in the Hells. Maybe this was some curse Sairché laid on her. "I just need to lie down, all right?"

"Lie down in your cloak with a haversack for a pillow?" Dahl said, corralling her up another set of stairs. "You were running away."

No, Farideh thought. I was trying to keep my word. I was trying to get out of this horrible deal alive. I was trying to protect Havilar. "I was going for a walk," she lied.

"I'm sure." Dahl was silent a moment. "You know, I thought Tam could trust you. It's not such a leap to see hidden agents and traitors in what I've heard of your tale, but I was sure that couldn't be the answer."

"I wasn't *here*," she said, as he marched her the rest of the way up the stairs. "I don't even know who you're fighting." But he said no more, as they continued past two guards who spat bursts of yellow and black stars and streamers of red, past a ward he disarmed with a wave of an arm, and into the offices of Tam Zawad.

"Dahl? What's wrong," Tam said, silver bursts of light blooming over him like ice flowers across a windowpane. "Shar pass us over, Fari, are you all right?"

Three steps past the door, the protection grabbed hold of her again, strong, icy fingers of magic wrapped around her arms, her chest, her throat. She stopped, but Dahl urged her on. Another step, another two—the lights surged. Her legs buckled, and she stumbled backward before she could fall.

"I can't," she said, panting. "Something's wrong. And I need to go. I need to leave." Don't tell them, she thought. Don't bring them into this. "I'm not feeling well."

"She was in the taproom," Dahl said, "dressed for a journey."

"Sit down," Tam said.

"I have to stand," she said. If she sat, she couldn't move, couldn't correct for the protection's pull.

"You'll sit," Tam said. "Before you fall. Dahl, get a chair." He turned to the sideboard, and through the shroud of lights she could hear the clink of glass. "I don't have a better cure for nerves," Tam said with a lightness she didn't believe. "And perhaps then you can give us a better explanation."

The popping was no longer her imagination, she was certain. The sound of a fire built high and damp, the sound of a thousand bullets from a thousand slings hitting the walls. She could hardly see for the lights and shadows. Though they seemed to grow, to surge off the two men, they swirled around the room like something alive.

Farideh shoved a hand in her pocket and felt the ring there. Whatever was happening to her, Tam and Dahl didn't need to be pulled into it. Let them think she was a traitor, let them think she'd been corrupted in the Hells, let them think she was beyond saving anyway—just let them be safe.

The lights seemed to overtake her, as if they were boiling over from some source beyond the fabric of the world, like ethereal lava. She heard, dimly, the sound of Tam asking her something, the clink of a bottle being set down. The sound of the chair falling and Dahl shouting her name. She felt, at a distance, it seemed, her finger slip through the warm circle of the ring, and Dahl's hands on her back as she collapsed into the space between worlds.

When Tam turned back from the sideboard at the sound of Dahl's shout and Farideh's wordless grunt, he expected his erstwhile charges puddled on the floor, one highly annoyed and one insensate and much heavier than expected.

Instead, there was only the chair, lying on its side on the well-worn rug, and the *clink* of the glass Tam dropped on the desk. Dahl and Farideh were gone.

Sairché waited until Farideh had left the library, off to assemble her things, and smiled to herself. Matched against a warlock in a game of wits? Even Farideh had to realize by now how unsporting that was.

Still, Sairché thought, it paid to make absolutely certain that she was defeated. Sairché knew better, after all, than to leave loose ends. She pulled a scroll from her sleeve, unrolled it and tore a large corner from it, making sure to catch just enough from the Netherese missive she'd snatched out of Rhand's study. Enough to imply Farideh knew something about supply chains to the High Forest. Enough to be interesting to meddling Harpers. Enough to make even her family doubt Farideh's innocence.

Sairché tucked it beside the ugly woodcut of a pit fiend. She tapped the little guardian on the nose. Farideh was going to wish very soon that she'd submitted quietly.

CHAPTER SIX

18 Ches, the Year of the Nether Mountain Scrolls (1486 DR)
Somewhere north of Waterdeep

THE FLOOR DROPPED OUT FROM UNDER DAHL'S FEET, THE AIR around him evaporated, and the only thing he could be sure of was the weight of Farideh slumped against him. But with his next heartbeat his feet slammed into a stone floor, the air condensed around him once more, cold and clammy, and there were six shadar-kai men standing around them, looking startled.

"Gods' books," Dahl spat, and he dropped Farideh to her knees. He drew his sword and cut at the nearest of the shadar-kai—the blade slashing deep into the scarred, gray skin of the man's arm, opening a vein. The shadow-damned creature looked down at the blood pumping from the wound, surprised. A wild grin spread across his face, thrilled by the sensation stirring up his nerves, anchoring his soul to his body a little firmer.

Dahl cursed. One didn't wait for shadar-kai to bring the fight, and one didn't count on a surrender.

Dahl moved quickly, taking out the fellow behind the wounded shadar-kai with a quick, fortunate strike to the side of the head. Still spraying blood, the wounded one pulled a pair of sharp sickles and with a crazed yell hooked both around toward Dahl's back. Dahl twisted, slamming the hilt of the sword into the man's face.

All around him, the sound of blades being pulled from scabbards, chains being unhooked from carriers, bodies primed for violence and *eager* for the pain of that violence, set into motion. He glanced around as he wrenched one of the sickles out of the wounded shadar-kai's hand. They were all grinning.

Farideh was still on the floor, fingers curling against the stone, eyes on the backs of her hands. Gods damn it, Dahl thought, stepping between her and the shadar-kai. He flung the scythe at an approaching guard, a thick brute with a missing eye. He didn't even flinch as it hit his collarbone. A long spiked chain slithered over the floor beside him, twitching as if preparing to strike.

It lashed out, but Dahl was ready. He leaped out of range and into the reach of another shadar-kai, this one shaved bald and pierced all over with silver barbs. He caught Dahl and slung him down to the stones, so quick Dahl couldn't stop his head from smacking the floor.

Up, up, up! he shouted to himself. His head was spinning and the pain was intense, but it was nothing compared to what would come if the brutal shadar-kai got ahold of them. The chain struck him hard in the ribs as he pushed up, sending a lightning bolt of pain through his chest. One elbow buckled, but he kept moving, twisting up to face the shadar-kai who'd thrown him and slamming his elbow into the side of his knee. The pain lit the man's face, and the dagger that was arcing toward Dahl slowed, enough to give the Harper a chance to sit up and get out of the way of the chain that hit its owner's ally instead. Dahl's sword finished its work.

But, Hells, there were still too many. He looked around, past the advancing thug with his chain, past the swordsman shifting around Dahl's side, past the fellow who'd knocked him down, now holding a pair of sharp-bladed carvestars in hand, ready to throw. There had to be an exit, a way to retreat, but even then, could he get Farideh—

A crackling gust of magic streaked through the air and

devoured the carvestar as the guard threw it. An explosion of metal shards and sparks made the guard flinch back. Farideh stood now, eyes wild, the powers of the Hells suffusing her arms and tinting her veins black. She hissed another unholy word and Dahl scuttled back, as several bolts of burning brimstone streaked out of nothing to hammer at the three guards.

The big fellow turned on her, but when his chain lashed out, she stepped into it—and vanished, reappearing at the guard's back. She threw another bolt of bruised-looking energy. Dahl took advantage of the guard's surprise and punched his dagger through the seams of the shadar-kai's leather armor, deep into his belly. The chain slipped from the man's grasp.

He heard Farideh's shouts of Infernal and the sound of one of the swordsmen crying out and hitting the floor. When Dahl turned she was bleeding from one nostril and a cut on her arm below where the sleeve of her shirt had torn loose like a flapping sail, but the heel of her hand was also slamming into the philtrum of her assailant. The shadar-kai's head snapped back, but he kept his feet.

"*Adaestuo*," she hissed, and the pulse of energy came again, bursting out through her palm and over the man's face. He screamed—that horrid scream the shadar-kai had, half pain and half mad laughter—and dropped the sword, stumbling back into Dahl and his dagger. Dahl cut the creature's throat, ending his ecstasy.

"Oghma, Mystra, and lost Deneir," Dahl said, panting. His ribs ached, his elbow was screaming, his head pounding hard. He couldn't take another fight like that. He scanned the room—no more shadar-kai, but stairs up to some other level ahead and a path behind him into the torchlit gloom.

He sheathed his sword and took hold of her unwounded arm, dagger in the other hand. "We have to get out of here."

She didn't budge. "*You* have to get out of here." She tore her sleeve at the elbow, wadded the cloth up and pressed it to the side of his head. Only when he took it, only when her hand came back smeared scarlet, did Dahl realize how much he was bleeding.

He cursed and pressed the cloth harder to the wound. "Come on," he said. "We'll find somewhere to lie low. There's got to be—"

"No." She looked from one exit to the other. "You shouldn't have followed, Dahl."

"Followed?" Dahl squinted, the wooziness of blood loss catching up. "You came here on purpose?"

"It's not what it looks like."

"It had better not be—it looks like you're a godsbedamned Shadovar agent. Where is this place?"

"Whatever it is, it's not safe for you to be here. Please. Trust me, I—" She jerked her head toward the sound of footsteps echoing down the stairway. "*Karshoj*," she hissed. "You have to go. Before someone finds you." She drew her sword and pushed him toward the dark corridor.

"I'm not leaving you!"

"You are, because they aren't going to kill *me*."

"What in all the planes are you—"

"Gods damn it, run!" The shadows of approaching bodies slunk down the stairs like the fingers of a reaching hand. And though a chorus of old instincts shouted at Dahl to stay, to draw his sword, to find out what in the Hells was going on, to protect her or stop her or *something*, Dahl had enough sense to know he wasn't going to do any of that while bleeding from the head, Farideh fighting him every step of the way.

Farideh shoved Dahl hard toward what she hoped was the exit, and ran back to the circle of dead guards. It had to look like she'd come alone. It had to look like she'd done this, whatever the consequences. She drew her sword and bloodied it with the mess of one guard's belly wound. Kept the rod in her off-hand.

Didn't dare look after Dahl as six guards—humans this time, but still armored in the same spiked and studded armor the shadar-kai had favored—came into view.

You can do this, Farideh thought, drawing herself up and trying to look dangerous.

The guards considered her, considered the dead shadar-kai. Considered the sickly looking light dancing around Farideh's rod. But they didn't move.

Not until the seventh, a man in robes of emerald so deep and dark they might have looked black were he not flanked by the guards in ebon armor, came up behind. The guards parted for Adolican Rhand, and Farideh's heart stopped dead in her chest.

"You?" she said, suddenly no more dangerous than a stunned deer.

Adolican Rhand smiled at her, his blue eyes piercing and predatory, even if his next words were innocent enough. They always were, she thought.

"Ah, your mistress didn't tell you," he said. He clucked his tongue—at Farideh or at Sairché's omission, she couldn't say. "Nor did she mention that you planned to sacrifice half a dozen of my guards."

Farideh didn't dare move, didn't dare look away. The memory of Rhand smiling at her while the poison he'd slipped her made her thoughts slip out of reach like little fishes in a dark pond. What had Sairché promised him?

Anything she wanted, Farideh thought. And Havilar and Lorcan will answer if you don't.

She looked down at the dead guards. Adolican Rhand was still watching her, one part amused, one part hungry.

"If you didn't intend them as a sacrifice," Farideh said calmly, "you should have told them to let me pass. I didn't come here to be tested."

"My apologies," Adolican Rhand said. "I suppose it was in their nature. To see how far something can be pressed before it breaks." He smiled. "Obviously further than they thought."

"Much further," Farideh snapped.

"Well met, and I will warn them they should avoid it in the future." His smile wavered, as if he might laugh. "Though you must promise me you won't press them back. Come, I have quarters prepared for you."

Run, every muscle of her body urged. Go. *Go.*

But instead she sheathed her sword, put away the rod, and sent the quickest, most secretive glance in the direction of the dark hallway. Dahl was gone, and despite her fear, she nearly sighed in relief, as she headed up the stairs, into the reaches of a man she'd had every intention of never, ever coming near again.

Dahl cursed and cursed again, as he wound through the passageway away from Farideh, away from the dead guards. He should have stayed. He should have gotten her away—she might be a traitor, she might not, and he wouldn't be able to find out which if she was dead.

She'd come here on purpose, and if she hadn't expected the shadar-kai, she'd expected something bad. Something dangerous.

But she told you to run, he thought, pulling the second dagger from his boot before edging around a corner. She could have kept you there, let whomever it is kill you.

Shade, he thought, easing open a door and finding a cistern and storeroom. That many shadar-kai in Faerûn and who else could it be? But why would Farideh aid the Shadovar? And if she would, why would she tell him to run?

A deal with a devil, Havilar had said. If the Nine Hells worked in concert with Netheril . . .

Then Toril had best all pray together, he thought, because anyone would make a better hero than *you* in this case.

Dahl moved quickly and quietly, checking for exits, and

though he heard the sounds of more guards behind several doors, none of them opened on him.

He ducked behind a stack of water barrels, checked his wound. Still bleeding. He pressed harder and tore strips off his own sleeve to tie the packing on. He wriggled the flask out of his breeches' pocket and took a mouthful—just enough to think straight. Until he knew what was happening, until he could get reinforcements, he was the only hero Toril got.

Stop the bleeding, he thought. Send a message back to Tam. A group of human guards passed by, talking in low, tense voices. Dahl waited until they passed, then—after another swallow too tiny to count—he edged down the corridor in the direction they'd come from.

He tried a quiet door—found a pair of human guards, dead asleep in their uniforms—and quickly shut it. A second—filled to the edges with casks. No exit. A third—an armory. Dahl slipped inside, his head getting lighter. He needed to sit.

Racks and racks and racks of swords. Spiked chains dangled from hooks like hideous vines. Hooked knives, vicious katars, long black whips—he counted back over the rooms he'd passed, considered the unused weapons. Whatever this fortress was guarding, it was well armed.

All the more reason to get out, he told himself. Not for the first time he was glad of the little sending kit he'd convinced Tam to have his Harpers carry. Even lost in the middle of gods-knew-where, he wasn't cut off entirely from support. And Dahl carried a spare besides.

He found a dim corner and pulled out the pouch, the vials of powdered metals and salts, the little scroll. He poured the vials out in neat lines, one eye on the door, half his thoughts on the right words to send. Weapons. Fortress. Farideh. He cursed again, and read the ritual.

The lines burst into brief, bright flame.

"Netherese stronghold," he whispered. "Soldiers, shadar-kai, *heavily* armed. Somewhere cold," he added, spotting a single fur-trimmed cloak on a rack, and he nearly cursed again, recalling his thin breath. "High up." He hesitated. "Farideh came intentionally. I've lost her, both wounded. Have one reserve sending, sword and dagger."

The magic crackled like a fading fire, as the spell carried his words across Faerûn, to Tam Zawad's ears. A moment later the reply came.

"Lie low. Get me better idea of your location, quickly, so rescuers can find a portal. Find Farideh. Determine where she stands. Stay safe."

Dahl opened his mouth to protest, but the magic was spent, there was no replying. There was no insisting that he didn't need to be rescued, that wasn't what he meant. And the way Tam had said "find Farideh"—did he think Dahl had fumbled that too? That he ought to have stuck beside her, regardless of wounds, regardless of what she told him to do—regardless of the fact that it was likely she wasn't exactly in need of rescue from the Shadovar? He couldn't even be sure this *was* a dangerous place—what if what he thought was a Netherese fortress was only some Shadovar nobleman's pleasure house?

He dragged his hands over his face. Gods, he thought. You're a mess. Even Tam knows it. He sighed, sure there was no farther for him to fall. He'd missed the signs Khochen had picked up on, and let a probable Shadovar agent into the Harper's hall—and then let her flee. He had botched recapturing her when he'd had the chance, and as much as he'd have liked to blame that on being hit on the head, he knew better. And just to confirm how little anyone trusted him to manage, there was a rescue party coming for him. Like some kidnapped noble in sullied hose.

Dahl was sure down to his bones that if his colleagues had to save him, he would dig the tattoo out of his arm himself. He would find out what they were dealing with. He would find the way out.

And then he'd find Farideh—and whatever had passed

between them before wouldn't cloud his judgment again.

He stood, a little better for his rest, but his vision still swirled. He untied the makeshift bandage—the blood had clotted—and wiped the remaining smears away in the dull reflection of an axe head.

This is just information gathering, he told himself. You're just in the field instead of behind a desk.

A fortress this stocked, and he'd be hard pressed to get out past its guards. He scanned the walls and racks of the armory before spotting the leather armor uniform of the Shadovar guards he'd seen earlier. If there were so many guards in the fortress, maybe one more wouldn't faze the rest.

Dahl slipped out of the room moments later, his old clothes shoved back under a rack of pikes. The armor wasn't fit for him, but the spare cloak covered the looseness around the chest and the gaps in the bracers. He pulled up the hood and continued searching for an exit.

The air was definitely thinner, he thought, as his pulse clattered along like a runaway wagon. Up in the mountains? Floating city? (Gods' books, please, he thought, *not* a floating city.)

He found a way out at the back of a cellar, past vast stores of roots and kegs (ready for a siege, Dahl thought), and came up and out into a yard. A smithy sat to one side, still and seldom used. A trio of goats looked up at Dahl from a small pen, bleating uneasily. A handful of shadar-kai threw dice in the corner by the light of the moon. Dahl watched as one threw a bad round and was rewarded with a stiletto through the back of her hand as a prize.

While her companions laughed, Dahl slipped around the pen and past a stable, then past another stable where something big and growling stirred the shadows. He peered in a window and saw a massive creature, all leathery wings and gasping mouth. Veserab, he thought. Shit. Whoever ran this place had clout in the city of Shade to ride one of the monstrous mounts.

Another building—this one made of the same strange, craggy stone as the tower only windowless—cut off Dahl's path as it stretched across the space between the tower and the wall.

The tower reached high enough to make a powerful caster a strong concern—you could see an army approaching from any direction up there. The wall around the courtyard would not hold against siege engines, though—too low, not fortified enough. And the forces . . . there were more guards on the wall, but the racket they made suggested there was a brawl on and they were clustered near the large building. Not watching. Curious.

Dahl eased up a watchtower's stairs to the wall's top. The shadar-kai guards were circled around two of their fellows, both bleeding and bruised. Two of the guards looked back at him, and Dahl caught his breath. He made a face and waved at them, as if telling them to continue, to keep to themselves. The shadar-kai sneered back, but it was a good enough imitation. They returned to their battle, muttering insults about fragile humans to each other. Dahl nearly vomited in relief.

He walked quickly along the wall, looking for a likely landing place, and surveyed the surrounding land as he did. On the other side of the wall, the castle was surrounded by smaller buildings. Barracks? he thought. A village? No way to tell in this light but to pull one of the inhabitants out and ask. Beyond the buildings, the sliver of a moon reflected off a lake, and traced the edge of a mountain peak. Starmounts? he thought. Sword Mountains? Something farther afield?

Dahl dropped down the other side of the wall and quickly slipped into the darkened spaces between the squat, square huts. Woodsmoke hung on the air—scores of cookfires leaking out the twig-thatched roofs—but there were no lights hanging in the dark alleyways. Only the moon keeping watch over her wicked sister's Shadovar followers and whatever they were up to. Dahl kept moving toward the edge of the settlement.

Beyond the last of the buildings the land rose to a steep

hill scattered with rocks and low brush. Mountain sedge, frills of mauve orclar edging the rocks, clumps of snowstars shining bright in the moonlight against dark leaves—he was well north of Waterdeep. Dahl climbed, keeping to cover. A crater, he thought.

Near the peak of the slope he nearly crossed the path of a shadar-kai patrol. He crouched beneath a scraggly yew as the two women passed, jangling with blades and chains and spikes and arguing with one another in the tongue of the Netherese.

Dahl frowned. He'd seen more attentive guards patrolling Waterdeep's sewer. He glanced back the way he'd come and marked the edge of a crater that went nearly all the way around the fortress and its settlement. Beyond the land dropped away into dark forest, blurred by clouds or maybe the thin air. Long scramble down, he thought.

Long scramble back, he thought, to get Farideh. Old worries, old thoughts surged up in him. Oghma, let that have been the right choice. The farther he got from her, the less sure he was.

When the shadar-kai were out of sight and out of earshot, Dahl sprinted across the distance, toward the next patch of brush.

As he crossed the trail the guards used, his foot hit a rill in the dark, and he stumbled. Arms outstretched to cushion his fall, Dahl caught himself instead on the invisible barrier surrounding the strange village.

The *crack* of something hitting the wall jerked Havilar from her slumber. She sat up, tense and ready to attack whoever had made the noise. But the room was empty. The banging came again, and she considered the wall. Farideh's room was on the other side. She pounded against the wall and smacked her knuckle crooked on the boards. Pain shot up her arm and forced a curse out of her mouth.

She sucked on the scrape, glad no one had seen that. All her anger and grief welled up—no. She didn't want to do this. She didn't want to be awake. She reached for the wine bottle again, and spotted the note beneath it.

Havilar, she read.

There's nothing I can say to fix what's happened. But I hope you know I did what I thought I had to, what I thought I needed to do to protect us both. If anything happened to you I would never forgive myself, and the worst thing to bear is that now, I've made something happen that's more terrible than I could have imagined.

You should know that our imprisonment wasn't the price of Sairché's protection. I owe her a favor, and she's come to collect. I hope I come back, but if I don't, I love you and tell Mehen I love him too. I am so sorry. I hope this makes things easier

The necklace is yours. You were right. Rubies suit you better.

Havilar stared at the letter for several breaths, uncertain whether she wanted to cry out and run after her sister or crush the note into a ball and forget she ever saw it. She wanted to crush it, she realized. Even if she was scared and sad and aching in every corner of her heart, she still wanted to crumple up the foolscap and kick it under the bed.

The knock came again, and Havilar's anger lit. As if she couldn't *hear* Farideh gathering her things. As if a letter made the difference. As if Farideh running off into danger weren't just another way she didn't trust Havilar. If Farideh was going to go, then she ought to get on with it.

She stood woozily and caught herself on the table . . . and noticed the ruby necklace Sairché had given Farideh balled against the wall like a frightened viper. As she watched, it uncoiled, the largest stone falling over with a *clink*.

That necklace, Havilar thought. That *stupid* necklace. What was it but a great big sign that no matter what Farideh did, she'd be rewarded and Havilar would be left behind? The big ruby in the middle hung crooked, as if someone had bent it toward the door. She scooped it off the ground, and slammed the largest stone against the corner of the table.

She expected the gem to rattle her hand and make her feel stupid.

But the ruby shattered under her palm, and the necklace exploded.

Havilar was thrown backward into the door by the force of the cloud of ash, knocking the wind from her. Her eardrums ached, but there was little sound beyond the tinkle of glass, the rush of smoke, and the sound of Havilar coughing.

And someone else coughing. Havilar rolled to her feet and peered into the room as the smoke thinned. She drew the little knife from her belt as the shape of a person came clear.

Lorcan, slowly standing.

"Shit and *ashes*!" he all but howled. He loomed over Havilar, looking like nothing so much as the sort of devil that crept into her nightmares, fierce and murderous. Ready to tear her apart. His hands were curled into weapons, and all Havi had was her little knife. "Do you have any idea what you've done?" he snarled.

Havilar might still have been drunk, might have been frightened out of her mind. But she was still wise enough to reach into her shirt and clutch the amulet of Selûne that had settled between her breasts.

"*V-Vennela*," she said, the trigger word sliding up, unimpeded by her frozen thoughts. A flash of silver light and Lorcan hissed as the binding spell crackled over him.

"Is that how we're doing things now, you ungrateful little—"

Something about the air seemed to snap and whip past Havilar. Lorcan broke off with a cry of pain that had nothing to do with the binding, and fell to the floor. Havilar blinked at the strange sensation, gone so quickly she thought she might have imagined it.

Except Lorcan was still lying on the floor, panting.

Lorcan's wings snapped open, sending the last of the smoke swirling. "Does your new mistress know you have such a sweet trinket?" he said, still seething. "Or have you played her just as false?" He looked up at Havilar, and there was no mistaking the surprise in his expression.

Havilar narrowed her eyes at him. "Wrong sister."

He eyed her a moment, a change as clear as when he wore a human skin coming over him as he turned calm, charming. "On the contrary. You're just who I'm looking for."

"Liar," Havilar said, climbing to her feet. "She's *gone*. Like you ought to be."

Lorcan spread his hands wide, still looking as if he'd prefer to tear her limb from limb, but at least looking like he was thinking better of that. "We're on the same side here. If you think I'm happy . . . well, whatever you've endured, I did it in the comfort of that shitting necklace. So tell me where your sister is, I'll find *my* sister, and I'll get to making both of us a little happier."

Havilar shifted and glowered at the broken bottle on the floor. At least he knew Farideh was wrong. "I have nothing to say to you," she said, sliding the knife into her belt. She missed and it clattered to the floor.

Lorcan peered at her. "I see wine is no cure."

"Oh *thrik-ukris* and *karshoj arlorcanominak*," Havilar spat, the vilest curse she could think of. She scrambled for more. "You shitting bastard of a *tiamashkosj* . . ."

"Calm down," Lorcan said edging toward her. "No one's saying you don't deserve that wine. Hells, I would gladly take what you're not using. But to start with, Sairché won't be through—"

I don't have to listen to this, Havilar thought. "I'm going to find Mehen," she announced and turned on her heel. "I'll bet he has a *lot* to say to *you*."

The alarm that blared through the safe house's hallways stopped her in her tracks. Suddenly there were people—so many people—pouring out of rooms, and the tide of bodies dragged her through the hall and down into the taproom. She couldn't see if Lorcan had followed her—no one screamed about devils, but he might have changed. Every other soul in the Harper safe house was there, and the doors were barred. Several wizards with wands out seemed to be separating the ordinary patrons—now dazed and glassy-eyed—from the Harpers, who were clearly being counted up.

Mehen found her then, his scaly arms catching her in a close embrace. "Here you are," he said. He waved away the wizard who approached with raised brows. "Where's your sister?"

Havilar scowled. "Ask Lorcan."

"Lorcan?" Mehen looked up and over her shoulder, scanning the crowd. "What are you talking about?" He fixed a yellow eye on his daughter. "Where is your sister?"

Havilar turned and searched the milling crowd of people, but there was no sign of the disguised cambion. She made a face. "He's here. I didn't imagine it."

"*Where* is your sister?" Mehen said again.

"Gone," Havilar said. "She ran away. Didn't even say where she was going." She shoved the crumpled note at Mehen. "There."

Mehen took it from her gingerly, as if he were afraid of the note—which was silly, Havilar thought, watching him. Mehen wasn't afraid. But then he tapped the roof of his mouth nervously, and she wondered. He read Farideh's message, and when he looked up again at Havilar, there was so much fear and horror in his face that she wished he would just be nervous again.

"Did she go with Lorcan?"

Havilar looked away, out into the crowd. "No. He was looking for her too. Everyone's looking for *her*."

"Now is not the time, Havi. Where did she go?"

The crowd around them parted for Tam. "You two," he said, to Havilar and Mehen, "come with me."

Tam's study was at the top of too many stairs, but Havilar kept her complaints to herself. The room already held plenty of people—the handsome half-elf fellow she'd chased off when he'd watched her too long, the lady Harper who'd been with Dahl when they arrived, Brin. Havilar found herself a corner and tried to disappear into it.

But Tam wouldn't let her. "Your sister vanished from my office with Dahl."

Worse and worse—she'd run off, run off to save the day, without Havilar and *with* some good-looking fellow. Because Farideh got everything. She clung to that angry, spiteful thought because under it, powerful as a tide, came the panic. They couldn't stop Farideh if she'd vanished. They couldn't make her come back if she'd disappeared.

"And?" she said, surlier than she meant to.

"And I want to know who took them," he said. "Where they went. Whether I need to clear this safe house. This sort of thing doesn't happen."

"This sort of thing happens to *her* all the time," Havilar said, feeling bold. "I don't know why you're so worried."

"Havi!" Mehen gave her an awful, shocked look. Even the strange Harpers looked appalled, and Havilar wished she could vanish too. She didn't dare look at Brin. The panic squeezed her chest.

"I don't know where she went," Havilar said. "You'll just have to find her."

"They left no sign?" the half-elf man asked. "No trace of where they might have gone?"

"Nothing," Tam said. "They were there, I turned my back, they were gone. No trace of a spell, no marks of a portal." He waved his hand. "This room is warded against that sort of entry—so is it some new spell we weren't ready for?"

"Have you tried locating him?" the woman asked.

"Briefly," Tam said. "The spell didn't find him, but such things . . ." He spread his hands. "We'll try again. In the meantime—"

"You have to find her," Havilar said again.

She was in the library," Brin offered. "Looking for something."

"I'll search it," the Tuigan woman offered.

Tam turned to Havilar. "Why has she been acting so strange?"

"How should she act?" Mehen said hotly. "World turned her upside down."

Havilar thought of the note, still crushed in Mehen's hand. A devil. That Sairché. That's who took her, she thought. Maybe who took Dahl. But Tam wouldn't want to hear that—what would he say? That it was Farideh being wicked. She wasn't wicked—she was just stupid.

Tam was still staring at Havilar. "What was she looking for in the library?"

"I don't know," Havilar said.

"She's not in trouble. Not yet. But you have to help me here, Havi. Where might she have gone?"

"I don't *know*," Havilar insisted. "She wouldn't have left. She knew better. Someone else must have . . . Someone could have taken her."

Mehen sighed. "She left a note," he admitted. He handed it over to Tam. "Doesn't say where she's going."

Tam cursed. "Who's Sairché?" Havilar covered her face. This was everything she didn't want. "Havi," Tam said sharply. "Who?"

"The devil," Havilar said, her voice squeezing tight. "The one who—"

Havilar's reply was overtaken by a voice coming out of the air—Dahl's voice, whispered and quick.

"*Netherese stronghold. Soldiers, shadar-kai, heavily armed. Somewhere cold. High up.*" Dahl's voice hung for so long Havilar was sure he'd finished, but then he added, "*Farideh came intentionally. I've lost her, both wounded. Have one reserve sending, sword and dagger.*"

Tam hissed as if he were trying not to curse. He scowled at the desk a moment more before saying to the air. "Lie low. Get me better idea of your location, quickly so rescuers can find a portal. Find Farideh. Determine where she stands." He blew out a breath and shook his head again, as if there were no *end* to the curses he wanted to say. "Stay safe," he finished instead.

" 'Rescuers'?" Brin said. "Is that necessary?"

"We're in the midst of a war and someone in a Netherese fortress just pulled a high-level handler out of the heart of our operations," Tam retorted. "We're not taking chances."

"And the tiefling?" the half-elf man said. Tam was silent.

Mehen bared his teeth. "She stands exactly where she did before."

"With a devil?" the half-elf said skeptically.

"You can't think she's a traitor," Havilar said. "You can't." There were a lot of bad things she could say about Farideh, after everything, but not traitor. Never traitor.

The woman threw open the door, out of breath and clutching another scrap of paper. "Netherese," she panted. "Was in one of the books she had out."

Tam took the paper—and Havilar marked the writing, the same sort of writing she'd seen all over the place, when they'd sought out that creepy Netherese arcanist before. Tam considered the paper, his expression becoming harder and harder.

"Havilar," Tam said gravely. "If you know *anything* about this, you need to speak up."

The wine was turning sour in her stomach. Farideh might be stupid enough to listen to Lorcan's sister, but she wasn't on the devils' side. She wasn't a traitor. And if Havilar said the wrong thing—if all her anger tricked her clumsy, tipsy tongue . . .

"I don't know anything," she said quietly. "Can I go to my room?"

Tam studied her, as if he might search out what she wasn't saying written on her face. But after a moment he nodded, waved her toward the door. "Don't leave," he said tersely.

Mehen followed her out of Tam's offices.

"They'll find her," he said. "They'll know she's not a traitor. And I will make *sure* of that. Everything will be fine." When she didn't stop, he grabbed her arm. "Havi, wait."

She squeezed her eyes shut. "I drank too much, all right? I'm no good to them, not now. I'm just going to sleep."

Mehen didn't look as if he believed her either. "We could sit. Talk about this?"

Havilar shook her head. "Tomorrow," she promised. She hugged him tight and kissed his scaly cheek. He held her so long she felt guilty for turning him down. But she slipped away anyhow, went back to her room, to her half-empty bottle of wine, to her sadness and her quiet. She pulled the blanket up over her head and resolutely did not think about anything at all.

The door opened. She didn't look out.

"So the Harpers think Farideh is a traitor," Lorcan said. "And they don't know where she is. Anything else?"

Havilar curled up tighter. "How much did you hear?"

"Enough," Lorcan said. "It sounds like you've gotten everything you wanted."

"What's that supposed to mean?"

"It means she's not coming back. Not this time."

"Of course she'll come back," Havilar said, throwing back the cover and sitting up. "She always gets out of these things."

Lorcan shrugged. "I won't pretend I know her better than you. But I do know that my sister has a way with her deals. Whatever she's caught Farideh in is no simple task. And if your Harper friends do find her, well, there's a war happening out there. They're going to treat her as a traitor from the sound of it. How could they do anything else? So if her captors don't do her in, her rescuers well might." He turned away to toy with the window latch. "I'll admit, I never thought you'd be the sort who could wash your hands of her. But then if it were my sister, I would do the same without thinking. Maybe we're not that different."

"You and I are *not* the same."

Lorcan smiled. "And yet both of us would be much better off as only children."

Havilar balled her fists as if she could squeeze all the fury out of her. "I know what you're doing," she said, her voice shaking. "You think I'm stupid, but I know what you're doing. You want me to feel bad for her. To feel like I have to save her. It won't work. She can save herself."

Lorcan tilted his head. "Can she? Who killed the plague-touched succubus before she could kill Farideh? Who stared down a Zhentarim assassin? Who rescued her sister from a green wyrmling at the tender age of twelve? Farideh would be dead a dozen times over without you, Havilar. Make no mistake."

Havilar's fists loosened. "Who told you about the dragon?"

"Farideh, of course," he said.

"She said you didn't talk about me." She *had* said that once, Havilar felt sure, after Havi had been jealous and demanded to know.

"I don't," Lorcan admitted. "But she's always been impressed with you. Always a little envious of your skills."

"You're doing it again," Havilar said. "I'm not stupid."

"No," Lorcan said. "You're not. And you know I'm right. Those Harpers will be too slow in the first place. And then they don't have all the facts, and even if Mehen would never turn on Farideh, they will outnumber him by a dozen. If you want to save her—and I think you do—we're her only hope."

Havilar folded her arms across her chest and glared at her glaive leaning against the wall. "I hate you," she said after a moment.

"We can work on that," Lorcan said. "But first we need to get far away from here."

"You don't know where to go," Havilar pointed out. "She could be anywhere."

"She could be, but she isn't," he said. "They had no clues?"

"Cold. Up high. And there was a note in Netherese."

Lorcan smiled. "Then it sounds as if we start by heading north." He tensed and magic crackled over his frame, dissolving his wings and horns and turning his red skin pale. He blinked and his dark eyes were human. "Let's find some horses, shall we?"

CHAPTER SEVEN

19 Ches, the Year of the Nether Mountain Scrolls (1486 DR)
Waterdeep

FARIDEH DID NOT SLEEP. SHE SAT ON THE BED WITH HER BACK against the wall, watching the door. Every time she started to doze off, she thought of waking in the dead of night with Adolican Rhand standing over her, and she jolted into alertness.

She kept her cloak pulled close around her, her rod in her hand, her sword in easy reach. The room was cold—like a cave more than anything, all smooth-planed black glass—same as the halls they passed through to reach it. The rich furniture—a canopied bed, a raised chest with a ewer and bowl beneath a large mirror, and a brazier burning hot and magically smokeless on the thick carpet—couldn't hide it, nor did it blunt the faint vibration the stone seemed to give off. Not enough to hear. Just enough to make her even more on edge, as she sat and waited for Rhand's inevitable return.

Coming back into the world from Sairché's confinement had been so like waking from a nightmare, only to realize she was still trapped within another dream—one where she couldn't control her powers and monsters she was sure she'd vanquished rose up out of the ground, undeterred.

"I seem to recall we had unfinished business, you and I," Rhand had said after he'd shown her into the room. "What a fortunate coincidence your mistress's plans aligned with mine."

One of the guards stirred up the brazier and a second laid out a pale nightdress on the bed—he'd draft her proper servants tomorrow, he'd said. Farideh didn't dare look away from her captor even as her nerves sent up plumes of shadow-smoke, as if they could blur her edges and hide her from his sight. "I seem to recall you drugged my wine," she said. "And then set your guards after me and my friend."

Adolican Rhand wagged a finger at her. "Ah, but you were the one who destroyed the site I was so close to reclaiming. A score of my men died in the blast, you know," he said, as if these were impish pranks. He smiled and it was still unpleasant. "Shall we let bygones be bygones?"

The way he'd looked at her while she drank the poisoned *zzar,* the feeling of his hands on her waist where they didn't belong, the way he'd smiled like she wasn't a threat at all and asked if she wanted to lie down while the crowds around her dissolved into laughing devils and her feet stopped obeying her—Farideh suppressed a shudder. Nothing is bygone, she thought.

She wondered what Sairché had promised him.

A common enemy—that was the deal. The favor would bring down a common enemy. But Sairché hadn't said who that was. Did Rhand know? Was Farideh meant to turn against him? Was there some fourth wicked source in this arrangement?

But Rhand had given her no sign, and merely bid her good night, saying that he'd send up a maidservant in the morning to help her find her way down to morningfeast. As much as she hadn't expected to see Rhand again, she'd expected even less for him to make conversation with her like a long-lost friend and then walk out the door, leaving it unlocked.

She wondered if Rhand would remember Dahl from before if the Harper got caught. She wondered if Dahl had seen Rhand come down the stairs and if he'd come back for her. Dahl had gotten her away from Rhand the first time, when she couldn't walk straight let alone say what was happening to her. But the middle of a revel where everyone was at least *acting* innocent and the middle of a fortress crawling with shadar-kai and devil-dealers were very different.

And, Farideh thought, picking at the embroidery of the coverlet, Dahl only came back for you by accident that first time.

She took a deep breath—again. You can handle this, she thought, staring at the closed door. You are the daughter of Clanless Mehen. You are a Brimstone Angel . . .

You are an idiot, a little voice said. You are in well over your head.

As soon as Rhand and his guards left, she'd thrown the nightdress over the mirror. She couldn't bear to look at her face with all its subtle strangeness, all the minute reminders of what she'd done. In the hardness of her jaw was everything Havilar had lost—including her trust in Farideh. In the slight widening of her cheekbones, Mehen's broken heart. In the paleness of her skin, there was Brin's sad expression and the uncertain way he looked at Havilar. In the faint lines around her mouth, there was Lorcan.

Farideh's throat tightened and she laid her head against her knees, trying to swallow her tears. *Do you really think you're still his warlock now?* Sairché had said. Because he was done with her or because Sairché had him locked away? If this was how she protected Farideh, how had she "protected" Lorcan?

It doesn't matter, Farideh thought as the tears started flowing. There is no reason to think you'll ever see him again. He wouldn't forgive you either. She wept and wept for all of them, and without meaning to fell asleep.

The sound of the latch made her leap off the bed, all adrenalin and instinct. The sun had risen, she noted as she caught her breath and tried to slow the hammering of her pulse. How long had she been asleep? She wiped her face as the door opened—long enough all her tears were gone.

So were the rod and the sword.

It was not Rhand who opened the door but a human woman in a threadbare gray skirt and blouse, a black cloth tied around thick auburn hair shot through with gray. She curtsied before entering, trailed by a guard in spiked armor holding a wooden case.

The guard was shadar-kai, and shorter than Farideh by a head and a half, but by the way she moved every ounce of her seemed to be muscle, encased in black leather and trimmed with chains. Her silvery hair was cropped short and stuck out from her head in a wild halo. Piercings of blackened metal pulled at her face, giving her a strange grimace. There were knives at her hips and crossed on her back. The guard looked Farideh over and smiled, displaying teeth filed into points.

The human made another little curtsy. "Well met, my lady. I'm Tharra," she said, with a familiarity that didn't fit. "They've asked me to dress you for morningfeast."

"My lady," the guard added, dropping the case on the table.

"My lady," Tharra said, smoothly, as if she'd merely paused a moment too long. As if the guard weren't terrifying.

"What am I supposed to call *you*?" Farideh said, Sairché's warnings echoing in her thoughts.

The guard's eyes were black as Lorcan's but colder, much colder. She curled her lip, displaying a row of filed, pointed teeth. "Nirka." She turned to scowl at the maid. "Be quick about it!" Tharra bobbed her head and went to the wardrobe.

"I'm already dressed," Farideh said. Tharra considered Farideh's torn and gore-stained blouse, and raised her eyebrows. She looked to the guard who snorted.

"You'll change," Nirka said. "He'll have things to say if you come down wearing that."

"I'll suffer them."

Tharra straightened her apron. "There are lovely gowns in here," she said, and whether it was her tone or the worry of what Rhand might do, Farideh found herself curious. It wouldn't be such a concession to change . . .

Farideh frowned. That wasn't like her, not at all. She wondered what Rhand—or Sairché?—had done while she slept.

"There are combs and a necklace, as well." Tharra opened the case to show a wide collar of jet and rubies that would sweep over Farideh's collarbones. The combs were decorated with little clusters of lacquer poppies spangled with more rubies and weeping drops of pearl milk. "They won't suit your current clothes. And Nirka tells me the wizard would like you to wear them."

I'll bet he would, Farideh thought.

Farideh thought of Sairché's cool confidence. She thought of Lorcan's sly sharpness. She thought of Temerity's stillness in the face of a Brimstone Angel. She could do this.

Farideh steeled herself and sneered the way she had when faced with Rhand and the dead guards to answer for. "Are the gems what's making me so interested in dresses?"

Tharra stiffened. "What?"

"What do they do?"

Tharra stared at her, and Farideh had the strangest sensation that she was keeping herself from looking to Nirka. " 'Do,' my lady?"

"How are they enchanted?"

Tharra smiled and shook her head. "They aren't. Do you prefer they were?"

Farideh touched the gems tentatively—no itch or buzz or tingle. No sense there was anything magical at all about them. She frowned.

"Put her in the dress and come along," Nirka said. "Your morningfeast is getting cold and Master Rhand is growing impatient."

The maid pulled several items from the wardrobe—a dark green velvet gown; a gauzy silver one, matched with a long corset; a third, glittering black and red with long, carefully placed strips. Tharra's amused expression showed clearly through the very transparent red sections.

"That one. A fine gown," Nirka said, though her disgusted expression showed she didn't agree. "Put it on."

"I'm not wearing that," Farideh said, feeling her stomach knot. "Ever."

"It will suit your figure," Tharra said. "You could try it on?"

She could. She could just try it. There was no harm in—

Farideh flinched as if she could shy from the embarrassing, intrusive thoughts. "Hold it up again?"

Tharra had no more than lifted the dress, but Farideh pointed a finger and spat a word of Infernal that carried with it a shiver of energy. The middle of the dress exploded into cinders and tatters of thread. Tharra and Nirka jumped back in surprise, the guard catching the hilts of her hip daggers as she did.

"I am not," Farideh said again, "wearing that." She considered the open wardrobe. "Haven't you any armor for me? Anything with breeches?"

Nirka eyed her impassively. "What do you intend to do, little demon? Fight your way out?"

"I intend to wear what I want," Farideh said sharply. "Or not leave this room. So you can decide—do *you* want to explain to him where I am? Or do you want to find me something I'll wear?"

Nirka looked her over slowly, as if thinking of all the ways she could cut Farideh into pieces. "You will wear the jewels and the combs. And you will tell him what you did to the dress." She stepped closer to Farideh—close enough Farideh thought about which spells she could cast, which tender spots she could strike if the shadar-kai grabbed her around the throat. "But do remember, it won't make any difference." She gave Farideh another horrible grin that bared her pointed teeth. "It may even make it worse."

The powers of the Hells coiled around Farideh, ready to lash out if the guard so much as moved—

A claw of pain gripped the back of Farideh's skull. The lights began blooming around her vision again and clustered in shadow-black and foul green around the guard's heart, and a shimmering purple and bruised yellow around the servant's. Blue sparked around the corner of her silvered eye. Farideh held steady, trying to channel someone cold and dangerous and not at all afraid of what was happening. Trying not to cry out.

"Don't leave," Nirka snapped at Tharra as she swept from the room.

Tharra shut the door behind the guard. "Shall I dress your hair while we wait? My lady?"

"Where are my weapons?" Farideh demanded.

Tharra smiled, the purple light in her pulsing. "I wouldn't know. They brought me into the fortress just this morning. If I had to guess, I'd say someone took them to the armory." She gestured at the chair before the mirror. "Nirka would be the one to ask. My lady."

Farideh sat, her nerves ready to shatter. Nothing felt right, and she couldn't shake the sensation that at any moment, she would be surrounded by all the things she feared. That if she stopped preparing, tensing for them, they would sweep her away as neatly as Sairché had swept her out of the world.

And then there was Tharra, who was so calm and falsely pleasant, it set Farideh's nerves on edge.

"I'm afraid I don't know what's fashionable in Shade," Tharra said. "Or have the skill to make it happen. But I can plait—"

"Do what you want," Farideh said. She could tie the whole mess up in a bow, and it wouldn't make a difference. Instead of watching her unwelcome reflection, Farideh watched Tharra in the mirror, as she deftly separated hanks of Farideh's purplish-black hair, plaiting them into smaller sections and twisting them up into knots under Farideh's horns. A pang of heartsickness hit Farideh—Havilar would have cheerfully pinned her hair up. Although she would have spent the time trying to convince Farideh that the combs would look much better on her.

"Do you come from Shade?" she asked Tharra. The woman's expression turned curious.

"No, my lady," she said. "I don't think any of us do."

"You just serve him for your own reasons?"

For the barest moment, Tharra's eyes turned hard as flint. "For food. We take the best we can get in hard times," she said. "My lady. How is it *you* plan to serve him?"

Farideh flushed at the unspoken implication and started to retort, but the blue lights that had been flickering in the corner of her silvered eye flashed again in the mirror's reflection, just over Tharra's head and behind her. Farideh pursed her lips and tried to quiet them. Sairché would have to come eventually. She'd have to tell her what it was then.

But as she watched, the lights grew and clung to each other. And, for a moment, took the shape of a woman, a tiefling.

Farideh leaped to her feet, jerking her hair out of Tharra's hands. But the lights had gone out once again, and there was no sign in the little room that anyone but Farideh and the maid had been there.

"Is something wrong, lady?" Tharra asked. She'd taken a good two steps back from Farideh, watching her carefully. The lights around Tharra had vanished too.

Farideh blinked several times, but whatever she thought she'd seen didn't return. She sat back down. "No. Just finish."

Nirka returned a moment later with black leather jacks, marked with lines of gold-colored studs. Nirka made a slit in the back seam for her tail, and Farideh mutely pulled them on, still watching the empty air over the bed. The necklace looked preposterous with the high-necked armor, but Tharra draped it around her neck anyway.

"Come on," Nirka said. She nodded to Tharra. "Clean this up, and I'll be back for you." Nirka locked the door behind them, and led Farideh downstairs.

Adolican Rhand waited for Farideh at the end of a long table laden with delicacies she had no stomach for. He stood as she entered, chuckling at her garb.

"I'll admit," he said sitting again. "I was hoping you would choose something more flattering. The red one is terribly fashionable in the city, I'm told."

"Not in any city I've been in," Farideh said, and the wizard laughed.

"Too true." He gestured at the meal between them. "Please. You'll have to forgive me, I did not wait."

Farideh didn't move. The last time she'd taken food from Adolican Rhand, it had taken tendays to get the poison out of her system. "I ate from my rations."

"I assure you, my kitchens are much better. Have some fruit at least." When she didn't, he chuckled again. "Ah, still holding a grudge. Nirka—reassure her."

Farideh tensed as the guard stepped up from behind her, a furious sneer twisting her pierced face. But Nirka only took Farideh's plate and filled it, cutting and eating a bite of each item as she did. Then she stood, glaring at Farideh, as if this indignity were purely her doing.

"I can promise you," Rhand said, "I'm aware of where we stand now. Of what you can do for me and my patrons. Of what your patron desires. Whatever you think of me, I hope you realize I wouldn't jeopardize such a privilege unnecessarily."

Farideh hoped none of her puzzlement showed. She thought of Rhand's notes, of his crude intimations, of the drugs he'd slipped into her wine, muddling her thoughts and senses. There didn't seem to be another way to take any of that.

But she remembered Dahl insisting that it was probably nothing, Havilar saying that Rhand was likely no worse than Lorcan. Maybe she was wrong to be so on edge. Maybe he was only an overeager suitor. Had he slipped her anything after all? Or was it only the sedative tea Tam had given her and the stirring of her pact magic?

You're not wrong, she told herself. But then again, she'd been wrong and wrong and wrong lately.

"Sairché wasn't very forthcoming about details," she said, studying her plate. "What is it exactly she said I could do for you?"

"Isn't that so like a devil?" Rhand said. "Vagaries and half truths? It must be a chore to work with them. Is your patron like that too?"

"Yes." Farideh looked across the table, not knowing what he meant by "too," but knowing it was better to seem sure. "So enlighten me?"

Whatever his own assurances, Rhand's gaze still had an unsettlingly predatory quality and his eager smile did nothing to blunt it. Anger—at him, at Sairché—squeezed her chest.

"You are to assist my grand experiment." He nodded at the plate of food in front of her, and since the guard was still standing, still clearly full of focused dislike for Farideh, she obliged and nibbled at a bun.

"In fact," Rhand went on, "with the assistance of your particular powers, I should be able to make the advancements I've been stymied from reaching."

Pain gripped the back of her head again, like a living creature latching on with many-bladed legs. Her eyes watered, and for a moment she could not focus on anything except the agony in her skull and getting her own breath in and out of her lungs.

Then the lights started again, shivering purple and black and deeper shades around Adolican Rhand—who hadn't seemed to notice her discomfort.

"I don't care for the term," he was saying. "Not in this case. Though some come near that mythical status. Not many. Not enough to warrant such a melodramatic title." He filled his goblet from a near pitcher. "At any rate, they are far trickier to identify in time than one would expect. Finding those with a trace of the divine about them, that's a trifle. But"—he held up a hand, as if to stop her inevitable argument—"there is a difference, as you can imagine."

"Yes. Well. I would think so," she said, nearly choking on the words. Nirka was watching her, a jagged, lashing green light at her heart.

"My first attempts," Adolican Rhand went on, "were focused

only on those traces. It works well enough to gather some, but then I end up with too many false identifications, clogging up my experiments."

Blue lights appeared into the empty space over his head, one after another. They grew and bled together, even as more popped into being. Farideh winced and she could hardly hear Rhand now, saying, "You can imagine the mess. It works but it's no good for the rest of them, waiting."

The lights once more took shape, becoming a tiefling woman trailing tattered robes. She shifted and flickered, like light cast across the surface of water, and the movement made the image of her peel away and build back up, showing skin, then muscle and viscera, bare bone, black shadow and back again—all drifting back and forth at different times, different speeds. As the light drew smooth skin over her face, the woman smiled at Farideh, and laid a bony finger to her lips.

Farideh leaped out of her seat and the ghost vanished.

"Eager indeed!" Rhand crowed. He stood as well. "Come, I'll show you my arrangement, then we can see how you fare. Garek, Sharit, go get a group ready. Come," he said again, holding out an arm for Farideh to take. Farideh steeled herself and took his arm, uncomfortably aware of the similarities to the last time he'd offered—the sick feeling in her stomach, her unsteady gait, the strange visions she couldn't control.

But the lights had come on twice before she ever put a morsel in her mouth. The lights had to be something else . . . some symptom or side effect . . . some clue . . .

She had just worked up the courage to excuse herself, to try and get back to her room where she might have a modicum of privacy to sort things out, when they reached a pair of doors flanked by two more shadar-kai. Rhand eased her in ahead of him, releasing her arm.

Equipment cluttered the room—glass retorts, shelves full of components in jars and pouches and envelopes, shelves of scrolls. Another brazier, burning hot and fragrant with dried herbs. Two large tomes lay open on lecterns at either end, and between them sat three vessels of water the size of shields, magic bristling around their edges. Windows lined one wall of the room, and the guards pushed the shutters open to let in more light. Two younger men in wizards' robes hunched over open scrolls. They stood straighter as Rhand entered, but he didn't acknowledge them.

"This tenday's draw," Rhand explained gesturing at the basins. "It has to be distilled carefully, with much of the ordinary water removed. A score of buckets full, and this is what's left."

Farideh peered at the water. It swirled gently in its confines, looking thick and cold and gleaming with an oily opalescence in the light that streamed through the wall of windows. "And what is it?"

He was silent so long that Farideh wondered if perhaps he'd already said, and now she'd exposed her inattention. When she looked up, though, he had a faraway expression as he gazed at the basins. He looked at her and smiled.

"They are what remains of the fabled Fountains of Memory."

Dahl crept back down the hillside as dawn broke over the mountains. Late, he thought. Which meant he was farther north than he'd guessed. The dozens of buildings he'd seen multiplied to scores—no, *hundreds* in the gray light. He slipped in between them, down alleyways, past dark doorways, past closed windows . . . past gardens with the last weedy tops of carrots and parsnips gone to seed. Past laundry lines, a hobbyhorse carved from a gnarled branch. Dahl frowned.

Lord of Secrets, he thought, ducking into the open door of an empty hut at the corner of two larger pathways. Don't let me have sent such a dire message over a *village*.

But a village should have had more than just huts—there

were no smiths or markets or farmlands to be seen. No pigs in the streets, no dogs. No horses or carts. No taverns, he thought, all too aware of the faint headache he'd woken with. He had his flask still—a sip here and there would keep it from getting worse.

He took another before he nudged the shutters open and watched, crouched in the shadows as people started coming out into the streets. With each one, his suspicions were confirmed: the "villagers" didn't belong, all mixed together, by the shores of the icy lake.

Dahl counted men, women, and children. Skins of every hue. Humans, elves, a dwarf, a pair of half-orcs. A *full* orc walking alone and cutting his eyes back and forth across the street. If it were a village, he thought, *everyone* in the North would have heard of it.

Not enough to warrant using the second sending. There was no doubting this wasn't a village. There was no being sure—not yet—what exactly it was.

Dahl peered closer at the group of humans standing outside, at the villagers who passed by in the meantime. Not one person wore a weapon of any sort, not even the fishing knives you'd expect to see in a lakeside village.

Except for the shadar-kai. Dahl heard the gang of three jangling up the street before he saw them. The villagers heard as well, and quickly got out of sight. A woman, her auburn hair gathered under a black kerchief, leaped in the door of Dahl's hiding place.

Dahl froze. The woman stepped behind the wall between the door and the window, watching past the doorjamb as the shadar-kai, dripping chains and blades and sneering laughter, passed by. The woman cursed softly and rested her head against the wall.

Not villagers, Dahl thought. But not Netherese soldiers either.

"I'm going to ask you to be quiet," Dahl said, low and quick, "and tell me if you can see any of those guards from where you stand."

To her credit, the woman didn't jump at the sound of Dahl's voice. She stood a little straighter, and without looking over at Dahl swept her gaze over the street. "No." She turned and looked Dahl over, not a little fear tensing her frame. She wore the same faded, mended clothes the rest of the villagers wore—as if she had only the one set. All the buttons were missing from her padded jacket and she'd tied a string around her chest, to keep it shut.

"What are you doing out of the fortress?"

Dahl held up his hands. "I'm not with the guards."

The woman's eyes flicked over Dahl's stolen uniform. "Is that a fact?"

"Tharra!" a child's voice shouted from outside. "You can come out!"

"Go on without me," the woman called back, eyes on Dahl. "Tell Oota I'll be there shortly. So whoever you are, keep that in mind," she said more softly to Dahl. "Obould's shieldmaiden'll care if I disappear. Is your scheme worth that?" She shifted back from Dahl, making her jacket gape. Out of the corner of his eye, Dahl registered the edge of something rounded and metal that dragged on the fabric of the woman's shirt.

"I don't know what that means," Dahl said, coming nearer, hands spread. "And I don't have a scheme."

It was the wrong move, and Dahl should have known it, he'd realize later. Not a sign he trusted Tharra so much as giving the woman the opportunity to strike out, punching Dahl hard enough to make the Harper see stars and fall back onto the cot. When he sat up, Tharra had fled.

Idiot, he thought, pressing gently on his nose and wincing at the blood his fingers came away with. Even a stranger would rather hit you than help you. At least Tharra hadn't pulled that weapon in her coat—

He frowned to himself, looking up at the reed roof. Not a weapon. A pin. The edge of metal under her jacket had had the same shape, the same curve as the old Harper pin Dahl had worn for a time. Watching Gods—he rolled to his feet and went to stand in the doorway of the hut. There was no sign of the woman, no sign of the child who'd called to him. Only the strange villagers passing this way and that, bundled in their thin cloaks and worn jackets.

And a trail of white daisies peeking merrily through the half-frozen mud, too early in the season to be in such bright bloom.

Mehen made himself wait for Havilar to wake up and come down for morningfeast, uncertain it was the right course. He had hardly slept, arguing late into the night with Tam and his Harpers, until Brin made him leave. They weren't saying Farideh was a traitor. They weren't planning to hunt her down. But Mehen knew Tam well enough to know he wasn't going to throw out the evidence for being absurd, and no amount of shouting from Mehen would make the difference. They'd go as soon as Dahl had better information.

He wished he'd kept Havilar close all the same. He wished he'd bundled both girls up and whisked them out of this filthy city, out of harm's way.

He'd made the Harpers swear to take him with them. No one was going to tell Clanless Mehen to cool his heels while Netherese and devils and planes knew what else menaced his daughter. Just the thought enraged him—and he held tight to that rage, knowing the alternative would undo him all over again. He wouldn't lose Farideh again.

Mehen considered the stairs up to the inn's rooms, and tapped his tongue against the roof of his mouth. Havilar would need to come as well—a thought that nearly made him willing to stay behind. She wasn't strong enough yet.

But he couldn't abandon Farideh. And he couldn't abandon Havi either.

Mehen sighed and stretched the tension from his neck.

The sun was well up and still no Havilar. Probably nothing, he thought. Probably just wants to be alone a bit. He went up the stairs anyway, unable to stand another lonesome moment.

Once upon a time, Havilar had insisted on sleeping on the floor beside his bed—not crawling in like a *baby*—and once she'd drifted off, Mehen would have lifted her in beside him, off the cold boards. But Havilar wasn't his wild little girl anymore, seeking comfort from a nightmare. He sighed as he turned down the hall. So many years without them—he felt as clumsy and out of practice being their father as Havilar did with her glaive.

Listen to your gut, he told himself, because there was nothing else he could do.

Brin was standing in the hallway, staring at Havilar's shut door. Mehen paused, watching the young man for a moment, wanting as much to leave them both to their privacy and to run him off before he could do something to break Havilar's heart on top of everything else.

There was no word for the knowledge you weren't supposed to have—how differently would things have turned out if Mehen had found out about the Cormyrean lordling and his daughter a few short tendays after the fact? He couldn't imagine being anything but furious. But years after? When the boy had become something like a son, something like a friend? Mehen didn't know what to hope for anymore, except that Brin would be kind to her.

Brin looked up at Mehen and gave him a wan smile. "Well met."

"Well met. Any news?"

Brin shrugged. "Lot of talk. Tam's pretty convinced this is bigger than just Farideh. He wants a full expedition, but the others are trying to hold him off until Dahl gets another sending through with more information." Brin sighed. "Assuming he can. Tam won't admit he's worried about Dahl too."

"Worried he's a liar," Mehen said. "Why would she work with Shade?"

"Tam knows," Brin said. "Still, it bears investigation. Why else would Dahl mention it?"

Mehen bristled. "Because he's excitable and he doesn't like her. He said as much."

"He told you they fought because you scare the piss out of him, much as you do everyone," Brin reminded him gently. He shook his head. "And who *doesn't* Dahl fight with? But all I mean is, there are Netherese involved. So the Harpers need to be involved."

"They could be involved faster," Mehen said. If they were too slow, too cautious . . . He tapped his tongue against the rough roof of his mouth, reminding himself to be calm. "Did you sit down with her yet?" Mehen asked, nodding at the door.

"Almost. I will. It's not easy." Brin shook his head. "You know. You know exactly. Terrible and wonderful and . . ."

"And the words aren't there," Mehen finished. "Might be best. You lay everything out too quick, you'll send her running. You don't need to be the thing that breaks her."

Brin nodded, as if he didn't believe it, but he didn't have a better plan.

"Might be the gift hiding in all this," Mehen said. "There's more time before we have to go back."

Brin chuckled once, bitter and aching. "Not much of a gift." He turned away from the door. "She's still asleep."

Mehen squeezed past him and pounded on the door. "Havi? Havi, you need to get up!"

Silence.

Mehen pressed the side of his head to the door and tapped his tongue against the roof of his mouth. There were *no* sounds—not the faint drone of Havilar's sleeping breath, not the slight shift of her, awake and annoyed—and the taste of her scent was dull and old. Mehen's heart thundered in his ears as he wrenched the door open.

The bed was empty. Her glaive, her haversack, her cloak—all gone.

There was only a note on the bed.

And Clanless Mehen, for the first time since Brin had shown up in Suzail and told him his daughters were gone, felt panic sink its frozen claws into the deepest part of him, and pull him earthward. *You think the world has hurt you?* it might have whispered. *There is so much more pain for you.*

Steady, he told himself. Steady.

Brin pushed past him, read the note, and cursed. "She's left. With *Lorcan*. They've gone after Farideh." He scanned the note again. "They took horses."

Mehen reached for the note. "She wouldn't have gone with Lorcan."

Brin held tight to the sheet. "No. He says he has some way to find Farideh, so they're following that. North. Gods damn it, Havi."

"That *karshoji henish*!" First Farideh, now Havilar—you fool, he thought, you utter fool. He should have killed the devil when he'd had a chance. He should have stopped this, all of this, ages ago. "Tell Tam I've gone."

"Wait!" Brin called. "Mehen you can't—"

"Don't you tell me I can't," Mehen roared. "I know what I can do. I'm not going to sit here and—"

"Mehen you *can't* get to them both," Brin said. "You know it. There isn't a horse in that stable—in *any* stable—that can carry you that fast. By the time you get Havi back, the Harpers will have gone. And they'll have made up their minds about Farideh, with or without you."

It was true. He couldn't be sure how long Havilar had been gone, how far she'd traveled, but with the scent of her so cold and stale it had to be hours and hours.

"If I go now," Brin said. "I might be able to get her back before the Harpers leave. But if I don't, you can still go after Farideh."

There was no part of Clanless Mehen that didn't rebel at the plan—he would not sit back like an old man and wait for others to do his duty He would not let the boy who held his daughter's heart in his hands shatter it out in the wilds, where that devil might pick up the pieces.

But they were both out of his reach, and there was nothing he could do in that moment—Brin was right, Tam was right. He had to rely on others and wait.

Mehen grabbed the younger man's arm, hard enough and suddenly enough to make Brin try and pull away, frightened. Good, he thought viciously.

"You *listen* to me," Mehen said. "You find her, you bring her back. You don't lose her and don't you hurt her, or I swear on every bit of esteem I have for you now, I will make you wish you left me in that cell."

"I know," Brin said. He pulled free. "I don't want her hurt either."

Mehen grabbed hold of Brin again, this time in a fierce embrace. "Be careful yourself, lad. Don't leave me wondering."

CHAPTER EIGHT

19 Ches, the Year of the Nether Mountain Scrolls (1486 DR)
Somewhere North of Waterdeep

Farideh leaned over the strange waters of the so-called fabled Fountains of Memory. A spark of magic arced through the air and popped against her fingertips. She clutched her hand and stepped back. "That's not a fable I'm familiar with," she said.

"Would you like to give them a try?" Rhand asked. He laid one hand lightly against the small of her back and pressed her forward. Farideh edged nearer, if only to step out of his reach.

Her reflection looked back, rippled by the magical current stirring the waters. The air around the vessel chilled noticeably and her breath made faint clouds as she looked down into the thick, dark water, waiting for something to happen.

"There's a trick to it—be specific enough to see what you want, but vague enough to find what you don't know you're going to miss." Rhand reached around her and tossed a scattering of dried blue petals into the water. "Show us when this dear lady's patron first took notice."

The waters' swirl changed direction, the ripples widening as the center of the basin seemed to pull the water inward. Farideh's reflection broke into a hundred smaller patches of color and light . . .

That reformed, bled together . . . and reflected back not Farideh but an open room, the ground floor of an old stone barn that had been converted before she was born into a home for an outcast dragonborn, come to the hidden village of Arush Vayem. Below Mehen's lofted room was a circle of chalked runes, and in the center of that circle was Lorcan.

Farideh's breath caught. She knew enough now to see the frank appraisal in his gaze as he spoke to Havilar, standing in front of him—assessing the tiefling, looking for a warlock to complete his set. Havilar settled herself on the floor, utterly unconcerned with the devil she'd caught instead of an imp or the strength of the binding circle she'd only mimicked.

Farideh watched Lorcan, her heart aching.

He looked up, past Havilar, and something in his demeanor changed, relaxed, as Farideh came into the room. He smiled, showing the faint points of his canines, and Farideh remembered how undone she'd been to see that smile the first time.

She watched as Havilar left, after convincing her nothing would happen if she stayed with the devil in the binding circle. "You're not like her," he said, his voice tinny and strange. "Like night and day. Like sweet and sour. Like the ocean and the desert. It's astonishing." She watched herself try and fail to ignore Lorcan, falling into the bickering conversation that would change her life, Havilar's, Mehen's, and countless others along the way.

"Who could blame you?" he said. "Who wants to be held responsible for something they can't control? Turned away because of something their foremothers and forefathers did to gain a little power?" She shut her eyes wishing the waters would cut off her protest, but it came anyway: it might have been anything that led her ancestors to mingle with fiends. It might have been love.

And Lorcan laughed. "My darling, let me tell you a secret: devils don't love."

She watched herself try to leave, watched Lorcan stop her

with all the right words and warnings. "You'll live in this village for all of your life," Lorcan said, keeping pace with her along the border of the circle. "You'll spend every day, trying your hardest to be what they want, and you'll never meet their expectations, because you were not made for this . . ." She watched him list all the ways she was trapped already, all the ways she couldn't save herself—couldn't save reckless Havilar. At least not alone. Watched herself curl into her chest, covering her face, as if she could hide from what was coming.

As much as she regretted the pact in that moment, Farideh felt only pity for her past self. She would have done the same thing over again, she knew, as Lorcan crossed the faulty line of runes to hold her near, whispering promises and coaxing her toward the agreement that would catch her in a pact. She would have taken the magic no matter what—because every word he said was true. She was trapped. She was powerless. She was so afraid. She watched herself look up, horrified, as she realized what she'd done and at the same time, her chest ached. She wished Lorcan were here, were offering her a way to save herself again.

The image vanished in a wall of flames.

"Interesting," Rhand said, snapping her back to the present. Farideh straightened, wiped her face and realized she'd been crying. Missing Lorcan, but missing, too, the girl in the reflection. She would never be so innocent again. Rhand gave her another unpleasant smile.

"Fascinating things," he said. "Before the Spellplague, the water formed a number of pools in a cavern here—at least, that is what the deep gnomes say. If pressed. They kept the location a secret, as much as one *can* keep such a thing secret." He chuckled. "Harder to hide when the mountaintop was torn off and floated away. The cavern went with the peak—off drifting somewhere over the North, I suspect—but the springs that fed the pools remain. They muddle with the ordinary springs now, so the waters aren't as powerful if you come upon them naturally." He dipped a hand in and stirred the waters. "But with a little ingenuity, a little careful magic, a little discipline . . . they can do miraculous things. Even better than before."

"Indeed," Farideh said, still rattled. "What do you use them for?"

Rhand sighed. "Originally, I had *hoped* to use them for their other abilities. Legends hold that the Fountains of Memory would spontaneously open portals to the locations they showed—past and present. You can imagine how useful such a thing would be. I wouldn't have to identify anything—only send back some eager guards to stop any manifestation before it took hold."

"Yes," Farideh said, wishing she'd heard his earlier explanations. Manifestations of what? Devils? Gods? Something worse? She thought back to all the things she *had* heard, searching for a clue.

But too many of her thoughts were stuck, clinging to the phrase *portals to the locations they showed—past and present.*

"Alas, I haven't managed to unlock that particular secret. Portals to elsewhere, yes. But not the past."

"Do you think you will?" Farideh asked. If Sairché couldn't undo the past, could he? She met his piercing blue gaze.

"I never pursue things I don't think I can achieve."

Farideh didn't dare look away. "What would it take?"

"If I knew that," Rhand said irritably, "it would be done. Nevertheless," he went on, "the Fountains are still useful enough—ask the right questions and it will show where the likeliest candidates are to be found. Set a body before it and ask when their patron took notice, and you can weed out many of the accidental choices. Slow, and not as accurate as I would like. But four in ten is better than two in ten."

Patron, as in Lorcan, as in pact holder. But patrons might mean devils, Farideh thought. Might mean demons. Might mean gods. Might mean just people. And still, she had no idea what Sairché meant for her to do, or who the common enemy was. The waters shimmered, showing no sign of the scene they'd just reflected.

"At any rate," Rhand went on, "I hope this becomes merely my own amusement. Lady Sairché has assured me you are capable of vastly improving my rate of success." With his hand again at the small of her back, he steered her to the open windows.

Beyond the jagged turrets of the fortress, beyond the castle wall, lay scores and scores of square huts with reed roofs leaking smoke from cookfires, aligned on a tidy grid of roads dotted with people. From so high, Farideh could see that the fortress and all the buildings around it sat in an enormous crater—the remains of the sundered peak Rhand had mentioned. On the far end of the village, a large lake lapped a pebble-crusted shore, and over its edge was the peak of another mountain.

"You can just see," Rhand said, pointing across to the edge of the crater, "in this light, the traces of the Wall." The low sunlight sparkled nearly seventy feet from the ground, as if catching on the edge of something invisible. "It's quite impressive," he said. "Completely impregnable and hides everything within. Keeps everything quite tidy." He gave her another unwelcome smile. "Nothing gets in or out unless I let it."

Including Dahl. Ghosts and shadar-kai, Rhand and Sairché and her guilty conscience—she wouldn't have thought there was anything else that could happen to top those. But if Dahl was trapped inside the magical wall as well, he was in grave danger. She watched the people flowing up and down the narrow streets and wondered if he was among them. "You've never had an escape?"

His smile thinned, and he held her gaze a bit too long for comfort. "Never." He leaned out over the sill, looking down at the ground below. "Ah—it looks as if they're ready. Come," he said, taking her arm again. "Let's see what you're capable of."

Through the winding passages of the fortress, Farideh

scrambled to pull together the details of Rhand's experiment she'd managed to hear. Patrons, manifestations, ordinary somethings masquerading as extraordinary somethings? And she could help.

No killing, she told herself. No stealing souls. Rhand led her out onto a balcony with no balustrade, the guards fanning out around them. As they neared the edge, Farideh could see the enclosed courtyard nearly twenty feet below and the dozen people standing in it, staring up at her.

She took an involuntary step back.

Rhand chuckled and urged her forward. "Go ahead."

The villagers stared up at her, puzzled and maybe repulsed. They all wore the same faded garb, tunics and breeches and skirts. It was like being faced down by an army. Her stomach tightened.

"What is it you're looking for?" Farideh said. The wizard considered her a moment, and there was no missing his displeasure.

"Your mistress assured me," Rhand said, "that she could get me someone to assist my efforts. That she would bring me someone who could read their little souls and tell me which of them were . . . special."

Farideh looked up at him, but he seemed no madder than before. "Special how?"

Rhand spread his hands wide. "You'll have to tell me." His piercing gaze speared her in place. "If you can."

Farideh made herself look down at the crowd of people, her nerves rattling and shadowy smoke seeping off her skin as her pact drew up the powers of the Hells. They were all staring at her, all waiting for something. Good or bad. *Someone who could read their souls.*

The lights. Farideh caught her breath—the flickering colors and shadows that had come out of nowhere, the strange magic Sairché had infected her with. The lights were souls.

She shut her eyes. The magic was lurking in her somewhere, crouched in the recesses of her mind and waiting to spring forward. She'd been angry the last two times, she thought. The other came when the protection spell had been overstretched.

She drew up the powers of her pact, while thinking of punching Sairché in the mouth for good measure. Again, the pain in the back of her head started to bloom, and then her throat began to itch.

And there in the middle of her thoughts, was a sensation like a dangling thread, waiting to be pulled. She focused on it, opening her eyes.

The lights exploded over her field of vision, crackling across the staring crowd. They lingered on the people, little spots of brightness and color radiating strands of gray and gold and red and more. As she watched, the lights intensified—and around three of the people, the colors coalesced into the blurry shapes of strange runes. A tall man who shone with vibrant green and yellow, a brand of darker emerald thrumming at the core of his chest. A woman whose lights left streamers of violet-red drifting around her, curling at her heart into a sharper glyph. Another woman, much older, whose lights seemed to overtake the whole of her body, shining bright as one of Selûne's tears come to earth—the symbol there was hard to spot, only a shade lighter than the silver around it.

They were beautiful.

"Nirka," Rhand said mildly. "Hold. Give her a chance."

Farideh looked over her shoulder at the shadar-kai guard, her hands on her knives, her cold black eyes on Farideh. Farideh looked back down at the crowd—she stood at the edge of a twenty-foot drop onto paving stones, surrounded by shadar-kai ready to kill her. And Rhand, ready to give that order.

Sairché promised you wouldn't be killing anyone, she told herself. Wouldn't be taking their souls. Promised this would turn against a common enemy.

"The tall man in the back," she said. "The Turami woman on the far right. The old woman in green at the front."

Rhand smiled. "Well done." He gestured to the guards

below, who seized those three and ushered them through one of the doors. The rest of the people were herded back out the larger gate. An uneasy feeling built in the small of Farideh's back, and her tail flicked nervously.

"What happens to them?" she asked, watching the old woman hobble after the guard holding tight to her arm.

Rhand did not speak for long moments, until Farideh looked back up at him. He smiled, as if she'd given something away with that question. "Nothing much. I'm merely going to see if you're right."

"How will you do that?"

Rhand shrugged and took her arm again. "These things show themselves eventually. Close attention and study. Time. A little carefully applied pressure. If you're right, though—and I do hope you are—we should be completely certain in a day or so at most. Come," he said, leading her back into the building, "let me show you the rest of the castle."

There was little Lorcan hated as much as the feeling of not having any kind of a plan. Even when the world was trying to leap out from under his feet, usually, Lorcan had some scheme, some strategy, some charm in his back pocket that would help him land safe.

But riding ahead of Havilar, now nearly a day out of Waterdeep, Lorcan could hardly form even the most basic plan aside from getting away from Mehen and the Harpers and heading north. Every time he tried his thoughts scattered, driven like sheep before the wolves of his anger at Sairché, at Glasya, at Farideh.

Give me some gods-be-damned space to figure it out, because if you make me choose right here, right now, I choose to be done. He should have expected it. He should have been prepared, not counting on Farideh like some fool mortal would.

"What are you going to name your horse?" Havilar called up to him. Lorcan drew a slow breath and steeled himself. If someone had told him a few hours ago that he would wish she were grousing and moaning about her aching head and upset stomach, he would never have believed it.

"It doesn't need a name," he said.

"Of course she does—how else will you call her?" she said. "I'm going to name mine Cinnamon. Or maybe Alusair."

Lorcan glanced back over his shoulder, at the tiefling astride a placid bay. "That's a gelding."

Havilar made a face at him. "*Fine*. I'll call *him* Alusair."

Lorcan turned back to the road, to the marshy ground surrounding it, and swallowed his speculation about how *impressed* Brin would be about Havilar naming her gelding after his fabled great-grandaunt. It was too simple a barb, and if Lorcan had made it this far without prodding her unnecessarily, he could certainly hold out until the pact was done. He hoped.

"Are you truly more concerned about your horse than your sister?" Lorcan asked.

"I can care about her and name a horse. I'm not simple. Besides," she added, "I'm riding out sick as a hound. With you. I think it's pretty *karshoji* obvious I *do* care."

"Not sick," Lorcan reminded her. "Hungover. And your sister may be in mortal peril."

"Fine," Havilar spat. "She wins. I never said she wasn't worse off. I said *I* don't feel well and it doesn't mean anything if I want to name a stupid horse. Stop trying to turn everything around." She hesitated before he heard her add, "Sorry, *Alusair*. You aren't stupid. You're just a horse."

"You misunderstand," Lorcan said silkily. "She's trapped and in danger. You've managed nothing more than some drink-sickness—and you're awfully calm about the whole matter. I suppose," he added, trying to sound reluctant, "I underestimated you." He let the silence stretch before glancing back at Havilar. She watched him with narrow eyes.

"Probably," she said, just as reluctant.

"I sometimes wonder," he said, turning back to the road ahead, "if I made the right decision. Giving Farideh the pact. It seems to only cause her trouble."

"Do you think she's all right?" Havilar asked, after a few moments.

Of course she is, Lorcan thought viciously. Sairché had made it clear how she intended to reward Farideh's shift of loyalty. He knew better than to believe what Sairché said without question—the idea that Farideh had sought his sister out and asked for her patronage was, on the face of it, madness.

But the hurt and the fury and the desperation in Farideh's expression—the last thing he'd seen before Sairché brought him around again in the Hells—made it all the easier for Sairché's version of events to burrow into his brain and make itself at home.

"What did you tell her?" he had asked Sairché.

"What goes on between a girl and her patroness is private," Sairché said. "Isn't that right?"

"I'm not a fool," Lorcan said. "She didn't call you down. You used Temerity."

"To find you," Sairché said, standing a careful twenty-five steps from Farideh's unconscious body. "But I didn't need Temerity to convince Farideh to come around. *You* tricked her, after all—did you really think you were the only one who could manage that?"

"Of course not," Lorcan said, a heartbeat too slow. He'd tricked her, true, but then he'd let himself get pulled into an argument that he hadn't shut down as quickly as possible. He'd left Farideh ready to jump into another devil's pact. He'd practically handed her to Sairché.

No, he told himself. She wouldn't leave.

Sairché chuckled. "Oh. You thought she was different. How funny."

"They're all the same," Lorcan said off-handedly, furious that his heart was racing. "That said, they're all a fair bit cleverer than you give them credit for, little eavesdropper. Why should I believe anything you tell me?"

Sairché had shrugged. "Well, what you believe or don't believe is immaterial. She turned on you—that much is plain. She didn't trust you. She hasn't trusted you for a long time. The magic circles, the dealings with priests, going to the wizard. Does that suggest a long-term plan for the pact in your mind?"

"Lords, Sairché, you can surely spin something together without making up players. Point out the paladin. Point out all the books of lore and legend. Hells, tell me her sister was the key. But there's never *been* a wizard."

Sairché's grin was a terrifying thing, brimming with glee and giddy surprise, and Lorcan knew in that instant he'd miscounted. "Oh," she said. "Oh, my dear brother. She never mentioned an Adolican Rhand?" Sairché giggled. "Oh, Lords of the Nine—truly? Where did you think she got her ritual book?"

Lorcan scrambled—from Dahl, that scowly fallen paladin, though clearly that wasn't the answer. "A ritual book she needed to rescue me," he scoffed. "Terribly clever of her to do that instead of taking the opportunity you presented her with and running off to learn spells."

Sairché had shrugged. "Mortals are complicated. Maybe you're right. But it makes *me* wonder"—and she'd smiled at Lorcan, as if she'd already won—"why she decided not to buy a book from any of the myriad sellers in the City of Splendors, and instead accept the gift of a wealthy, fine-looking wizard who was very clearly taken with her? And why she never spoke a word of him to *you*?"

"There's no telling," Lorcan said, finally answering Havilar's question, "until we find her. She might be at the mercy of untold enemies. She might be curled up with that *wizard*." He spat the word as if he could rid himself of the notion entirely. Godsdamned Sairché. The wizard didn't matter.

"What wizard?" Havilar asked. After a moment without

an answer, she asked, "That creepy Netherese fellow? The one from Waterdeep?"

"As I said, there's no telling, is there?" Lorcan asked.

"He was shady," Havilar said. "Even if his revel was nice. Until the poison and the assassins and things." She paused. "I suppose the fight was sort of a thrill, too, although I wouldn't call it nice. Anyway, she's not curled up with him, whatever *that* means. I mean she might put up with you, but there's shady and then there's *shady*."

Lorcan gritted his teeth. "We'll have to see."

"And how are we going to do that?" Havilar asked. "You have no idea where we're going. I could have gone off on my own and found her quicker than this."

Lorcan had left the ruby necklace in Havilar's care, certain even without examining it that his prison was only one element of Sairché's gift. The other gems wouldn't be ordinary. One would surely be a beacon for Sairché to trace Farideh by. A few days, a tenday, a month—however long it took, eventually Sairché would check in on Farideh. Eventually she'd have to. And then Lorcan would strike.

In the meantime, he had a replacement heir to pact.

An heir that a part of him was rapidly reconsidering how dearly he wanted. He tried to ignore it, but every time Havilar piped up with some new nonsense, with some new insult that had no spark to it, with some new sigh or whine or sadness, Lorcan missed Farideh. He missed arguing with her. He missed the nuances of steering her. He missed the furtive way she looked at him and perhaps the less furtive way he looked at her. He even missed the constant pull of that damned protection spell. Farideh might have always been a difficult warlock, but Lorcan had to admit that she was interesting.

"If you'd gone off on your own," Lorcan said, biting back his irritation, "you'd find yourself walking straight into Sairché's hands."

"Why should she care about *me*? I'm not a warlock."

Lorcan smirked to himself. Not yet. "To begin with, you decided to push yourself far beyond your limits and then pour a bottle of wine down your throat."

"Half a bottle," Havilar protested.

"Does that change anything? Don't tell me you don't know better," he said. "If those aren't the actions of someone ready for easy answers, I don't know what are."

"I think I *deserve* some easy answers at this point."

He clucked his tongue. "Easy answers lead to a perilous road. Though," Lorcan added, "if you're as eager to divest yourself of a troublesome sister as I am, no one would blame you."

Havilar made a face at him. "First, *everyone* would blame me. Second, I don't want her to die." She rubbed her arm, a strange, subconscious mockery of her twin's familiar gesture. "And anyway, it's *your* stupid sister who messed things up, isn't it?"

That wasn't what Lorcan had been expecting her to say, and he cursed his clumsy maneuvering. She should be turning on her sister, eager for Lorcan's approval. He reined his horse in and turned to consider her. "*Your* sister's the one who made the deal. You don't need to defend her. Not to me."

"Right, but . . . she didn't have a whole lot of choice. Not that I think she should have gotten into that position in the first place. You don't have to be a master strategist to see making a *karshoji* pact means eventually a devil's going to make you do something dumb because you have to."

Lorcan weighed this, shifted his tack. "There are always possibilities. If you're clever enough. If you're determined enough."

Havilar snorted. "What should she have done then?"

Lorcan didn't have an answer for that that he wanted to give. Not started that ridiculous argument about Temerity. Not doubted his protection. Not tossed him aside. "What would you have done?" he said.

"Chopped your sister with my glaive," Havilar answered. "But I'm not Farideh. She would have been more careful—I don't care if I hit you too."

Lorcan kept his thoughts to himself.

"Why are you doing this?" Havilar asked. "Going after her. I mean . . . I have a *guess*, but . . . well, devils *shouldn't* care."

"She's my warlock," Lorcan said simply.

"And?"

"And it's part of having a pact," Lorcan said. "Besides I need to pay Sairché back for her little stunt. As you said—it's her fault." Hers and Farideh's, he reminded himself.

"So you're dragging me across the world to make Sairché mad?" Havilar said skeptically. Lorcan didn't answer, he just kept staring ahead at the road—let her learn that foolish questions got no answers.

But Havilar wasn't silenced. "Are you in love with my sister?"

Lorcan yanked the reins and pulled the horse around to block Havilar's path, studying the tiefling for long, painful moments—long enough she should have time to consider for herself what a foolish question it was. She stared right back, unblinking.

"You shouldn't assume," Lorcan said, "that I think anything like you do. That any of us do. Devils aren't mortals. That's another way Sairché can claim you."

"But we think the same when it comes to sisters?" Havilar demanded. "You can't have it both ways."

Lorcan laughed. "My sisters have spent my entire life tormenting me, trying to end my life or use me against some other devil. They have beaten me until I could see the swirling mists of oblivion closing in on me. They have thrown me to the mercy of archdevils. To them, I am only half a proper being, hardly worthy of concern." He gave her a nasty smile. "So to say we would both be better without siblings, I'll admit, takes some liberties with the details."

"You're a devil, you're not a devil. We're alike, we're nothing alike. It can't be all of those things."

Lorcan kept smiling at her. "Then you have a very poor imagination."

Havilar glared at him. "You never answer questions, do you?" she said.

"Not the foolish ones."

"She doesn't love *you*," she blurted.

Pathetic, Lorcan thought, his patience with Havilar evaporating. She doesn't listen and she doesn't learn. "Would she tell *you*?" he said nastily. "Last I recall you were too busy finding the edges of the lordling's mouth to have much of a conversation."

Havilar flushed deeply. "She thought you were dead," she shot back. "That you were gone and never coming back. And she was *glad*. We were all *glad*."

Did she think that? Had she been glad? It doesn't matter, Lorcan reminded himself. She betrayed you as soon as she listened to Sairché. "That's interesting," Lorcan said. "Since I'm the only one who apparently gives two coppers that she's in trouble. Go back and sulk over your broken heart if you can't think past it. I'm sure the lordling will find *that* more interesting than whatever princess he's gotten up the skirts of."

She startled as if he'd punched her, right in the base of the lungs. Lorcan gave her a wicked grin in return and urged his horse down the road once more. He'd pay for that—he'd have to be careful with her and redirect her attention to other matters, which were clearly more important than how much she hated Lorcan or why he was doing what he did. What he thought about her sister.

Havilar's horse gave a sharp whinny, and suddenly she was pounding past. Lorcan's horse shied and laid its ears flat as her bay blocked its path, too close for comfort.

"Don't you *ever* say a word about me and Brin again," she shouted, her voice shaking. "You don't know what you're talking about. You're just being cruel."

Lorcan held her furious gaze. "And what are you doing?"

Havilar looked away, off at the forest encroaching on the landscape to the west. Leave her, a part of him said. This is never going to suit. He ignored it.

"Shall we stop trying to wound each other?" he asked. "I think even in your sorry state you can see what a poor course of action it will be. Whether you hate me or not, I am your best option at the moment for finding your sister. Truce?"

Havilar watched him as if she'd rather put that battered glaive right through his skull. "You promise," she said, still raw and angry-sounding. "You *promise,* right now, you will *never* say another word about Brin and me. I don't care what you think. I don't care how much you hate him or you hate me. I don't care if you think I'm an idiot or hopeless or what. You don't say a *word* about it."

Lorcan regarded her a long moment. "Fair enough." He urged the horse forward again.

"You're not going to ask me the same about you and Farideh?"

"Why would I do that?" he asked, without turning. Let her wonder. Let her be stuck on that nonsense notion. Better than trying to unravel his motives. Better than questioning his dedication. Better than realizing he'd not answered any of her questions.

Lorcan eased his horse to the side of the road as the hoofbeats of a distant rider coming up behind them became distinct. He hoped—for both of their sakes—that it was an overeager highwayman, set on overtaking them. They'd both be more inclined to civility if they could vent their anger on some unfortunate villain.

As the hoofbeats neared, they slowed, as if some wicked god had heard Lorcan's prayers. And then a voice shouted out, reminding Lorcan why he never prayed.

"Havilar!"

Lorcan looked back, at Havilar, at the rider on a sleek dun mare, prancing to a stop: Brin. "Havi," he said. "Thank the gods, there you are."

Havilar had frozen, like a rabbit trying to hide from a hawk. "Yes," she said after a moment. Lorcan cursed to himself—this would not help things.

"What in the Hells are you doing?" Brin demanded, ignoring Lorcan. "Mehen's in *pieces*. You have to come back."

She'll agree, Lorcan thought. She'll do anything he asks. She's too angry. He scrambled to form a new plan, some way to make her side with him once more, to forgive Farideh a little and get back to following him.

But then Havilar shook her head. "I have to save Farideh."

Brin stared at her, as if she were a little mad. Lorcan reconsidered. He might be able to use this.

"What do you think you're going to do?" Brin asked. "Leave the Harpers to it. They know what they're doing. You've been through a lot. Rest for this one—the world won't end."

"I can't," she said. "Do you think I'm going to sit on my hands while bad things happen to Farideh?"

She would have, Lorcan thought, smiling to himself, if he hadn't been there to prod her into action. And she knew that.

Havilar looked over and glared at him, as if she knew his thoughts.

Brin followed her gaze. "This is your idea, isn't it? You convinced her."

"Well met to you, too. And there was little to convince her of." He looked at Havilar, who was watching Brin uncertainly. "She's loyal even when others are . . . less so."

Brin bristled. "The Harpers are leaving the moment they get better direction. They're better equipped than you two. Or did you tell her you have some magic tool to help you get lost faster?"

Lorcan nearly laughed—for once, things seemed to be turning his way. The little lordling had no idea what damage he was doing. If Lorcan was out of practice, Brin had gone to seed.

"Havilar?" Lorcan said. She looked up at him. "What would *you* like to do? I'm hardly going to 'drag you across the countryside' if you'd rather go back to the Harpers' hospitality. But I hope," he added more seriously, "that I don't end up needing a quick blade at my side if you do. As I said before, there's no telling what we're dealing with."

"Shade," Brin said hotly, "isn't going to be brought down by a blade and a stlarning half-devil."

Lorcan held Brin's gaze and wondered if perhaps someone was listening to his prayers after all—Havilar was more of a certainty than ever. "Well," he said. "Perhaps we'll leave Shade to the Harpers and worry about our own plans."

"We're not going back," Havilar adjusted her haversack. "Be angry if you have to. But I'm doing this."

"And what about Mehen?" Brin asked.

"Mehen . . ." She looked at Lorcan again. "Will keep. And he should know I'm not going to wait when I can do something."

Brin sighed and threw his head back to stare at the cloudy sky. "Fine," he said after a moment. He wrapped the horse's reins once around his wrist. "Then I'm coming with you."

Havilar's eyes widened. "Oh. Are you?"

Lorcan cursed to himself. Bad, bad, bad. "Don't your Harpers need you? Doesn't *Mehen*? You are the best equipped to ferry a message back, after all."

Brin scowled at him. "I'll send a message from the caravansary. There's a waystation outside the Goldenfields, a few hours down the road. Then we'll get a reply—maybe they've worked out more details by now."

Lorcan calculated, considered, and cursed to himself again. This could be fixed. "Wonderful," he said. "Lead on, then."

Brin turned to Havilar once more. "You're right," he said, and he smiled. "I should know you'd never sit on your hands."

Havilar gave a nervous laugh as Brin nudged his horse into motion and rode to the head of the group. Havilar watched him go, then gave Lorcan a dark look as if daring him to say something.

But Lorcan only turned his horse to follow Brin. After all, *he* kept his promises.

The waters of the Fountains of Memory well up from the center and pour down the sides as if a spring beneath refreshes them, although not a drop enters or leaves the basin. Farideh has stood here for over an hour, watching scene after scene after scene. Meanwhile the apprentices come and go—never leaving her alone, never speaking above a whisper—trading scrolls and worried expressions. She gets the impression that somewhere in the fortress, Rhand is unhappy, and the implications clench around her stomach. She wonders if he's discovered the Harper in his camp.

"Show me where Dahl was . . ." Farideh catches herself. The wizards aren't watching her, but they're not as dedicated to their tasks as they'd be if they weren't listening at all. She lets the rest of her question—"an hour ago"—disappear. She isn't such a fool as to think they won't report every single thing she tells the waters to show. If Dahl's still trapped behind the wall, it might mean his doom. The waters turn, waiting for the rest, waiting for something they can use.

"Three midwinters ago," she blurts—long enough that it shouldn't matter one bit what Dahl was doing. She shouldn't watch, but if she doesn't, the wizards will notice that too.

The waters spit back a street scene—Proskur, Farideh realizes, surprised—and Dahl coming out of a dark doorway into an alley. A fine snow falls, trimming the dirty ice of the streets like lace. Dahl wraps his cloak close and hurries down the road toward the market.

Farideh's fingers itch to touch the surface of the waters—the frustration and anger that seem to vibrate Dahl's frame might make the waters shiver too. He is turned inward, scowling, his mouth twitching as if he were trying not to argue aloud with someone who wasn't there. She sighs despite herself—that was more Dahl than a doppelganger could make.

He winds through the crowded market of stalls and carts and other bundled-up people. The light is fading and lamplighters thread through the crowd. Past an unlit corner, Dahl eases around a pair of arguing merchants, cutting into a bookseller's shop to do so. He is watching the fight when he crashes into the third man, hidden in the shadows. Farideh watches as Dahl is thrown off, as if pushed away, and falls into a stack of books. They tumble, some falling open, their pages rapidly speckled with melting snowflakes.

"Gods stlarning hrast it!" Dahl shouts. "Watch yourself!" The man just chuckles. The lamplighter brings her torch up to the streetlamp, and the flame reflects off plate armor, elegantly wrought and inlaid with gold and copper.

"It's you that's turned the wrong way, my good man," the man says, and his voice sends an eerie, slow shiver down Farideh's back. It's like a song. It's like a prayer. Dahl freezes. The man keeps walking, looking over his shoulder to call back. "Surely you can figure that out."

Dahl sits, stunned, amid the fallen books, staring after the man as if he's seen a ghost. He looks as if he's frozen to the cobblestones, as if he'll never move . . .

"Wait!" he shouts, leaping to his feet like the ground beneath him has exploded. But the ice is slick and kicks his feet out from under him as he stands. He falls onto the scatter of books again, catching himself inches from an open page. The red-inked print of an angel with a herald's horn and a flaming sword standing before an elf hero stripped of his weapons, and leaning on a crutch. The line of text beneath it: You believed yourself unmatched, good Fflar, honest and wise beyond all measure. But you never set yourself to find the whole truth, and that was your undoing.

Dahl lets out a breath as if he's been punched. The bookseller is shaking the Harper's shoulder, demanding to know who will pay for the ruined books. But when Dahl sits up, his gray eyes are locked on the crowded street, where the strange man with the elegant armor and the song for a voice has disappeared. A smile eases over Dahl's face, as if someone has snatched away a heavy burden. He starts to laugh.

The vision disappears, leaving Farideh to wonder what happened between then and now, what took away that moment of lightness. And what exactly caused it.

CHAPTER NINE

20 Ches, the Year of the Nether Mountain Scrolls (1486 DR)
Somewhere North of Waterdeep

WHATEVER THIS PLACE WAS—VILLAGE, PRISON, LONG-TERM military encampment—Dahl still couldn't make sense of it. He'd spent the first sleepless night under a thick yew bush near the wall, nibbling at the bitter orclar lichen and emptying his flask sip by sip. Before the sun was too high, he sneaked down into the village again and stolen clothes—a tunic and cloth breeches—off a line. He'd tucked his dagger into a boot, hidden his sword and the armor in the thatch of one of the empty huts' roofs, and made his way around the perimeter.

He'd estimated close to five hundred stone huts. Spotted something like an infirmary. Garden patches, a lot more than he'd have expected in such close quarters. Meager piles of food stores left by the guards in two places, and quickly divvied up by a score or more. Later, he saw familiar faces doling out gruel from wooden buckets.

Near the lake, the villagers were mostly elves, and the shadar-kai more frequent. Up on the higher slope, the huts were crowded and the mix of villagers more dramatic—humans, orcs, half-orcs, half-elves. He even found a contingent of dwarves all packed in together in six huts. Wherever he went, the villagers watched him cautiously, but no one tried to drive him off, the way he would have expected if he'd wandered into the wrong quarter of some other town. Whatever this place was, whoever these people were, they seemed to know he was either on their side . . . or he was with the shadar-kai and not to be provoked.

And then there were the flowers.

Dahl had found another trail of them, a scatter of crushed violet petals, and followed it to the crowded quarter. He asked about Tharra, and everyone played dumb. He asked about Oota, and everyone looked at him like he was madder than a mouther.

He might be one of them, their looks seemed to say, but he also might not be. They gave him a little gruel, though, and asked where he was from, when he'd come to the camp. His answers weren't the right ones, and everyone seemed to keep their distance.

Dahl cursed, nipped whiskey-flavored air from his flask, and cursed again. What he wouldn't do for an ale, he thought for the third time that day. What in the Hells had Farideh gotten him into?

He found a bench before one of the dwellings and sat down to eat his gruel and think. He looked up at the dark fortress, looking comically wicked against a blue, cheery sky. He'd have to get back inside, somehow. Climb over the wall. Bluff his way through a gate. Discover how the villagers interacted with the fortress and slip in with someone who did belong.

"Hey!" a child called. "Hey! Hey!"

Dahl looked down the road a short ways, where a trio of children watched him from another bench several dwellings down—a blond boy, a blue-skinned girl with the marks of a water genasi on her bare scalp, and a long-legged Turami boy, his knees drawn up to his chest.

"What's your name?" the genasi called out, her little legs swinging back and forth.

Dahl considered them a moment. "Dahl. What's yours?"

"I'm Vanri," she said, pointing to herself, the pale boy, and the dark-skinned boy in turn. "He's Stedd, and that's Samayan."

Samayan watched him cautiously over his knees.

"Well met," Dahl said. "Are your parents around?"

Vanri shook her head. "No, they didn't get took."

"Taken," Stedd corrected. "When did *you* get taken?"

"Two days ago," Dahl said. He stood and crossed over to the children. *Taken*—interesting. "Have you been here long?"

"I've been here longest," Vanri said. "Then Samayan, then Stedd."

"But she's the youngest," Stedd said. "She's only seven. But I'm ten. And Samayan's almost eleven."

"How old are you?" Vanri asked.

"Twenty-seven. Do you know a woman named Tharra?"

"*Everyone* knows Tharra," Vanri said. "She makes everyone talk to each other, and keeps all the people safe. Most all the people, if they listen." The dark-skinned boy hissed something at her, and Vanri made a face at him. "What?"

"Safe from what?" The children traded glances. "Does she tell you what this place is?"

"It's like . . . a farm," the little blond boy said, and he smiled, pleased with himself.

"No, it's *not*," Vanri said.

Dahl shook his head. "Like a what?"

"A *farm*," Stedd said more loudly. "A farm for chosen."

"Chosen what?"

"You know. Chosen of the *gods*," the little boy said. "The wizard makes them grow, then he harvests them." He thought a moment. "But not really. Because they're people."

"Ah. *Chosen*," Dahl said. He ruffled the serious little boy's hair. "Of course."

The Chosen of the gods—if there were any such people walking Toril—were individuals the gods imbued with uncanny powers, to serve their interests in the mortal world. But even in stories such people were so rare as to be apocryphal. You didn't fill a mountain village with them, even if you managed to capture every Chosen in the world. Even if you were a wizard *and* a high-ranking Shadovar . . .

"Have you ever seen the wizard?" he asked. The children eyed him like he was a lunatic.

"You don't *want* to see the wizard," Vanri said.

"Nobody does," Samayan said quietly.

"Sometimes Tharra sees him," Stedd said. "I mean, I bet she does. 'Cause she goes into the fortress. For food and things," he explained to Dahl.

"She doesn't see him," Samayan said, sounding worried.

"Where can I find Tharra?" Dahl asked.

"She just left," Vanri said. "She had to go and meet Ol' Sour-Fey, so we're waiting for Hamdir." She wrinkled her nose. "You ask a lot of questions."

"Which you are *very* good at answering," Dahl said. "Do you know where I can find Tharra right now?"

"I told you," Vanri said. "Ol' Sour-Fey."

"Cereon," Stedd said. "You're not supposed to call him that."

Samayan's dark eyes watched Dahl. "Why do you want to know about Tharra?" he asked. Dahl weighed his options—all the while Samayan watched him nervously.

"Because I think she can help me," Dahl said.

"If you want help you're supposed to go to Oota," Vanri said. "*Everyone* does. Except Ol' Sour-Fey and the elves."

"Can you tell me how to find Oota?"

Vanri wrinkled her nose again. "How come you don't know where *Oota* is?"

Dahl held up two fingers and smiled. "I only got took two days ago, remember."

"*Taken!*" Stedd cried.

It was more information than Dahl had gotten anywhere else, even though he wasn't sure what to make of half of it. It did not answer his questions of the daisies. It did not tell him who the wizard was. It didn't give the other villagers much reason to stop playing dumb with him, particularly when he broke down and asked about the farm for Chosen.

Though, he had to admit, that might well have been more because it was a foolish question than because they weren't going to answer. Dahl felt foolish enough asking. If the villagers were somehow Chosen of the gods, one of the dwarves pointed out, they would have been able to breach the wall with those fantastical powers and escape. Why would any one of them be sitting there, at the wizard's mercy, if the gods had granted them powers fit for a chapbook?

It sounded like the sort of puzzle Dahl's masters in the Church of Oghma would have handed down: A god grants powers to a mortal, but leaves the mortal trapped in the hands of a madman. What is the god's will?

And after all the possibilities, the ultimate answer: We can never be certain of the will of the gods. We can only trust them to know their own minds.

The thought dredged up old pains Dahl always managed to believe were buried down deep. *A god grants a mortal powers, but then takes them away without saying why. What is the god's will?* The answer, Dahl had found, was much the same: *We can never be certain of the will of the gods. We can only be certain they know you aren't worthy.*

He stopped and blew out a noisy breath, as if he could spit out the shame of falling that still crept up on him from time to time and plant it in the cold mud. Now was not the time.

When night fell again, he tried to re-enter the fortress, but the gates were locked tight, and there was no climbing the stone wall without risking the bored guards. He retreated to the cottage he'd stored his things in and cast the second sending. At least he'd puzzled out one answer: he'd scaled the crater's edges, high enough to look down on a trackless forest stretching off to the east and south and north, a ribbon of river to the west, just past the wood's only visible edge.

"Southernmost of the Lost Peaks," he said, while the ritual's components burned away. "A camp of some kind—inhabitants were kidnapped. Definitely Shadovar work. There's a wall around the place I can't breach."

Eight days to reach you from Everlund, came the reply. *Find Farideh and wait for them to contact you.* Dahl bristled. He spent the evening praying indignantly to Oghma.

The next day he tried again, and while the villagers seemed to be less wary of him, they weren't welcoming. He made his way, winding through the alleys, toward the crowded quarter where the children had said he could find Oota, wondering if there were better ways to track down Tharra, the elusive Harper who might have a way to get into the fortress. Instead he found a trio of villagers, all muscle and grim expressions, weaving through the scattered people and alleyways, searching for Dahl. He lost them without much trouble, but every time he came back out into the open, he saw them again. Tucked into a narrow passage between houses, he crouched over someone's fallow garden, puzzling over what to try next.

He reached the street again and found a delicate line of violets peeking out of the dirt.

Perhaps they bloom early here, Dahl thought. It wasn't warm on the mountain, but it wasn't as cold as it should have been. Perhaps . . . it's warmer this year. Perhaps the mountains have volcanos' hearts, and the seeds stay warm. There were a dozen answers more likely than flowers signaling the presence of a . . . what? What did he expect to find?

Chosen growing in the mud, he thought. Waiting for a wizard to harvest them.

"Cakes, some sweetmeats, lovely grapes only a little bruised." A woman's voice stopped Dahl in his tracks. "And half a ham on the edge of spoiling—I suppose she doesn't much appreciate the wizard's hospitality."

Dahl peered around the building's corner—there was Tharra again, holding open a sack. She was talking to a half-elf man with broad shoulders. Beside them, Samayan perched on a windowsill, while little Vanri hopped one-footed around them, squelching in the chilly mud.

"Brightnose lady?" the man asked.

The woman shook her head. "She's odd. But I don't think so. Wants to wear armor, not frilly dresses. Looks embarrassed half the time she gives an order. She puts my nerves to the blade, but she's better than the wizard—so far."

The man shook his head. "Small comfort. Is she certainly on his side?"

Tharra gave the man a look Dahl was all too familiar with. "Look at the signs. You don't deck an enemy in gems."

"Right," the man said, with the air of a chastened pupil. He scratched his forehead with the back of his hand, and Dahl noticed the cages—the man's fingers were locked into awkward curls by metal brackets. "Wish I could help in there. You still think it's worth it?" he asked. "Walking among the guards—they could figure you out any time now."

"Then they will have to reckon with the fact I'm not just a servant," the woman said. "But don't worry. They don't *want* to figure me out."

"That's what I'm afraid they'll notice—Vanri, stop. You're getting mud everywhere."

Vanri made a face at the man, then looked across the road. Right at Dahl. Her eyes brightened. "Hey! Hey! There's that jack!"

And now all of them were looking where Vanri pointed.

"Dahl," Samayan said.

"Yeah, Dahl," Vanri said. She looked up at the woman as Dahl walked over. "He got took two days ago."

"Three," Samayan said.

Tharra pulled the little girl behind her, her eyes on Dahl. "We've met already. Armas?" The half-elf man took hold of Vanri's hand. She pulled against it.

"Dahl, Dahl, Dahl!" she said. "Want to see how far I can jump?"

"Later perhaps," Dahl said. "I need to talk to Tharra right now."

"Vanri, Samayan," Tharra said. "Go with Armas, please."

Armas frowned. "Are you sure?"

"She knocked me down pretty quick the last time," Dahl said. "I wouldn't worry."

Tharra looked over at Armas. "I've dealt with worse. I'll meet you later. You too," she said to Vanri and Samayan, as she passed Armas the sack of food. "Go with Armas now."

"Bye, Dahl!" Vanri said, as Samayan slid off the window-sill. Dahl waved, but at the same time he was thinking about how fast he could get the dagger out of his boot. Tharra only smiled pleasantly at him, as Armas and the children headed up the road.

"You're a pretty incautious fellow," Tharra said. "Strolling around in your uniform. Walking right up to me like this. I hear you've been looking, though, asking around. But not getting anywhere."

Dahl blinked at her. "You told them to stay away from me."

"Guilty," she said. "But I have to say, you've done better than expected—you went to the children. Good instincts."

"Thank you," Dahl said.

"And you've managed to keep ahead of Oota's enforcers," Tharra pointed out. She straightened her apron, her hand reaching into the front of it briefly, as if adjusting the pin Dahl knew hid there. "They've been trailing you all day."

"They're easy to spot," Dahl admitted. "Do you think I need to talk to Oota?" Dahl frowned. Why would he talk to Oota? Why wouldn't he just talk to Tharra, here and now? He had to show her . . . something. "Wait," he said, shaking his head. "I need to talk to you. I need to get back in the fortress."

"Well, we can talk about that. No problems there. But I need to go, I'm keeping someone more powerful than me waiting." She smiled. "You can wait in my house here. I'll even leave some bread and wine to keep you company."

He nearly agreed—bread and a seat and some stlarning wine was all he wanted in the entire world, and a chance to talk to Tharra besides? She smiled, and he nearly thanked her profusely and followed her in.

But it didn't sound nice, a little part of him thought—in fact, it sounded like an ambush meant to catch a complete imbecile, even if a *little* of the wine would be fine, drugged or not. "Something's not right here."

Tharra gave him a pleasant smile. "We could talk about it inside."

She looked past him, up the street. Dahl followed her gaze to where three powerful brutes—two humans and a half-orc— were marching down the street toward them.

"Ah, never mind," Tharra said, and the urge to follow her dissolved. "They've finally found you. Give Oota my regards, would you?"

"You stlarning—" But Dahl stopped, transfixed—not by the approaching toughs, but by the trail of tiny wine-dark violets running up the path between them, beginning in the spot where Samayan had stepped down from his perch.

As bad as having Rhand loom over Farideh's shoulder was, being left alone in the fortress for two days was almost worse. Alone with her thoughts, with nothing to do, she alternated between sudden, racing plans to escape, to unravel Sairché's deal—or at least speed her way through it somehow—and deep, smothering sadness.

She might well die here, and she couldn't even hope for someone to save her. If she didn't uphold her end of the deal, Sairché would have her soul, and anyone who might manage their way past the wall would be in grave danger.

Tharra still came in the mornings, to help her dress and style her hair. Farideh made no protests—not any longer. What was the point? She took out Dahl's cards and made a game of them just to keep Tharra from talking to her any more. Dahl was right: the game did still her thoughts, for a time.

Once the maid had left, Farideh searched nearly every inch of the black glass castle, spiraling down from the battlements to Rhand's study, into the dark cellars. She passed storerooms and servant's quarters; barracks and an armory where she found her rod, dagger, and sword; more guest rooms and a strange little kitchen. She walked the wall around the fortress, hunting for Dahl among the people passing through the little village. She never found him. The shadar-kai guards watched her pass, their coal-black eyes glittering, but their weapons still. Rhand was as good as his word—not a one moved to stop her.

It wasn't until she stood before a pair of iron-banded doors that the shadar-kai reacted, blocking her passage and herding her back to her room.

"What's behind there?" Farideh had asked Nirka.

"If you're lucky," Nirka said, all but walking on Farideh's heels, "you won't find out."

Farideh looked back at the guard. "That's where he's working, isn't it? Where he brought those people."

Nirka scowled at her. "If you need to know, he will tell you. Keep walking."

But she couldn't stay another moment in the little room. As soon as Nirka had left her, Farideh went back to the study at the top of the tower. The waters still swirled in their basins, two apprentice wizards murmuring questions over them. The third stood unattended, and Farideh looked down into the stirring waters once more.

"May we help you, lady?" one of the apprentices, a heavy-set young man, asked. Farideh regarded him, unsure of what to say, for so long that he started to fidget—and she realized he couldn't read her gaze any better than most of them. They didn't know what to make of her.

"No," she said, and she reached for the bag of petals. And though the wizards watched her, agitated and unsure of what she thought she was doing there, Farideh didn't budge. Vision after vision after vision—she knew without a doubt that Sairché wasn't done, that Rhand was no innocent. That there was so much on her to solve. At first, she pulled past events from the water like fishes, hoping one of them would hold a secret in its belly.

But even as she called up the first of those visions, Farideh knew in her heart of hearts she wasn't asking for answers. She was asking for penance. She was asking for comfort. She was asking the waters to condense her guilt and sorrow into something she could hold and handle, and make into something useful—she owed them all a solution.

She was asking to see that all wasn't lost, something the Fountains of Memory couldn't possibly know.

The questions whose answers might make a damned bit of difference to her predicament, she couldn't ask, not while the wizards were watching her.

That night, she played the cards while Tharra took her hair down and plaited it, and didn't look up as she bid Farideh good night and left. Farideh did not sleep until the early hours of the morning, when she couldn't keep her eyes open and watching the door any longer.

She woke up alone, unharmed, and still frightened to her core. Tharra brought water and soap, and a scowling Nirka, and once Farideh had convinced them both that she wouldn't be so much as shifting a sleeve while they were there, she washed in the chilly water, trying to sort through her thoughts and figure out an escape—

There is no way out, she told herself. You have to make it through.

Rhand did not come to morningfeast, and after, Farideh went back to the iron-banded doors, wondering what went on behind them, wondering what wonders or horrors she might have made possible. Nirka came again and escorted her back to the cold, dark room.

"That place is not for you," she said. "And the wizards want you *out* of the study. You stay here."

Farideh looked up at her. "And what if I won't?"

Nirka raised an eyebrow and folded her arms, standing directly in front of the door. "Then I will make you."

Farideh stared at Nirka—*if you die fighting shadar-kai,* she told herself, with absurd mildness, *then Havi is in just as much trouble*—then turned to her dressing table and pulled the cards out again.

"What is that you have?"

"Cards," Farideh held up the painted deck. "To pass the time."

The shadar-kai woman considered the deck a moment, muttered, "Wroth," and spat wetly. "What do you ask them?"

Farideh spread the cards out in a fan, considering the faces and stalling for an answer. Dahl had said they were for fortune-telling, even if they could be used for games, but he hadn't said how they were consulted or who used them or why. The shadar-kai refolded her arms nervously.

"Right now?" Farideh said slowly. "I'd like to know how much longer I'm needed. It seems as if your master has gone ahead without me. If I'm going to sit in a room and dawdle uselessly, I'd like it to be my own." She laid out the first row.

"He will tell you when you have a use. Put away the cards."

Farideh looked up at her and very deliberately laid a second row down. "What use does he have for you?"

Nirka gave her a jagged smile. "He knows what it is to battle with the Shadowfell—a cleverer master than most. If we do not have as much to do at this stage, at least he knows how to keep us amused."

Farideh did not flinch, but she could not stop her tail from flicking across the thick rug, and Nirka smirked at her. Farideh laid the third row.

"Lot of superstitious nonsense, Wroth."

"Are you afraid of it?"

"You can't fool me. I think you ask them how to escape."

The face-up card, a stern-looking man in a crown, riding a chariot drawn by displacer beasts, might have made a decent start, Farideh thought. "Why would I do that?" she asked, mildly. "Master Rhand mentioned it hadn't been done. Are you suggesting he was lying?"

"Put them away, little demon."

"Or what?"

In Nirka's smile there were a thousand threats, a thousand ways she would be thrilled to kill Farideh. Farideh narrowed her eyes. "Or I'll cut off your hands," Nirka said. "See if you can manage without."

"Did you forget what I did to your fellows when I arrived?" Farideh asked.

"You'll find I have no fellows."

"I've asked the cards how you'll die," Farideh said. "I see a castle on a mountain with nothing to occupy you, nothing to keep the Shadowfell at bay." Nirka's hands twitched toward her weapons. Farideh held her gaze—the guard couldn't kill her, not without angering Rhand, and Sairché, and who knew who else. "Quiet," Farideh said. "Lots and lots of quiet."

"Mad witch." Nirka snorted. She turned on her heel and slammed the door shut. The heavy *clunk* of the lock punctuated her departure.

Farideh laid the last row of cards down with shaking hands—*The Offering*, number twenty-two; *The Companions*, number six; *The Rising Dragon*, number twenty—trying to keep her focus on the painted faces, the numbers, the flow of the game. She might well be mad after all, provoking Nirka like that.

You should have let her stay, Farideh thought. You should have made her tell you what's happening here. You should have made her tell you what she knows about Sairché, about Rhand. Another time, another Farideh, and that was exactly what she would have done.

But in that moment, all she wanted was to prove she wasn't

a pawn. Maybe Sairché and her strange powers were changing her more than she'd realized.

These powers, she thought bitterly. She laid down another card—number thirteen, *The Herald*—and bit her lip. They weren't from her pact—even if Sairché had stolen that from her brother, she would have had to give Farideh the new spells explicitly. If she hadn't been so quick to snap at Sairché, the cambion might not have sent her into the fortress with no idea she was toting strange powers around or what their purpose was.

A potion, she thought, furious at Sairché as much as herself. An infection. Some charm she didn't realize she carried. There were ways to do it. They were all ways that might run out, and there was no telling when that would happen or what would happen to *her* when they did.

As if to assure her they had not run out, her headache sank its claws into her brain, and she dropped the hand of cards in shock, clutching her skull with a hiss of ripe Draconic. Bit by bit, the pain receded, as if the claws were being drawn slowly out of her head, and when she looked up, the cards were strewn over the floor, and the ghost was back.

Farideh turned to fully face the figure, too startled to speak. The apparition didn't vanish as she had before, but tilted her head, considering. Her horns were slim and sharp as a mountain goat's, and her eyes seemed to glow silver.

"Who are you?" Farideh asked. The ghost pointed down at the scattered cards. Three were faceup: a woman holding a child in her arms, an elf standing over a pool that reflected a battle, a woman in dark robes. *The Ancestor; The Seer; Tethyla, the Dark Lady.*

Farideh considered them. A seer . . . who came before her. A seer and a dark lady . . . "You . . . Did you help Rhand before me?"

The ghost smiled, but said nothing. The light shifted so that half her body wore away, down to the bone.

"You can't talk," Farideh said.

The ghost wagged a finger at her. She swept her arm over the cards and a breath later a gust of cold wind blew through the curtains and stirred up the cards again. Again three landed faceup: a monstrous man with a bloodied sword, a whirling creature with a tail of flames, a pile of gems and flowers. *The Reaver, The Firetail, The Offering.* The ghost touched her mouth. She pointed to Farideh, to the combs lying in their case, to the brazier on the other side of the room.

Blood, jewels, fire.

The ghost pointed at the scattered cards and one trembled, then flipped over. A green-skinned angel pursuing a devil that chased after her in a whirlwind. *The Adversary.*

Farideh picked it up. Was the ghost her predecessor, the angel chasing the devil? Or was she instead the devil, and some *new* enemy to consider and plan around? There was little telling.

"What do you want?" she asked.

The cards stirred. *Tethyla, the Dark Lady* again; a grim-faced specter called *Loskor, the Gatherer;* a robed man named *Iolaum, the Arcanist.* Dark lady, death, wizard. Farideh raised her eyebrows. "You want to stop Rhand."

The ghost nodded gently.

"And the first set," she said, "that's . . . how to do it?"

The ghost shook her head, regretful, then touched her mouth again. How to help her to speak. Farideh looked down at the card in her hand. It had the sort of buzzing, itchy feeling she'd noticed magically touched things had, a sense they were reacting to her pact. It hadn't done that before, she was certain. Farideh held it up to the ghost. "And this?"

The ghost drew her hands together, interlocking fingers that were nothing but bone and sinew. Farideh took one of the combs and wove the card in between the teeth of it. The ghost held up one hand and drew a line across her palm. The blood—Farideh's stomach twisted.

"I don't have a knife."

The ghost stared at her.

Farideh blew out a breath, her gloom evaporating as if this new element shone a bright, hot light on it. If she could get the ghost's help, she might be able to unravel Sairché's plan—or at least figure out what it was Rhand was doing.

She scanned the room. She could shatter the mirror and cut herself on that, but what would Nirka do when she saw it? The cards' edges weren't crisp enough to cut her. Smashing a shard of wood from the chair or the chest would make as much mess and probably damage the stone walls—

The walls. Farideh stood and went to one, running her hands over the slick surface. Here and there the black glass wavered as if the room had been chipped at, and the edges of the chips were sharp as razors. She'd caught her sleeve on one walking around a corner too close and sliced a neat line through the dress's sleeve.

Near the corner, she found a peak sharp enough to slice a small cut through the center of her palm, so quick and neat Farideh hardly felt it at first. She turned her palm up to cup the blood that oozed up.

"Now what?"

The ghost smiled. And dissolved into a cloud of vapor.

Farideh nearly cursed as it swirled in the air over her bed for a moment, but then the cloud streaked across the room and vanished through the mirror, fogging the whole glass.

A line slowly appeared across the surface with the long squeak of a finger drawn over the glass. The line became a letter, and the letter a word as inch by creaking inch the ghost spelled out a strange phrase down the mirror.

Farideh moved to stand beside the brazier, transferring the card to her bleeding hand. "*Ibaatori pherognathis molochai.*" The flames leaped up, licking at her hand. A drop of blood sizzled into the fire. "*Adaachinis labolas maniria.*"

The flames surged and Farideh dropped the card and comb, jumping out of the way. The fire turned brilliant red, then fell back, then died down into the glowing coals that had filled the brazier before the spell. On top of them, the comb rested, the card balanced on its ruby flowers merely scorched. Farideh fished them from the brazier. The card was once more ordinary, but the comb had the same faint feeling of something strange that the card had had before.

The ghost reappeared, smiling. Waiting. She gestured to the side of her head.

Farideh set the comb down carefully on the dressing table. This was how she fell into trouble. This was how Sairché had caught her and Lorcan before her—giving her an answer she didn't have time to consider carefully.

"Not yet," she said. The ghost's expression was lost as the light shifted peeling her face back to the bone.

The lock clanked open and Nirka pushed in again. "You have to go, up to his study." She grimaced at the scatter of cards across the ground. "*Now*."

Farideh's stomach knotted up again, and the pain of the strange magic curled around her skull, as she hurried up the stairs.

"Perfect!" Rhand declared as she entered the room. "Every one of them. And it took no more than confinement to force the manifestation." His blue eyes were dancing. "A pity for my guards, but a boon for you and I."

"Good," she said. "Are . . . we finished?"

"We are only just begun!" he crowed. "With your assistance, we might sort the camp in mere tendays. I can bring in double, triple the possible subjects and clear them out as they prove unlikely."

One of the younger wizards sprinted into the room, skidding to a stop before the basins. "Saer?" he said.

Rhand did not so much as look back at him. "Mere months and they will see how right I have been, how dear my work is. All to the glory of—"

"*Saer!*" the assistant said, louder now. Rhand whirled on him. "There's been a message," the younger man said tremulously.

"From the city."

Rhand smiled, a mirthless empty thing. "I trust there is more to it if you think it worth interrupting."

The aide wet his mouth. "The Nameless One arrives tomorrow evening."

"What?" Rhand said, and it was not a question so much as a dagger stab. A chill ran down Farideh's spine.

"Sh-she will stay four days, the message said," the younger wizard went on, apologetic. "The Church of Shar is eager to see our—*your* progress."

Rhand did not move, did not speak. *He knows what it is to battle with the Shadowfell*, Nirka had said. Farideh still wasn't sure what that meant, but she imagined all the darkness in the room sinking into Rhand, condensing around his rage. She did not dare move.

"Well," he said, sharp and brittle as the black glass. A silence just as sharp hung in the air a moment. "Prepare her rooms. Make a stable ready for her mount. And get me more subjects." He turned to Farideh. "We have much time to make up."

Shortly after sunrise, Mehen stared at the edge of a vast forest, and wished the breath that stirred in the corners of his lungs were made of fire not lightning. Miles and miles of *karshoji* trees between me and Farideh, he thought, tapping his tongue nervously. He would burn them all to cinders if he had the chance.

"Are you all right, goodman?" Mehen looked down at the little Tuigan Harper, Khochen, and bared the edge of his teeth. No laying waste to forests with Harpers on his heels. Khochen and Vescaras flanked him as they neared the High Forest, while another flock of them purportedly waited in the damnable wood.

"I'm fine," he said.

Khochen smiled at him and kept her pace. "They say

dragonborn are tricky to read. But you could be a faceless thaluud and I'd still say that was a bald lie."

"It was," Mehen agreed, turning his eyes back to the forest. When Brin's sending had come, with an apologetic admission that he could not convince Havilar to give up her quest and come home, that Lorcan was still there, that they were still headed north . . . well, Mehen hoped his response made Brin wish he'd turned the lightning breath on him instead.

"You're still upset about that scrap I found aren't you?" Khochen said.

"Khochen," Vescaras warned. To Mehen he said, "You needn't worry. We'll find her."

Mehen would find Farideh. And Havilar. And Brin. Then he would lock the three of them in their rooms until . . .

Mehen blew out an agitated breath. There were no rooms to lock them in. There was no sense in doing it. They were grown, all of them—and Brin, for all the boy had been like family, was not. Was in fact Mehen's patron at this point and a lord of Cormyr. If Mehen so much as raised a hand to him, there'd be payment in kind, whether Brin liked it or not.

Still the need to do something—anything!—ate at him like rust at old armor. He'd felt as though he'd been sitting still for seven and a half long years. When Dahl's voice had broken the tense silence of a palace hallway, two little words—*they're alive*—had dissolved all that stillness and left him free falling, unsure of what to catch hold of. He'd stuffed that urge down, moved carefully.

And what good had it done him? Mehen had lost them all over again.

No more sitting still, he thought. No more waiting.

"And Dahl is with her," Khochen added. "He'll see that she's safe."

"Once he sees she's not a traitor?" Mehen said.

"It's only caution," Khochen said. "If she's honorable as you say, that will prove out."

It had been caution that kept Tam talking and planning and thinking instead of striking while there was still time. When Brin's message had come, when he'd heard that Havilar was not coming back, Mehen had nearly broken down the door to Tam's offices, demanding the Harpers make up their *karshoji* minds and go after his daughters.

"I'm not raising an army here," Tam told him in private. "These people are skilled infiltrators, not infantry ready to march at a moment's notice."

"Every moment we wait puts them farther out of reach and closer to danger."

"Enough," Tam had said. "You will give me the time to make arrangements so my people can do what they do best. I can promise it won't be more than a day. In the meantime, collect yourself—we may be old friends, but I won't hesitate to leave you behind if it's in this mission's best interests."

"And I won't hesitate to go without you," Mehen said. "And damn your missions."

Which was when Mehen had stormed out, cursing Tam, cursing devils, cursing Brin who had not managed to keep his word. Snapping at every Harper who had crossed his path. He'd spent the day as far from Tam as possible, knowing there was nothing left in him to keep quiet and polite while his girls were in danger, and he needed the Harpers' resources to do anything about that.

Tam at least was true to his word, and a brief and bone-jangling portal trip later, they were in Everlund, far to the North. Closer, they hoped, to the spot Dahl indicated in his second message. Mehen shuddered—if he never traveled by portal again, it would be too soon.

The Lost Peaks, the Harpers said, would take at best eight days to reach from Everlund. Mehen tried to imagine eight more days of this uncertainty, this *stillness*, and fought the urge to take off into the ancient wood himself, alone. Somehow, even after seven and a half long, awful years, this was worse.

"May I ask, goodman," Khochen said, interrupting his thoughts, "how you came to adopt tieflings?"

Mehen kept his eyes on the treeline, the path vanishing into the emerald shade. The air was turning warmer every step they neared the ancient wood. "Someone abandoned them at the village gates," Mehen said. "It was winter. No one wanted them. I'm not heartless."

"Fortunate," Vescaras said. Mehen gave the half-elf a glare that did not wilt the good Lord Ammakyl. "There aren't many villages out there that would take kindly to a delivery of tieflings in cloths."

"Arush Vayem is different."

"Not that different if they were going to leave them in the snow," Khochen said. "Though I suppose there are blackguards everywhere."

"Not just Westgate," Vescaras murmured. Khochen snickered.

Mehen sighed and shook his head. The villagers had been cowards, not blackguards—even the tieflings among them. If you came to Arush Vayem, you'd already heard every bad thing about yourself and believed half of it. Tieflings might well be little demons, even in the cradle. Twins might easily be a dark portent. "It was the eye," he said out loud, and regretted it immediately. "Farideh's silver eye," he explained. "That mark is an ill-luck sign to some of us, and the tieflings didn't want trouble."

"Dragonborn and tieflings no one wants," Khochen mused, as they crossed into the wood. "Interesting village. Did you grow up there?"

"No."

"Where is home, then?"

"Where my girls are," Mehen said tersely.

Khochen began to reply, when the rustle of a fern brought them all up short. No one moved for a moment, their hands hovering near their weapons. Vescaras made a face.

"Daranna, if you please," he said, "I'm not going to hoot like a bloody owl when you've given yourself up that way."

"That's not me," a woman's voice spoke from behind them. An elf woman with hollow eyes and loose dark hair dropped down from the spreading limbs of an elm tree. "Ebros," she said sternly. A young half-elf man with mussy blond hair rose out of the patch of ferns, looking abashed. Daranna sighed. "Next time not the ferns."

"If we hadn't been allies, you'd be dead, lad," Vescaras said.

"No," Daranna said. She nodded to their right, where two more rangers in dyed leather had appeared out of the wood, both holding bows trained on the intruding trio. "You make a great deal of noise," Daranna noted, her voice soft as the moss underfoot.

"It's a fair concealment technique in the city," Khochen said. Vescaras gave her another sour look, as Daranna's green eyes flicked over the other Harper.

"Don't do it anymore," she said. "Get yourself killed." She looked up at Mehen and sighed. "You, do your best." And with no further introduction or warning, Daranna started into the High Forest, her scouts falling in behind her, and Clanless Mehen close on their heels.

CHAPTER TEN

21 Ches, the Year of the Nether Mountain Scrolls (1486 DR)
North of Waterdeep

Havilar brushed the loose winter hair from Alusair's coat as if there were nothing more interesting in the world, and hoped in equal measure that it would be enough to keep Brin away and that he would come and take the brush from her hand and make her have the conversation she was hiding from.

Fortunately—or maybe not—Lorcan did a pretty fair job of keeping Brin away himself. "Build it up, will you?" Lorcan snapped as Brin fed twigs to the meager flames of a small campfire. He'd shed the human visage he wore during the day, and his leathery wings were pulled close as a cloak. "Shitting winter."

Brin glowered up at him. "We don't have enough firewood, and I'm not interested in fighting off the sort of things a great bonfire will lure out of the hills. Cover up. Or better yet, go home."

"Oh, come now," Lorcan said, dripping venom. "How will you find your way without me to scout for you? How will you find this mysterious camp if you have no one to search from above?"

Havilar peered over her horse's back and wondered if she ought to worry about one or the other starting a fight. If she could stop it. She brushed Alusair's withers. If she wanted to stop it. They could both probably stand to get some sense knocked into them.

I'm not an idiot, she wanted to say, ever since Brin had shown up on the road north. I'm not weak.

"How could you think that?" she murmured to herself.

Lorcan turned his attention to her, as if he'd heard, and she dropped her eyes to her task. Too late—the cambion strode over to stand beside her. "I see why you're fond of him," Lorcan said, too quiet for Brin to hear, thank the gods. "You're both stubborn."

"Farideh's the stubborn one," Havilar said. "What do you want?"

He smiled. "To offer you a pact," he said. "I think you could handle it."

Havilar blinked at him, surprised. "No," she said. She watched Brin, gathering more sticks to feed the fire from the grove they'd stopped near to. "Why would you think I'd want a pact?"

"For safety. She told you, I assume, about the Toril Thirteen. About Bryseis Kakistos. About the collectors. If Sairché doesn't try to claim your pact, someone else will."

"Someone like you," Havilar said.

"That's what I'm saying. Make a pact with me, don't use it—I don't care. But it will slow down everyone else. You have to be deliberate about breaking a pact. You can be terribly careless about making one."

Havilar watched the comb dragging faint lines in the bay's coat. "How'd you get Farideh?"

Lorcan didn't answer right away. "You," he finally said, as if he'd decided to tell her the truth. "She is so afraid of something happening to you that she will do a lot of very foolish things to make certain you're safe."

Havilar bit her tongue. He was right and it made her heart ache—she loved her sister, and she didn't want to scare her—and it made her temper flare. She wasn't Farideh's problem to worry about.

"I guess we're more alike in a lot of ways, you and I," Havilar said bitterly. "She thinks she has to save us. I don't need her saving me, you know? I don't need her help. That's a stupid reason to bind yourself to a devil."

"I didn't say she was right," Lorcan said.

Havilar was quiet a long moment. "I always figured it was something indelicate," she admitted.

Lorcan gave her a wicked smile. "I didn't say it wasn't both."

Havilar rolled her eyes and took the comb to the horse's mane. "She wouldn't like it if I made a pact with you."

"When did you start caring what Farideh would like?"

Havilar gave a single mirthless laugh. He really did think she was an idiot. Just like Brin.

She fixed him with as hard a stare as she could muster. "So you'll give me the pact and nothing else," she finally said. "But those others, those collectors . . . they'll offer me more."

"Whatever they offer you," he said, "it will only make your life worse in the end."

Brin was still sorting branches beside the fire. He looked up at the pair of them, glowering at Lorcan again. "It can't get worse than this," Havilar said.

"We've established you have very little imagination."

Gods, he was awful. "*Henish*," she grumbled. She turned from the horse, dropping the last clumps of hair from the comb into the damp grass. She was still smarting from what he'd said the other day, from what she knew he was thinking every time he looked at her and Brin. "I know what I'm not imagining."

Lorcan didn't rise to the bait. "What is it you want?" he said quietly. "Hmm? You want him to love you again? Let's say you ask my sister for that—she'll tell you it's a simple matter. She'll give you some charm or potion. You'll use it. He'll love you, oh yes. But let's say he has got that princess back home—you forgot about her. You didn't say he loves only you, and now his heart is split between the two of you. Is that what you wanted?" Havilar looked away, but he kept going. "And she certainly knows something's wrong. That isn't like him, is it? You might be the most innocent, sweetest thing that ever walked this plane, but look in the mirror—her first guess is that you've worked dark magic on her sweetheart. And in a sense, you have. You'll catch all the blame, so then my sister will come to you and offer you a way out—for another deal. Or for your soul. Or for that princess's soul. Or something worse. You're trapped, and if you try to wriggle your way out, you'll only sink deeper."

Havilar fidgeted. "I can be careful."

"Not careful enough," he said. "How do you think your sister got caught?"

"By you," Havilar pointed out.

"I am making you a special, once-only offer," he said, "based entirely on a desire to thwart Sairché and get out from under her thumb."

"And make Farideh happy?"

Lorcan gritted his teeth a moment, and she was pleased she'd gotten to him, finally. "That's a very dull barb," he said with a forced smile. "You jab much harder with it, it's liable to break right off. Might hurt yourself." He straightened. "Besides, you're right. She won't like it."

"That you've saved me from all those wicked devils?" Havilar said. "I think she'll be so happy she won't know what to do with you first."

Brin came back, dropping a load of branches beside the fire. "That should be enough. What have you two been talking about?"

"Farideh," Havilar said, without missing a beat.

Lorcan smiled. "All sorts of things. It's a new world, after all. Havilar has . . . all manner of prospects she hasn't explored." He stood. "Enjoy your meal." He leaped skyward before either of them could say another word.

Havilar watched Lorcan disappear into the fading light,

acutely aware of the silence he left behind. The fire crackled and popped and still she and Brin said nothing, and she didn't feel as if she was strong enough to push aside the weighty silence and change that, awkward and awful as it felt. The nights before they'd stopped too late for chatting, or they'd stayed in shabby inns where she'd had her own room, or Havilar had gone off to catch rabbits. Or Lorcan had stayed there, between them. But they didn't need more rabbits, there was no room to hide in, and she'd chased Lorcan off, sniping at him. She was stuck.

She took out the leather pouch of clean bandages and unwound the ones from her hands. The broken blisters were still raw and red, even though the blood had stopped. Havilar sighed. Ten years to get the good, strong calluses she'd had. Would it take another ten to get them back? As a girl she'd begged off practicing when her hands were too chapped— maybe if she kept on, she'd get used to the pain and her hands would thicken up faster. Beside the fire, she tested the bubble of an unbroken blister with her nail and winced.

"Will you let me heal your hands?" Brin asked.

That would have been nice. No more pain and he'd be holding her hands too. Havilar flexed her fingers against the burning skin. "No."

"Havi, don't be proud," he said wearily. *So weary of me,* she thought, and she nearly agreed to make that feeling go away.

"If I don't let them heal on their own," she said, still studying her palms, "I won't get my calluses back. Your magic will just put me back where I started." *Weak,* she added to herself. *Useless.* She wrapped fresh bandages loosely over the blisters.

"I didn't think of that," Brin admitted.

"Does Torm like you better, then?" she asked. "Are you a priest now?"

He chuckled once. "Hardly. Still the holy champions' curious problem." With the firelight dappling his face, Brin looked so sad, so much older, and it wasn't just the beard. He looked up from the fire and gave her a sheepish smile. "I don't even use the powers most of the time," he admitted. "I always feel like a fraud when I do."

"You know that's stupid," Havilar said after a moment.

Brin blinked at her. "Beg pardon?"

"It's stupid," she said again. "You're not a fraud. If Torm didn't think those powers were yours he'd take them back, wouldn't he?" She shrugged—what was she doing giving Brin lessons on the gods, anyway? "I mean, maybe you know better than Torm, but I doubt that."

A smile crept across his mouth, and Brin laughed—really laughed. It made Havilar's heart ache. "I missed you," he said after a moment.

I still miss you, she thought, but didn't dare say. Everything was still a mess, still had to be sorted out right, before she tried anything as rash as telling Brin she loved him. Might as well try to leap the Underchasm with a cat tied to your tail, she thought.

She didn't mean to let the prickling silence grow—she hardly noticed until Brin cleared his throat.

"We can't really avoid it, can we?" he said. "Can't go on, because who even knows where to start?"

Havilar looked at the fire. "I suppose I don't really even know you. Not anymore."

"You do," he protested. "Not everything changes." From the corner of her eye, she saw him shift closer to her, the better to knock the ashes from the fire and stir it up. "Do you remember," he asked quietly, "what happened in those seven and a half years?"

Havilar shook her head. "First I was there, with you, and then I was pushing open the door. And then we were waking up in the forest and everything was wrong." She nudged one of the stones deeper into the fire, and heard Brin's sharp intake of breath as her foot breached the fire. She smiled at his surprise. Then she added, "I dreamed the other night. A nightmare. It was so hot and close and dark. Like being trapped in a stove, maybe, only the stove is alive." She looked over at him. "And

I dreamed of being shocked and being pricked with needles and being talked about in some other tongue. But I couldn't see any of it, you know?" She turned away from his sad face. "Maybe that's what happened, or maybe I just invented it. Mostly it all just vanished."

"I'm so sorry."

Havilar kept watching the flames, remembering the smell of something burning, something alive. She shut her eyes and shook her head. "If you could have changed it, I'm sure you would have." Or maybe not, she thought, sunk in her sadness. Maybe he was glad to be done with her. Maybe the Hells just made things easier—

"I tried," he said, so much emotion in his voice she was almost afraid not to look at him, and all those self-pitying thoughts scattered. "I tried," he said again. "I waited three days there, until I was almost out of coin and food. I was so afraid to leave, but what else could I do? I rode hard the whole way to Suzail. I nearly killed the horse." He cleared his throat. "I went home. I had to. I needed their help. I got Mehen free—Helindra let me go, I think she knew she couldn't keep me and that I'd keep my word and come back. We went back to the inn. But you weren't there."

He rested his head on his hands. "I thought it might be a cycle, you know? I came back in a tenday, in a month, in a season, in a year and then two and then three and then four. But you were gone. Every time you were gone."

"Four years is a lot of trying," Havilar said. "I don't blame you for giving up." Would she have given up on him? No, never, she thought.

"I never gave up," he said fiercely. "I went back every year, and every time I took the road past Proskur. You were never there, but I didn't stop looking—I let all sorts of unsavory people take my coin to find some hint of how to get you back and I didn't care. One of them might have managed, after all." A bitter smile crooked his mouth. "Even Helindra couldn't make me stop. I'm afraid my family has invented some pretty unfair things about us. About what we were. I suppose it's been good practice, though," he added with a chuckle. "If I wouldn't promise Helindra that I'd stop going to that inn, I suspect I'll keep from buckling on more than that."

Eight years ago, Havilar thought, I would have known what to say. But there by the fire in the middle of nowhere, her tongue felt like lead. She was sorry her disappearance tangled Brin back up in the family that sought to control every part of his life. She was glad he didn't sound so scared of his old terror of an aunt anymore. She wanted to tell him how glad she was to know he hadn't given up. She wanted to tell him she was so glad, because maybe—maybe—it meant he still loved her back.

But then he might tell her that he didn't.

"Thank you for saving Mehen," she said finally. "Thank you for sticking with him."

Brin sighed. "I can't believe we just left him. Again."

"I know." Havilar drew her knees up to her chest. "But he would have stopped me going. I'm not going to leave Farideh to die just because she's ruined my life." She shut her eyes. Gods, she couldn't even keep it in that long. No one wants to hear how angry you are, she thought. The horse lifted its head and nickered.

"I know." Brin sighed once more, and Havilar wondered if he was angry at Farideh too.

Something popped in the underbrush, and Havilar whipped her head around toward the sound. The shadows of the forest were deep and not even Havilar's sensitive eyes could pierce them. Beside her, Brin's hand went to the sword on the ground.

"Lorcan?" he whispered.

Havilar shook her head. Lorcan would fly back. She checked the bandages and stood carefully, glaive in hand. The crackling and popping came again, the shiver of leaves too low to the ground to be wind. A flash of light and then another.

"Lorcan!" Havilar shouted, as loudly as she could. "Come

back!" She and Brin shifted, fanning out without a word to better meet whatever was about to come at them, out of the portal opening in the brush beside the road north.

If someone had told Sairché the forest was older than the arch-devils themselves, she might have believed them. Broadleaf trees towered over her, too ancient and imposing for common names like "oak" and "alder." Despite the fact it was late winter in this part of Toril, their leaves stayed, emerald and viridian. Sairché twitched her cloak over her wings. She couldn't shake the feeling the trees were watching her wait in the ruins left behind in the little grove.

However old the High Forest was, it'd had time to accumulate its own layers of magic. This spot, in particular, bubbled with long-dead powers from some failed civilization, stirred to wakefulness by the Spellplague, and simmering now as the Weave shifted and changed. Perfect for conversations you didn't want people eavesdropping on.

Sairché counted the glowing, pale green crystals protruding from the crumbling stone wall for an eighth time, when the second devil finally stepped free of his portal.

"You're late," she said.

Magros of the Fifth Layer regarded her as one regarded a furious imp—unconcerned, unimpressed. The misfortune devil looked as much like a human as Sairché did—only instead of wings to name him a fiend, his feet were cloven hooves the size of an erinyes's fist.

"I thought that was how we were doing things," he said. "How *you* were doing things, anyway." Magros shed the heavy furs he wore, draping them over a spike of crystal. He rolled up his sleeves and patted a cloth to the sweat that had sprung up between his tiny horns. "Blasted heat. Your Chosen is finally in play, I take it? Better late than never. I suppose."

Sairché gritted her teeth. That stlarning phrase.

"Much better," Sairché said. "Or will you claim that the Chosen you used for your prince's personal efforts—the one that died far too early—was a better played piece?"

Magros gave her a withering look. "What can we do for the frailty of mortals?"

"Not get them killed unnecessarily?" Sairché offered.

"And what of your wizard?" Magros said. "My agent in the camp reports witnessing—over several nights—a carrier landing in the courtyard of the fortress." He settled himself on a fallen pillar. "Seeing as how there were not more guards in the camp after, and the beasts that bore the carrier had a harder time leaving than arriving, I'm beginning to wonder if you even know what your pieces are managing in your absence."

Sairché's eyelid began to tic again. Ferrying prisoners out of the camp—that was not what she and Rhand had agreed to. That was not what Farideh was meant to assist. It would have to be corrected, and damn Magros for noticing it first.

"How is it your agent knows so well the count of the guards?" she asked coolly.

Magros chuckled. "Perhaps the guards were a guess. Still, with or without the loss of souls, your wizard seems to be working most inefficiently."

Sairché bristled. Rhand's unexpected speed at completing the camp had thrown her off schedule—for seven months he'd been acting as if he had all the resources he needed, sifting through his captives and singling out only a third of the ones with potential. She cursed the wizard's willfulness to herself. "He's done well enough. He'll do better now that he has help."

"So you say. She has a tenday to make things work more smoothly, remember?"

"We need to adjust the timeline," Sairché said. "Give me another tenday before you act."

Magros chuckled. "Is that why you asked me here? I think not. After all, this isn't the only effort Prince Levistus is concerned with. You'll simply have to catch up, cambion." He smiled nastily. "You wouldn't want His Majesty's efforts to be in vain."

Sairché held the misfortune devil's gaze. "Of course not. So why not give me the time to be sure of her?"

Magros clasped a hand to his chest, affronted. "Are you suggesting Asmodeus has given us pieces that might fail?" He gave her another unpleasant smile. "Perish the thought. I have every confidence in you, Sairché."

You have every confidence that I'll be the one caught holding the bag, she thought. The longer she played a part in Asmodeus's plans, the clearer it became that the archdevils who served him were using what was happening on Toril as an excuse to advance their own personal agendas. And that some of those personal agendas amounted to unseating the god of sin.

"His Majesty is indeed wise and powerful," Sairché said. "But let us not forget the lesson of the Eighth."

Magros's attention was piqued. "What lesson is that?"

Sairché smirked. "Oh, didn't you hear? His Grace, the Archduke, seems to have overstepped. He had claimed a fraction of a spark. He doesn't have it anymore."

"Everyone has heard that," Magros said. "Have they found the spark?"

Sairché shrugged as if that weren't the important part, but in fact, everyone was still scrambling to find out what had happened there. "His Majesty hasn't. But he has specially tasked Lord Mephistopheles with recovering it or replacing it." She gave Magros a knowing smile. "Since of course he and his agents have always maintained that it was an attempt to gain more power for His Majesty. Asmodeus would be sure they carry through."

"So His Majesty's attention remains on the Eighth's efforts?" Magros said thoughtfully.

"His Majesty's attention is everywhere," Sairché said, an answer that was all but catechism for a devil in the Hells. "But

I would not wish to be in Cania."

"Hmm," Magros said. "Is that all? I have much to do."

"Of course," Sairché said. If he looked into Cania, he would see she was right enough, and with any luck, Magros would be as incautious as he'd been with the first Chosen and do something stupid, thinking the god of sin wasn't watching.

"Give my lord's regards to your lady when you speak," he said, gathering his fur.

"The same," Sairché said, knowing he wouldn't and neither would she. Sairché would have to go back to Toril, to lean on Farideh and make sure the tiefling wasn't shirking her responsibilities. It could be done in a tenday if everything kept in place.

She returned to the skull palace of Osseia, bypassing her chambers once again and steeling herself before heading back to the portal room, all too aware of her half sisters' eyes as she passed. She activated the portal linked to the beacon she'd given Farideh, swearing to herself if Rhand's godsdamned barrier spell threw her off course one more time, she would vent all her frustration on the first person she saw. She hoped it was the wizard.

Sairché stepped out of the portal and saw Farideh at once—there was that, at least. The wizard must have fixed his blasted spell—

But then she noticed they were standing outside near a fire, beneath a scraggly bunch of trees on a riverside, Adolican Rhand was nowhere to be seen, and there was a young man with a sword standing nearby.

"You little idiot!" Sairché snarled. "Run away? You're lucky I haven't got time to go snatch your sister, because I would gladly trade today. What have you done to my wizard?"

Farideh took a step back, and glanced at the young man.

"What? All your bluster gone?" Sairché said. The gold-eyed woman braced as if she were going to lunge at Sairché again. "You'd better find answers for me. What are you doing out here? Where is—"

Gold eyes, Sairché thought. Lords of the Nine.

"Wrong twin," Havilar said. She pulled an amulet out from under her shirt. "*Vennela.*"

Sairché's shield shattered around her and the blood in her veins seemed to fill with crystals of ice. Bound, she thought. Lords of the Shitting Nine. She took a step back. "Well," she said. "You're quicker than your sister."

"Much," Havilar snapped.

Sairché turned on the young man, expecting an attack, but he was only watching, sword drawn. "You'll have to forgive my outburst," she said to Havilar, all calm. "I'm sure I'm not the first to make that mistake. I see your sister didn't follow instructions. You have the necklace don't you?"

"She left it for me."

"You don't want it," Sairché said, eyes still on the sword. "Give it to me."

"You tried that already," Havilar said. "Lorcan gave it to her, and she gave it to me."

"Lorcan didn't give it to her," Sairché said. "Give me a little credit. I only said that so she'd hang onto it—clearly that didn't work as I'd like, so kindly hand it over."

"Where is she?"

"Paying me back," Sairché said. She turned back and smiled at Havilar, but the tiefling's expression was hard. The necklace was in her hand, rubies glinting in the firelight. "Don't worry— the punishment's equal to all those lost years. I like things to be fair, too. Now, give that to me, before . . ."

Sairché trailed off, staring at the necklace in Havilar's hand. The largest ruby was missing. Lorcan had escaped.

The thought had no more gone through her head but the entire weight of her brother crashed down from the sky and slammed Sairché into the ground, driving all the air from her lungs. If the fall set him off-balance at all, he recovered quicker than Sairché, pinning her flat, one hand on the side of her head.

"Oh, you like fairness?" he crooned in her ear. "Let us see about fairness."

Whatever weakness, whatever softness she had marked in Lorcan, it was nowhere in evidence as he set one red thumb deliberately below her right eye.

"She knows where Farideh is!" Havilar cried. "You have to ask her! You have to ask her first!" Lorcan didn't move, didn't speak. He smiled down at Sairché as if Havilar hadn't said a word.

"I won't tell you if you intend to kill me," Sairché said. She might be able to throw him aside, but he wouldn't let her go and she couldn't hurt him back, not safely—she'd promised to protect him, after all. "You won't find her if I don't tell you where."

Lorcan chuckled. "I think you mistake my goals."

"If you wanted to ruin me, you've had chances already," she said quickly. "Hells, if you'd just slit *that* one's throat, you'd have caused enough chaos to make my life a slog through the Abyss." Sairché tried to twist an arm out, but he held her secure. "You kill me, you make an enemy of Glasya."

"Because she is such a friend to me these days." He pressed against her eyelid, hard enough to distort her vision, and no further. "I have a lot to pay you back for."

"Stop," Havilar said. "Please." The pressure stopped increasing. "You don't want to save my sister—fine," the tiefling went on. "And I don't care what happens to your sister, pop her eyeballs out and hand her over to those erinyes things, just do it somewhere else." She stepped closer. "But I care what happens to Farideh. And you said you'd help."

Lorcan was silent such long moments, Sairché wondered what schemes he was weighing, what prior agreements were in play—or if he had gone too mad for such things.

"Give me your knife," he said to the tiefling. She tossed it down to land before Sairché's face. He aimed the tip of the blade at Sairché's right eye, just a hair's breadth from her lower lid.

"Ask your questions."

"How do we get her out?" Havilar asked.

"The necklace," Sairché said. "Every one of those gems is a failsafe, a tool to help Farideh get out of this alive. And now she doesn't have it."

Havilar held the strand up to the light by one dangling ruby. "What do they do?"

"Nothing, likely," Lorcan answered. He drew the tip of the blade over the thin skin beneath her eye, drawing blood. Sairché didn't dare flinch. "She's quite the liar."

"Throw it!" Sairché said. "Throw the last shitting ruby, for gods' sake, and see for yourself!" Havilar twisted off one of the dangling jewels.

"Havi, no!" the young man cried, but it was too late. Havilar hurled the ruby across the glade, against the side of the rocky outcropping. As it struck its target, the gem detonated, the explosion large enough to send a rattling avalanche of stone off the face of the outcrop and a hot wind rushing past the camp. Havilar and her young man tumbled off their feet, but Sairché was not so lucky, and Lorcan weathered the concussion.

"Another bomb," Sairché panted, blood dripping down into the corner of her eye and over her nose bridge. "A charm that will help her pass through the wall undetected. A portal bead that will pull her back into the stasis chamber in the Hells. A beacon for me. And Lorcan."

Havilar looked up at Lorcan, who had gone quiet again. Sairché twisted against him—if she could get her hand up to the chain of rings she wore, she could find the one that activated her portal . . .

"Bring it here," Lorcan said. The tiefling laid the necklace out just beyond Sairché's reach. "Now," he said. "Which is which?"

Sairché eyed the chain of jewels, weighing the risk of a lie against the risk of the truth. "Bomb, beacon, portal, passwall. The passwall charm is the only thing that can open the wall without resorting to planar travel. She very well might need it."

Lorcan reached out, snapped the portal bead off. "Let's see if you're lying."

Before Sairché could react, he'd slammed the bead against her mouth, past her lips and over her teeth. He kept his hand pressed against her face, looking down at her without even a scrap of emotion she could use. She tried to speak, to convince him that he would lose so much more with her trapped in the Hells. The bead slipped, lodged in the gap of her molars, and Sairché froze.

Lorcan smiled at her. "Sleep well, Sairché," he said, and he slammed the hilt of the knife into her lower jaw. The bead shattered, the glass cutting her gums and tongue, then the portal's rough magic wrapped around her and dragged her back, deep into the caverns of Malbolge.

CHAPTER ELEVEN

21 Ches, the Year of the Nether Mountain Scrolls (1486 DR)
Three days ride from Waterdeep

Lorcan took hold of Sairché's necklace of rings and leaped aside as his sister vanished in a tangle of glowing threads and a gust of flame. The chain snapped as its wearer was pulled through the fabric of the planes, sending magical rings scattering over the forest floor.

He had expected to feel a rush of triumph, a certain glee as she was sucked away to the same cage she'd trapped Farideh and Havilar in. But the utter calm surprised him: their quarrels were finished, his revenge complete. Sairché would stay, trapped in the stasis cage for as long as he liked—one of the rings would open it.

"Now what?" Havilar demanded.

Lorcan turned to her, relishing the moment. "Now? Now I take my new trinkets and return to the Hells." He stooped to pluck the rings from the deadfall, nearly a score in all.

"And then?" Havilar asked after a moment. "She knew how to get to Farideh, and you just . . . did you kill her?"

"I sent her away," Lorcan said, stringing rings onto their chain. "Back to where she kept you all those years." He looked up at her. "You're welcome."

"She *knew* where to find Farideh," Havilar repeated. "She

knew and it's not like she was going to attack you."

"You underestimate Sairché."

"I don't underestimate Sairché, I *listen* to Farideh!" Havilar shouted. "We needed her to find Farideh, you *karshoji* bastard!"

"*You* needed her," Lorcan said savagely. "Your sister threw me over—did you really think I was eager to rescue her? To swoop in like someone out of one of your silly chapbooks and go on like she hadn't betrayed me? You're a lot more foolish than even *she* thinks you are."

Havilar's cheeks reddened. "Farideh was trying to protect us!"

That was just a twist of the knife—Lorcan ought to save her because Farideh was only doing what was in her and Havilar's best interests. *You thought she was different,* Sairché had chuckled. They all try and scale the hierarchy eventually. They all choose someone else. He twisted the broken links together and put the chain of rings around his neck.

"Well I do hope that works out for you," he said snidely. "Good luck finding her without Sairché's help." He spread his wings and flapped into the air.

"Don't you run away!" Havilar shouted. "She's in this because of you, don't you *karshoji* run away!"

"Havi," Brin said. "Let him go."

Lorcan didn't wait to hear what followed, what entreaties, what insults, what outbursts. He was done. There was nothing Havilar or Brin could say to change that. Done with warlocks. Done with Brimstone Angels. Done with Farideh . . .

Are you in love with my sister?

And he had nineteen new magical rings to distract him from *that.*

But he had gone only far enough to lose sight of Havilar and Brin's fire, when the air in front of him peeled open like a rotten wound. Lorcan dropped back as three enormous insects with bladed arms darted out of it, surrounding him.

Shit and ashes, he thought, hanging in the air. Hellwasps.

The leader dropped down to the level of Lorcan's face, tilting its head as it considered him. "You are Lorcan," it said. "Son of Invadiah."

"None other," he said, wondering if he jammed his fingers into as many rings as he could whether he'd find the one that took him away from Glasya's monstrous messengers before he found the one that turned him to stone—or worse.

The hellwasp clicked its mandibles. "Her Highness wishes to speak to you." Its bladed legs extended toward Lorcan. "You will come."

Havilar watched as the night sky swallowed Lorcan and with him her last scrap of hope of finding Farideh. She clutched her glaive, hardly daring to move.

"It's better this way," Brin said behind her. "I promise."

She whirled on him. "How? How is this possibly better?"

"Havi," he all but sighed. "With Lorcan? This was never going to end well."

"He said he could find Farideh, and—"

"And he lied," Brin said. "Can't you see that?"

"He didn't lie," Havilar said. "He doesn't lie—Farideh said so."

"He was playing you all along, to get back at his sister."

"He wouldn't do that."

"Damn it, Havi! He just did!" Havilar took a step back, and Brin shook his head. "Look, the Harpers will go after her. They'll get her back, I promise. Let's just go home, all right?"

Havilar's chest tightened around her heart. She'd been right the first time: she didn't really know him anymore. "I don't *have* a home," she said fiercely. "I have a sister. And no matter what *miserable* nonsense she's put me through, if something happens to her . . ." Her voice caught and she clapped a hand to her mouth. She swallowed the fear and the tears. "I'm *not* going back. Not without Farideh. You'll have to knock me out and sling me over a horse to make me, and *best* of luck with *that*. So go back alone if you have to."

Brin looked at her for a long moment, as if he wanted to say something but couldn't. As if he wanted to say a whole swarm of somethings, Havilar thought, and was swallowing them instead. Finally he sighed. "All right. Then let's get moving. We have too much ground to cover in too little time."

Havilar held her glaive closer. "You . . . you'll come with me?"

He smiled wanly. "I already said I would. Besides, as much as I'm sure Mehen will threaten to beat me senseless for not stopping you, I *know* he'll do it if I let you go on alone. And you know as well as I do I'm not slinging you over any horse. Let's go."

"But the sun's gone down," Havilar said. "You're not supposed to ride in the dark."

"Trust me," Brin said. "I'll break camp. You get the horses ready. There's a jar in my saddlebag, about the size of a walnut, and a pouch of herbs. Smear the unguent on their fetlocks and haunches, and get a pinch of the herbs in behind the bit. And tie Lorcan's horse to mine," he added, packing up their bedrolls. "We'll see if it can keep up."

She did as he said, still smarting from Brin's outburst, still puzzled by his reversal. When the horses were saddled again, she rubbed the greasy paste into their muscles.

"My hands feel like bees," she said to Brin as he loaded their gear onto Lorcan's horse. She flexed her fingers—they were definitely buzzing. He laughed to himself, and for a moment he looked so familiar she wanted to fall into his arms.

"It's the unguent," he said, grinning. "Has a kick to it."

The horses pranced as if they'd been shut up tight all day— not exhausted after miles and miles of traveling. Alusair started off before Havilar had even settled herself in the saddle.

"South," Brin told her, turning his and Lorcan's horses to the road.

Havilar bristled. "I'm not going back to Waterdeep."

"No," Brin said. "We're going to an inn."

The herbs, Brin explained, were for darkvision. The unguent, for speed. The horses would be no good to anyone for a tenday or so, but they'd recover.

"Just hold on tight," he advised.

There was enough moon for Havilar to see, vaguely, where they were going, but it was still dark enough that barreling up the road felt like she imagined flying would—utterly thrilling.

At first. After a few hours, she was only sore and sleepy and tired of riding. When the walls around the inn appeared on the edge of the moor, she nearly sighed in relief. Brin talked to the guards at the gate, who—despite the hour and the sour looks they gave Havilar—let them in. The horses had slowed down, plodding through the muddy field between the gate and the inn. They seemed almost grateful when Brin handed them over to a stabler in exchange for a small purse of coins.

"Won't we need them?" Havilar asked.

"Not for a tenday at least," Brin reminded her. "Come on." They hiked up the short hill to the sprawling inn at its peak.

" 'The Bargewright Inn,' " Havilar said. "Is that a joke?" Brin chuckled and held the door open for her.

"*Havilar.*" She looked back—he was rubbing the base of his throat.

"What?"

Brin shook his head, smiling pleasantly. "I didn't say anything."

She looked around the taproom, still full of travelers—most sleeping on the floor, but more than a few still drinking even at the late hour. "What are we doing here?"

"Come on," he said, crossing the taproom and heading straight for the tired-looking innkeeper, stacking flagons behind the bar. "Goodman Bargewright?"

"Aye," the man said. "What's your pleasure?"

"I need a room," Brin said. "Your *best* room."

A room. Havilar's breath caught and a flush spread across her cheeks.

"One with a fireplace," Brin added.

The innkeeper looked at him, brow furrowed. "I have one," he said slowly. "But the chimney's blocked up."

Brin smiled and shrugged. "Might be fine. It's plenty hot down here." He pulled on his collar, as if to let in the air . . . and flashed the dark edges of a tattoo inked across the left side of his chest. Havilar wondered how far it went, and realized she was very likely about to find out.

The innkeeper's eyebrows rose a fraction. He rummaged beneath the bar and pulled out a tarnished-looking key. "Through the door on the left, near the end of the hall. Can't miss it."

"Many thanks," Brin said, sliding the man a pair of gold coins.

"Any news I should worry about?" the man asked, pocketing the coins.

"Nothing new," Brin said. "We haven't passed a soul on the road."

Havilar frowned. That wasn't true at all. She started to correct Brin, but he grabbed her hand and squeezed it, and she stopped. She squeezed his hand back.

"Though I meant to ask in Beliard after a cousin of mine who was passing this way, out of Noanar's Hold," he said. "Called Laird Harldrake?"

The innkeeper nodded thoughtfully. "Haven't heard tell of him. But, I've heard no news out of Noanar's Hold since Marpenoth. Good or ill." He picked up another flagon and dried it carefully. " 'Course, I never do hear bad news out of Noanar's Hold. Get a little fuss from the farther reaches, mind."

"Hmph," Brin said. "Well many thanks. We should leave quite early tomorrow." The innkeeper nodded again and told Brin to be careful. Havilar flushed—a blur of shyness and anger. Did he mean *her*? What else would he mean?

"What was all that about cousins?" she asked Brin, as they passed down the hall.

"I'll tell you in a bit," he said, peering at the frame of each door they passed.

"I didn't know you had cousins in the North," she said, looking at the doors herself. They all looked the same, but it was better than worrying. She'd been trying very hard not to think about the last time they'd shared a bed, the last time he'd had his arms around her. She tried not to get her hopes up too quickly, to be brave and above all, careful.

And here was Brin, being the not-careful one. And all at once she found it thrilling and *awful*. She wasn't supposed to be the careful one, after all.

"Brin," she started, "I don't know if—"

"Ah!" he cried, his fingers on a particularly battered door-frame. He looked back the way they'd come, and then down the hall again. "This one."

"Brin," she tried again. "Can we . . . can we talk first?"

"In a moment," he said, unlocking the door. "Come on."

Her stomach flipped as she stepped inside. The "best" room looked like every other inn room Havilar had ever seen, clean and shabby and sparse. A bed, a table, a chair, a window, a little fireplace that Brin had crawled half-into . . .

She frowned. "What are you doing?"

Clink. Thunk.

Brin scuttled back and Havilar saw a hole where the fire would have sat . . . a hole with the edge of a ladder peeking up out of the darkness. He smiled at her. "There we are."

Havilar peered down into the darkness. A faint, greenish light hinted at the bottom of the ladder, fifteen feet down. Brin dumped their packs and weapons down the hole, then gestured for Havilar to go ahead.

She stepped down onto the wet stone ground, scanning the dark passage as Brin fixed the stone back into the fireplace.

"If this were a chapbook," she said, slipping her glaive and harness back on, "this ends with you being killed by some madman, and me running screaming through a hundred tunnels."

"Don't be silly," Brin said, coming to stand beside her. "You and I could handle some madman." He took up his pack and strode ahead, toward the greenish light. "This is a secret portal the Harpers have made use of for ages. If there were a madman down here, we'd have heard of it."

"Oh," she said, holding tightly to her haversack's straps. "So before, with the innkeeper, that was all Harper code-talk."

"Right," he said. "Don't repeat any of that, would you? I was just asking if the portal's behaving and such. Letting him know we're not running from anyone."

"Oh."

"Sorry," he said. "I should have told you what was going on."

"It's fine," she said, even though it wasn't.

The portal sat in a dead end of the cave, a flickering green pool in the floor. Beside it, a woman waited, the perfect picture of a chapbook witch. Wild eyes flicked over Brin and Havilar through a snarl of steel-gray hair. Purple motes of light swam around her gnarled fingers as she pointed at them. "You got a key?" she demanded.

Brin handed over the tarnished key the innkeeper had given him. She turned it over, sniffed it once, then fixed an eye on Havilar. "What're you? Some kinda demon?"

Havilar stiffened. "A tiefling."

"Huh." The woman spat. "If you say so. Where you going?"

"Noanar's Hold," Brin said.

The woman sent the purple motes into the portal with a whispery trail of magic. "You could walk there cheaper, you know?" she said, once the portal glowed bright and ready.

"Next time," Brin said, clearly unfazed by the portalkeeper. He held out a hand to Havilar. "Ready?"

Havilar stared at his outstretched hand. "If this were a chapbook, this would be the part where the portal eats us, you know." The woman guffawed, and Havilar scowled at her.

Brin took hold of her hand, smiling again. "Then how would they sell more chapbooks about us?" he said, teasing. She flushed all over again, not sure of what to say, and instead of guessing, Havilar stepped into the pool of green light.

Passing through the portal felt almost like riding through the dark had—lightless, rapid, death defying. There was no wind to blow through her hair as they traveled through the fabric of the planes, and a peculiar scent like wintergreen and old wine filled her nostrils. The air around her—if it *was* air—was no temperature at all. Not hot, not cold, not even *there*.

She only felt Brin's hand, holding tight to hers.

And then suddenly they were stepping out into the world again, through a stone doorway and into a root cellar that made the previous cave look cheery. Havilar stumbled, narrowly avoiding a thick patch of cobwebs, heavy with dead bugs. Brin, still holding her hand, pulled her back on balance.

"Thanks," she murmured, embarrassed at her clumsiness. That wasn't going to impress him either. She took her hand back. "How do we get out?"

"Cellar door," Brin said, pointing to a crack of grayish light off to their left. The portal's shifting green light flared briefly, painting his face in stark shadows. "Not better than a room at the inn, but much closer . . ." He trailed off. "Wait, did you think, back there, that I meant . . ."

"I didn't think anything," Havilar said.

"Gods, I'm sorry."

She pressed through the maze of old crates and barrels. "I said it's fine."

"Havi . . . we *should* talk. When you're ready, I mean."

No, she thought. No, no, no. If they talked now, he'd only tell her what she didn't want to hear. If they talked now, she wouldn't even know what to tell him she wanted. *I* don't really know me anymore, she realized.

"Later," she said. "Definitely not down here." She moved

through the darkness toward the angled doors and heaved them open. Outside the sun was just beginning to tint the sky gray and blue. A handful of stone buildings peeked out from the edge of a forest so thick and dark that Havilar wondered if there were any way to walk through it at all. A shattered keep stood behind them, spilling stones down a rise toward the river, while new timber held new masonry in place.

Brin came to stand beside her and pointed over the forest, toward the tips of two mountains peeking over the trees. "There," he said. "That's where we're heading."

Gray morning light rushed into the cell Dahl spent the night in, wrenching his pupils wide. He flinched as the headache that had been pounding harder and harder since his flask ran dry surged up behind his eyeballs.

"Get up," a man said. "Oota says she'll see you now."

When Dahl didn't get up fast enough, the man—a big human fellow—hauled him to his feet and out the door. A second man—a half-orc—wrapped a rope around Dahl's wrists, tying them behind his back.

They didn't go far—down the road a ways, every step guarded by a third man and a woman sweeping the cross-paths. A door opened, and the men pushed him through it. He blinked as his eyes readjusted to the gloom.

It looked as if the villagers had torn down one of the huts to make a courtyard, and what thatch they could reclaim had been built over the space, sheltering it from the weather. Dahl was dropped in the middle of the muddy space, facing a hut whose front wall was missing and a mountain of a man standing there.

Not a man, he corrected himself. A half-orc. A half-orc woman in men's clothing, her dark hair cropped short, her bosom crushed into a hide chestplate. She was taller than Dahl by a head and a half and outweighed him, surely, by himself again. One parent's blood had claimed her brutish features, her massive frame. But the cleverness in the single black eye that watched him struggle to his feet was something a human would gladly claim.

A shiver ran down Dahl's back: Oota, and she was no one to trifle with, he was certain of that. A gesture and the big man untied Dahl—he knew as well as Oota did that it would be suicide to try anything.

"People tell me," Oota said, "you've been asking how to find me. People tell me," she continued stepping down from her dais, "you've been asking a *lot* of questions. Stirring people up. Making them worry." She stopped in front of him. "I don't like my people to worry."

"You make it sound as if I were specifically harassing *your* folk," Dahl said, "when I was asking everybody I found. Half-orcs, humans, elves . . ." His throbbing eyes had settled enough to see that in the dimmer corners where the firelight didn't touch, there were scores more watching—humans and half-orcs . . . and dwarves, and half-elves, a tiefling, a pair of dragonborn. All Oota's charges. Dahl cursed.

"You rule this place?" Dahl asked, trying again.

"I *run* it," Oota said. "The parts that matter. There's a difference." She stooped so that their faces were nearly level—still too far for him to reach—and said softly, "One which you should appreciate, whoever you are. If I ruled this place, I'd have executed you already."

She straightened. "First Tharra tells me she clashed with a man about your height and description, wearing one of the guard's uniforms. Tells me I need eyes and hands ready, because someone else has a fool idea about serving the wizard and it might cost us in the end."

"Are you going to wait for my end of it?" Dahl asked.

Oota chuckled. "What is it you think we're doing here, son?"

Dahl tried to think of an answer. None made any more sense than "a farm for Chosen." He saw Tharra ease in a side door, Oota's guardsmen watching. He was caught—another mission falling apart. Time to be honest, he thought, and see what happens.

"My name is Dahl Peredur," he said. "I was taken by accident, brought to this place with another. I stole the uniform to escape the fortress. And then I stole these clothes when I realized walking around in that uniform gets me punched. I'm not with the wizard, I don't *know* the wizard. I'm just trying to figure out what in all the Hells and farther planes is going on so I can get word out to the proper people and maybe—maybe—save you all."

"How soon?" Tharra asked from the shadows. Oota shot her a dirty look.

"What makes you think we need saving?"

"Look, you're not military—the children make that clear," Dahl said. "You're not a village—you have almost no way of feeding yourselves beyond the rations and the gardens, and I haven't found a drop of bloody liquor in this whole town. That wall says this is a prison—a war camp—but I can't figure out what it is you've done to deserve that. You clearly weren't here before. If you're displaced, then *no one* has good intelligence on what Shade is doing. What is it?"

Oota gave him a toothy smile. "We like to say 'the misfortune of being blessed.'" The crowd tittered.

Dahl bit back his frustration. "What does that even *mean*? You're all being so damned cryptic—I can *help* you." He looked over at Tharra and rolled his right sleeve up past the elbow. He rubbed his forearm, as if it were bothering him, and muttered under his breath, "*Vivex prujedj.*" Under his fingers, a harp and moon sigil burned up through the skin, shining blue with hidden magic before fading to a normal, indigo tattoo. He moved his hand to his wrist, so that Tharra could see the mark.

"You have something to say, Goodman Peredur," Oota said, "you need to speak up."

"I'm on your side," Dahl said to Tharra. "What do I need

to do to convince you of that?"

Oota laughed once, as if he'd made a weak jest. "Hamdir," she said, and one of the human guards stood. "Our guest complains he's thirsty. Get him a flagon of the wizard's finest." She looked to Tharra. "Unless you object?" she said, all false compliance.

Tharra stared at Dahl. "It's the only way to be sure." Dahl's stomach knotted.

Behind Oota, the guard poured a measure of dark liquid into a plain flagon, then an equal measure of water. He held the flagon as far from his body as possible as he carried it to Oota, but Tharra intervened and took the vessel from him.

"Who do you intend to share the vision with?" she asked.

Oota lifted her chin. "Do you imply I can't?"

Tharra gave her a look of disappointment. "When did we become enemies, Oota? Of course that's not what I mean." She looked into the vessel. "I'm offering to do it myself. Take the headache off your hands," she added with a friendly smile. "You've too much to do."

Oota watched her, guarded. "We're not enemies," she said, somewhat warily. As if she were saying it as much for the crowd's benefit as Tharra's. "We are good friends and allies. But why," she added, slyer, "are you offering yourself?"

Tharra considered Dahl again. "Well, I did give him that bruise. I like to know I'm right. Or at least, take my lumps if I'm wrong." She kneeled beside Dahl. The fumes of alcohol were enough to tickle Dahl's nose even at that distance. Twenty-five ales behind schedule, he thought, and he'd take what he could.

Tharra gave the murky liquid a distasteful grimace. "I'd like to say you should have told me you were one of the Shepherd's flock right at the start," she murmured. "But I suspect you'd tell me that's not how you do things." Tharra swirled the flagon. "And I'd wager Oota'd demand you drink anyway."

"If that's all I have to do—"

"Two things you ought to know: This dungwater is what

the shadar-kai drink when they're feeling bored. I don't know what they distill it from, I don't care to know. It's potent, rough, doesn't slow you down like regular alcohol will. Sweeter than a penniless wastrel with a sick old granny."

"But it's just spirits? I can handle a rough round." Dahl gave a short laugh. "Right now, I could take a few rough rounds."

"Not just spirits," Tharra said. "You drink it straight it's as like to make you blind as mad. Or worse. You want something better than our bucket-brewed scrap-wine, you have to water it down."

"What's the other thing?" Dahl asked, after she'd been silent a moment.

Tharra looked up at him. "You shouldn't drink the water around here either. Welcome to your first taste of 'the wizard's finest.' " Tharra looked down into the cup. "How did you get here?"

Dahl frowned as Tharra pushed the liquid toward him. He started to answer, to repeat what he'd said before, but she tipped a measure of the drink into his mouth. Even watered, it was sweet as honey and burned like fire as it tripped over his wind-pipe and set him coughing. He managed to swallow it down.

Tharra forced another gulp on him and another, and by the third drink, Dahl's head was already spinning—potent stuff. Tharra seemed to steel herself and drained the rest of the cup.

"That it?" Dahl asked, his tongue feeling thick.

And then everything went black.

When Dahl's vision cleared, he was standing in the middle of a temple. Rust-colored tiles. Pews and reading stands. A high domed ceiling. And a familiar face walking toward him. The bottom of his heart dropped out.

"No," he shouted. "No! I've lived this enough."

"Nothing happened," he heard himself say, as he had eleven years before. Dahl turned around and saw a younger version of himself, sad and sick with fear.

"Oghma, Mystra, and lost Deneir," he said. "Don't make me do this."

"I know," Jedik said, walking straight through Dahl, to stand beside his younger self.

"I tried. I tried, and tried," the younger Dahl said. "It's still broken and I can't fix it, I can't *fix it*!" The paladins behind the old loremaster looked on, stern and cold. Looking for all the world as if they had never thought anything of Dahl but that he was trouble and a nuisance. A poor use of the order's charity. A millstone.

"You smug bastards," he cried, the words he wished he'd said. "Stop standing there gloating and help me fix this or go to the Hells." They didn't move. "I don't care what you think!" But he caught himself: he did. He *had*. Dahl blinked hard as if he could clear the illusion from his eyes.

"Can't hear you," Tharra called. She was standing a distance away, watching. She shook her head. "Not that you're going to realize that in a few more breaths."

"This isn't your business!" Dahl shouted. "This is *nobody's* business."

"Apologies," Tharra said. "The wizard's finest can be a bit particular. I should have been more specific this time. But it will be over soon enough."

Behind Dahl, his younger self was weeping uncontrollably as everything he'd worked for, everything he'd sought was ripped away without warning or reason. He squeezed his eyes shut as he heard Jedik say, "Tell me, Dahl, how does it serve Oghma to simply give you the answers you've been sent to seek? When you are sworn to the God of Knowledge, you are sworn to serve knowledge, to seek it, to free it." He shook his head. "It is in your power to know. So find the answers."

The world blurred away from him, stretching Jedik's words into a buzz of nonsense. Tharra's voice spoke over the clamor, *How did you get here?*

"I have a name for you," Jedik was saying. It was nearly three years later, and Dahl had returned from another fruitless quest to find the answer to Oghma's question. "Aron Vishter.

Go to Waterdeep."

"And what will he tell me," the younger Dahl said bitterly.

"Lies," Dahl said. Aron Vishter had been a traitor of the highest order. But he hadn't known that then, and neither had Jedik.

"He will give you another path. When you stare ahead too long and hard, you miss what passes by the side." Jedik squeezed his shoulder. "Let the Harpers give you something else to look at."

How did you get here?

The loremaster's quarters were abruptly gone, replaced by a shabby tavern, and Dahl was sitting on a stool, beside his younger self—their edges blurring together. He was shuffling papers nervously, sipping an ale, waiting to meet Tam Zawad for the first time. That was when the twins came in.

"He's not here," Farideh said, and it was strange to feel his younger self's revulsion and fear. Was there something there he should have known? "We should wait." She looked up at Dahl, and they were suddenly sitting nearby at the bar as well. She frowned at Dahl, at his younger self. "Can we help you?"

"No," his younger self said, all full of venom and anger. Dahl winced.

"*Gods*," Havilar said. "Are you listening to yourself? This is probably how you attract such creepers. One fellow—one good-looking fellow!—in this whole taproom is giving you notice, and you jump down his throat." She grinned at Dahl. "Excuse my sister. She's better at worrying than enjoying herself, but she's in the market for a good tutor."

Tharra snorted from behind the bar, and Dahl scowled at her as the room turned blurry, and things jumped around. Tam was suddenly standing in front of him.

"Good gods," Tam said, looking Dahl up and down. "You? Where did you get the impression that eavesdropping like a gawping spectator made for good spycraft?"

Dahl colored, even though this had happened years ago,

even though he'd been right. He started to answer, but the tavern was gone, and they were in a cave, deep under the Nether Mountains, the warped mummy of a mad arcanist stomping toward him, away from a cluster of devils. Farideh looked back at him. "Go," she said to Dahl. Her expression softened. "Many thanks. For coming back for me."

He was lost in the jumbled memories now. "No—are you mad? That thing—"

How did you get here?

Between steps the arcanist turned into a pillar of flames, the cavern, the library burned all around him. He was standing in the flames. He was sitting in the woods, showing Farideh a ritual while her sulking devil watched over them. He was talking to the devil in a shabby inn, handing him the rod he'd gotten her as an apology. Did she still have that?

Still? he thought. You just gave it to her.

He was in Baldur's Gate, collecting the evidence he'd gathered in Neverwinter, then slipping out the door he'd used in Proskur to visit the woman he'd been seeing while he kept tabs on the Dragon Lords. A man in ornate armor passed him by, laughing, and Dahl shivered at the avatar's passing. He wet his mouth, but the dryness persisted.

The skin of his arm seared and he flinched against the tattooist's needle. "This will be safer," Tam was saying. "You can't lose it, can't show it accidentally, can't have it stolen." The shape of the harp and moon surged up under his skin, the tattoo filling in, healing over seconds, not days. "It might take a while to get used to."

He looked up and saw Tharra, watching him curiously. The wizard's finest, Dahl thought, rubbing his arm. This isn't real.

And then they were in Procampur.

"Whatever you think you've discovered, it's clear Oghma was right to oust you from our ranks," the stern paladin told him, while Jedik sat watching, at a loss for words. "Whether it was your own doing or the poor advice of your companions, you participated in the destruction of priceless wisdom."

"Wisdom that would have destroyed tens of thousands of people," Dahl protested. "Especially when the Shadovar closing in took hold of it."

"And the knowledge is not to blame for the actor's use of it!" the leader of his order had shouted. "You made your decisions. And Oghma has made his."

How did you get here?

The desk became his father's grave, and Dahl was kneeling before it, in the middle of the night, clutching a bottle and trying to get numb. He'd died after Dahl admitted he'd fallen, and the Oghmanytes didn't want him back. He'd died thinking Dahl was a failure. He toasted the headstone, tipped the bottle back, and he was in Nera's taproom.

"I think you need some time out of the field," Tam was saying.

"A demotion," Dahl said, angry, aching.

"Not a demotion," Tam said. "You're clever at analyzing reports, I've said it before. I could use that." He drank from his own ale. "Some would say I could use someone who keeps me from going out and seeing what's happening for myself. And I trust your eyes."

"But it's a demotion."

Tam regarded him seriously. "*Not* a demotion. There's nothing wrong with honing your skills inside the house—it's where I spent most of my early years, and here I am." Then he added quieter, "But as your friend, I'll not deny, I think you could use some time out of the field after the last year."

A desk, a desk, a desk. More parchment than Dahl could remember blurring into a drift of the stuff, then a blizzard. A mission in the city here and there. And pinning down Rhand, that one hot summer. The desk melted into the figure of the brown-haired apprentice, hastily dumped in the alley near to Rhand's manor, before the Shadovar fled. One eye missing, one hand at the wrist, the fingers of the other hand blunted short with a sharp knife. He bolted far enough to vomit. When he stood, his Zhentarim agent was standing there. "From what I understand," she said carefully, "they are dead. Killed between here and Suzail. Maybe Brin has better details." And he closed his eyes and thought of Farideh, missing a hand at the wrist, a silver eye, a bloom of blood staining half her blouse.

"Dahl?" Farideh said, and he was in the taproom once more, Tharra beside him instead of Khochen. The urge to repair things Farideh didn't know were broken was hard to fight. He looked down at the deck of cards in his hand. It wouldn't fix this. It would only slow it down.

Farideh stumbled into him again, again acting oddly. She didn't look at him, but somewhere in between. Was she drunk or drugged or something else? No time to tell—he reached out to steady her and they both vanished.

They fought the shadar-kai again. She told him to run. He stole the armor, sent the message, found his way to the wall. All over again, he made his way to Oota's court, to the cup of the wizard's finest easing toward his lips. Not again, he thought. Not again . . .

But it came again, fast and hard. Dahl's fall, that first mission to find the library, the blur of grief and anger, Farideh, Rhand, the shadar-kai. Tharra and Oota and the cup of the wizard's finest easing toward him.

How did you get here?

And it started again. And again. It would go on forever, he felt sure, and Dahl would be trapped, reliving the painful past, battered by moment after moment, until—

"No!" he shouted. Dahl opened his eyes, years and years and years later, looking up at a patchy thatch roof. He lay spread-eagled in the dirt, his head pounding and his stomach rebelling against his ribs. He shut his eyes again and that sent the world spinning. "Gods' books."

"So does he lie?" a too-loud voice said. Dahl curled away from it, hands over his head. Oota—the name sifted up through his memory like a lost coin drifting in the sand. With it came the rest: the camp, the fortress, and the wizard's finest. He shuddered.

"No," Tharra said, sounding hoarse. "Not a word. He's what he says." Dahl tried opening his eyes again. She was standing over him. "Bit more too."

"Tell me there's an antidote."

Tharra smiled. "Time. Few good heaves. The spirits aren't the worst of it, but you can't much avoid the visions." She hauled Dahl to his feet, and Dahl swallowed the saliva that flooded his mouth. He wasn't going to vomit in the middle of everyone like some common drunk.

Again, he thought, noticing the puddle of sick near where he'd fallen.

"Get him out of here," Oota said. "We can talk later."

"Come on," Tharra said. "Let's get you somewhere quiet." She helped Dahl back out into the sunlight, and Dahl's resolve failed. He was messily sick in an alley before Tharra got him back into the hut he'd spent the night in and ducked back out. She came back shortly with a bundle of rations and a small bucket.

"Here—this is safe. From the cistern," Tharra said, handing Dahl a dipper of water.

Dahl gulped it down. Tharra grinned at him. "So. You're out of Waterdeep. They always said you lot were skilled. How in the Hells did you get past the wall? The waters skipped over that."

"Luck," Dahl said, *Bad luck*, he thought. "I got pulled in by mistake. I got a pair of sendings out to Waterdeep already. Tam's sending reinforcements." That sounded better than res-cuers. "If I can get more components I might be able to find out how many and how soon."

Tharra took the dipper from his shaking hands and filled it again. "You Waterdhavians," she said, sounding like his eldest sister-in-law. "Excess is in your blood, isn't it?"

"I'm not from Waterdeep," Dahl said. "I'm from Harrowdale."

"Harrowdale?"

"Near enough. My father's farm—" Dahl stopped—not his father's, his brothers' now. "It's to the west of New Velar. About a day."

Tharra's smile widened. "My brother-in-law had family outside Harrowdale. Tassadrans originally, but they've been there since the Sembians invaded. Did you know a fellow called Melias by some happenstance?"

"Bearded fellow with a field full of beehives?"

Tharra laughed. "Second cousin."

"He traded honey for my mother's apple butter every year." He finished the dipper. "So you're from the Dalelands too?"

"Mistledale. Though lately," she said, with a wry smile, "I wander. A Harper's lot."

"I suppose."

"Funny though," Tharra said. "I've got watchers up along the border line. Not a far reach to grab a Harran lad clever enough to slip out of a fortress that well-guarded. A few different turnings and you might have been my fledgling instead of the Shepherd's."

More than a few, Dahl thought. And if he had? He wouldn't have gone to Procampur, he wouldn't have become a paladin. He wouldn't have lost his powers. Would he have let the contact in Rhand's manor die? Would his father have died? Would he have been prouder of Dahl if he'd stayed in Harrowdale and kept a farmer's cover?

Tharra gave him a thin smile. "You spend a lot of time with tieflings?"

"No," Dahl said, rubbing his eyes "That's . . . new. Temporary."

"Hm. Seems slippery," she said. "A pity we don't have more resources."

"Do you have agents coming?" Dahl said.

Tharra chuckled. "No. We're not all wizards like you lot, hauling around scrolls, casting sendings like they were stones into the sea."

"That's not . . ." Dahl shook his head and winced when it started spinning. "Look, I'll defer to you here. Clearly, you know what's going on better than I do. But for the love of every watching god, you have to tell me what's happening."

Tharra shook her head, as if all the words in every tongue on Faerûn couldn't sum up what was happening in the camp. "Something strange and something wonderful and something far more dangerous than we can comprehend. The gods are stirring, mark my words, and in a way we've never seen before. The wars? The way powers who were content to bide their time have all leaped at each others' throats?—if that isn't the hand of the gods moving things, I don't know what it is."

"Politics," Dahl said. "Tensions past their breaking point. Wars happen, then people think 'Why not us too? Why not our problem?' It spills over."

"And the earthmotes? The plaguepockets fading? The world is getting ready for something," Tharra said. "These people, all of them, were stolen out of their lands, their homes. Gods above know what makes him choose them exactly, but he's not grabbing at random. Sometimes he takes a whole village. Sometimes he takes a single child." Tharra dropped her voice. "But the ones he takes, some of them, when the time is right, gain powers by the grace of the gods. Right out of the blue. Strange powers."

"Like the boy trailing flowers."

Tharra nodded. "Samayan? Chosen of Chauntea, near as we can figure."

Dahl eyed Tharra. "Funny way for the Earthmother to spread her influence."

"Depends on what it is She's trying to do."

A god grants a mortal powers, but not the powers that can save them, Dahl thought. "It doesn't sound like any Chosen I've heard of."

Tharra shrugged. "They call it what they call it. A lot of the ones we find are like Samayan—their gifts are modest, but you can't deny they're something rare. No use against the shadar-kai, but the wizard gathers them up as if they're precious things—the ones they catch. Those powers usually come on quiet, and the wizard doesn't always notice it's happening. We can keep them away, shifting them around the camp ahead of the guards' sweeps. They haven't caught on yet. Others you get are like Oota—can't put your finger to it, but you know something's strange. Your thoughts just go a little crooked, a little changed. If we weren't noticing daisies and such, we might not realize it was something unique. They can usually blend in.

"A few gain much more impressive powers. The sort of thing you expect when you hear 'Chosen.' They don't tend to be quiet. The guards come for them much quicker, catch them as they manifest." Her expression darkened. "Not all of them survive for the wizard's use."

"And you? Or do you Dales Harpers get that odd influence with your pins?"

Tharra flushed and shrugged, and Dahl realized there must be an etiquette here he didn't know. "Not all of us get a clear message. And the majority of us are just ordinary. Or ordinary for now. We've found signs the powers are coming—a persistent ill-feeling, or sometimes a euphoria no one can explain, vertigo or dreams about the gods. It's not perfect, but everyone knows to look out for strangeness."

People touched by the powers of the gods. People disappearing—whole villages disappearing. Was that what had happened to Vescaras's farmstead? Or any of the missing Harpers? Were Vescaras's lost agents, or Dahl's Sembian handler, among the dead Chosen?

"If you're all touched by the gods," Dahl asked, "why are you still here?"

"Because the wizard is very prepared." Tharra scooped another dipper of water for Dahl. "Drink it and get some rest. You can sleep off the vision's side effects, but your head's going to feel like it's the Chosen of Tempus's Warhammer tomorrow."

Glasya's words echoed in Lorcan's thoughts as he flew low over a dense forest, searching for the devil Sairché was meant to meet with that evening, according to her imps.

"Your sister understood my particular needs," she'd said. "Asmodeus's particular needs. I cannot say I was pleased with her results thus far. But I had my hopes." She had smiled, and Lorcan had been too terrified to breathe for a moment. "You have her tools. Prove to me the children of Fallen Invadiah don't repeat their mother's weaknesses."

Lorcan searched the ground below. Whatever Sairché had been planning, she had been careful not to leave the details lying around. The erinyes only knew about scattered schemes involving cultists who largely ran on their own. The imps told him about a devil named Magros who sent an avalanche of scrolls. And he'd found the empty case that had held the original orders, passed down from the god of evil himself, buried in a box of useless rods, tucked beneath a settee and behind a rolled up skin-rug.

This wasn't just about Sairché's revenge on him.

Lorcan spotted the violet-and-white flash of a portal in the trees below, and dropped straight down, catching the air again to hang near to the clearing, out of the portal's lingering light.

There was the devil, Magros, decked in heavy furs . . . and there was a cluster of strange creatures besides. Leashed ghouls. A boneclaw, towering over its companions with fingers like scimitars dragging in the litterfall. A handful of robed humans. A woman in red robes with a pale line of hair down the center of her skull. A palanquin besides, hauled by a pair of massive zombies too degraded for him to be sure what exactly they had once been.

"You are no more than four days from the site," the devil said. "I trust you can find it."

"Of course," the woman said. "As much as I trust you'll be

there to see the ritual through and claim your prize."

"A prize for all the Hells," he corrected gently. Unctuously, Lorcan thought. Oh, this one would be trouble. The necromancer said something else that Lorcan couldn't hear, then she and her macabre retinue disappeared into the ancient wood, their way lit by globes of floating light.

Magros turned, and before he could wake the portal once more, Lorcan dropped to the ground in front of him, earning a gratifying cry of surprise.

Lorcan sketched a little bow, marking the hooves, the small horns, the oily expression—a misfortune devil. Smug bastards, he thought. "You're Magros, I presume," he said.

"You have the advantage of me." The misfortune devil's eyes flicked over Lorcan, resting a moment on the flail-shaped pendent he wore. "A Malbolgian?" He narrowed his eyes. "Did Sairché send you?"

Lorcan smirked. "In a sense."

"Ah—you're the brother, aren't you? The resemblance is uncanny."

"I doubt that," Lorcan said. He was supposed to ask, supposed to wonder why it was uncanny. But he didn't.

"Word was Sairché made short work of you some time ago," Magros said. "I take it I shouldn't be expecting her to keep our appointment."

"She's indisposed," Lorcan agreed. "So I have the pleasure of taking her place."

"Is it a pleasure?"

"It could be."

"I doubt that if you've seen what a mess your sister left behind."

Lorcan smiled—Magros must have driven Sairché mad. He was hardly *trying* to provoke Lorcan into defending his position, revealing what he knew. "*Is* it a mess?" he said. "The site looks quite . . . sharp."

"Do you have a better leash on the wizard, then?" Magros

asked. "Or the armies?"

Lorcan gave him a pitying look. "Did she tell you there were *armies* involved? How adorable."

Magros considered Lorcan a long moment—likely Sairché had said no such thing. Likely Magros was simply trying to trick Lorcan as much as Lorcan was trying to trick him. But there would be no chance his erinyes half sisters would not have had plenty to say about Sairché's handling of an army. The wizard who wouldn't behave was a better bit of information.

The out-of-place Thayans better still.

"I can tell from her notes that she doesn't care for *you*," Lorcan said. "So we should get along very well."

"She does have quite the little temper. Takes after your storied mother?"

Lorcan smirked. "You've obviously never met Invadiah."

"I have little reason to travel to Malbolge." Magros sat on a boulder at the edge of the clearing and crossed his hoofed legs. "If you're here in Sairché's place, I assume you have some information. Have you gotten things back on track?" He gave Lorcan a wicked smile. "Or are you the one who's going to fall in your sister's place?"

"Please," Lorcan said witheringly. "Unlike my sister, I know where I stand. If you decide to step on my neck to advance, you'll have to clamber down the hierarchy to do it. I've long since realized there's nothing to gain by rising above my station—if I could escape *this* honor, believe me, I would. If there's any devil in the Hells you can trust—for the moment—it's me."

Magros smiled politely, and the effect made Lorcan want to shudder. "You'll forgive me. I wasn't promoted yesterday."

Lorcan shrugged. "And I wasn't born a fool. There's a great deal more going on here than it seems. More than even our archlords would ever say—more than my sister was ever going to be foolish enough to leave written. Why would I try and overtake you, Magros? I have enough to do trying to make sure this looks like it was all Sairché's fault."

"Will blaming a corpse catch your mistress's eye?"

"Corpse?" Lorcan said. "I said indisposed. Not dead. Why would I waste a perfectly good piece?" He took a risk and sat on the ground near to Magros. "And why would I care about catching the eye of a mad witch who dragged me right out of my comfortable life?"

Magros raised his eyebrows. "Your words."

"Indeed."

"So you're looking to cross layers?"

"If you threw in the furs, perhaps I'd consider it," Lorcan said. "But at the moment, all I want is room to make sure whatever collapses lands in Sairché's hands and not mine."

Magros tilted his head. "His Highness can offer many perquisites for a little assistance."

And all the same dangers, Lorcan thought. Stygia might be as far from Malbolge as a mind could imagine—a frigid sea, encased in perpetual ice, the waters below stirring only for hungry, mindless beasts. Its master, Prince Levistus—leagues from beautiful, terrible Glasya with her voice in every devil's ears—present only in mind, his body sealed in a massive iceberg.

But there was no layer of the Hells where Lorcan's situation would truly be improved.

"In exchange for your indulgence, I could consider it. What is it he wants?"

"A trifle," Magros said. "I need someone who can get past the wall your sister's wizard has around that fortress and take care of my own agent." He stood once more and gathered up his furs. "Do it right and we shall neatly entrap Sairché. All I need is for you to use this." Magros suddenly held a gleaming knife, the length of a long bone in one hand. "Shadar-kai make. Run my little traitor through and leave it near. Or better still, run that troublesome wizard through as well and put the weapon in her warlock's hands. Sairché hasn't prepared her nearly enough—Lords of the Nine know . . . she might snap."

The blade's hilt didn't warm in Lorcan's hand, but the center of his chest burned hot. "So that's where her warlock is," he murmured, hoping it would cover anything else his face showed. He would have to go there next. He would have to face her. And a wizard who wouldn't behave.

"What's the wizard's name?" he asked idly. "She didn't mark that down, I'm afraid, and I'll have to go sort him soon." Magros gave him an oily smile, and for a heartbeat Lorcan thought he might be wrong, the wizard might be some other nuisance. Sairché might have been lying.

"Rhand," Magros said. "Although Sairché doesn't know I know that."

Even though Lorcan had been expecting to hear the name, his temper threatened to make Invadiah blush.

"Well," he said. "That should help."

Draped once more in fur robes, Magros gave him the sort of smile that shone politeness but oozed condescension.

"At least you don't need to recall it long. Here." He pulled a bundle of cloth from a pocket hidden in the robes and held it out, peeling back the cloth to reveal an iron cube, its sides etched with frost. "When you've taken care of things, let me know. Just squeeze the cube tight." He dumped it into Lorcan's hand, and the cambion bit back a cry of pain at the sudden, intense cold. Magros chuckled and dropped the cloth on top. "You'll have to get used to that."

The portal gaped and exhaled a frigid breath that made Lorcan fight not to shiver. The misfortune devil vanished, along with the obvious markers of the portal.

He hadn't mentioned what his agent was doing, Lorcan thought. He hadn't mentioned why he wanted that one dead. He hadn't explained about the Thayans. Worse, Magros clearly thought he was an idiot if he was going to go around murdering his pieces and taking the blame.

Lorcan pieced through the details he knew of Sairché's plan, of Glasya's. Of Asmodeus's. There was nothing that would suggest the best course of action lay in allying with the followers of Szass

Tam. If rumors were true, the calculating lich was keen to repeat Asmodeus's feat of snatching the divine spark away from a god and canny enough to manage it. Not the sort of being to hitch your fortunes to, if you were concerned with hanging on to your own ill-gotten gains.

Lorcan wondered whose mistake that was, and if they even knew, before reopening his own portal and stepping back into Malbolge to prepare for his next meeting.

His feet had no more than touched the bone-tiled floor when his mind registered that something was very, very wrong on the other side of the portal. His knees buckled, slamming his body down into a supplicant's bow. His vision turned black, as if someone had plucked his eyes entirely from his skull. The air burned hot enough Lorcan imagined it would burst into flames if he exhaled too hard. There was only the sound of his frightened breath against the floor.

And then Asmodeus spoke.

The ancient wood swallowed Mehen and the Harpers, the sun lost behind a canopy of emerald leaves. Even in the heart of Ches, the forest felt mild, the air brisk but nothing compared to Everlund's chill. A carpet of feathermoss and brittle bracken muffled their footsteps, but the sharp, grassy scent of broken plants marked their path wherever they trod.

Daranna checked Mehen's pace often, but he wouldn't give her the satisfaction of being the slow, ungainly creature she expected. He knew how to move through the wood, quickly and stealthily. They made camp late and broke early the first night, and by the time they stopped on a high hilltop for the second night, Mehen had to admit at least that the Harpers weren't the worst folks to be traveling with.

Not as good as his girls, he thought sadly, digging an acorn cap out from beneath one of his foot-claws. He rubbed his sore foot.

"I may owe you a boon," Khochen said, dropping down beside him. "Daranna swore it would take eight days with you along. I wagered a gold piece we could do it in five. I think you'll win me my gold yet, goodman. Many thanks."

"Thank me when you've won it," Mehen said. "Don't tempt the gods into your business."

"But they are so easy to tempt, goodman." Khochen tilted her head. "You must tell me what to call you, at least. 'Goodman' is terribly stiff, 'Mehen' is too familiar, and no one can tell me your clan or family name—"

"Mehen is fine. And don't pretend you don't know perfectly well I have no clan name." He scratched the empty piercings along his jaw frill. "You know the difference between clan and family, you know what this means."

"A hit!" she said clasping a hand to her chest. She considered him silently, that twitchy smile mocking him. "I have guesses," she said. "The size of the holes, the placement. I'm no scholar of Tymanther, but I think you were somebody once."

Mehen glared down his snout at her. "I'm still somebody: I am Clanless Mehen, Son of No One, Father of Farideh and Havilar."

Khochen's smile softened. "But you were Verthisathurgiesh Mehen. Once."

All these years, and the sound of those words spoken aloud still sent a shock of shame and anger through Mehen. "Don't you dare say that name," he said, his voice a hiss. "I am *clanless*, and that means forever."

"Indeed," Khochen said. "I know that well enough too. But someone is looking for your old self."

Mehen sighed and folded his arms, and all that sudden shock turned back to annoyance. "Let me guess: a dragonborn, clanless, but freshly enough to tell you that they, too, were Verthisathurgiesh once. Wears a symbol of the Platinum Dragon big enough to stop an axe. Tracked me out of Tymanther, but then the trail runs cold. They start asking, you think of Lord Crownsilver's bodyguard."

Khochen smiled. "An excellent guess, goodman."

"I get one every five or seven years. They get themselves expelled from the clan for swearing too loudly to Bahamut. They're lost and lonely. They've heard the tale of the favored son who called Old Pandjed's bluff and took exile over obedience and they assume—every *karshoji* one—that it was the same 'sin' as theirs. That I will know their hearts and be their mentor, and turn them into the sort of warrior Verthisathurgiesh will be so proud of, that they will make an exception and bring them back into the fold." Mehen fixed Khochen with a hard stare. "They are wrong on every count. Don't encourage this one."

Khochen's eyebrows raised. "Your clan doesn't talk about what you did?"

Mehen snorted. "Doesn't sound like it."

"That's peculiar. Can't warn anyone off unless an example's made."

"There are some things, where if you make an example, you give the young ones ideas," Mehen pointed out. "Pandjed is nothing if not canny. He knows the difference."

"So what did you do?" Khochen asked.

Mehen held her gaze. "I told you," he said. "I told Verthisathurgiesh Pandjed he could exile me."

"Does Verthisathurgiesh Pandjed do everything you tell . . ." Khochen trailed off and peered into the distance over Mehen's shoulder, down the hillside and into the depths of the darkening forest.

Mehen traced her gaze—nothing there. Not at first. Then the flash of magic, purple and gold, far into the distance peeked through the trees once more. He narrowed his eyes as it flashed again.

"Company," Khochen noted, coming to her feet and retreating to Daranna's side. A few quick, whispered words and the four scouts were on their feet once more, slipping through the trees toward the strange lights.

"Goodman," Daranna said softly. "Hold. Let them do what

they do best and get us information before we decide whether to strike."

Mehen didn't look back at her, watching the faint lights instead, and trying to pick out where the scouts had vanished into the fortress. He had no way to gauge the time this deep into the forest, but it might have been another seven and a half years before the four scouts returned one by one with the sort of answer Mehen was craving.

Thayans.

"What in the name of every dead god are Thayans doing in the High Forest?" Vescaras asked. Daranna remained silent, pondering the point between the trees where the lights had flashed.

"They've had trouble with them up in Neverwinter," Khochen noted. "Maybe whatever they're after's not there but here."

Mehen tapped the roof of his mouth with his tongue. *Karshoji* Harpers. "Are they supposed to be here?" he demanded. Daranna looked up at him through her hair.

"No."

Mehen slid his falchion from its sheath. "Then let's get rid of them."

The sun has started its downward path, when one of the apprentices returns, his robes scattered with a constellation of blood droplets. Farideh studies them as he crosses the room, her pulse speeding with every step. Whose is it? The old woman's? The tall man? The woman wrapped in red light? He bends his head in conversation with his fellows, his voice rushed and excited. Something has changed. The wizards all look up at her, like a herd of spooked deer, and out of habit, she looks away, down at the waters. Mehen would be disappointed—there are times a warrior shouldn't back down.

She summons a memory of her father. The vision of Mehen plaiting her hair, before she heads out on patrol duty for the first time, back in the village of Arush Vayem, washes up as sharp-edged as it is in her mind. She is so young and gangly at fourteen—she knew it then, and the image only makes her want to hug her younger self close.

"Is it . . . ," the younger Farideh starts. She tries again. "It's just it's supposed to be so dangerous."

"It's not dangerous," Mehen says. "Stop listening to Criella."

"If it's not dangerous, then why is there a wall? Why do we need patrols?"

Mehen ties her hair off, tucks the end of the braid into the band at the nape of her neck, and steps around her to check her armor, her sword belt. "There is dangerous," he says, "and there is dangerous. You're watching for signs of bandits and monsters migrating through. Getting a little hunting in. That's it. The day patrol is nothing, or they wouldn't let a fourteen-year-old do it."

" 'Make,' " the younger Farideh corrects.

"You will be fine," Mehen says. "You'll have your sister with you. A blade at your side." He pauses and his great nostrils flare. "Hmmph. But keep her from running off. She needs you to be her . . . voice of reason."

Farideh looks away. "She doesn't listen to me."

"She does," Mehen says. "She doesn't listen to everyone, but she listens to you, Fari. Even when it doesn't look like it."

He looks her over once, then hugs her tight. "Remember: keep your wrist firm and your grip gentle. And don't worry about the day patrol."

Two fat tears send a series of ripples over the scene. Farideh wants to ask if Havilar would have listened this time, if it would have been wiser to tell her the truth about Bryseis Kakistos, the collector devils, and the Toril Thirteen. But the waters don't know the answer any more than she does, and Farideh is running short of time.

Though not as short as the people she's doomed, she reminds herself. She steels herself and looks up at the apprentices, who watch her back, appraising. Whatever it is she's done, their opinion of her is shifting, and it doesn't soothe her at all.

CHAPTER TWELVE

23 Ches, the Year of the Nether Mountain Scrolls (1486 DR)
The High Forest

MEHEN CROUCHED BEHIND A MOSS-COVERED HUMP OF STONE, peering past at the moonlit clearing. The Thayan party had stopped, lowering the palanquin carried between two hulking zombies so that the two necromancers inside could exchange places with two more of their fellows. The remaining two clutched the leads of eight ghouls between them, as the creatures pulled like errant hounds, scenting the air wildly. The Harpers had moved carefully, staying downwind of the pack. The smell was thick, and every time Mehen nervously tasted the air, he fought not to gag.

Eight ghouls, six necromancers of unknown skill, two zombies, one towering creature with fingers like sharpened stakes that one of the scouts had identified as a boneclaw. And a Red Wizard.

"She's sleeping in the palanquin," Ebros had reported back. "The other wizards swapped in about half an—" He caught himself at Daranna's furrowed brow. "Eight songs ago."

"Now's the time, then," Vescaras said. "Let's move."

"Send your scouts around," Mehen said. "Fire arrows from behind."

"I know how to stage an ambush, goodman," Daranna said.

She had nodded at the scouts, gestured quickly in a rough circle, and they'd sped off into the forest.

Now, crouched and ready to attack, Mehen could just mark Ebros in the rustle of a tall oak tree. Daranna peered into the dark, checking for a sign of each.

"Ready?" Khochen murmured.

By way of answer, Daranna gave a nightjar's looping trill, summoning the scout's arrows as surely as she might a trained hawk. Two hit ghouls—one straight through the eye, one with a thud and a screech in the meaty part of its back. Their keepers turned toward the source of the arrows, loosing the ghouls. The two wizards who'd just woken pulled globes of light into being. More arrows struck more ghouls in the dark. Then a wizard dropped, clutching an arrow in the gut. The ghouls found the scent of the hidden Harper scouts, scrabbling at the bark of the trees.

The curtains of the palanquin twitched.

"Go," Daranna said.

The arrows kept coming, but now the wizards aimed their spells at the scouts' hiding places, splashing the trees with dark magic. Branches withered, leaves dropped. One scout yelped and fell to the brush as Mehen swung his falchion and took the wizard who'd brought her down across the chest. The wizard fell, a look of shock on his features, and Khochen's dagger froze them that way with one sharp motion. A ghoul leaped on her, but Khochen turned it aside, and toward its former master's body as she rolled under. The ghoul took the offering, and Khochen took the opportunity to run it through.

The Red Wizard burst from her palanquin, all fury and fiery light, and turned against the scouts and the Harpers that harried her undead and her apprentices. No taller than Khochen, but thicker, her skin was ghostly in the moonlight. Her inky hair stood out in a plume down the center of her shaven head and ran down her back in a thick queue.

Mehen shoved aside another ghoul and slammed against

the zombie that had broken free of its harness and come at him, claws raised.

The Red Wizard cast a splatter of flames at the battle beyond, catching Vescaras's sleeve and sending Daranna scuttling back from the boneclaw she'd been harrying. The scouts aimed their arrows at the boneclaw, and as they hit, they burst with a vibrant green light that made the boneclaw scream. It threw a hand up and the tapered blades of its middle fingers stretched impossibly far, up into the trees. Mehen heard Ebros cry out, and Daranna threw herself at the boneclaw again.

The Red Wizard started shouting orders to her remaining apprentices—only three now—to fall back, to pull in toward the palanquin.

But before she could finish, Mehen had reached her and her dangling braid.

He grabbed hold of it and yanked hard. With a yelp, the Red Wizard toppled backward, off the palanquin and to the ground.

Mehen set one clawed foot on her forehead and pressed the edge of his falchion against the woman's throat. "Call them off," he hissed. "Unless you can raise things when you're the one beyond the grave?"

The woman's dark eyes flicked down to the blade, shocked and fearful. Hesitantly, she raised a hand to the amulet she wore. Shadows twined around her hand.

The undead all froze and looked to the necromancer. Vescaras ran another ghoul through—the creature died with an inhuman screech—before he realized something had changed. The last three apprentices held their spells, dancing in their palms, and watched their leader.

The amulet still clutched in her hand, the Red Wizard looked up at Mehen. She was younger than he'd guessed—younger than his girls. "We surrender."

"No need," Daranna said, advancing with her blade out.

"Hold," Vescaras said. He sheathed his rapier, eyeing the boneclaw, swaying in place, its skinless face impassive. "My friend doesn't like trespassers in her forest, Lady Red. You might make her mood improve if you tell her what you're doing here."

The wizard's eyes never left Mehen's. "We have a mission. One you might be interested in for your own sakes. Parley?" Daranna snorted.

"You'll forgive us," Khochen said, "but parleying with zombies breathing down our necks is hardly appealing."

"One zombie," the wizard corrected. "One boneclaw. Four ghouls. Three necromancers. All held at bay. And myself. You have—I must admit—the advantage. In more than one fashion—I am Zahnya, of the Red Wizards of Thay. Who are you?"

"Your doom," Daranna said. Vescaras sighed.

"Would you happen to be enemies of Netheril?" she asked. Her first fear at Mehen's sudden presence had slipped behind a facade, but Mehen could see it, lurking behind her eyes. Not a lunatic, not a bluff—someone's daughter, he thought. He kept the sword where it was, though.

"Because I might have information to trade," Zahnya went on. "A partnership to offer, perhaps."

"In trade for what?" Vescaras asked.

"Not killing me?" Zahnya squeezed the amulet more tightly, her eyes still on Mehen. "There's a fortress, in the mountains. A wizard of Shade has a prison camp there. That is our mission: find it, destroy it, claim what weapons we can."

The Harpers did not speak. Mehen felt as if every eye were on him in that moment—as if the Harpers and the undead knew that Mehen would be the one to decide the fate of this unlikely party. She can find Farideh, he thought.

"What wizard?" he growled.

"A very evil man," she said. "I can show you the way to his camp. I can help you destroy him." She swallowed hard. "We're on the same side, for the moment."

Mehen's pulse pounded. An evil man. Fari, he thought. Fari, Fari—what have you gotten caught in? He knew where he stood—if it meant they got where they needed to be faster, he would lead the slavering ghouls himself.

Vescaras and Daranna traded glances. Khochen's eyes shifted off the boneclaw and to Mehen's. "A caster would be handy," she said.

"No," Daranna said. "She'll turn on us."

"I can give you assurances," Zahnya said. "The amulet—you can keep it. Control my creations, and the boneclaw."

"Unwise." The boneclaw's hissed word made all of the Harpers jump. Its burning eyes pierced Mehen. "They will betray you."

"Or they kill us now," she said to the monster. Zahnya pulled the amulet from her neck and held the jewel up to Mehen. "It is, unfortunately, their choice."

Tharra hadn't been exaggerating. The next morning Dahl's stomach had settled, his head had stopped spinning, and he felt far less fatigued. But his skull felt as if someone had filled it with nails that flexed and pierced his brain as he moved.

You don't have time for a hangover, he thought. He shuffled out into the sunlight, nearly vomited from the sudden pain, and found Oota's two guards waiting for him.

"Better, Harper?" the half-orc grunted. Dahl cursed to himself: Tharra clearly had different opinions about the need for secrecy.

"Oota has questions for you," the human, Hamdir, said. "Come on."

The little courtyard was empty this time, and Oota was sitting on a makeshift camp stool, making it look like a chieftain's throne. She smiled when Dahl entered, and Dahl had to wonder what god's hand had touched her, as a chill went down his spine.

"I assume Tharra has told you what we're up against," Oota said. "What we are."

"More or less," Dahl said. "Though that poison you dumped down my throat didn't make things easier to make sense of. What do you want?"

Oota's dark eye shifted off Dahl, to the entrance. "Tharra and I," she said, "are on the same side. Let me make that absolutely clear. However, she and I have different ideas of how to *be* on the same side. How to run things. You understand?"

"Go on," Dahl said.

"Tharra thinks it's a death wish to take up arms against the wizard. She thinks we should bide our time until rescuers arrive. I say *that* is a death wish. There is no way into or out of this camp that the wizard doesn't make. He picks us off, one by one. Some day—soon—we'll have to take a stand, and the longer we wait for that day, the more people we lose."

"You have no weapons."

Oota smiled to herself. "We have *some* weapons. Some of us *are* weapons. Enough that if we had a clever strategist—someone who could even the odds from inside the fortress perhaps?—we could stand a chance. She says you stole a uniform."

"I'm not about to stroll in there and start cracking skulls. I'd be dead in heartbeats."

Oota's attention shifted back to him. "Son, I know what you think of me—but whatever my kin have shown you, people don't follow me because I'm a fool. I wouldn't send you in alone. And I wouldn't send you in without a plan. All I'm asking is if you have the means and the stones to do it."

"Doesn't Tharra know how to get in and out?"

"As a servant," Oota said. "They offer extra rations for those of us desperate or foolhardy enough to take on tasks. But every breath there's a guard on their back, and no one works down near the armory." She sat back. "You can certainly use that, if you find a way. But you're right, we need weapons. We need to deal with present threats first."

"What do you want me to do?"

"Word is," Oota said, "the wizard has a new pet. A tiefling witch who's making his life a lot easier."

Dahl held in every curse he knew. "Does he now?"

"He's picked up plenty of prisoners over the months, for the gods know what purpose. About thirty all told. But in two days she's picked out that many of my people—all folks we suspected of having the gods' good graces—and who knows how many of the rest. Tharra is out asking the longears for their count. Speck's chatting up the remnants who don't follow either of us."

Dahl nodded, as if he were considering the numbers, but all he could think was that Khochen had been right. His younger self had been right. He thought of the distant way Farideh had acted, the way she'd snapped at him before she teleported them to the fortress. There was no questioning it—Farideh was an enemy.

No questioning it, he thought, but some stubborn part of him still didn't believe it.

"This keeps up," Oota said, "the rest of us will be next."

"What do you want me to do?"

"I need someone to get into the parts of the fortress they won't let servants go to. Recover some weapons and deal with the tiefling. Cripple the wizard somehow."

"Just that?" Dahl said. "I'm guessing based on that wall and that castle that we aren't talking about some dabbler."

Oota shrugged. "Rumor is, he's not as powerful as he lets on. Maybe there's something in there that will make the difference. Tharra knows where the witch is—she can get to the tiefling, but as I said—"

"Oota." Dahl turned and saw Tharra standing in the doorway.

"Ah, my good friend," Oota said. "What do the longears say?"

"Sixteen. Speck's found eight more missing." Tharra nodded

at Dahl. "Did you tell him what's happening?"

Oota stood. "We were just discussing what comes next."

Tharra gave Dahl a dark look. "Well, good to see you're up. Can I talk to you a moment?"

Dahl followed Tharra out into the sunlight.

"She's asking you to help her attack the fortress, isn't she?" she asked. "Gods be *damned,* her mind runs like a mine cart."

"Infiltrate," Dahl said. "She makes some good points."

"Good points? Aye, well, here's the one Oota will never make: attacking the wizard will kill more people than it will ever save. Starting with you." She pointed up over the rooflines, at the fortress's tower rising up to vanish in the low clouds. "Six points to that tower. He has a full view and at least four novices who can cast better than any of us. He doesn't even have to come down to our level to destroy the entire camp. A few spells and we're all ash."

"Not when the clouds are this thick," Dahl said. Anyone on the tower's heights would be hard-pressed to see the ground. "You time it right, and—"

"You don't have to aim much with a meteor swarm. And if you're right and he doesn't bother? Then he sends out the shadar-kai. They'll mow through us like we were wheat stalks in a drought. Better to bide our time."

"You must have casters."

"He's seen to that. You met Armas? My fledgling? He was a sorcerer. Can't cast a thing, though, on account of the cages on his hands—every one of them is the same. They wake here, already hobbled, none of them the sort of wizard gifted enough to cast without hands. And if you think he's let a spellbook slip by, you're madder than a mouther. They come in here with nothing but their clothes."

No weapons, no casters, no resources to speak of. Except perhaps for Dahl's sword and stolen armor. And the Chosen that the wizard hadn't claimed. "I can get in. Dressed like a guard."

"And you'll die before you pass the gatehouse. The human

guards don't come out of the fortress," she said. "You're lucky none of the shadar-kai saw you. If you head back in, pretending like you belong, they're going to know something's funny when they don't know why you went out."

"Nobody?" Dahl asked. "You don't get soldiers fraternizing or—"

"You think a single one of these people are going to cross paths with a godsdamned Shadovar?" Tharra said. "They don't come out here. They send the grays—they want us to stay scared. You get in as a servant—*if* they'll take you—and you have a guard on you every single heartbeat. Think, would you? I know you're cleverer than this," she said gently, but Dahl bristled all the same.

"So what's your plan?" Dahl asked.

Tharra stared up at the fortress. "Stay alive."

"You can cling to every soul you find, but what's it matter if the wizard just kills them?"

"He doesn't kill them," Tharra started. Then her eyes fell on something behind Dahl and she cursed. Dahl looked back over his shoulder. A shadar-kai guard was heading up the alleyway, shouting at them in Netherese.

"Run," Tharra murmured. "Get back to Oota. Tell her they're sweeping—"

A second guard stepped around a hut, blocking their escape. "Let's go," he said, herding them both down to the wider road where a score of other villagers gathered. Dahl wished for his sword as the half-dozen guards drove them like wayward sheep toward the fortress.

Patience, he told himself. Even if he'd had his sword, striking in the dense crowd would have been too dangerous. He kept his eyes on Tharra instead—watching as she took careful stock of the faces around them.

Twelve at a time, they were herded through a narrow stone passage, jammed cheek by jowl together, before shuffling out into the open. Into a wide courtyard with a smooth, black stone floor. High walls. A platform above—high over his head—on which stood several more of the shadar-kai guards, looking down at the villagers as they filtered in, and a wizard in dark robes, talking to a pair of robed novices and a woman in dark leathers.

"But, saer—" one began.

"You will wait," the wizard interrupted, "until I am present. How many left?" he shouted down to the guard in the pit.

Dahl felt his lungs freeze: the wizard was Adolican Rhand.

"Two, master," the guard called back.

Dahl ducked behind Speck, Oota's big half-orc guard, hoping the wizard hadn't seen him—Rhand might remember him and he might not, but now was not the time to find out. *Hrast. Hrast.* How in all the Hells could Farideh be helping *him*?

She wouldn't, he realized, sure as he'd ever been. She couldn't. Which meant she *was* in trouble, that Dahl shouldn't have run. Which might mean she was *dead*—

Then he realized that the woman standing behind the novices *was* Farideh.

And she was staring straight at Dahl.

She'd traded whatever homespun clothes the Harpers had given her for snug black leathers and pinned her hair up between her horns with a jeweled comb. Gone was the grief-drawn young woman who'd haunted the Harper hall for the last half tenday—she looked like nothing so much as Rhand's pet, the shadar-kai's deadly ally.

Except she was staring at him.

He still wasn't sure he could read her expression—not with those focusless eyes—but there was no triumph in that stare, no anger, not anything he could place on an enemy.

"Well?" Rhand asked her.

Farideh shifted away from him as she turned to survey the crowd. Her gaze swept over them, her mouth tight, until she was looking at Dahl again.

Rhand reached over and set a hand on the small of her back. Farideh did not flinch, but a certain rigidness overtook her frame. The gesture might look comforting but it would also take the merest effort to shove her right over the edge. "What do you see?"

Farideh kept staring at Dahl. She bit her lip. "The short man with the green tunic. The halfling woman in the apron near the front. The moon elf at the back. The big fellow . . . the half-orc with the tattoos." As Farideh identified the prisoners, the guards in the pit came forward and took hold of them—gently but with horrible smiles. They led them out the smaller door, one by one, ending with Oota's struggling guard. Dahl took a step to the right, into the thick of the crowd.

Beside Dahl, Tharra cursed quietly.

Farideh hesitated, half a breath in her mouth, as if she were about to speak. "That's it," she finally said, turning back to Rhand. When she spoke next, her voice shifted, sharp and dissatisfied. "Now, I need rest. There's nothing in our agreement about being made to stand in the cold for hours."

Rhand gave her a slippery smile and reached his other arm around to guide her away from the edge. "Of course. Just once more."

Before Dahl could so much as consider what to do, a guard shoved him toward the larger gate, along with the rest of the villagers. They were crowded in so close, he felt like a beast headed into a slaughterhouse. And then abruptly the bodies in front of him broke free into the open, and the guards were laughing as their captives scattered back into the strange village.

"Piss and *hrast*!" Dahl cursed. He had to go back. Whatever was happening, Farideh was not on Rhand's side, he would drink a bucket of the wizard's finest to prove that. He had to get her out—where Rhand wouldn't be a factor.

But getting into the fortress would be nigh impossible, as Tharra said.

He spotted Tharra, hurrying south, away from the fortress and toward Oota's makeshift stronghold. Dahl sprinted after her.

"He has *Speck*?" Oota said as Dahl came in.

"More than Speck," Tharra said. "That witch picked perfectly. I don't know how she spotted those four. Speck came to me complaining of a headache yesterday, and Perdaena and Laencom have had their powers for months—too quiet for the grays to spot." She sighed, and spotting Dahl, beckoned him in. "The elf was a surprise, but even if she's not what's he's looking for, that's no better news. If Rhand's witch can hunt the Chosen among us without even coming near them, nothing we've managed so far will matter. You need to get people down into the buried rooms, before that witch—"

"She's not his witch," Dahl snapped. Tharra frowned at him. "Why did nobody tell me the wizard was Adolican Rhand?"

"Doubt anyone thought it would matter," Tharra said. "You know him?"

"After a fashion. He slipped my grasp before. Twice."

"And her?" Oota asked.

"She brought him in here," Tharra supplied. "Apparently *not* because he was pursuing her. Bit of the visions maybe we ought to reconsider."

Dahl scowled at the other Harper. "She wouldn't work with him, not willingly."

"Nobody was making her pick those people out of the crowd." Tharra shook her head. "She's seemed right at home in her fancy jewels these past few days."

Dahl dragged a hand through his hair. This was too many pieces all at once: Chosen and gods affecting the wars. And what was Adolican Rhand doing with those he gathered? What could Shade possibly do with a boy who trailed flowers? Tharra and Oota and the plain fact that whatever plans they had wouldn't make a damned bit of difference without a means of escape. And Farideh, wearing shadar-kai armor and standing beside Rhand. For all you know, he thought, she has dressed that way every day of the last seven and a half years.

But never at Adolican Rhand's side. If he could count on nothing else about Farideh, he could count on that.

Oota eyed him, patient as a hunting cat. "It sounds like we have a disagreement," she said. "How are we going to settle it?"

"I have to get in there," he said.

"You head in there," Tharra said, "and the grays will kill you and never care why you were there or how well you might know Rhand's pet tiefling."

"And it's no skin off your back if they do," he said. He turned to Oota. "You want a better idea of what's happening in that fortress? You're not going to know what she's doing or why unless someone she trusts asks her. Help me find a way in, and I'll get your answer. Maybe some weapons, too."

Oota cocked her head. "Can't do that, son." She smiled, and beside her Tharra folded her arms over her chest. "But I may know someone who can."

Some time later, Oota paused in front of a little shack, glancing around for errant guards before knocking five times on the wooden door. She looked back at Dahl. "This is as far as I'm sure I've still got them on my side."

"What else is there?" Dahl asked.

"The elves to begin with," she said. "Few packs of dwarves playing the odds. And the stragglers in between—don't want to throw in with the rest of us, just want to keep pretending everything's going to right itself one morning."

"Like Tharra?"

Oota looked at him out of the corner of her eye. "I didn't say that." She knocked again, harder.

The door opened and shut so quickly that the squat dwarf man who stepped out seemed to appear out of thin air. He scowled up at Oota, and ran a hand over his bristly black beard. "Did Tharra send you to pester me about that third level?" he asked. "I don't know if the ground—"

"Tharra doesn't send *me* anywhere. You know the dirt. Do

what needs doing. Let us in." Oota looked back at Dahl once more, as if to remind him to keep his mouth shut. The dwarf followed her gaze.

"That the Harper?"

"Let us in, Torden," Oota answered. "I need to talk to Phalar."

Torden snorted and threw the door open, ushering them down a rough-hewn stairway that led deep into the ground. The entire building had been filled with excavated dirt. Dahl thought of the other buildings, all shut up tight, and wondered how many had been similarly used.

Despite being built of pounded dirt and uneven, the stairs were blessedly stable. They ended in a level tunnel, where Torden lit a lantern that smelled of old cooking oil and handed it to Oota.

"The bastard's in a right mood today," he said. "Don't let him fool you—he's bored and he wants to get out." He looked at Dahl. "Best of luck."

"Many thanks," Dahl said, wondering privately at a dwarf guarding a hidey-hole in the territory of a half-orc chieftainess everyone seemed to listen to. Stranger and stranger.

Oota started off, leaving Dahl to follow past several doors. "This is where we hide the ones who've manifested. The ones we can catch before the guards do." She shook her head to herself. "It's not enough."

"You do what you can," Dahl said. "Someone down here can help us get into the fortress; that's a good start." He considered the doors they passed. "If you managed to dig this passage, why not dig under the wall?"

"That's what we were doing," Oota said. "The magic goes deep, deeper than we could manage without drawing too much notice. Torden keeps going, a little at a time. It's a lot of dirt to hide." The tunnel ended shortly after, in a makeshift door. Oota turned to face Dahl, sizing him up. "Son, I need you to promise that you won't panic."

Dahl frowned. "Why would I panic?"

Oota smirked, and by way of answer, unlatched the door. The lantern's light fought its way into the room beyond, illuminating a large cell and a slight man with ebony skin and moonlight hair, flinching away from the light.

"Put that *iblithl* light out, you one-eyed brute," he snarled, brandishing the book he'd been reading at Oota. "I thought we agreed to be civil."

Dahl only just stopped himself from shouting "Drow!" and drawing weapons. If one didn't take chances with shadar-kai, one certainly didn't ask for favors from the spider-worshiping elves of the Underdark, unless one wanted to be tortured and sacrificed. Still he took a step back.

Phalar placed a cupped hand over his pale eyes. "Tell me what you want, *cahalil,* and get out."

"Dahl," Oota said, "this is Phalar. Phalar, this is Dahl. He wants a favor."

Phalar chuckled to himself. "Does he?" He spread his fingers just wide enough to see through, making a mask of his hands. "Oh. You didn't tell him who I was, did you?"

"I hear you can get me into the fortress," Dahl said, making himself look at the drow. "That you've got some skill with breaking into places."

"You could say that," Phalar said. "In fact, in certain company that's *all* you should say." Dahl frowned.

"Dahl didn't come here like the rest of us," Oota said to Phalar. "He got pulled in by accident with Rhand's new associate." Dahl could hear the words Oota hadn't said buried in that comment. "If you get him into the fortress, he thinks he can stop the wizard. And maybe get us some weapons."

"That," Phalar said, "is the stupidest thing I've heard all day. And Tharra was here earlier, trying to convince me to help my jailor dig holes."

"All I need is someone to get me in," Dahl said stiffly. "The rest is my problem."

"Cocky, aren't you? What's in it for me?"

Dahl shrugged. "Escape?"

"*If* your plan succeeds. *If* you find your 'associate.' *If* the guards don't flay you alive." Phalar peered at Dahl through the mask of his fingers. "You almost certainly think I'm mad, but you still have to know the difference between mad and stupid." He dropped his hand, wincing at the light. "Give me your dagger."

"Give a drow a dagger, then follow him into a fortress under cover of night?" Dahl said. "I'm not stupid either."

Phalar's chuckle sent a shiver up Dahl's back. "Oh good. I assumed you were like the rest of them, thinking I'm tamed because I'm trapped here too. But it's the dagger or nothing. I don't have to help you. It's not as if I came to the surface to make friends. Give me the dagger when we part. Then all you have to do is stay out of my way."

Dahl glanced at Oota out of the corner of his eye. Giving the drow a weapon might upset the careful balance she had crafted. But Oota merely shrugged.

"Fine," Dahl said. "After."

Phalar smiled. "Aren't you going to ask me to promise I won't try to kill you?"

"Why should I?" Dahl asked coolly. "You said it yourself: you aren't stupid. You won't try."

"Be careful with Phalar," Oota said as they climbed the dirt stair once more, a secretive smile playing on her mouth. "He tends to make people act a little"—she blew out a breath—"rash."

"I'm not afraid of him," Dahl said too quickly. Oota glanced back at him. "I mean," he amended, "I can keep my head."

"You have to be a *little* afraid, or he acts up. But he's no fool—whatever he'd like to do to the lot of us, he's outnumbered in the end, and he needs what people will trade him for the use of his powers. He's only alive because of my good graces and Tharra's silver tongue. He can't afford to go around stabbing people and he knows it."

"Why else would he want a dagger?"

Oota stopped walking. "You're trapped in enemy territory full of people you don't think much of, who are always arguing about whether they ought to just kill you and be done with it? You'd want a dagger too." They slipped out the door and waited while Torden latched it behind them. "All the same, you get Torden a good crossbow when you find that armory. He'll bury Phalar if he decides to prove me wrong with that dagger and then the whole tunnel will end up collapsed. *Everybody* would rather Torden just shot him in that case."

All through evenfeast, Rhand was agitated, matching bouts of excitable conversation with as many sulking lulls as he watched the entrance to the dining hall. Farideh ate mechanically, answering his questions with whatever entered her head, spouting opinions that weren't hers—it didn't matter. She didn't matter. To Rhand the only important thing was when his guest arrived.

And the only important thing to Farideh was the knowledge that Dahl had not managed to escape. She still had no idea what she was tangled in—the people who stood before her in the courtyard might be prisoners, might be displaced, might even be Sairché's "common enemy." She might have landed in the midst of worse evils with both feet. She didn't know. She couldn't.

But it was clear to her this was nowhere she wanted Dahl to be.

Rhand's assistant appeared in the entry, white-faced, and before he could say a word, Rhand bid her good evening, and servants appeared to clear the table, taking little notice of Farideh. Rhand stopped in his rush and looked back at her.

"By the way, Nirka tells me you have been enjoying the castle grounds," he said. "Should you be interested in a walk tonight, I'd suggest you forgo it."

"Why is that?"

He gave her a wicked smile. "To begin, she will be locking your door. For safety. Our guest can be particular." Without further explanation, he swept from the room.

His guest can be Asmodeus himself, Farideh thought, *and it would not stop me. Not now.* She had to save Dahl. She had to find out what she was doing here.

"Leave Tharra outside, would you?" she said as Nirka loomed over her. "I'm tired, and I'd rather go to bed than wait on you and her. I can get myself out of my armor."

Nirka narrowed her eyes. "I will have to go and tell her to leave."

"Then do that," Farideh said. "I shall be in my room. Dealing Wroth cards."

She climbed the stairs, feeling Nirka's suspicious gaze on her the entire time. But the shadar-kai said not another word until they reached her room.

"Whatever you're thinking," she started.

"Good night, Nirka," Farideh said sharply, and she shut the door. A moment later, the latch *clanked* violently, as if Nirka could somehow wound Farideh with the key in the lock.

Farideh waited, but didn't hear the guard's footsteps leave. She took the cards up and flipped them loudly, one after the other—*snap, snap, snap.* Shuffled. Dealt. Beyond the door, she heard Nirka curse and storm off, and Farideh sighed in relief. She looked down at the haphazard pile of cards—the top one was flipped, facedown. She turned it and found a faintly scorched painting of a devil, horned and winged and hoofed, chasing a green-and-gold angel in a circle. *The Adversary.* Farideh fought back a shiver.

The second ruby comb still sat under the mattress where she'd hidden it, still buzzing with the magic from the ghost's strange ritual. She hadn't touched it—and she was trying hard not to wonder if the ghost was still watching her, unseen.

Farideh pulled her haversack from the wardrobe, still heavy with the ritual book Rhand had left her, but her thoughts were on the comb, the itch of its waiting spell like a plea—*Pick me up. Bring her back.*

Farideh hesitated a moment, before pulling it from its hiding place and stuffing it into the sack. She'd decide for herself what to do with it once she knew what she was up against.

Then she took another deep breath and went to the window. She pulled herself up to kneel on the ledge, leaning out as far as she dared. The night was cold, and though the wind had died down, it was enough to make her glad Tharra had plaited her hair. She could not miss.

Across the way, another of the fortress's starlike points loomed. Two floors down, one window waited, not quite covered by its heavy curtains and leaking faint candlelight. The stairwell. Farideh pulled herself up to stand on the window ledge.

It was, perhaps, thirty feet away. Or perhaps fifty, perhaps a hundred. In the dark of night she couldn't be sure. She held in her mind the way it had looked when she'd considered it several days before—close enough, she thought, to make this work if you just *do* it. She found her balance, held her breath. There wasn't much a body rebelled against like this, and in the space between panicked thoughts, Farideh leaped, into the empty air.

And started to fall.

But in that heartbeat, she pulled hard on the powers of the Hells. The fabric of the world split and swallowed Farideh, spitting her back out into the air much farther on. Still not to the opposite point, and as soon as the gape closed, she was falling again.

I'm going to die—but the thought had no more formed, before she caught hold of the ledge, two floors below where she'd started, knocking the wind out of her. Farideh clung to the stonework, lungs screaming as she caught her breath, and hauled herself into the tower again.

She leaned against the wall—it had worked. She wasn't

dead. It wasn't a hundred feet. Farideh pressed her hands to her face to smother the giddy laughter that shook her bruised ribs. For the first time in ages, she felt a little like her old self.

Composing herself, she looked up the dim stairwell, illuminated by the light of a few unclaimed candles, and hoped that the escape from her room would not turn out to have been the easy part.

Up, first—Farideh crept toward Rhand's study, her nerves sending Hells magic through her and blurring the edges of her frame with shadowy smoke. At the top she peered in both directions, and saw no sign of guards. Odd, she thought, and she waited a few moments more, in case they were merely out of sight and quiet. Nothing.

She thought of Rhand's warnings about his guest, and shoved that fear aside as she made for the study.

The door was open and she found the room beyond empty. A faint light emanated from the magic limning the vessels and from a crystal hanging overhead, and the brazier glowed with hot coals. Rhand's open spellbook and ritual book sent a shiver through the space, pulsing with magic. Farideh slipped inside.

The heat from the brazier had no effect on the air over the vessels, and through the cloud of her breath, she watched the waters ripple. With no wizards to watch her, she might be able to find the way out.

Farideh scattered a pinch of the dried petals across the water's surface, the way Rhand had. Specific, she thought, but vague. "Show me the last time someone found a weakness in the wall around this camp."

The waters did not change. It hadn't happened.

"Show me the last time someone came *close* to escaping the camp alive."

The waters remained, stirring gently.

Farideh leaned farther over the waters, tension closing around her breath. She'd asked scores of questions in the days before and seen all manner of visions in return. But the

Fountains of Memory had nothing to say about escaping the camp. No one had managed. Rhand hadn't lied.

She'd been sure he had. There was something odd about the way he'd responded. Something that reminded her too much of Lorcan—that half moment where he decided to tell her the truth turned sideways.

Her heart buckled at the memory. Without thinking, she threw another pinch of petals into the waters. "Show me what happened to Lorcan when I made the deal with Sairché."

There was Sairché, there was Farideh. There was the agreement, turning the room inside-out. The waters shivered and showed the Hells—and Sairché was right, there was no mistaking anything on Toril for such a place. The ground itself seemed to quiver, as if it were alive and hurting. There was a cave—a hollow of bone sunk deep into that evil ground and filled with writhing, shadowy forms. A cage formed of what looked like insect legs, thick and thorny, the spaces between crackling with lightning, and at its center, herself and Havilar. Sairché and Lorcan watched.

"What did you tell her?" Lorcan asked Sairché.

"What goes on between a girl and her patroness is private," Sairché said. "Isn't that right?" Farideh's chest tightened, and she wished perversely she could be there, that she could tell him the truth.

The lightning of the cage snapped, popped, leaped outward to spark against the sides of the bowl. The center of the waters dropped nearly to the bottom of the basin, as if a drain had opened below. A sickly light shone from the whirlpool and the smell of brimstone wafted off the waters. Farideh stepped back.

A portal, just as Rhand had said—to the Hells, but when? If she reached in, could she save Lorcan? Or only trap herself a second time? The magic holding the waters sparked and crackled as the light built. Farideh reached toward it, feeling the pressure of the air change as she approached the portal's edge.

The light surged and collapsed into itself like a dropped cloak. The portal was gone.

In the waters' reflection, Sairché held up the ruby necklace she'd given Farideh. A greenish light—the color of a rotting limb—began to build around it. Lorcan stepped back, but caught in the protection spell, he could only go so far. The light flashed and the vision ended.

Farideh swallowed against the sudden lump in her throat and drew her hand back. The portal might not have worked, she reminded herself. It might have only made things worse.

And you wouldn't be able to save Dahl, either way. She rubbed her hand. It had been stupid to even try. Lorcan was safe—Sairché had promised that much. Dahl wasn't.

The water smoothed out again, waiting for the next request. Farideh chewed her lip, trying to puzzle out the right words, then scattered another pinch of the petals across the surface.

"Show me the conversation where Rhand denied anyone had escaped this place."

Again the water swirled, and again the waters reflected the wizard and herself beside him, looking out over the camp below. She asked the question, her expression far more closed than it had felt. And there again, the flicker of annoyance across Rhand's face before he spoke.

If there were nothing to find there, Rhand would have been smug, triumphant. Something hidden in her question irritated him. Reminded him of something he'd rather forget.

But what? Farideh turned from the waters, considering the lecterns, the tables spread with maps of Faerûn and scrolls, the shuttered windows. She crossed to the open shelves of spell components and pulled her torn and bloodstained shirt from her pack, laying small bottles in the open cloth. If she didn't know how to escape, she couldn't guess what might be useful—or what might be missed. She chose things she recognized and hoped for the best.

Swiftly, she turned to the rack of scrolls—spells that could be cast regardless of the reader's skill—and pulled down several, eyeing the runes, the detailed diagrams. The remains of the destroyed ancient library. There was a spell to call the clouds down low. A spell to open caverns in the ground. A spell to turn a river to ice. There were half a dozen altogether, smudged and scorched but bristling with magic—not a one useful against an army of shadar-kai.

The sound of Rhand's voice carrying from the staircase broke her reverie. Farideh shoved the scrolls back into place and bolted for the door, but his voice came again, too close: "The Lady of Loss should not be disappointed. More now than ever."

Farideh turned and sprinted for the far corner of the room, behind a table covered with parchment and instruments, into a wardrobe hung with heavy leather aprons and stained robes. Farideh pulled the doors as close to shut as she could, before crouching low, out of the sight line of Rhand and the young girl he followed into the room.

CHAPTER THIRTEEN

23 Ches, the Year of the Nether Mountain Scrolls (1486 DR)
The Lost Peaks

FARIDEH NEARLY LEAPED FROM HER HIDING SPACE AT THE sight of the girl—she could not have been more than thirteen. She was slight as a willow switch with dark hair unbound to the middle of her back. Her skin had a dark, grayish cast, though, and her eyes were faintly luminous. Rhand watched her back as she walked calmly into the study, his expression sending a curl of terror through Farideh.

She knew that look. She knew what was going to happen.

"This . . ." Rhand stopped and cleared his throat. "Ah. This is where we bring the waters for further use." Rhand stopped before the table blocked Farideh's view of him, looking drawn and beaded with sweat. "My lady," he added.

Jump out, Farideh thought. Grab the girl. You can cast without the rod, well enough to get out the door . . .

Then what? Run and find Dahl? Run and hit the barrier? Somehow kill every guard in this place and wait for someone who could break her out?

She couldn't just watch, that much was certain.

What else are you going to do? a little voice in her thoughts seemed to say. *You're trapped and so is she. There's nothing you can do.*

Fatigue settled on Farideh, and though her nerves were drawn, ready to whip her to her feet and out the door, all her muscles drooped. She sat back and heaved a breath as softly as she could to shake the feeling. It didn't work.

"So you look into the past," the girl said, unconcerned with Rhand looming over her, "holding tight to what was."

"Not at all, my lady," Rhand said. "It's a tool. The waters will show the point at which a potential—" He cleared his throat again, hard. "When one of the possible . . . ah . . ."

She turned and gave him a beatific smile. "You dislike the term."

"I think it overstates what we are dealing with," Rhand said irritably. "In most cases."

"But not all."

Rhand gritted his teeth a moment, before continuing. "If you ask the waters when a likely person's patron took notice of them, it separates those with such blessings from imposters. Would you like to try, my lady?"

They will catch you, the little voice in Farideh's thoughts went on. *You might as well come out.* The hanging robes felt as if they'd smother her. Her own armor might smother her. She dug her hands into her hair, the pain sent a shock of sense through her.

Focus, she told herself. That girl will be dead if you can't focus.

" 'Patron,' " the girl said. "That seems like it will give you many unwanted answers. Lords. Benefactors. Weak entities with ideas above their station. Plenty of things the Church of Shar is not remotely interested in. Why not say 'god'?"

"It would reject too many," Rhand said patiently. "There is no way to know where the waters draw the line. If an exarch has reached out, must we say 'exarch' or 'god' or 'demigod'? 'Saint' or 'devil' or else? 'Patron' covers all options—any who might bestow the powers under any guise. If it gathers a few artisans with nothing to mark them, that is a minor difficulty,

I assure you. My lady."

"Is it?" the girl said. "There are those who would say it's a drain on the princes' coffers. A waste of Shar's clemency."

Rhand looked at the girl, as if he were fighting once more with something dark and powerful inside himself. "And have you listened to them, my dear?"

"I haven't decided yet," she said, and through the confusing swirl of panic and despair, Farideh dimly thought it was the first time she'd actually sounded like a young girl. The girl prodded the edge of the magical field surrounding the basin, making it spark. "It does seem awfully involved. And expensive."

"As I mentioned," Rhand said. "My system is improved. I have someone capable of spotting them before they know they aren't merely captives, finding even the most minor ones hiding among the fold, before they are ready to claim."

You, Farideh thought. He means you. And when he's done with her, you'll be next. Go—grab her. Run. She imagined Nirka and her knives coming after Farideh. The blades slicing into her skin. It would drive away this awful, smothering feeling. Cut the heavy layer of skin off, that would do it—

Farideh bit down hard on her tongue, disrupting her runaway thoughts. What was happening?

"And what 'patron' bestowed *that* blessing?" the girl said, disinterested. She crossed the room, toward Rhand. Toward the door. "Who chose her?"

Farideh had to get out. She had to get away. It felt too much like that revel in Waterdeep, with the pull of Rhand's poison dragging her down. But if she so much as moved, Rhand would find her. She concentrated on the sound of her breath, hissing in and out of her nostrils.

"I have an agreement with someone from the Nine Hells."

"An agreement?" the girl said. "If you're venerating someone other than the Lady—"

"Your pardon, but nothing could be further from the truth.

The devils have their purpose, but godhood is not one of them. What happens to her patron is irrelevant. All will aid Shar in the end, by their assistance or by their destruction."

The girl looked back at Rhand, her expression peaceful. Farideh leaned forward enough to see Rhand, paler still with a wildness to his eyes and his breath coming hard, as the girl stood just within reach. The silence stretched out. Farideh held her breath.

"Nothing is everything," the girl pronounced. "Shall we see what you *have* managed?"

Rhand drew a single, shuddering breath. "This way, my lady."

You have to move, Farideh told herself. You have to save that girl. But she felt as if her bones had turned to stone, and it took an eternity before she could haul herself up. Rhand and the girl were long gone.

You have to find them, she told herself, even while a little voice seemed to murmur, *Why? So you can fail her too?* Even once she'd left the study, the feeling that she didn't quite have the strength in her to continue in her own body persisted.

A good thing the guards are gone, she thought, pausing on a landing to catch the cold air on her face. She needed a weapon, she needed to find Rhand, she needed to stop him. The armory—she all but tumbled down the stairs, all traces of stealth long gone.

What was she doing? she thought. She couldn't manage this—even if she could save the girl from Rhand, there was nowhere to run. If Dahl couldn't save himself, then maybe he was doomed too.

You'll never get out of here, the same little voice said, as she made her way down to the lowest level. No longer sure of her plans, no longer sure of anything except that if she didn't follow through, she didn't know what to do next. Get a weapon. Get the girl. Get out.

You'll never manage. You can't save her anymore than you could save Havilar. If you try you'll only make things worse.

She pressed a hand to her head. What was the matter with her?

By the time she found the armory, she felt as if she was drowning. Nirka's strange words popped into her head—*He knows what it is to fight the Shadowfell.* The home plane of the shadar-kai, the path—they said—to the world of the dead. The shadar-kai feared fading away into it, their essence drawn away into the shadows of the plane. Was that what this was? Was that what was happening to her?

In the armory, she stood amid the wicked-looking weapons, unable to hold her thoughts together, unable to decide what to do next.

The air shivered, and when the tiefling woman's ghost appeared again, Farideh nearly wept in relief. She tore the comb from her haversack, not caring if it doomed her or damned the whole fortress. She slid it into her hair, the teeth scraping her scalp.

I'm glad you changed your mind, the ghost said. She didn't move her lips, but her voice rang in Farideh's thoughts as clearly as if the dead woman had spoken. *And not a moment too soon.*

"What is this?" she asked. "What's happening?"

You've been poisoned, the ghost observed. She made a sound, as if she were clucking her tongue, but again, her mouth did not move.

"I didn't eat anything," Farideh said. "Tell me what to do?"

It's a poisoning of the mind. The ghost's face peeled back to muscle and bone, the globe of one silvery eye laid bare in its socket. *It will take a blade and a stern stomach. An act to shock the thoughts out of you.*

Farideh shuddered. Of course—that was how the shadar-kai fought off the Shadowfell, wasn't it? They would tear each other apart and make it stop. She made her way to a rack of short, cruel-looking knives, and picked up one with a scarlet handle. Sharp enough to part flesh easily. Broad enough to cause a lot of pain. She imagined how it would feel, plunging into someone's back.

She shuddered again, so hard she nearly dropped the blade. Even if she found a guard . . .

It won't end on its own, the ghost chided. *You have to take action. A little suffering now, greater rewards later.*

Farideh took a firmer grip on the knife. Perhaps she could use it on Rhand . . . and then Sairché would say she hadn't kept her deal, and Havilar was as doomed as the rest of them. Besides, she couldn't go after Rhand with her head spinning like this. *It will take a knife. An act to shock the thoughts out of you.*

Farideh squeezed the knife's hilt hard enough to make her palm ache, and steeled herself for what she had to do.

Once the sun had set and the moon was low, Dahl—dressed once more in his stolen uniform—met the drow near the fortress's postern gate, near where Dahl had made his initial escape. The walls swarmed with guards.

It's impossible, Dahl thought. They're waiting for exactly this. But at the same time, his pulse started drumming with excitement, and he found himself sizing up the wall, the guards, the entrance. There were ways to do this, if you were bold enough to seize what you deserved.

Phalar chuckled under his breath. "Oh good. You're ready."

Dahl blinked, suddenly aware of how out of place those thoughts were. Oota's warning came back to him.

"Stay close," Phalar said, and he walked toward the wall, toward the spot where the shadows clung close. As Dahl sprinted after him, a ball of darkness formed around Phalar, so complete the drow seemed to disappear.

Clinging tight to that sense of boldness, Dahl stepped into the dark as well, one hand shooting out to catch the drow's shoulder, trying to keep track of how many steps they'd taken, before the drow crashed them both into the stone wall.

A clammy sensation rushed over Dahl as he counted too

many steps. Phalar stopped, then pushed him backward—into the other side of stone wall. The darkness dissipated. They stood at the edge of the courtyard, alongside the large stable Dahl had noticed earlier and behind a disused smithy. The veserabs inside stirred with a sound like leather cloaks slapping in the wind.

Phalar smirked. "There you are. Blessed be . . . Let us say you owe someone a very quiet favor."

"I owe *you* a dagger," Dahl said. "Your god can keep his blessings." He scanned the courtyard—there were a handful of shadar-kai at the door, and more still dicing in the courtyard. "Which wall do we hit next?"

"We don't," Phalar said. "I'm not a ghost. I need a chance to recover."

Dahl turned to him. "So what are you planning?"

"Oh calm down, *cahalil*. I've done this scores of times—do you think I leave a body behind every time?" A deep booming sound echoed off the crater's ridge. Phalar peered around the edge of the shack. "Ah! There's what we're waiting for."

Through the low clouds, a great dark shape descended into the courtyard—a long, deep box big as a barque, dangling from a half a dozen cables. The booming came again as the carrier landed, and six enormous, shadow-winged drakes swooped low.

Phalar turned and scaled the wall of the building beside them where it met the curtain wall, finding footholds in the rippling stone. Dahl followed, saying a quiet prayer to Selûne that she kept herself hidden behind the thick clouds.

No cry of alarm followed, and Dahl shortly hauled himself up onto the low roof. Phalar had not waited, but stretched out on his belly and crept along the slates toward the tower. Crouched, Dahl hurried to catch up to Phalar, where he'd slowed beside some damaged tiles.

"Does that come every night?" he panted.

"It came tonight," Phalar said. "It's come on other nights."

"What do you do when it doesn't come?"

Down below, the drakes squalled and boomed, and the shadar-kai and humans holding on to their lines struggled and shouted at each other. The clouds split, revealing Selûne in all her glory. Phalar cursed and flinched back, away from the edge of the roof, away from Dahl.

"Make the darkness," Dahl hissed. "Hide us!"

"I have a better idea," Phalar said. And he kicked Dahl into the patch of damaged tiles.

The tiles fell in, and so did Dahl, slipping between the broken beams of the roof to land roughly on a loft piled with detritus and old hay. He'd hardly gotten his breath back, but the veserab's flexing mouth appeared beside his head, as likely trying to take a bite of the intruder as goading him into riding. There were two of them now, thrashing and fighting the lines that held their harnesses in agitation.

Dahl rolled to his feet—all too aware of the shouts outside, the nearing voices. He climbed down from the loft, cursing Phalar and skirting the veserab's wild wings. There were two doors, he noted, one on the side where the carrier had landed, one on the farther wall.

Two shadar-kai men came into the stable, weapons out, muttering to each other in Netherese. Dahl ducked behind a bale of hay, landing in a pile of the veserabs' stinking shadowstuff castings. He watched the shadar-kai split up, edging around the stable. Looking for the intruder.

Oghma don't forsake me, Dahl said to himself. He eased from his hiding place enough to gauge the distance, and when the shadar-kai were as far behind the fitful veserabs as they could be, he leaped out. He pulled loose the tethers holding down the veserabs one by one as he ran for the door.

Behind him the shadar-kai shouted, and Dahl dared to glance back. One veserab threw itself at the nearer guard, battering him to the ground. The other disentangled itself quickly from the ropes and threw itself at the other door, knocking it wide.

Dahl didn't wait to see what happened next. He ran through the opposite courtyard, wondering what in the world had possessed him to do something so mad. As he reached the shadows of the fortress wall, hands seized him and pulled him into the darkness.

"See?" Phalar said. "A much better idea."

Dahl tried to shove the drow back, but Phalar was quick and the darkness, complete. "You nearly killed me."

"Yes," Phalar said. "Because I *like* you, *cahalil*." Dahl felt the drow clap him on the arm, and the darkness evaporated. "So you get to be 'nearly' dead." He chuckled again. "Come along."

They skirted the fortress wall, before slipping in through a trapdoor that led to the cistern.

"There you are," Phalar said. "Swim through and you'll come out in the fortress."

"You really think I'm an idiot."

"It's rainwater," Phalar said. He pulled a pair of skins from his pack. "No one *wants* to drink the tainted stuff." He held out a hand. "My dagger?"

"You're supposed to get me into the fortress," Dahl said.

"I don't *go* into the fortress," Phalar told him, filling the first skin. "All the stores I steal from are in the outbuildings—where I can get out quickly. A drow in the fortress would be a little suspect, don't you think?"

"So how do I know this doesn't end with me drowning in some underground river?"

"You don't," Phalar allowed. He gave Dahl a wicked smile. "I *could* snatch that blade, cut your throat, and leave you here for some jack to find the next time the wizard gets thirsty."

Dahl was sure Phalar wasn't lying—the drow likely had plenty of practice cutting throats in the darkness. But he was also sure that he wasn't the easy target Phalar expected—especially with the drow god stirring up his adrenalin, urging him to keep the dagger, or maybe leave it buried in Phalar's gut.

"You could," he said evenly, pushing down that alien

brashness for all he was worth. "But then your chances of getting out of here get a little slimmer. I can't imagine you like being caged up, put to work for a stlarning half-orc. But maybe you're more of a *cahalil* than you think."

Phalar smirked. "Well. You're no fun."

Dahl waded into the water, up to his waist. The water moved from the small pond he stood in through a narrow passageway. He could see lights beyond, filtered through the cold, dark water. He swam right up to the passage, turned and threw the dagger to Phalar, before ducking under and swimming to the other side.

The cistern room within the fortress was empty, thank the gods. Dahl squeezed as much water as he could from his cloak and shirt, and poured out his boots before donning them once more, half-hoping that the drow would swim up from the cistern and attack him after all—

Dahl shook the urge off and said a little prayer to Oghma as he slipped down the hallway, looking for the armory once more. Much as he'd like to pretend Phalar's powers were nothing notable, the force still thrumming through him called his bluff. Even with Phalar far behind him. How long was this going to last?

Dahl found the armory and slipped inside. He considered the array of weaponry. Blades, arrows, whips, chains—how much would fit in the sack?

How much can you take before they notice? he thought, looking for a new dagger. He was certainly cleverer than some shadow-kissing mercenaries. Dahl stopped to collect himself—he knew better. He'd worked hard not to be the sort of man that took everything as a challenge. After all, look where that had gotten him.

You'll be fine in a bit, he told himself. Just don't make any decisions you can't undo and keep your steel sheathed. Find a dry uniform, stay calm—

As unexpectedly as she'd appeared in the taproom, Farideh

stood in front of him, holding a dagger. She looked up at him lazily. Unconcerned.

Dahl hadn't planned this far ahead, what to do or say when he found her, and all the options he'd considered crowded up into his thoughts. For once, Phalar's damned god had a use.

She'll cut you down if you don't take her first, the voice in his thoughts murmured. Dahl reached for his sword, his sureness bolstered by Phalar's powers. Good, he thought. He wouldn't be able to do this without it.

"Drop the blade," he said.

Farideh blinked at him, as if she didn't quite believe he was there. "Dahl?"

"Drop," he said again, "the blade."

She looked down at the knife, as if she weren't sure where it had come from. The dagger fell out of her hands and she threw her arms around him in a way he was very much unprepared for. "You're all right. Oh gods."

He froze and let go of the sword. Not even Phalar's god had an answer for this.

"You're all right," she said again. "I didn't know which was the safe one. I was sure . . ." She exhaled again, as if it were taking all of her effort to talk.

For a moment, he was entirely too aware of her—the curve of her breasts, the strength of her arms, the faint wind of her exhalation, damp with tears on the edge of his collar. She was tall enough to rest her chin on his shoulder, and he noticed this, too, without meaning to.

"What are you doing here?" he said.

She pushed back from him, looking . . . tired? Dazed? Embarrassed? Gods, he was still so bad with tiefling eyes. "I don't know. Something happened. Everything's going wrong. I was coming to save you . . . but I have to save the girl first, before . . ." She inhaled as if she'd forgotten she ought to be doing that. "But I can hardly keep my thoughts . . . ."

"What girl?"

"With Rhand," Farideh said. "She's so young. But then she's so strange too. Like a shadow? Like a nightmare? But he's the nightmare."

She was squeezing his arms, her hands over the sharp buckles of the bracers, and she was swaying on her feet. "What's wrong with you?" he asked.

She met his eyes, and the shade of them shifted, darkened. He wondered if she was trying to focus on his face. "I think I was poisoned."

Horror poured through Dahl. "What did he give you?"

"Not like that," she said. "He calls her 'my lady' like he doesn't want to. The Nameless One."

Dahl steadied her. "Gods damn it, *concentrate*. What happened?"

"I looked in the waters," she said. "The Fountains of Memory. There's no way out, we're trapped. And then I hid in the cabinet. There was Rhand and the girl, the nameless girl. There's something . . . he seemed ill too—like he was falling apart and couldn't stop it. Like he hated her and was afraid of her. And . . ." She swallowed. "And now I can't bear it. It's like I'm smothering in my own skin. I thought I could drive it out with the knife. But I'm not brave."

"You tried to fight an arcanist's mummy alone, last I recall. You're brave enough," he said, his mind racing. "This started in the study? Had you seen that girl before?"

She shook her head. "She came today, from Shade. To see about Rhand's works."

Dahl cursed again. A girl that Rhand feared and deferred to must be something terrible indeed. If Phalar's god could fill Dahl with reckless nerve, then someone blessed by the Lady of Loss might fill a soul with melancholy and numbness. He thought of his darkest days, the feeling of despair settling down on him, heavy enough to stop his breath. If a body were swallowed up by that feeling, without a source, without an outlet . . .

That body would look for a cure, he thought. Something to

shock it out of them. Like a knife through the palm.

"I have to save her," Farideh said, tears welling in her eyes. "And I can't save her. Not like this. I can't save anybody."

"You shouldn't save her," Dahl said, trying to think of a solution. "She's a bigger problem than Rhand."

Farideh stared at him a moment, horrified. "She's just a girl."

"Would he be scared of a girl?" Dahl demanded. "She's got powers over him. You need to stay far away from her. Let Rhand handle her."

"I'm not leaving her to be *handled*—or worse—by that monster."

Dahl's mind turned to the mutilated apprentice, and he pushed it aside. "He wouldn't dare do anything of the sort," Dahl said. "Not this time. Not if I'm right."

Farideh drew back from him, rigid with fury. "Right," she snapped. "Just like he wouldn't have done anything of the sort at that revel."

Dahl felt himself color. "Gods' books," he spat. "Truly? Now?"

"You could say I'm reminded. Clearly it's *well* out of your mind."

"Do you think I don't regret that?" he demanded. "It's plagued me for years, that mistake. When I found out you were dead, I was convinced it had been Rhand's hand that did it and my fault that it was you. But you're *not* dead, and I've apologized, and this is not the same situation, gods damn it!"

"You most certainly did not apologize," Farideh said. "You said I wasn't allowed to blame you—which is not a *karshoji* apology."

"Fine!" Dahl shouted. "I'm sorry. Did you really think I wasn't? It's probably the worst thing I've ever done to someone— of course I'm sorry. How could I not be?"

"You're unbelievable. How is it you can turn an apology into an insult about what an idiot I am?"

"I didn't say you were an idiot."

"You didn't have to," she said. "Because I'm *not*."

Dahl bristled, churning with Phalar's recklessness. "Yes. Terribly wise getting us dragged off to a Netherese prison camp. Perhaps *you* ought to be the loremaster."

"You don't even know what—oh." Farideh gave a little laugh. "It *doesn't* take a knife." She giggled again, covering her mouth as if to stem the mad laughter.

"Oh gods," Dahl said. "Is this a fit?"

"I'm not having a fit. I'm fine. It's passed. Whatever it was, apparently it doesn't go well with being really *karshoji* angry." She smiled. "So thank you for being unpleasant."

Dahl sighed, still on edge and annoyed and ready to argue. But at least he'd fixed it. Sort of. That was something. "You're welcome. And I am sorry."

"I forgive you," Farideh said, still fighting back giggles. "Gods, sorry—the difference is really nice." She frowned at him. "Why are you all wet?"

"This girl," Dahl said, trying to steer her back to the matter at hand, "you didn't feel strange until she was there, right? And Rhand didn't look well?"

"He looked like he was about to fall down."

"But you were fine before," Dahl asked, "when you were alone with Rhand? She's got to be the source."

"She's just a girl," Farideh protested.

And a girl could channel the powers of the gods as easily as a half-orc or a Rashemi woman or a Turmishan boy who trails flowers. "She's probably one of them," he said. "Are you likely to run into her again?"

"I have no idea," Farideh said. "I keep thinking I've figured out what's happening, and then it all changes." She told him what she'd overheard, what Rhand had shared with her and what she thought she'd missed, and about the waters pulled from the Fountains of Memory. "I don't know what he's doing exactly," she admitted, "but it's important. And complicated."

"You *don't* know," Dahl said, overwhelmingly glad that he'd been right. She wasn't a sympathizer. She wasn't a traitor.

Farideh scowled at him. "I'm trying, but he keeps me out—"

"That isn't what I mean," Dahl said. He narrowed his eyes at her. "Why are you helping him?"

Her expression shifted—was that sadness or annoyance or confusion? "I made a deal with a devil," she said finally, and he decided it was something in the middle of all three. "Seems Rhand made a deal with the same devil, and that's my payment. If I don't help, she gets my soul. Worse, if I don't help, she'll go after Havilar. A very stupid thing to do," she added swiftly. "I know that."

Dahl sighed. "I'm not going to tell you it was wise. But we are both in this now, however it happened, and it might be for the best. I don't know when—or if—we would have found this place otherwise. And then it might have been too late."

"Too late for what?"

Dahl frowned at her. "You really don't have any idea what he's doing."

"Will you just tell me?"

"These people are Chosen of the gods," Dahl said.

"Like in chapbooks?"

"Somewhat." He told her about Oota and Phalar and Torden, about Samayan and the trail of daisies. About the strange things Tharra had told him. Her look of shock was unmistakable.

"So you think the Nameless One is a Chosen of Shar?"

"Fits, doesn't it?"

She turned from him. "So what does Rhand do with them?"

"No one seems to know," Dahl said. "They disappear. But no one's finding bodies."

"But knowing Rhand, it's nothing good." Farideh hugged her arms to herself. "And I'm helping him do it. *Karshoj.*"

"What *are* you doing?"

She shook her head. "Something happened in the Hells, I think. I can make myself see things. He says they're people's souls. I don't know. I tell him which ones look different. Which ones are tied to the gods, I suppose, if they're Chosen."

He hadn't been expecting that. "Did you look at mine?"

"Only for a moment." She gave him a sideways look. "It's—"

He flushed, unexpectedly embarrassed. "Don't. Please, don't."

She regarded the blade lying on the floor. "Sorry. I won't. Not anymore."

Dahl considered her. "He needs you to tell him which people are and which aren't. So if you lied . . ."

She pursed her mouth. "He can't tell if I'm telling the truth. Not until later on, after he does whatever he does. Makes their powers come out, I suppose. So I'll just start telling him there's no Chosen in each group. Send everyone back out into the camp, until we can figure something out. I've looked at a hundred people easily," she said. "Maybe I found all the Chosen already? He said he gets a lot of ordinary people. It could be that they're all ordinary."

"A *hundred*?" Dahl said. "No, that's too many. He'll notice if you suddenly can't see anything."

"What choice do I have?" Farideh demanded.

"We'll think of something else," Dahl said. "Don't make him angry." An awkward silence passed. "He hasn't hurt you has he?"

"No. It's odd. He's being so polite. I'd started to wonder if I had remembered wrong. If maybe everything from before was in my head."

A hand, an eye, a foot at the ankle—Dahl shuddered. "It wasn't. In fact, I'd really rather you came back out of here with me. Safer."

"That's going to make him just as angry. And then we're still trapped behind the wall," she said. She turned, searching the racks of weapons. "I haven't found a way around that either. I asked the waters, no one's even come close to escaping or damaging the wall." She hesitated. "But the waters, they make portals too." Farideh pulled a battered sword and belt from the stacks. "They don't last long, I don't think you can control where they open."

"So we end up on another plane, maybe in another time, and we leave all these people to their probable doom, and Shade to reap *some* sort of reward." An option, Dahl thought. A last resort. Grab a few, fight their way in and go. "Does he have any maps? Anything that shows where we are?"

"There were some in the study. Nothing marked."

"I sent a message to Tam, but I could only guess at where we are. A map would be handy if he passes another sending along."

"Right." Farideh yanked open her haversack and slid a blue silk-bound ritual book and a bundle of dark cloth out of it. "Here—if it helps. I don't have any more than when you taught them to me," she added apologetically. "So nothing spectacular. And I grabbed the components more or less at random."

Dahl leafed through the book—a sending spell, a spell to control fire, a sentinel, a magic circle, a spell to unlock doors, and the amplification ritual he'd inked in there for her, too powerful for her to cast just yet. "Still, thank the Binder, this is something." The bundle was small—good for maybe a ritual or two if she had taken the right things. "And thank you. Pity there's no one to buy components from."

"Tell me what you need and I'll find it," Farideh said.

"No. Don't let him catch you raiding his stores."

"I'm not the one sneaking through the fortress hoping no one realizes they've never seen me before." She pulled a rod off a shelf, a battered-looking thing with cracked and cloudy amethysts at its tips. Dahl smiled, the last of that strange rashness evaporating.

"You still have it."

She gave him a puzzled look. "Why wouldn't I?"

The rod had been a peace offering, an apology for all the things he'd said all those years ago. He'd had to give it to her devil instead of Farideh, and he'd half expected to find out that Lorcan had thrown the package out first chance he had.

"Lorcan's not going to swoop in here and rescue you, right?" he asked. "And if he is, would he mind a few passengers?"

It was a shoddy joke, and she didn't smile. "He's not coming for me."

The sound of the door unlatching made both of them freeze. The wedge of light from the torches beyond cut through the gloom the hanging glowballs couldn't disperse. Farideh dropped from the shelves, and she'd no more than touched ground but Dahl grabbed her around the waist and pulled her behind the racks where he'd stuffed his clothes that first night. They slipped into the low, dark space, pressed to the floor, peering out as two pairs of feet came around the swords' rack, jingling with each step.

"Anything missing?" a man's voice said.

"How could you tell?" a woman sneered. "This place is a mess."

"Nirka," Farideh breathed.

"What does it matter?" the man said. "You grab a weapon, you have what you need."

"It matters if there are intruders stealing from us," Nirka said. She paced across the room, toward Farideh and Dahl's hiding place.

"And who said there are intruders?"

"A rumor," Nirka replied.

Nirka came to stand beside the rack of implements, where Farideh had been, and chuckled roughly. "Ah. The little demon's rod is gone." Dahl felt Farideh tense against him. "She's the one been snooping."

"It's her weapon," the man pointed out. "I'd drag my chain out of here if someone tried to hide it. And then maybe I'd find somewhere to hide it in *them*." He paused, then added, "Are you going to ask her about it?" He sounded as if he'd like to watch that.

Nirka sniffed. "Not tonight. Not with the Lady's Handmaiden up there."

The man laughed. "Chavak says you can master it if you prick your hands four times every step."

"Best of luck to Chavak," Nirka said as they walked back out the door. "I'll give him a day and a half before he fades, trying that nonsense."

The latch clicked again, and Dahl let out a breath he hadn't realized he was holding. "You know her?"

Farideh nodded, her eyes still on the place where the shadar-kai had stood. "She's the guard they put on my room most of the time."

Dahl thought of Phalar. "Does she guard the wall when she's not with you?"

"I don't know," Farideh said. "I assume they all do at times."

And Dahl had to assume that if a voice whispered from the darkness about intruders in the armory, any one of the guards would leap at the chance to root them out. Stlarning drow.

"Help me thin these weapons out," Dahl said. "And we'll make a plan for what comes next."

CHAPTER FOURTEEN

24 Ches, the Year of the Nether Mountain Scrolls (1486 DR)
The Lost Peaks

THE NEXT MORNING, FARIDEH DIDN'T ARGUE WHEN THARRA pulled down a deepnight-blue and gold tunic and breeches, with high boots to match. She didn't quail at the jewels or ask her for quiet. Her eyes were on Nirka, waiting by the door, her thoughts on whether Dahl had made it back out into the camp after they'd parted ways, agreeing to meet back in two nights.

"Leave a sign if you can't make it," she'd said before he'd disappeared down the corridor. "Some mark on one of the roofs near the wall so I know you're safe."

Dahl agreed. "You too. Hang something out the window?"

"I know just the thing," Farideh had said, thinking of the selection of skin-baring dresses.

In the cold light of day, their scrambled plans seemed flimsy as the awkward gowns. She was supposed to find the rest of the components for Dahl to make another sending—salts of copper and dried formian blood.

"Or brain mole," Dahl had said. "Or intellect devourer. It will be labeled. But don't touch anything. Just find it."

"I can palm a little silver," Farideh protested.

"Don't," Dahl had said again. "Don't give him a reason to be dangerous."

As if he weren't dangerous already, Farideh thought. As if she weren't setting scores of people into his hands. Dahl had had a point about her misidentifying Chosen. But what else could she do?

"You're quiet, my lady," Tharra said, as she finished fastening the laces of the tunic.

"It's a quiet morning," Farideh said. Hardly morning anymore—Rhand had spent the early hours in his study with the Nameless One, blessedly leaving Farideh alone for a time.

Now finally dressing for highsunfeast, her head was starting to throb again, as if the strange powers were tired of waiting to be used and going to start up whether she liked it or not. She thought of Dahl's embarrassed expression when she'd admitted she'd seen the lights of his soul and felt a blush creep up her neck. Whatever Sairché had done, Farideh hoped dearly it could be undone. She didn't want to go around peeking in on people.

There was a tapping at the door. Nirka ducked out, her rapid Netherese carrying through the door.

"Is Dahl all right?" Farideh asked. Tharra blinked at her.

"I assume so," Tharra said, stitching the end of a braid up to its root. "Don't think they would have come asking for servants among the prisoners if they'd caught that fool sneaking out."

Farideh frowned at the woman's sudden chilliness. "He says you're a Harper."

"Not like he is, apparently," Tharra said. Before Farideh could respond, Nirka opened the door again, sneering at Farideh.

"Your devil is here."

Sairché. A chill ran down Farideh's spine as she stood. Time for answers. She shoved the ruby comb into her braid, just in case. "Take me to her."

Keep your calm, she told herself as she trailed Nirka through the shining corridors. You need answers right now, not revenge. You need to look as if you're happy to be protected by her. You need to keep everything in balance.

Farideh had almost succeeded in quelling her anger, her nerves, when Nirka opened the door, and Lorcan looked back over his shoulder at her.

She did not think about how her face was set. She did not think about the words she was going to say. She didn't think about where Sairché was or what she needed to know or what Rhand was thinking.

Lorcan was safe. He was here. She nearly cried out in joy.

Lorcan's dark eyes studied her for a moment more, and without a word, he turned back to the wizard. Farideh closed her mouth.

"There you are," she heard Rhand say. "We've just been discussing your progress."

Farideh's eyes darted to the wizard. To Lorcan. He was still not looking at her—they were still in danger, after all. There was still Rhand to fool.

"Have you?" she said, scrambling for something to say. "Have you mentioned how many sessions you've put me through? Standing out in the cold?"

Rhand smiled. He eyed her, looking like nothing so much as a starving, frostbitten jackal after his time with the shade. "Not as many as I would have liked."

"Do what you need to," Lorcan said. "She's not made of glass."

Farideh faltered. Lorcan wouldn't look at her, wouldn't give her any sign of what she was supposed to be playacting. "I never said—"

"Not to worry," Rhand said to Lorcan. "I'm happy to find motivation for her."

Farideh stiffened, and she looked to Lorcan, ready for him to respond with sharp words or quick spells or worse. The muscle in his jaw flexed as he clenched his teeth.

"Well, kindly return her in one piece," he said eventually. "I can't do much with a corpse."

Rhand chuckled. "You'd be surprised."

Lorcan didn't blink. "I don't *like* surprises, you'll find. I need her in one piece, as it happens, and still breathing."

"Can I talk to you?" Farideh blurted.

Lorcan raised an eyebrow. "I'm sure you can."

Farideh stared at him in disbelief. "Give us a moment alone, will you?" she said to Rhand.

Rhand was silent a long moment. "Of course." He turned to Lorcan and offered a hand. "Well met. I trust you'll make your own way out." Lorcan glanced at Farideh, then slowly took Rhand's hand.

"Well met," he said.

The wizard shut the door behind him, and still Lorcan watched her, emotionless, distant. Farideh swallowed.

"I assume," he said, "that between him and Sairché, you're well appointed. So far as I'm concerned, you can continue as you have."

"That's it?" Farideh said. "That's all? I am *not* well appointed. I have no idea what Sairché put me here for, I have no idea if I'm doing things right. Which is all *aithyas* at the moment: I cannot tell you how glad I am you're safe." She reached for him. "She promised, but—"

"He seems pleased," Lorcan interrupted airily. "That's enough for me."

Farideh let her hand fall. It wasn't an act for Rhand's sake, she realized. Sairché hadn't been lying about that. "I know you're angry with me; I'm sorry—I didn't see another way. But I'm glad you came back anyway."

"Make no mistake," Lorcan said, "this has everything to do with what my betters' have demanded and nothing else."

Farideh shook her head. "So do you have a plan?"

"Plan?" Lorcan said.

"How are we getting out of here? Or at least, what am I doing? What happens when I've found all these Chosen?"

Lorcan stared at her, his expression so empty and cold she felt for the first time since she'd met him that she was looking at a creature as far from mortal as it was possible to be.

"Why should you know my plans?" Lorcan said. "You don't tell me yours."

"What are you talking about?"

He smiled, and it reminded her, terribly, of Sairché. "Just that I'm so *pleased* to see Sairché's desires lined up with yours. Felicitations on the wizard. I'm sure you'll suit each other well."

Farideh's felt as if her chest were pulling into itself. Tatters of shadow-smoke leaped from her skin. "What did she tell you?"

"Everything you didn't."

"And you believed her?"

"*You* did!" Lorcan snapped. "No, I didn't believe her—I'm not a fool. But she told me enough to see clearly that you're not so innocent in all of this. You *didn't* tell me about a wizard."

"She told you about Rhand, but did she tell you why I know him?" Farideh said, her face growing hot. "Why I didn't tell you? Why I don't even want to talk about it now?"

"Where you got that lovely ritual book?" Lorcan asked. "He seems *charming*, by the way."

"He *isn't*," Farideh started.

But Lorcan plucked one of the rings from Sairché's necklace. "Spare me—I don't care about your lovers' quarrels and thanks to you—" He drew a sharp breath. "Thanks to you, I suddenly have a great many eyes on me I could do without. Just keep to your task, darling." The pet name seemed to slip out, and a look approaching embarrassment crossed Lorcan's handsome features. He didn't look at Farideh as he blew through the circle of the ring, casting the whirlwind that sucked him back to the Hells.

Farideh stared at the space where he'd stood, as if she could will the portal to reverse, to reopen again. He was gone. He wasn't going to save her. He was done with her. After so many upsets, so many upheavals, being left behind by Lorcan made her feel as if she'd been shattered into pieces. There was nothing left but hurt.

She thought of the ritual she'd managed to cast once, the spell that pulled Lorcan to her, out of the Hells. If she could just bring him back . . .

Then he would turn it all on her anyway. This was always going to happen. He was always going to leave her. She thought of Temerity, the warlock in Proskur—how betrayed she had felt by Lorcan, but how betrayed Temerity had actually been.

She didn't hear Rhand return until he spoke. "Good," he said. "You're finished."

You have no champion, Farideh thought. No one else is going to keep Rhand from hurting more people except for you and Dahl.

"Are you ready?" Rhand asked, offering her an arm.

Ready as I'll ever be, she thought. She ate the offered high-sunfeast mechanically, repeating Lorcan's words in her thoughts again and again, just to harden her heart.

A dozen prisoners were waiting in the courtyard. Despite the flurries of snow, the guards had stripped them of any sort of cloak. Farideh edged closer—even without trying she could see several of them glowing like firebrands. An old, straight-backed human man, another with a hooked nose, a willowy elf woman with short-cropped hair.

A sturdy-looking man, deep browns and reds flickering over him—blurring together with the colors surrounding the dark-skinned boy he carried on his back. Both carried a rune, sharp and dark—like fresh soil for the boy, like charcoal for the man. The boy met Farideh's eyes with a dark, steady gaze.

And in that moment, Farideh was sure: she couldn't send another soul into Rhand's fortress.

"Is there a problem?" Rhand said.

Farideh shrugged. "There just aren't any."

"None?"

"Nothing out of the ordinary."

Rhand stared at the crowd. He gestured to the guards, and the prisoners were led out the larger door as a second group was led in. Farideh eyed them as they entered—that dwarf with the thick black beard, that half-elf wreathed in green, that little blond-haired boy who eyed Farideh back, deeply serious.

Farideh swept the crowd twice and shook her head. "None of them."

Rhand's brows raised. "None of them?"

"Perhaps we've found them all already?" she said. She hardly dared move as his blue eyes pierced her. But after a moment that seemed to stretch taut and thin as a tripwire, he waved to the guards, without ever breaking his gaze.

"Perhaps they've realized what you are doing," he said. "Perhaps they're hiding their little lights."

"I don't think so," she said, the picture of calm. "I can see . . . their souls still shine. Only none of them have the markers that the others did." She considered the group that filed into the courtyard—another four in this one, a young man whose copper rune seemed to pulse with his heartbeat; an elf wound up in lines of green that framed her mark; a little blue-skinned genasi girl, sniffling and hiccuping and shimmering like light on the water with a blurry, uneven rune; and a dragonborn with silvery scales that shone a little too brightly around his chest.

"Perhaps I'm overtaxed from the last two days. Or perhaps there aren't as many as we thought."

Rhand was still looking at her when she glanced back. "Perhaps."

Farideh again considered the group. He might be suspicious, but he had no reason to believe she would lie, and no way to prove that she was. Even proving she was right took days. She bit her tongue, as if deep in thought, then shook her head again. "None."

"None," he repeated.

"Perhaps the guards are bringing back the ones we rejected yesterday," she said. "There's nothing here."

"Nothing," he repeated. He watched her several tense

seconds, before stepping entirely too close to her. He slipped an arm around her, and shouted a rough word of Netherese down to the guards.

The guards' grins flashed into being, one by one, like stars appearing in a suddenly dark night.

"If there is nothing here," Rhand said, low and in her ear, "then I have no use for them, do I?"

The first blade speared the young man, as easily as if he were made of almond paste, and no god on Toril or beyond stopped it. The coppery rune flared and vanished, as he pressed useless hands to his wounds. Farideh cried out in horror, but it made no difference. There were too many bodies, too many blades. Too much pain for the shadar-kai to pass up.

The little genasi girl froze in the middle of it, and started to scream.

The prisoners tried to flee, but in the little courtyard, the only exits were barred and blocked by more shadar-kai. Some fought. They died faster. Farideh tried to pull away, to get her hands up. The powers of the Hells poured into her, but Nirka's knives were suddenly pricking at her chin, and strange hands were holding her wrists tight.

Down below, one of the guards sliced an old woman's throat, bright red blood pumping from the wound. Rhand grabbed hold of Farideh's jaw and wrenched her face toward the carnage. "Oh, you will watch."

The lights around the elf suddenly caught fire in bright lines of green that surged out of Farideh's strange vision and into reality. The elf cried out, throwing her arms up to shield herself, as a fringe of vines erupted out of the cracks between the stones and twisted around her.

Beside her, a burst of silver motes surrounded the dragon-born, and even as shock gripped Farideh, she felt the passage to someone old and distant and stern crack wide as the rune that marked his god burned bright as a fire. In the same moment, the little genasi girl's screams reached a frantic pitch as the shadar-kai closed on her, becoming a roar like the waves ahead of a ferocious storm. They fell back, toppled by the noise, and the child's eyes were deep and unfathomable behind their swollen lids. A rune the color of storm clouds nearly wrapped itself around her tiny frame.

The shadar-kai separated these, shunting them toward the smaller door, even as their fellows were cut down.

"You see," Rhand crooned, stroking her jaw, "we managed fine before you. A little pressure in just the right way, and I don't have to guess who I need to pay attention to—they make themselves known. Perhaps less ideal than the arrangement you and I have. After all"—he looked down at the courtyard, at the swamp of blood and spilled innards—"who knows what the rest of them might have been good for, with time."

The dead man who'd worn the copper rune stared up at Farideh, as if he knew it was all her fault. She swallowed against the lump in her throat, against the feeling that she would surely vomit.

"Now," Rhand said. "If you are through being willful, shall we continue?"

Dahl folded his arms over his chest, then self-consciously uncrossed them, as Tharra and Armas considered the array of weapons he'd brought. He had never been so aware of the flask in his pocket, heavy now with stolen liquor. Stolen and *untouched*, he reminded himself, trying to focus on that instead of the headache he still hadn't shaken and the nerves that made the gruel in his stomach coil like snakes. He hadn't heard back yet what Oota had decided to do about Phalar, and in the stark light of day, he wasn't sure anymore what he thought the answer should be.

"To tell the truth, I expected you to be turned away," Tharra said, sitting off to the side. Dahl had asked her for sketches of the tower above the cellar rooms and she'd managed the beginnings of these with a charred twig and a swath of ragged fabric that had been clothing once. "You're lucky Phalar's trick didn't come sooner. I warned you it was dangerous."

Dahl scowled. "I handled it."

"You were lucky," Tharra said again.

"Luck's better than the alternative," Armas said, nudging the punch-daggers to one side with his clawlike hands. "The whips were a good thought. More drovers than swordsmen around here."

"Thank you," Dahl said. "I grabbed sickles for the same reason."

Dahl had slipped out of the armory, his pack heavy with weapons and Farideh's ritual book. He didn't dare swim out through that narrow passage, but a little searching led him through the storeroom he'd escaped through the first time.

And to the pyramid of sticky black casks, filled with the shadar-kai's special brew. Much as Dahl would have liked to swear he'd gone right past the stuff, the sight of it had given him a terrible thirst. He'd filled the flask and ever since found himself wondering what a *little* would do.

"There are enough weapons to make a run at them," Armas said. "Fortify Oota's court and mount a defense. Especially if we can steal some bows right before."

"Until the wizard lets his spells fly," Tharra countered. "There's no sense rushing into things. Just having these is an enormous step."

Dahl kept his tongue—a sip, he thought. A sip would be fine and you'd be a lot easier for everyone to deal with.

Armas sighed. "I suppose." He examined a sickle. "There's more prisoners every day. We can't protect them all."

"Especially with that tiefling at hand," Tharra said.

"She seemed fond enough of you when we spoke," Dahl said.

Tharra looked up at him and smiled. "Did she?" she said. "I suppose I've only got so much to go on. Like how many people are being taken thanks to her." She gave Dahl a serious look. "You really think she doesn't know exactly what she's doing? A tiefling? A warlock? A Netherese collaborator?"

Dahl ignored her. "We'll have to find an area to fortify that Rhand can't hit from the tower," Dahl said. "Close up to the fortress, maybe. Or perhaps up against the wall, out of reach. And we need to be prepared for an escape. Let's start with the Chosen—"

"I'm sorry—first you think you can beat the wizard and his shadow-warriors," Tharra interrupted. "Now you think you can pass the wall when none of us have managed?"

"I told you, Farideh thinks there's a way. Maybe she's wrong, but there's plenty of sense in preparing for either possibility."

"And so I come back to this," Tharra said, "how in the Hells are you so sure she's not going to turn on us? You don't have an answer for that."

Someone banged on the door of the little hut. The three Harpers scrambled to hide the weapons, but the door swung open before anyone could stop it. Dahl grabbed a dagger and got to his feet.

Oota's big human guard, Hamdir, leaned in and nodded to Tharra. "You'd better come. We've got a problem." He noticed the weapons spread across the table and raised his eyebrows. "Nice."

Tharra gave Armas a worried look, before hurrying out the door after Hamdir.

"Probably nothing." Armas sighed. "Oota likes making her jump, and what should she do? Complain she's being included?"

"You think Tharra's right?"

Armas shrugged. "They're both stuck in their ways, if you ask me. Tharra's right—we're not ready for a fight." He turned over a dagger. "But maybe we need to be." He peered out the window. "I need to go get the kids out of the underground rooms. Let them have some sunshine."

Dahl considered Tharra's hardly begun maps. It was clear

she wasn't interested in helping him. Or admitting she wouldn't help him. He sighed—more politics, more Harpers giving each other sidelong looks. "What about the elves?"

"What about them?"

"You carry them messages from Oota and Tharra, right? What is it they want? A battle? A long wait?"

Armas gave a short laugh. "The opposite of whatever Oota's offering, usually." He set his hands on the table, the finger cages clacking against the wood. Armas sighed. "Cereon—that's their Oota—wants out, that's for sure. His advisors feel the same. This place . . . it's not somewhere you settle down. The waters, the cold, the mountain itself. You know if the elves don't want to be somewhere, there's a damned good reason."

Dahl considered the array of weapons a moment. "But they don't want to fight the wizard."

"Oh they'd *love* to—who wouldn't? But"—he held up one caged hand—"the ones in charge are in the same straits. No gestures, no spells. I almost wish you'd smuggled out a good heavy hammer. At this point I'd let you try."

The cages weren't too large, Dahl thought. Smaller than a cup altogether . . . or a carvestar.

Small enough for Farideh's spell to destroy.

"If I found a way around the cages," he said, "do you think they'd throw in?"

"If you ask them right."

"So I'll ask them."

Armas snorted, but then realized Dahl meant what he'd said. "Oh. Take me along. Trust me. Cereon's . . . well, you know what people think of the eladrin? Make it a little haughtier. He won't talk to you. He doesn't even like speaking Common—they don't send me because I've got Dead Leira's touch. Do you even speak Elvish?"

Dahl scowled at the half-elf. *"Orth Quessin, arluth."*

Armas made a face. "Don't do that around Cereon. Flaunting your Dales-pidgin is exactly the kind of thing that will just kick his kettle. I'll bring it up. Trust me."

"It has to be now," Dahl said. He pulled Farideh's ritual book and the mix of stolen components out of the pack. Armas's brows rose.

"Gods. Where'd you get that?"

"The same place I'm going to get the magic to break your cages," Dahl said. "Go see if Hamdir will watch the little ones for a bit, while I figure out how to speak enough Elvish."

"Evereskan dialect," Armas said, his eyes still on the book. "That's more important than you think."

"Write a line before you go. We'll take the elves some daggers to sweeten the pot, and be back before Tharra and Oota are through."

"You're not going to tell them where we're going?"

"And let them argue over it?" Dahl said, plucking a tiny bottle of ink laced with potent magical salts from the jumble of components. "Let's be sure before we start anything."

The amulet hung around Mehen's neck, solid as an iron anchor. All too often, as the strange party tramped through the High Forest—Zahnya in her palanquin, her undead breaking brush ahead of them—Mehen found himself holding the onyx pendant in the flat of his palm. It didn't take the weight from his neck, though, and it tended to draw the boneclaw's soulless gaze.

Mehen smirked and held the pendant up, dangling it like a lure at the creature. The boneclaw rubbed its fingers together in response—*skritch, skritch.*

"You shouldn't do that," Daranna pointed out as she passed Mehen by. None of the Harpers had been eager to take Zahnya's amulet. Daranna, in particular.

"A calculated risk," Vescaras had called it, after Mehen had allowed the Red Wizard to stand.

"There is no 'risk' when allying with Thayans," Daranna had said. "There is certainty. We'll regret this."

"Eventually," Vescaras said. "But not immediately. At the moment, they make fair allies." Zahnya had, in fact, healed the scout who'd fallen from the tree, keeping the ghoul's terrible poison from felling her—and all before she raised her own dead. The fallen apprentices made for poor palanquin bearers and poorer ghoul controllers. But they would make more fighters to stand against the wizard and his forces, should it come to that.

"Surely you want the Shadovar fortress gone from these woods," Khochen said. "She promises that much."

"We're wasting time," Mehen had snapped, and undead or no undead, he had followed after Zahnya and her palanquin. A sad army, he thought, infiltrators and restless corpses. But if Zahnya had the means to stop the wizard and destroy the fortress, he would follow her. Albeit with a watchful eye.

He strode up to walk beside the palanquin and yanked at the curtains. Zahnya opened them a finger's length. "Yes."

"How much longer?"

"Two days? Perhaps more. My creations don't need to rest," she added. "I didn't plan to either. I need to be at the fortress at the appointed time, so——"

Mehen narrowed his eyes. "What happens at the appointed time?"

Zahnya shrugged. "My ritual works. If you want your fellows out of range, well, then I hope you can keep up." She twitched the curtains shut once more.

"She's hiding something," Khochen said, when Mehen walked alone again. "Do you notice, she never throws those curtains open enough for anyone to see in? There's something in there, I'll wager."

"You ought to stop wagering," Mehen said. "She says it will take us another two days or more. That she'll go on without us if need be."

"Well," Khochen said. "Then we'll simply make certain there

is no need." She dropped her voice. "Daranna carries a special waybread to keep us running. But let her be furious at the rest of us another day. She'll be likelier to share then."

Mehen grunted. He hoped so—broken planes he hoped so. As he walked he couldn't help imagining the fortress and camp. A sprawling keep? A fortified tower? Barracks? Tents? How many soldiers? He imagined Farideh—thrown in a dungeon, tied to a stake, locked in a tower, dead—and shuddered. For all he tried to keep his mind focused on what he might do to get to her, what he might have to plan around, his thoughts kept drifting there.

And Havilar . . .

Brin will keep her safe, he told himself. Or I will knock him senseless.

"Shall we resume then?" Khochen asked. "There's little else to do."

"Resume what?"

"Our discussion. About your latest friend."

"What is there to discuss? I want nothing to do with Bahamut's orphans."

Khochen regarded him mildly. "Goodman, I said you made an excellent guess. I didn't say you were right." Mehen stared her down, but Khochen didn't so much as blink.

"Will you stop with these games, little *verlym*?" Mehen spat. "Congratulations—you're very clever. Someone is after me, then name them. I'm not going to dance for you."

Khochen clucked her tongue. "Out in the woods with you and Daranna. Maybe I should have left you two stone-tongues together. Happy in your silence." Mehen bared his teeth, but the Harper only smiled. "Does the name Kepeshkmolik Dumuzi mean anything to you?"

"What does Kepeshkmolik want with me now?"

"What did they want with you before?" Khochen asked. "It's a fair question," she added, when Mehen growled. "I haven't a side in this. So make me choose."

"*Henish*," Mehen spat. "You only want a story."

Khochen smiled. "Sweetens the pot."

And it was an old pain, Mehen thought, far duller, far less dangerous than stewing on what might happen, what troubles might lay over the horizon. Much as he hated to give Khochen what she wanted. "I was meant to marry their scion. Kepeshkmolik Uadjit."

"A good match?"

"The best Verthisathurgiesh could broker. Kepeshkmolik is a wealthy clan, with many families. Uadjit is a skilled diplomat. A very wise, very proud woman with a very keen longsword."

"Pretty?"

Mehen shifted. "I suppose."

"But you wouldn't do it."

"I was in love with someone else."

"So you insisted you would marry your lover."

"There was no point in that," Mehen said. "In Djerad Thymar, you marry for alliances, for eggs."

"And those eggs wouldn't be good enough," Khochen finished, "for Verthisathurgiesh."

Mehen snorted at Khochen's sense of irony—it was a little funny—and startled the apprentices as much as the ghouls on their leads.

But then the Harper's superior expression fell and Mehen realized she'd meant it—broken planes she'd meant it *plain*. His roar of laughter made the ghouls howl and claw at the ground.

"Shush!" one of the ghouls yelped. "Stop it! Loud!"

"She was barren?" Khochen said, but she was guessing now, and he laughed until he thought his scales would shake off and the ghouls would go mad of the sound.

"She was from a bad family? She . . . wasn't a dragonborn?"

"Gods damn it!" the female wizard shouted. "Shut up, you brazen fool!"

"Well, well," Mehen said. "I suppose you're not as observant as you think you are, Harper."

Before Khochen could reply, the shrieking ghoul leaped away from its handler, yanking the lead from the apprentice's hand. The young man snatched at the line, missed, and worse, in his efforts let his grip on the remaining ghouls slip. Two more broke free.

"Catch them!" the other apprentice shouted. "Catch them, quick!"

Daranna ignored the apprentice's meaning, pulling her bow and nocking an arrow to it almost as quickly as she let it fly. It struck one fleeing ghoul directly in the base of its skull, and the creature dropped like a stone. Another fled past Vescaras and into the High Forest, scored by his rapier. Lord Ammakyl and two of the scouts ran after it.

The first ghoul turned, mad-eyed and slavering on Mehen. It barreled toward him, and Mehen hardly had time to pull his falchion free before the corpselike creature reached him.

But not an arm's reach from him, the ghoul stopped, flinched, and scrambled back. Mehen took hold of the amulet. "Stop!" it barked. "Shush! Stop it!" It threw itself at him again, as if it didn't care what the amulet did.

A blade reached out of nowhere, skewering the ghoul through its bony ribcage. "You are not behaving," the boneclaw thundered, holding the speared ghoul up like a tidbit of meat plucked from the spit. "Mistress Zahnya has decided to be unwise. Do not compound that."

"Ow," the ghoul mewled. "Sharp."

The boneclaw let the weaker creature slide to the ground. The apprentice who'd loosed it dropped beside the ghoul, casting dark magic that slithered over the ghoul's blood-blackened skin and muttering to himself. The other apprentice turned on Daranna, who was staring into the forest, after the lost ghoul. "You fool," she shouted, storming toward Daranna. "You've killed the other one, and we haven't got time to—"

Daranna replied with the butt of her bow, slammed into the apprentice's nose.

"Enough," Zahnya said, emerging from her palanquin. She surveyed the damage, clearly biting back her rage. "Harper, heal her. And then, Mayati, burn the corpse." She looked at Mehen. "What did you do?"

"Not a thing," Khochen answered. "Your pets seem a bit sensitive."

Zahnya glared at the Tuigan spymaster. "Give me the amulet," she said to Mehen. "You obviously can't be trusted with it."

"The amulet worked fine," Mehen said. "Just your ghouls aren't convinced of it." He tilted his head. "Maybe you ought to be out here, walking with us. Remind them of their place."

"Don't chide me," Zahnya said. Her gaze slid to the palanquin, as if she were thinking about what lay within. "Push on," she said after a moment, climbing back into her place. "And if you kill any more of my creatures, our deal is done."

"Excellent," Daranna murmured. She glowered at Khochen and at Mehen, who hoped dearly it wouldn't come to a battle before they reached the camp and Farideh.

CHAPTER FIFTEEN

The Palace of Osseia
Malbolge, the Nine Hells

If Lorcan's erinyes half sisters had little idea of what to do with Sairché as their commander, they had even less idea of what to do with him. The last few days, each one he passed watched him as if she were trying to decide just *how* severe the punishment would be if she opted to swat him with the flat of her sword, like in the old days. Lorcan had made a point of avoiding their haunts and posts—he needed a better plan than "look like you belong" before he tempted the elite erinyes of the *pradixikai*.

But when he returned from Rhand's fortress, full of words he hadn't said and retorts he hadn't made, keeping his guard up was the last thing on Lorcan's mind.

If possible the wizard was worse than he'd imagined: unbearably smug, not the least bit concerned that a representative of the Hells themselves was standing in his chambers. Lorcan still wished he'd broken that smug grin, wished he'd given Farideh something to look at.

What did she tell you? Enough, he thought, blood boiling. He wasn't an idiot. He hadn't lapped up Sairché's lies—and how dare she suggest it. He'd been at this long enough to spot the truth among the deceptions.

I cannot tell you how glad I am you're safe. What else would she say, faced with her betrayal come undone? *She promised.* Oh, Lorcan thought, I'll bet she did. He could just hear Sairché, "Not to worry. He'll be taken care of." *I was trying*—However she meant to finish, it only made him more angry. He'd told her not to trust Sairché, and she had. He'd told her not to talk to Temerity, and she had. He'd told her she was just another warlock and lied, baldly, for the first time he could recall.

He wished he'd prodded at Farideh, made her confess. Made her tell him every secret about that shitting wizard. Made her admit that she was in well over her head. Raged and threatened and made her remember he wasn't some accessory she could discard—

"Lost, little brother?" Lorcan looked up—a trio of erinyes, one of the *pradixikai* and two lesser. Noreia with her wooly black dreadlocks, and the twins, Faventia and Fidentia.

Lorcan looked around. "Oh I don't think so," he said savagely. If ever in his life there were a time he would gladly go toe-to-toe with his terrible half sisters, it was that moment. "These are still my quarters. Do I need to find something for you to do?" Faventia and Fidentia traded glances.

"Baby sister might have something to say about that," Noreia said.

Did she say how I know him? Farideh had demanded. *Why I didn't tell you?* Lorcan bit his tongue. "She'd find it difficult."

"Would she?" Faventia asked, lazily shifting her scabbard. "Where've you put her?"

"Why? Do you want to keep her company?"

Faventia smiled around her fearsome fangs. "Try it."

"Go sort out those godsbedamned cultists," Lorcan snarled. "Earn your bloody keep."

All three erinyes collapsed into laughter.

"*Lorcan,*" Faventia drawled, "telling *us* to earn our keep?" Wordlessly, he slipped a ring over one finger, and flames swallowed his arm. The erinyes shifted—more aware, more prepared. Not willing to back down though.

"Aw, little brother," Noreia crooned. "We were just starting to have fun."

Lorcan scowled. " 'We' have nothing . . ." His retort trailed away as pieces he didn't even know were missing locked into place.

I was trying—Farideh had said, and in his memories Havilar's voice finished the phrase she'd left hanging—*to protect us.*

Lorcan froze. Oh, Lords of the Nine.

"Maybe you don't," Noreia said. "But the three of us—"

"Shut up, Noreia," Lorcan spat. He'd put everything together wrong. He yanked the ring off as he turned on his heel. There was one way to be sure.

"What's wrong, little brother?" Noreia called, while the others hooted and cackled. "Did you just remember who you're talking to?" He made no response, but forced the portal open once more, slipping the ruby ring on his off-hand and concentrating on the necklace it was linked to.

He stepped out into the dim of twilight. Havilar was sitting as if at watch, her back against a huge oak. But her eyes were on the ground in front of her, lost in unhappy thoughts. Brin was nowhere to be seen.

Havilar startled when Lorcan called her name, a dagger in her hand as if it had leaped there. She glowered at him.

"Four breaths," she said. "And you're gone, or I kill you."

"Don't be silly," Lorcan admonished. "If you could do that, I wouldn't have come." He looked around at the forest. "You're a lot farther on than I expected. Brin didn't make you turn back?"

"Two breaths," she warned.

"Oh, calm down," he said. "I want to ask you something."

Havilar narrowed her eyes and didn't lower the weapon. But two breaths passed and she didn't lunge. "Ask," she said. "And go."

Lorcan wet his mouth, half-hoping he was wrong. "You said Farideh was trying to protect us—"

"She *was*."

Lorcan took a step back, just to calm her down. "I believe you. But who," he asked, "is 'us'?"

Havilar lowered her dagger, staring at him as if he'd gone more than a little mad in the last two days. "What?"

"Is 'us' you and her?" he said. "Or is 'us' . . . you and me?"

"Are you *joking*?" Havilar demanded. "You stormed off and left Farideh to die because you thought she'd suddenly turned into a sensible person and let your sister have you? Of *course* I meant me and you!"

That Farideh would throw herself into a deal with Sairché to protect Havilar, he had never doubted. But to protect him . . . "You didn't hear her talk that night," he said. "She was ready to dissolve the pact."

Havilar shook her head as if she couldn't believe the words coming out of his mouth. "She was angry at you—you don't kill people just because you're angry, you *henish*." Her gaze flicked over him. "Maybe *you* do."

"But it's fine and good to give them up to their enemies? You can't wish away that part of—"

"Why did you think your sister just laid there and let you pummel her?" Havilar cried. "She's not allowed to hurt us—that's the whole *karshoji* reason Farideh even said yes. Gods, you don't listen to anything. It's like double-Farideh."

Lorcan fell quiet, weighing his words, remembering Sairché's capture. She'd fought back a little, hadn't she? He'd been clever—caught her unawares, gotten her where she couldn't do anything to him.

"If I recall correctly," he said, "I was already protecting you just fine back in Proskur."

"And if I 'recall correctly,' you were frozen like a statue when I came in, and your godsbedamned sister was stalking around with a wand. Really, astounding job of protecting us."

She glanced off to her right. "Brin, don't!"

Flames poured into his hands as Lorcan turned to where the Cormyrean stood, not three feet from him with his sword out. Behind, near the edge of the brush, was a brace of rabbits. He hadn't heard a thing.

"Back away," Brin said to Lorcan, and the cambion wondered if there were a godsbedamned thing that had gotten simpler in the intervening years.

"Put your sword down," Havilar said irritably. "I don't need to be saved from Lorcan."

Lorcan narrowed his eyes. "Oh really?" he said. "I'm fairly sure I could burn you before your dear darling's sword hit me. Send you off to the cavern, plenty quick."

"You could," Havilar said. "But you won't. If you hurt me and then go save Farideh, she's not going to be happy with you." She folded her arms. "Besides, we're . . . What's less than friends? But not enemies, either?"

"Associates?" Brin said. "Collaborators?"

Lorcan shook the flames out. "Allies," he said.

"Good enough," Havilar said. Brin lowered his sword.

"She's near here," Lorcan said. "Maybe two days walking. Up on the mountain's peak. There's a fortress, a camp around it. She's in there."

"With the Netherese?" Brin asked.

"A wizard called Adolican Rhand."

Neither of them spoke to him for a long moment. "That's not funny," Brin finally said.

"It's not meant to be," Lorcan replied.

"You *left* her there?" Havilar cried. "With *him*? I told you he was—"

"You told me he wasn't your type," Lorcan snapped. He nodded at Brin. "And I can see that—they're not exactly a matched set, are they?" Havilar's cheeks turned bright red.

"Adolican Rhand," Brin said calmly, "is wanted for several murders in Waterdeep—grotesque murders. The watch would be after him for the rapes as well, only the victims are all dead and in pieces."

Lorcan shut his eyes, the fine edge of guilt threatening his certainty. Not one of Rhand's dark jests had bothered him in the slightest, aside from being not, in fact, amusing. Mortals said they'd do a lot of things, after all. They seldom followed through.

And if this one did . . . He wondered if what Asmodeus would do to him would be the worst of it, after all.

"Farideh can handle herself," he said, not sure of who he was trying to convince. "Besides, she has to stay. If she reneges on her deal with Sairché, she loses her soul." If she hasn't already, Lorcan thought. You still don't know what's happening.

"What are his forces like?" Brin asked.

"Well, it's overrun with guards. And he *is* a wizard."

Brin shook his head. "He's not that powerful. He makes as if he is, but we're pretty sure he's been trading on scrolls he recovered from the library's destruction."

"You don't have to be too powerful to hit a small force from a high point."

Brin shook his head. "The distance—"

"Stop talking!" Havilar shouted. "Lorcan, you go back and you save her. Brin, we have to—"

"Eat," Brin interrupted. "And rest. We can't walk for two days on fear and anger."

Havilar drew back as if he'd called her a filthy name. "How am I supposed to sleep knowing how much trouble my sister's in?"

"It's no more trouble than she's been in since we left," Brin reminded her. "And we're not going to get to her any faster if we collapse a hundred feet from the fortress. We're still doing what we can." Havilar turned from him, and Brin pursed his mouth.

"Also, I have some of Tam's sleeping tea," Brin added. "So, we'll try that."

Havilar glared at Lorcan. "What are you going to do?"

Lorcan held up the portal ring, glad at least for a plan even if he didn't particularly enjoy it. "To begin with," he said, "add to our list of allies."

Sairché wasn't sure at first that she'd woken. The world around her was little better than her nightmares: the bars of the cage, the dark shadows of the cave, the meaty gape of its mouth revealing Malbolge's virulent landscape beyond.

And between her and escape, Lorcan, scowling at her. Holding a red ring. The cage's control ring.

"Was I always meant to be a part of the deal?" he asked curtly.

Sairché fumbled for words, finding splinters of glass instead. She gagged and spat the remains of the portal bead. "What . . . deal?"

"The deal you made with Farideh," he said. "Did you intend to include me? Was that in the offer?"

Deal . . . Sairché shut her eyes and leaned against the cage's bars. Asmodeus. Dangerous . . .

A crackle of electricity jolted through Sairché's frame, throwing her off the bars, her muscles all contracting painfully. She fell backward, against the cage, too penned in to drop to her knees.

Lorcan released his grip on the ring. "Was I always meant to be part of the deal?" he repeated.

"No," Sairché said, panting. "It was a possibility. But I'd hoped to avoid it. I'd hoped she'd take the chance to rid herself of you."

"What did you give her?"

"Protection until her twenty-seventh birthday," Sairché said. "For her, for the sister, and for you. In exchange for two favors."

Lorcan goggled. "*Two* favors?"

"There was a premium for including you," Sairché said,

mustering a bit of venom. She looked around the cave, remembering the fight in the forest and the portal bead. She ran her tongue over her ragged gums. "How long have I been here?"

Lorcan held up the control ring. "It's still my turn. You have to protect me under her deal? That's why you didn't fight back."

"She wouldn't budge without it," Sairché said. "Besides, I was half hoping you'd come out mad enough to kill her or make her kill you, solve all my problems in one blow."

Lorcan stared at her for so long that Sairché wondered what she'd stirred up in his thoughts. "You *know* something," she said. She took in her necklace of magical rings, hanging around his neck like a badge of office. "Her Highness made you take over."

Lorcan smiled. "Indeed."

"So that's why you woke me? Can't handle the hierarchy alone?"

"You and I both know this is bigger than the hierarchy," Lorcan said. "I want to make a truce. I'll let you out. We'll help each other get out of this. You can't kill me, and you can't set me up to be snared by another devil—not till her twenty-seventh birthday. But you do what I say and I'll return the favor."

Sairché smiled. "Or what?"

"Or Glasya makes you suffer for your failure."

"She'll kill you too."

" 'Too,' " Lorcan said, "being the operative word."

Sairché considered him, considered the gaps that existed in the deal. Her thoughts were still slow and syrupy. But the alternative was unavoidable: stay in the cage until someone came to kill her.

"Fine," she said, slipping a hand between the thorny bars. "Until next Marpenoth."

Lorcan clasped it as though he'd rather crush it. "Not a heartbeat later." He took a step back. "Which of these unlocks it?"

Sairché would have dearly liked to point to the diamond circle nestled in the right-side stack. But even thinking of suggesting her brother slip on the cursed ring made her prior agreement prickle at her brain. She was devil enough to be bound by her agreements—at least he would be too. "The control ring will do it. Flip it over so the dark side is closest to you, and put it on your other hand."

The door sprang open, and Sairché stumbled from the cage. It could only have been a few days since she was trapped, and even still her muscles were confused and sapped. Lorcan made no move to assist her.

"Start with the wizard," he said.

"What about him?" Sairché said. "He's a nuisance and I can't wait to see him dead."

"What in the Hells is he doing?"

Sairché frowned. "Glasya told you nothing?"

"Little enough that I can guess she wants me to fail."

Sairché hissed. She glanced around the cave out of habit, but any watcher would be subtler than that. "Not here," she said. She took a few, tentative steps—the stasis cage's effects still clung to her nerves. "Do you have control of the portal still? Is it working?"

"That thing in your chambers? Yes, it's working."

Sairché stretched her wings. They'd hold her weight—she hoped. "The forest," she said. "The one you've almost surely met Magros in? It will be easier to talk. The magic makes scrying hard."

"No," Lorcan said, heading for the palace. "Straight to the fortress."

Sairché scowled at him. "Who are you to give orders?"

"The one holding all your magic rings, to begin with."

"Those weren't a part of our agreement."

"No," he agreed. "They weren't."

Sairché fumed. "I would have thought of that if I'd had a moment."

Lorcan gave her a nasty smile. "I suspect we are about to come across all sorts of situations that will make you reconsider having made such a quick agreement."

From Osseia, the portal dropped them this time on the sharp, black glass battlements of the tower's highest level and into the middle of a heavy snowfall. Sairché cursed. "That shitting wizard."

Lorcan looked around. "What's happened?"

"Nothing, that's what," Sairché said. "I've told him a hundred times if I've told him once to fix that stupid barrier so it stops throwing off my portals." The clouds hung low enough, Sairché imagined she might be able to drag her fingers through their icy coats if she stood on tiptoe. The snow they dropped collected in the dips and grooves of the obsidian tower, in between the irregular battlements. Sairché shook her wings off and curled them over her head.

"You shouldn't start with Rhand," Sairché said irritably. "He's incidental. Disposable. You ought to start with Farideh." She glared at Lorcan. "She can't leave. Not yet."

"Not until you declare her favor complete."

"I am not trying to trick you—you try and spirit her out of here, and we'll all suffer for it. This is dangerous terrain."

Lorcan gave her a significant look. "These are the plans," he said, "of Asmodeus."

Sairché blew out a breath—so he knew that much. "All the archdevils' actions are within the plans of Asmodeus," she said carefully.

"Of course," Lorcan said after a moment's pause. "It would be suicide to do something to upset His Majesty's plans. Especially plans that seem to be as complicated and delicate as these." He looked over the jagged battlements, as if considering the swirling snow. "But you must admit, these are particularly complex plans. One might say unnecessarily complex. From the outside, it seems as if you are aiding the Netherese in something. Something involving a great deal of divine power. And you have Stygia at your side—of all the layers—secretly recruiting Red Wizards and assassins."

"Red Wizards?" Sairché said.

Lorcan smiled. "Oh, was I not supposed to mention them? Give my apologies to Magros when you see him next. And tell him I am not such an idiot as to kill his Chosen for him." He pulled a strange, long blade out of his scabbard and held it up to Sairché. His eyes darkened. "He is *such* an asset."

"Half right," Sairché said dryly. She considered the blade. "Is it just a sword?"

"So far as I can see. He doesn't think much of us, does he? He suggested I kill the agent and the wizard, and leave Farideh to take the blame. Presumably so he could then act surprised I was driven so mad with rage." Lorcan rubbed his arms. "Apparently he's through with his agent. Shall we go in?"

"Not yet," Sairché said, though the cold bothered her too. "Too many ears down there. Magros's end was to put an agent in the camp—someone for the prisoners to rally around, someone to keep them from doing anything too drastic until arrangements could be made. And then to perform the harvesting."

"But?"

Sairché smiled despite herself. "But he decided to use the Chosen he was allotted to build up His Highness Prince Levistus's interests in the North. Around the time that Many-Arrows decided to give up on being civilized. A pity Asmodeus didn't grant the fellow an ability to deflect war clubs to the head. He had to find a new agent, and get that one into the camp. I have no idea what he told them or who they are. But if we were dealing with a Red Wizard, I would know."

"He seems intrigued by them outside the camp. Is he doing anything else?"

"He's not supposed to be."

"Then I don't see other possibilities here," Lorcan said. "What is it Glasya is having *us* do?"

"Follow the edicts of Asmodeus," Sairché said quickly.

"To what end?"

In the Nine Hells, there were none who didn't know exactly

where they stood in the hierarchy of the devils, from the lowest soul to the archlords ruling the layers to Asmodeus, the god of evil standing over all of them. To fall required only the displeasure of one's betters. To rise required their pleasure . . . which came chiefly from their own advancement. There was an art to pleasing one's betters, while not angering *their* betters.

And when one answered to an archlord . . . that art was very rare indeed.

"This world has been in turmoil for the last hundred and fifty years," Sairché said carefully. "The strain of chaos makes people hunger for answers, and the coffers of the Hells have swelled. We are powerful, more powerful by the day, because mortals ache for simple answers. Asmodeus is more powerful by the day," she added.

"Powerful and mad," Lorcan spat.

"For the moment," Sairché said, still careful. "The end of that chaos is coming. The crescendo. Asmodeus might have claimed the spark of Azuth, may have armored himself with impressive powers by claiming the succubi, the tieflings, uncountable souls, and more. But what comes next . . . even the gods are afraid of what it might mean. That something more powerful may take their divinity from them, or even wipe away the world. Everything will change soon, and who is as vulnerable, in the eyes of the gods, as the last to gain the spark of the divine?"

Lorcan watched the clouds. "If anyone could cling to the spark, it is His Majesty. But I fail to see how you're helping him do that."

"I am doing what is asked of me," Sairché said significantly. In each of these Chosen is a fragment of the gods' divine power, infusing their souls. "The wizard thinks he's gathering Chosen for his goddess's use, but he will soon find out we have other plans. When it's done, Asmodeus will have found a way to steal those sparks and thereby the powers of the gods themselves, and leave the blame on the goddess who thought she was gaining all the power. If it should fail . . ." She let the pause hang, filling with all the words she wasn't saying. " . . . then Asmodeus would not claim that power, our plans would be revealed, and the goddess in question might be very upset with him. Do you see what I mean?"

Lorcan's brows rose. "That is," he said, just as carefully, "a lot of pressure on such a delicate point. And we shouldn't pretend Prince Levistus has no argument with Asmodeus. He might have it in mind to sabotage these efforts and usurp the throne."

" 'Might'?" Sairché said sarcastically, before schooling her tone once more. "But that would be foolish—Asmodeus is a god. So long as he is a god, there is no chance another archlord might succeed him. So long as he remains a god.

"So long as he remains a god," Sairché repeated, "the archlords are all his grateful vassals, every one."

Lorcan blew out a breath. "And so your plan hinges on Farideh. She can't leave because then everything will come apart."

"That, and I would not repeat Magros's mistakes."

Lorcan turned to face her with such fury and horror in his expression that for a moment, Sairché feared he would break their agreement and throw her off the chipped obsidian battlements. "Magros's mistakes?" he said. "That's why Asmodeus wants her alive? Shit and *ashes*!" He rubbed a hand over his face.

Sairché frowned. "What are you talking about?"

Lorcan didn't answer at first, and once more, her brother's expression became a mask. "Nothing," he said. "A minor complication. I didn't mention it."

"You had better mention it. Are we allies or not?" Sairché demanded. "What's happened?"

He wet his mouth as if the words were threatening to choke him. "His Majesty paid me a brief call."

A chill that had nothing to do with the plane or the winter threaded through Sairché's core. "He gave you new orders?"

"No." Lorcan shuddered violently. "He wasn't interested in telling me any of this plan, or any of your adjustments to it.

All he said was that I had to keep Farideh alive . . ."

"And?"

Lorcan hesitated. "And then . . . he told a joke."

Sairché's brother had always had a way with the truth—a calculating stillness that made it impossible to discern how much he had twisted facts to make one hear a different story, how much irony was left to float gently into one's thoughts masquerading as verity. She studied him a moment—there was no mistaking his agitation.

There was also no mistaking how insane his last comment had been.

"He told a *joke*?" Sairché repeated. "Asmodeus?"

"Yes," Lorcan said, quieter. "He said he would trust me to do this because he knew I had no ambition in me, that I should keep it to myself and my trusted allies, and that he would reward me handsomely." He wet his mouth again, as if the very mention of the god of evil dried it out. "And then . . . then he said, 'Handsomely? Of course, for Asmodeus can do nothing in an ugly fashion.' And then he laughed." He shook his head. "I think."

"You *think*?" Sairché said.

"Have you ever heard His Majesty laugh?"

Now it was Sairché's turn to shiver. "Once. At a distance. My bones tried to jelly themselves, as I recall."

"Exactly," Lorcan said. He dropped his voice. "That didn't happen."

Sairché frowned. "Perhaps it was someone else. Perhaps it was a ruse."

"Who in all the planes has the unholy pluck to stand in the palace of Osseia and pretend to be Asmodeus?" Lorcan hissed. "Every *other* word he spoke, every heartbeat I lay there, was inarguably in the presence of Asmodeus."

"And then he told a joke." Sairché shook her head, wishing she didn't know that, wishing she were still trapped in the stasis cage. "Even the gods should be afraid of what that might mean."

She sucked her teeth. "What do you think it does mean?"

"I don't know. I don't care," Lorcan said, as flustered as she'd ever seen him. "This falls squarely into the category of things we should not consider."

"I would say 'things we should hold onto for later,'" Sairché said. "But for now, he wants her alive. He never said that before—not that I assumed he'd be pleased. But he didn't exactly throw Magros to Malbolge when he lost that Chosen. And he never mentioned that stricture in the orders."

Which meant he didn't want devils to know it mattered. He didn't want people looking for answers as to why. But it also meant it was critically important if he'd told Lorcan as much.

Sairché wondered if Lorcan realized that.

Lorcan was staring at the clouds again. "You didn't tell Farideh."

"Of course I didn't," Sairché said. "Do I look like Magros? She would have lost her mind at that sort of revelation."

"You don't give her enough credit." He sighed. "Ashes, we're playing a dangerous game here."

"Don't be dramatic," Sairché said.

He laughed. "You are a little mad these days, aren't you? You can't please everyone, and displeasing the wrong person—"

"Have you forgotten the story of His Highness, Prince Levistus?" Sairché asked. "You can seduce the king of the Hells' own wife, kill her when she refuses you, corrupt his only daughter, thunder around stirring up discontent, and in the end—so long as Asmodeus sees a use for you in the future—come out alive."

"And frozen in a glacier for all time," Lorcan said.

"Frozen and alive is still alive," Sairché said. "Still possible to come back."

"And what do you have to offer His Majesty that would rival an archduke?" Lorcan said. "If we fail—"

"We shall simply have to fail less spectacularly than someone else," Sairché said. "Asmodeus cannot afford to destroy perfectly good pieces in this game and he knows it. Better to keep us in play."

"But which is worse? Alive and under his notice," Lorcan asked, "or dead?"

"A very good question," Sairché conceded, and she headed down the stairs, trusting that her brother was, if nothing else, too curious to stab her in the back just yet.

The snow had started falling again, great fluffy clumps that melted away as soon as they landed on the blood-slicked courtyard. There was no covering the carnage. There was no washing away the deaths of the prisoners.

They are dead, Farideh's thoughts repeated, over and over like a terrible chant, they are all dead. This is what your bad decisions have wrought.

The shadar-kai had to shove the prisoners in, like cattle into a slaughterhouse. They passed by in a blur—angry, afraid, staring up at Farideh as if she were a monster. She could not tell them that this was safer.

Every time she closed her eyes, she saw the young man staring up at her, the old woman clutching her throat, the little genasi girl screaming and screaming.

I cannot save them, Farideh thought. I cannot save anyone. Not even myself.

She stared down at this—the last group for the day, Rhand had promised—the excuse hollow and dusty in her own thoughts. She ought to be planning. She ought to be counter-attacking, she ought to be figuring out how to outmaneuver Rhand, she ought to be clever—if there were one thing Farideh *could* do in a fight, it was think ahead, so why didn't she? It sounded so much like Mehen's voice, her heart ached to ignore it. She could be as clever as a general out of one of Mehen's bedtime stories, and Rhand would still win, because he held too many lives in his hands.

Every time she tried to outthink him, to pull herself out of the shock and grief for the sake of the prisoners who still lived, that truth lay as plain and ugly as the sticky gloss of blood the snow couldn't wash away. Every time she hesitated, the guards reached for their weapons, their excitement shimmering off of them like the heat off the cobblestones in the city of Proskur seven summers ago.

I should have cast, she thought as she named the Chosen. *I should have leaped down into the pit, put myself between the swords and them. I should have attacked Rhand, pushed him into the pit. I should have run,* she thought, and still she named the Chosen.

As each of those acts played out in her thoughts, the result was the same: The guards would react. Rhand would react. And with so many against her, she would fail, she would suffer. More people would die. She would die and Sairché would win. Havilar would be lost. It was as if she had already taken the wrong path seven and a half years earlier and there was no turning off it now.

Action was wrong. Inaction was wrong. She could not win without losing. She pointed to the last Chosen in the group—a human woman with her brown hair in long plaits. She glared at Farideh, a condemnation Farideh let soak through her. She deserved every bit of it.

"There now," Rhand said. "That wasn't so bad."

True, Farideh thought bitterly. There were more uncomfortable ways to damn your soul. If she could have hoped to find lenience for the Chosen she'd sorted before she knew what was going on—despite the fact she'd known well enough that Rhand was a villain—there was nothing, no justification, no appealing artifice, to lessen the deaths of the third group of prisoners, nor the Chosen she'd doomed afterward.

The tiefling woman's ghost appeared, hovering just behind Rhand, faint as Farideh's breath on the cold air. The ghost stared at her successor as she always did—cool and stern—before gesturing at her swirling locks. Farideh slipped the ruby comb from her pocket, jamming it heedlessly into the smoothed hair of her crown.

Now you see what he's capable of, the ghost said. *Now you see you must fight fire with fire.*

Farideh shook her head, knowing better than to answer. There were too many complications, too many ramifications. Rhand might not win, but she would always lose. And more importantly, innocent people would lose as well.

Do you know who you are? the ghost said. *What you can master? You have let a weakling—a robber, cloaked in magician's robes—outwit you by playing on soft feelings. He cannot afford to lose these people—you know that and so does he. Steel yourself—a few more dead, a score of dead, it is nothing compared to what he'll do. He cannot afford to lose you.*

Farideh turned from her, to look at Rhand where he stood giving arcane directions to his apprentices. He looked up at Farideh and smiled unpleasantly.

You have no choice, the ghost said. *You fight or you die.*

"Come," Rhand said. "My guest wishes to speak to you."

Even terror at facing the Nameless One again could not break through Farideh's numbness. She stared down at the snow landing on the blood-dark cobbles. It cannot be worse, she thought. You are trapped. They are trapped. You cannot save them.

And no one, she thought, remembering Lorcan's cold fury, remembering Havilar's refusal to meet her eye, is going to save you.

Maybe it was better that way.

Rhand took her by the arm, and there her gloom found its limits, and a spark of rage and revulsion seared through the fog. But she didn't fight as he led her up the stairs, trailed by Nirka and her unsheathed knives.

"She won't be happy," Rhand warned. "She'll want punishment." He lingered on the word in a way that fanned that spark of rage.

She owed the dead Chosen—but she did not owe Rhand or Shar.

At the top of the stairs, the shadar-kai woman stopped and went no farther. Farideh stepped out of the threat of her knives and into the grasp of the Chosen of Shar's powers—worse than the prior night. It wrapped her like a cloak of lead and threatened to stop her feet. Images of the massacre rose up with every step—the woman with the cut throat, the elf a shadar-kai had beaten with his spiked fists, the sound of the little genasi girl screaming. The Chosen whose ties to his god had been snapped with one sword stroke.

You fight or you die, the ghost's words murmured in her thoughts. Had the ghost not fought? Had she died fighting? The Nameless One's power smothered her curiosity. It might matter, but Farideh couldn't recall why. Only that she would like very much to stop, to sit, to curl into a ball.

Rhand stopped beside the door opposite his study, his breath growing unsteady, his eyes wild. The room beyond was far larger than her own, with a long table covered in maps and scrolls in addition to the bed and chests and chairs. A similar closet stood in the corner, its open doors displaying a similar variety of fashions—though far more were puddled on the floor, tried-on and cast-off.

The Nameless One sat beside the wide, open windows, and a cold breeze cooled Farideh's burning face. The strange glyph of power that marked the girl was not drawn in light but deepest shadow, glittering with traces of violet and blue. She looked Farideh over with colorless eyes, and numbness gripped the warlock, snuffing out fear and rage and every other thought.

Except one: *she looks like Havi.*

There was a ghost of Havilar in the way the girl held her pointed chin up, the way she tossed the long silky strands of her hair over her shoulder as her eyes fell on Farideh. There was the faint memory of the last young woman in the courtyard, the one she'd just sent to Rhand's tender ministrations, in the silver gleam of the Nameless One's eyes. The little genasi girl whose screams echoed and echoed in Farideh's memories in the way that dark cloud of Shar's blessing seemed too large for her to contain, in the delicacy of her features, in the way Farideh's heart suddenly ached for the Nameless One.

"Well met," the Nameless One said. "I see you're not as reliable as Saer Rhand insisted." She gave Rhand a cool look, and Farideh's heart threatened to break.

"Well met," she murmured. The ache in her chest reminded her of Mehen, of the grief in his gaze and the misery she knew she was putting him through. "Where are your parents?" she asked, her mind too tangled in the Chosen's powers to stop her tongue.

The girl flushed, but whatever dark magic imbued her and turned her flesh into shadows made the stain purplish and bruiselike. Her powers surged, and the force of Shar's emptiness made Farideh's throat tighten, her heart sink. "Dead," she said sweetly. "Buried under fallen Sakkors. I represent the Church of Shar now. We're the ones who determine Saer Rhand's success or failure. Your success or failure," she added menacingly.

I have failed already, a part of her sighed. But just as much of her noted that the Nameless One's superiority only made her seem younger, only sound like Havilar back in Arush Vayem, flush with success at some complicated attack she'd created.

"How old are you?"

The Nameless One lifted her chin. "Thirteen. And already more powerful than *any* other Chosen in this camp." Her gaze flicked over Farideh as if she were daring her to argue. "I saw your little stunt, and Saer Rhand's remedy." She turned to Rhand. "Was that truly necessary?"

Rhand cleared his throat. "I thought it so, my lady. A point needed to be made."

"You are very adept at wasting resources," the girl said scathingly. "You drain the Lady's coffers and destroy the powers she craves."

"Your pardon, my lady. There was a point to be made."

The Nameless One turned back to Farideh, and her terrible powers surged around the warlock, eager to wear her away like rough waves against a sandbar. *She looks like Havilar,* Farideh thought. *She should be trying to lie to her father and learning to flirt and practicing at adulthood.* Tears welled in Farideh's eyes. The Chosen of Shar smiled and her powers deepened, threatening to drive Farideh to her knees.

"Don't you wish your 'patron' could manage a gift like this?" she said. "Something useful. Something powerful." Farideh shook her head slowly, trying to cling to the parts of her mind that still made sense, even if they played neatly into the Nameless One's trap: *I cannot save them. I cannot win. I cannot. I cannot.* She looked into the girl's luminous eyes.

"I can't save you," Farideh said, tears breaking down her cheeks.

The Nameless One drew back, surprised, and her powers ebbed. "Save me?" She laughed, a short, shocked sound. "From what? I am the Handmaiden of Shar, powerful beyond my age and station."

"You're alone," Farideh said. "You're a child."

"A child and I command the blessings of Shar," the Nameless One said, smiling cruelly. "Who says I need saving?" She leaned forward, her powers washing into the room like a tide. "You're the one in need of saving, devil-born."

And no one is going to save me, Farideh thought, drowning in the emptiness of Shar. *Not Lorcan, who abandoned her. Not Havilar, who had washed her hands of Farideh. Not Mehen, who loved Havilar best. Not the Harpers, not Sairché, and not Dahl . . .*

And you can't save them either, she thought. *It's hopeless. Give up.*

She drew a long, shuddering breath, and made herself look away from the Nameless One, but the powers had already dragged her down like anchors chained to her ankles. It was hopeless. She could not stand alone. She had no one to stand beside her—

Farideh's eyes fell on the table, on the maps of Faerûn laid over it. On the scattered points marked in scarlet over the northern half of the continent. On the mark that lay on the mountains where Dahl had guessed the camp stood—the Lost Peaks. On the five other identical marks. Five other camps. Five other walls. Five other chances that someone had escaped.

Farideh's pulse sped. She forgot, for a moment, the Nameless One and Rhand standing beside her. She forgot the numbness and the weight of the Nameless One's powers. There were six camps hiding potential Chosen. And she had only asked about *this one.*

She had been right. Someone had breached one of the walls. There was a way out. She just had to ask the waters the right question to find out how.

"I don't think Saer Rhand's punishment is enough," the Nameless One said loftily. "You clearly don't know your place. And we value obedience above all else."

Stall, Farideh thought. Focus. She had to get out of there, and quickly. "If you think," she said softly, "that my patron will not be upset at the loss of so many souls, you are mistaken. I will pay for it."

"Is that why he's interested?"

Farideh shrugged. She couldn't guess what Lorcan wanted, what Sairché intended. Or why the Nameless One would care. But what did people expect of devils but a greed for souls?

"You will have a goodly number of . . . castoffs," she said. "Assuming you aren't just killing them all. Plenty of people looking for easy answers. My patron specializes in such things."

The Chosen of Shar considered her for another interminable moment, Shar's powers picking at Farideh's soul.

Six camps, Farideh thought. Six walls, and one of them had certainly been breached—concentrate on that, she told herself. There's a way out, and you're the only one who knows. You need to tell Dahl. You need to tell the prisoners.

Why would she think she could do that? Rhand was clearly

cleverer than her, the Nameless One clearly more powerful. Farideh could hardly even stand in her presence . . .

Farideh curled her nails into her palm and thought about the dead prisoners.

"Perhaps that is the way of the king of the Hells," the Chosen of Shar said, and the pain in Farideh's hands, the anger in her heart was no longer enough as the girl's god-given powers swallowed her up. "But the Lady of Loss demands we uphold the order of things. And you are too smug for my liking. Saer Rhand?" Her colorless eyes pinned Farideh, and when she spoke, once more she sounded ages older than she appeared. "You may not think yourself a tool, but you are. We all are."

Rhand was suddenly so close behind Farideh she could feel the rasp of his uneven breath against her hair. His hand clamped down on her left wrist, and swimming against the tide of the Chosen of Shar's powers, Farideh was too slow to pull away as he spread her hand flat on the table, pulled the knife from his belt, and sliced her ring finger off.

She heard the snap of the bone, saw the spread of blood across the parchment before she realized what had happened. There was no pain, her whole hand had gone as numb as her thoughts. But when Rhand released her wrist and she drew her hand back, the finger remained behind, curled in a pool of dark blood.

Her breath stopped in her lungs. Her mind seemed to scream and scream and scream, but not a sound came out of her. She was dying on her feet.

Rhand pressed a cloth to the wound and himself to her. She stared at the finger until the Chosen of Shar stood, plucked it from where it lay, and tossed it into the brazier.

"Not to worry," she said sweetly, the words echoing in Farideh's ears, "we'll not keep it as insurance. This time."

Farideh hardly understood the words, still reeling. Still realizing that Rhand was pressed against her, and that the unevenness of his breathing had a very different quality. Still trying to scream.

"Should you be driven to act out again . . . well, you'll have your reminder." The Nameless One smiled at Farideh and the pain burned up her arm, sudden and hot and enough to drive her held breath out in a single sharp cry. It pulled with it the swirling powers of the Hells and her arm became a sink of ruinous energy and agony.

Cast, the voice of the Hells hissed. *Show them what they've miscounted.*

But she had no air to speak the trigger word. Rhand and the Chosen of Shar exchanged words she couldn't pick up through the buzz of her thoughts, and the wizard steered her from the room, out into the hallway.

"It hurts doesn't it?" Rhand's whispered voice slid through the buzz of shock like a sharp blade between her ribs. He stood, still too close to her, his breath on her hair. "But it drives away the shadows. Puts the Lady at her ease. For the moment."

A knife does it fastest, the ghost had said. But which end? Farideh thought, turning to face him. The pain would do it, or the rush of adrenalin as you turned the blade on someone else—

"Her power over you won't fade," Rhand went on, taking her ruined hand in his. "Not completely. Not without careful . . . maintenance."

"Don't touch me," Farideh said, holding the bloody cloth tight against the wound. Holding onto her hand as if he could take it from her. He smiled.

"Oh, but you have so many more," he said. "Shar favors obedience, and the 'obliteration of the self'—what better approach than to whittle it away? And what remains . . . more lovely for the lack." His laugh sent a shudder up Farideh's spine, and the fear that traveled with it pushed more of the Chosen of Shar's effect away.

"She's a little demon, isn't she?" Rhand said. "Nearly as stubborn as you, but so haughty about it. She seeks to drag your fate out, but you've already set yourself against me. Against Shar. It's a waste of time trying to rein you in when you've decided not to be useful anymore." He ran a finger over the curve of her left horn. "More worthwhile to find a better use for you."

The Hells pulsed up her bones, hungry and fierce, ready to pour out, to fill the air with brimstone missiles, to pull lava up through the floor, to devour Rhand in a torrent of flames. Her face flushed, and a veil of sweat beaded up on her skin. *A better use,* she thought, feeling a sneer curl her lip. *I will show you a better use.*

The lights began to flash again, the muted purple and green of Rhand's tainted soul oozing into her vision. The shimmering blue of the tiefling ghost coming into being again.

What you're thinking, the ghost said, *is only going to make things worse.* She drifted down to hang in the air beside Rhand, her profile inches from his cheek. *You missed your chance to fight. Now he* wants *you to fight. He wants you to be something he can break, something he can overpower. That makes it sweeter. Trust me.*

Which left her with what? Farideh thought. Go along with him? Let him slice away parts of her until she bled out on the floor?

Be gentle, the ghost said. *Be cordial. Pretend this is nothing at all. He will be easier to distract that way. Remind him of your allies—the allies he believes you have.*

"As tempting as that sounds, I have to decline," Farideh said. "My head aches and . . . my patron will want to know what's happening. I need to speak to him."

The ghost smiled. *Perfect.*

Rhand drew back. "You speak with *him*?"

"Of course," Farideh said. She drew herself as straight as she could manage. "And he'll be very displeased with you if I let you keep me from him." She wondered how bald that lie was—how much Rhand knew Lorcan didn't care what happened to her—and that grief threatened her again. She held Rhand's gaze instead.

"Do you think he'll be *pleased* with your little rebellion?"

Rhand said, sounding angry. Sounding afraid. "If you lay the blame for *that* on me, I assure you it won't go well for you. We had an agreement, and I always read my agreements carefully."

"I think I need to bring it up. Lorcan will want to know, after all."

Relief lit Rhand's face. "His emissary? The cambion, you mean." He blew out a breath and chuckled nervously. "Of course. Tell him what you want. He and I are clear." He chuckled again. "Of course, of course. What did I imagine? You were calling down the god himself in my guest rooms?" He chuckled again.

Farideh kept her expression carefully blank, even as a new dread curled around her heart. He means Asmodeus, she thought. "No," she said slowly. "Of course not." But he was afraid of Asmodeus, not of her, not of Lorcan. "Lorcan is the one who calls him down," she said.

Rhand hesitated, as if trying to sift out her bluff. Farideh kept her face carefully blank, until he steered her toward her rooms once more.

My patron will want to know what's happening, her own words came back to her. *I need to speak to him.* And Rhand had assumed she meant Asmodeus . . .

Don't you wish your "patron" could manage a gift like this? Farideh's heart started pounding, the pain in her arm building as it did. *Patron,* the Nameless One had said in the study *Why not say "god"?*

"You keep saying 'patron,' " Farideh heard herself murmur. "And it means too many things."

"You too?" Rhand said. "By being vague we cast a wider net. And then?" He shrugged. "It becomes habit. I doubt *they* care."

"Some call Lorcan my patron," she said, the pieces falling together. He'd asked the Fountains of Memory to show the moment her patron had taken notice. The waters had shown Lorcan, Rhand hadn't asked to see her patron. Only the moment he'd taken notice.

Asmodeus had been watching, too—

Her breath stopped, sticky in her lungs. There was a moment where all Farideh knew was that things weren't making sense. And then the truth was just there, solid as a wall dropped around her. Rhand's horrible words come back to her in that moment—*more lovely for the lack*—and she was struck, perversely, how true that was of that moment she'd just lost. She might have been grieving and angry and lost, but that was the last moment she didn't know. The last moment she could claim innocence of any sort.

—and she was as trapped as the Nameless One.

"Perhaps," Rhand said, bringing her to the door of her room, "but we all answer to someone greater. Even him. Especially you." He gave her an evil smile. "Don't think it protects you. Your god is not as powerful as he believes."

Get in the room, Farideh told herself, above the frenetic buzz of her panicking thoughts. Get in the room. Lie down. You're going to faint. He can't see you faint. She grabbed at the door handle with her injured hand, the cloth slipping, more blood spattering on the shiny black floor.

Rhand's smile grew. "Remember," he said, as the edges of her vision started crumbling, "there is no god that could have chosen you who could protect you from the reach of Shar."

Dimly she heard the latch click, and someone grabbed ahold of her and pulled her into the room, and despite her resolve not to, Farideh's knees buckled in a faint.

"Your pardon, Saer Rhand," she heard Lorcan say in his silky way, "I need to speak to my warlock alone."

CHAPTER SIXTEEN

24 Ches, the Year of the Nether Mountain Scrolls (1486 DR)
The Lost Peaks

THE WIZARD—LORDS OF THE NINE NEVER TAKE YOUR EYES from him, Lorcan thought—looked up, surprised at Lorcan's sudden appearance. Farideh had fallen backward into Lorcan, her skin pale and grayish with shock. Blood— her blood—stained the front of her tunic, and Rhand's. A jagged stump remained of her finger, stark white bone and a fringe of torn flesh.

Don't kill him, Lorcan told himself, dimly aware of how tightly he was holding onto Farideh. Not yet. Not here.

If Farideh noticed at all as he hauled her into the room and slammed the door shut, she gave no sign. "Which of these opens your dimensional pocket?" Lorcan said to Sairché as she threw the bolt, locking Rhand and his curses on the other side. "She needs a healing."

Sairché considered the array of rings around his neck. "If I tell you, I get the ring."

Lorcan laid Farideh on the bed. "Lords damn you. Just tell me!"

Sairché shrugged. "Nothing in our deal about following all orders. She's not going to die of a missing finger."

The wound still wept blood and Farideh's breath came

shallow and rapid. "Tell me which ring," Lorcan said grimly. "And you get it."

"Emeralds in a serpent band. Left-hand stack," Sairché said, holding out her hand. Lorcan tossed it to Sairché, who slipped it over her finger. A spidery line of darkness cut through the air, widening when Sairché thrust her ringed hand past it. She rummaged in the unseen compartment, pulled out a glass vial the size of Lorcan's thumb, and threw it to him.

Sairché admired the ring. "Well met, pretty," she purred.

Lorcan ignored her, leaning over Farideh with the potion. He opened her jaw with one thumb and poured the syrupy liquid in. Her eyes opened wide. She choked and sat up.

"Swallow," Lorcan ordered. She did, flinching before she looked up into the room, and spied Sairché, spied Lorcan.

"What . . . ," she started, then all her breath went out of her. She inhaled in a horrible, throat-tearing scream and every muscle seemed to contract at once, as if trying to hold her struggling bones inside her flesh. Hells magic surged up her arms, tinting her veins black and ugly, creeping into the corners of her eyes. Lorcan pinned her to the bed, before she could cast accidentally or hurt herself.

Just as swiftly, the dark taint of Malbolge ebbed from her golden skin. Farideh looked up at him. A line of tears welled up in her eyes.

"How could you?" she said hoarsely. Her breath smelled of the healing draught, of char and cockroaches.

Lorcan didn't move. "Which time?"

She shoved him off of her with surprising strength and sat up, eyeing first Sairché, then Lorcan, as if she wasn't sure who to attack first. She would kill you, given the chance, Lorcan thought.

"Get *out*," she snarled. Lorcan held up his hands, a gesture of appeasement.

"Farideh, we're on your side. We're here to fix things."

Nothing softened in Farideh's expression, and she held her

hands up as well, bruised light collecting between her fingers. She caught sight of her previously wounded hand, now whole. The ring finger was ghost white to the line where its predecessor had been severed. Everything below was stained with blood.

"Oh gods," she whispered. The bruised light sputtered out as she stared at it. Lorcan crept a little nearer. If she kept her focus on the injury . . .

But then Sairché sighed. "If the color bothers you, I suggest taking that problem to someone else. Any cure I can get is about as pleasant as the last one."

Farideh's gaze snapped to the cambion and in a moment, she had crossed the room, forcing Sairché to retreat behind Lorcan. Farideh stopped, just out of his reach, her long frame gripped with rage so forceful, Lorcan was afraid what it might unleash . . .

"The color?" she cried. "The *color*? You threw me in here with no sense at all of what I was meant to do," she said, still hoarse from the potion. "You left me to flounder and *guess* and worry. You never bothered to tell me . . . to tell me . . ." Tears thickened her voice. She lowered her hands and gave Lorcan a look that cut right through his hope that any of this could work like in the old days.

"And we're going to fix it," Lorcan said gently. But that only made Farideh's expression grow harder.

"You can't fix this."

"Oh come now," Sairché said. "You couldn't have fumbled that badly." She edged out from behind Lorcan. "Although it does incite the question: why did he take your finger?"

Farideh gave a bitter laugh and all but collapsed onto the bench beside the dressing table. "Because your assurances mean nothing. Your deal is *aithyas* on a dead dragon's belly. I said I couldn't see any Chosen and so he murdered them."

"Well what did you expect?" Sairché demanded. "That he'd be pleased? He's a nuisance, not an idiot. That has nothing to do with our very respectable deal."

"You said I wouldn't kill anyone," Farideh said. "You said—"

"Who did you kill?" Sairché interrupted. "He killed them—or more precisely I suspect, his guards killed them—and you merely watched. I don't recall," she added coolly, "you negotiating anything about not watching someone being killed."

"Shut up, Sairché," Lorcan said. He had only the barest sketches of a plan, but one thing was certain: he needed Farideh to calm down. "You're going to declare her favor complete."

Sairché looked at him as if he were mad. "No, I'm not."

"We don't have a lot of time," he said, "or a lot of resources, and we have quite a lot of things to right if this is going to end with everyone important keeping hold of their heads. So to begin: her favor is complete. She owes you nothing else. Say it."

"If I do that," Sairché said, "then I've reneged on my deal with Rhand. I don't exactly keep my head in that case." She dropped her voice. "This isn't about making your pet happy."

"Find a loophole," Lorcan said, ignoring her. "The favor is done. Our plans hinge now on making sure of Magros. And since he's made it clear his intent is to kill Farideh, she needs to be removed from the situation. Is anyone going to argue with that?"

"I'm not going anywhere," Farideh said.

"Don't be silly—" Lorcan bit off his reply as he turned. In Proskur, Lorcan had begun to think Farideh was learning to mask her true feelings, to keep her anger quiet, her heart off her sleeve. Not well enough to hide from him—never that well. But enough that she thought she was hiding. Enough that she could be useful against Temerity, against some other mortal.

Whatever mask she'd crafted herself was torn away, and every bit of hurt and rage was writ as plain on Farideh as if it had been rendered in fresh blood. Lorcan recalculated.

"I take that back," he said. "You sound very much like a woman with a plan. Perhaps you ought to be in charge here." Her expression didn't flicker, and another thread in Lorcan's cold heart snapped. Careful, he told himself, even though another part of him wanted nothing more than to be very incautious indeed. Careful. Ease your way back. "Why are you staying?" he asked her.

"I won't let them die," she said. "I won't help and I won't walk away. I may be damned, but I won't go to my grave earning it."

"Who's sending you to your grave?" Lorcan said. "Who said you were damned?"

She laughed again. "Tell me the name of the god that's willing to claim a Chosen of Asmodeus. One—just one."

Dread coiled up Lorcan's core. "So you know," he said lightly. "Sairché apparently felt it was better you didn't."

"She was probably right," Farideh said. She rested her head in her hands.

Lorcan took a chance and moved nearer to her. "Darling, you're not damned. This is nothing. Favored status. A few silly powers to show off His Majesty's reach."

"Name the god, Lorcan."

"Stranger things by far have happened." The god of evil singling out his distressingly moral warlock for one . . .

"Why me?" Farideh whispered, as if she'd had the same thought. She shook her head, her face still buried in her hands. "I'm not . . ."

"You are," Sairché said. "And it doesn't matter if you did or didn't or never would have done any sort of thing. It's Asmodeus's decision, not yours. It's why they call them Chosen, not Choosers."

Lorcan spun on his sister. "Shut up," he hissed. "Or I do not care what deal we have, I will send you right back to that *shitting* cage. Every word out of your mouth is moving the axe closer to your neck, do you understand that?"

Sairché's golden eyes flicked over his face. "I don't take well to my pieces being impudent."

"And how well has that suited you? Shut up and let me do what I do best." He turned back to Farideh, who had lifted her head to glare at the both of them.

"It doesn't matter," she said. "I'm still not helping him massacre these people."

"No one's massacring anyone," Lorcan said. He frowned and glanced back at Sairché, realizing he wasn't sure what her plans had been for the prisoners. Sairché shrugged.

"If you don't help," Sairché said sweetly, "then you're the one who reneged. You're the one who bears the weight of the forfeit. Do you still want your soul?"

Lorcan started to silence her again, but then Farideh spoke, and she had never looked so terrible to Lorcan—so likely to be the Chosen of Asmodeus—as the moment when she turned to Sairché and said, "Would you steal a soul from your king's hand?"

Sairché froze, watching Farideh as if she'd like nothing better than to tear the woman's eyes out with her bare hands. "Not as such."

For a moment, Farideh held Sairché's gaze as if daring her to lunge. Then grief folded over Farideh again, dampening her fury. "All this time . . . you have nothing over me, do you? My soul's his as much as it can be. I've just gone along doing horrible things because I trusted you."

Lorcan kneeled beside her. "So we're not massacring prisoners," he said carefully. "Agreed. What are we doing?" Farideh shook her head.

"I could get you something to get you through the wall," Lorcan went on. "Sairché was kind enough to plan for—"

"Let me guess," Farideh said. "It will only let me out. Or it will snatch up anyone who passes through and drop them in Shar's hands. Or—"

"Hold on," Lorcan said. "We're as interested as you are in bringing Rhand down. Only we're interested in doing it the *right* way."

"Shar is not supposed to win here," Sairché added, for once following Lorcan's lead. "She never has been. That's your 'common enemy' after all. But if we break the deal with

Rhand—" She cleared her throat. "*We* can't just take the wall down."

"But that doesn't mean," Lorcan went on, "that *you* can't win a little too. Forget the passwall spell. How do you plan to rescue more than yourself?"

Farideh shook her head again, as if she couldn't believe she was listening to them. "I think someone's escaped before," she said.

Sairché sighed. "No one's escaped from here. I'm sure of that."

"Not from here," Farideh agreed. "From one of the other camps." Lorcan frowned and looked back at his sister.

"What other camps?" Sairché said, each word shot like a bullet from a sling.

"He has six camps," Farideh said. "He's moving Chosen from here to there. And in one of them . . . I think someone managed."

Lorcan smiled. "Well, I think *you've* found your loophole."

"Indeed," Sairché said, curling her hands into fists. "We are *well* into disputation."

"Don't be ridiculous," Lorcan said. "You dispute the terms and you bring Asmodeus's attention to us and pull her back to the Hells. Make Rhand *think* you're invoking the disputation clause. But don't."

Sairché narrowed her eyes at him, and for a brief moment he was very glad she was on his side. "A fair point. But I'm still offering him a proxy. A nice, antsy erinyes, I think. That gives you three days before the ruse is up." She looked at Farideh as if she'd like to give a few orders of her own. "Your favor's complete," she said instead. To Lorcan she added, "Remember what I said."

She opened the dimensional pocket once more and plucked another ring from it. A flash, a smell like burnt meat, and Sairché was gone.

And Lorcan was alone with Farideh again.

She turned from him, her eyes locked resolutely on her reflection in the mirror. She and Havilar might have the same features, the same face, but to Lorcan's eyes she looked ages older. And she wouldn't meet his eyes.

"I have *nothing* to say to you," Farideh said.

"Good," Lorcan said lightly. "I have a great deal to say to you, and I don't like being interrupted." Lords, he thought. He'd still set Asmodeus above anything else he feared, but this moment made the list.

"Don't bother," she said. "There's nothing you can say to me to change my mind. I know who you are now."

No, you don't, Lorcan thought. Even I don't know that anymore. There was a time when he would have said he did not have allies, and if he did by some twisting of the layers, he certainly did not try to win them back if they turned from him. He certainly wouldn't do it by admitting weaknesses. He certainly did not care.

But if he said that now, he knew he would be a liar, and if Lorcan was sure that he was anything, he was not a liar.

"I have never said this to another soul, another person on this or any other plane, and if I did, I am absolutely sure I didn't mean it," Lorcan said. "I mean this: I am *sorry*. I misjudged you. Terribly. I should have known, I should have realized from the very start you wouldn't have thrown me over. You were the only person in all the planes who wouldn't have thrown me over." He had never in his life felt so ridiculous, but he continued. "You were—you *are* the only one I trust. And for a time I was a fool, and I forgot that. And I'm sorry."

Farideh said nothing, still simmering with fear and hurt and anger. But there—a moment of softness where she looked his reflection in the eye, before she spoke. "You trust Sairché."

"I don't trust Sairché, I have a deal with Sairché. There are a multiverse of differences."

Farideh shook her head. "How can you stand at her side, when—were you ever even captured? Were you even in danger?"

"Yes," Lorcan said. "What does that have to do with anything?"

Farideh watched him a moment more, then sighed. "I'll never understand you."

"Don't sell yourself short," Lorcan said, acutely aware she had not forgiven him.

"I suppose I'll have to learn the ways of the Hells," she said bitterly. She started to say something else, but the words crumbled into a sob. She drew a slow, shuddering breath, trying to compose herself. She wouldn't, Lorcan felt sure. She couldn't. Everything he'd known would break her down—the fear of the dark sides of the pact, the fear that she couldn't escape, couldn't hold back the tide of the Hells herself—had come true in one terrible fact: she was a Chosen of Asmodeus.

Farideh stood—hardly able to straighten—and held her hand up as if she were going to push him away. "Please . . ." she managed. "Please . . ."

But Lorcan found he didn't care what she was going to ask him for. He seized her in a tight embrace. "Don't say a word," he said, trying himself to ignore the thickness in his voice. "Just don't say a godsbedamned word, all right?"

And she didn't. The stiffness in her frame fled and she buried her face against his shoulder and wept. He held her close, half folding his wings around them, and kept his own silence.

Because she'd said "please," he told himself. Because if she were still against you, she wouldn't have asked. This is the next step—you're her ally. Act it.

But that wasn't right. It was because he couldn't listen to her try and hold him off like an adversary, when she was too despairing to form words—that was the truth. Because he owed her better. Because she needed a moment to not be on guard.

"Take it back," she sobbed. "Please take it back. I'm not his Chosen. I can't be."

This is none of your doing, Lorcan reminded himself. This is nothing you could have stopped.

"If I could I would," he said. "You know that."

That triggered fresh sobs. "Why? *Why?*"

Lorcan shook his head. He didn't know. He didn't want to know. "It seems he's invested all the Brimstone Angels," he said. "Just an accident of your birth."

She went rigid again and pulled away. "All of them? Oh gods. Oh gods! Havi?"

Shit and ashes, Lorcan thought. "No. Your sister's fine. Nothing's shown up in her, I promise. I was at her side before I came here—several days now. I saw her only hours ago. Nothing."

"But it will?" Farideh said, panic edging her voice. "It will, and then what?"

"One thing at a time," Lorcan said. "Your sister has a protection laid on her too—and darling, it's heavier than yours. It may be Asmodeus passed her by. It may be that protection stops the blessing from awakening. The important part is that she's fine. She's not a day and a half from here, her and Brin. They'll arrive soon. And you and I had best be ready for them."

Farideh pulled away from him farther, shaking her head. "What's the trick?" she said. "Your god clearly doesn't go to all this trouble just to be perfectly happy when you go ahead and undo it all." She was back to looking at him like a demon, crawled out of the Abyss. "So what's the trick? You 'help them escape' by killing them all? You don't kill them, you just . . . pull them into the Hells? Is it me?—will I have to . . . Is it really my soul . . . ?"

"Gods damn it!" Lorcan cried. "The 'trick' as you put it, is not on you. It's on Asmodeus."

That stopped her. "On Asmodeus?"

"Or," Lorcan said more carefully, "perhaps a better way to say things is that Sairché's plan is flawed. As is her collaborator's, a devil called Magros. Both have made"—he gave her a significant look—"*mistakes.* Sairché was tasked with collecting Chosen. Magros was tasked with gathering their powers. We shouldn't be surprised if it falls apart. The concern, of course, is that any failure would reflect poorly on the person who caused it"—he nodded to Farideh—"the devils who made the plans . . . and the archdevil who oversaw it. We must make sure that isn't us."

"So I have to help you so your lady isn't punished."

"I'm more concerned about the fact that I'll be dead," Lorcan said. "And listen to what I'm telling you: there is another devil. Another Lord of the Nine with their fingers in the pie. And none of them care even a little what becomes of you or the people you're worried about. I do care."

She watched him warily. "So if Sairché fails, she'll be punished and so will you. And your lady. But if the failure is the other devil's it's him and his lady in trouble?"

"Lord," Lorcan corrected. "And yes."

"And none of you have an interest in making sure that Asmodeus's plan succeeds?"

Lorcan hesitated. "All devils in the Hells are invested in the success of Asmodeus," he said. "At least, all devils in Malbolge. Magros . . . One could surmise—if one stretched—that he and his lord might be pleased if Asmodeus didn't succeed. If Asmodeus *didn't* collect more divine power for himself." He told her what Sairché had said about the divine sparks, about Asmodeus's orders, and what Shar wanted. About what was happening to the world beyond. If possible she seemed to deflate further.

"What happens if he succeeds? If he takes the sparks?"

"Then his godhood is a little more assured in the days to come."

"And if he can't?"

"Weakened," Lorcan said. "He might even lose the godhead—no one knows."

Farideh sat on the edge of the bed, her expression drawn. "So you're worried," she said, as if choosing each word from a sack of razors, one by one, "that the other devil might sabotage the plan, stop Asmodeus, but make it look as if you were the one who failed. Do you think he's worried you'll do the same?"

"That would be clever," Lorcan said with exaggerated surprise. "But Magros seems to think Sairché and I don't have half a brain between us. He's already attempted to get me to kill his agent in the camp—an act that would place the failure squarely on me."

"So if I give up," she said, "then this . . . plan you've sold Rhand and Shar on might succeed."

"Perhaps," Lorcan said. "And who wants that?"

"Or Magros and his lord might succeed. But if I help you, your lady will succeed." She looked him in the eye. "I'm not gathering the divine sparks. Not even one. I don't care what she wants, I don't care what any of them want."

"Fair enough," Lorcan said. "I doubt either of them or Asmodeus are foolish enough to be surprised by that."

She shook her head. "Let's hope so. I think he'll find a great many things I won't do. Chosen or not."

"Darling, you know better than that," Lorcan chided. "No one wants to force you. That's our way—let the demons drag souls kicking down to the Abyss. The *baatezu* know you'll walk right in yourselves if we open the right doors." He smiled. "You just have to be wise enough to pass them by." And watch for the ones that open in your path, he thought.

She sighed. "You talk like this all day long don't you? Saying things without saying them? Whatever happened to not thinking about the plans of archdevils?"

Lorcan just shook his head. "The world's a different place. You and I are different. Something's happening and . . . it might be better to know."

"Who's the agent?" she asked. "One of the guards?"

Lorcan shrugged. "All I'm sure of is that it isn't a Chosen of Asmodeus. Magros managed to kill the Chosen Asmodeus allotted him. He had to find a replacement. But they'll be moving through the camp, not keeping to the tower." He blew out a breath, not wanting to say what he knew he had to. "What do you have in mind?"

Farideh looked up at him. "Is this where you try to talk me out of it?"

"No," Lorcan said reluctantly. "This is where we leave the tower, and I help you do something mad."

"We're not leaving the tower," she said, standing.

Much like Oota had, the elves had restructured a cluster of huts to mimic an elven high court, bringing in what scrubby brush and lichens they could collect from the hillsides in a defiant mimicry of the sort of lush green space Dahl found himself expecting. As if to set a seal on it, Cereon—the elves' Oota, as it were—was without a doubt the most eladrinish sun elf he had ever crossed paths with.

"You bring us empty promises of the goodness in an evil race." Cereon spoke as if he were reciting an ancient, elven spell, not dressing down Armas and Dahl. The cold planes of his face reminded Dahl of nothing so much as a marble statue. A very unhappy marble statue. "What a surprise," he said.

Ol' Sour-Fey, indeed, he thought.

"I would not call them empty, *solosar*," Armas said. His speech had shifted to mirror the sun elf's from the moment they crossed into Cereon's territory. "Nor would I call them promises. Say instead, 'potential.' My friend believes the warlock can help us."

"The tiefling," Cereon said. Two of the elves behind him, graceful women with their dark hair pinned up and ugly cages trapping their hands, exchanged looks. Half a smile cracked Cereon's stern facade.

"The tiefling," Dahl agreed, the words springing from his tongue in Elvish, thanks to the ritual. "Unless you have another way to get your hands freed?"

Cereon didn't look away from Armas. "I've heard what her help gains."

"You've heard what the wizard can make one do," Armas corrected gently. "Out of the fortress—"

"How do you intend to get this creature out of the fortress?" Cereon asked. Armas looked over at Dahl—that part they hadn't gone over, largely because Dahl was still plotting it out, looking for holes and traps and problems. There were too many, especially when so much of his mind was caught on the two score ales he hadn't had and the flask full of Shadowfell liquor still riding in his pocket. When his temper was still tangled around Cereon calling Farideh a "creature"—as if there weren't a hundred others who deserved Cereon's sneer before she did.

"We are working on that," Armas said finally. "We just want to know if you'd be willing to ally with Oota if we manage it."

"And I know better than to make assurances based on fancy. I know how this plays out—you take my agreement and next thing I know, you and your devil-child need sanctuary, because the guards are hunting for her, and as it happens, her magic doesn't quite work."

"Oota's willing to give her sanctuary," Dahl lied. "And I don't intend to have guards on our tail."

Cereon smiled thinly and considered Dahl with his fathomless eyes. "No one does. Trust me, young man, I have been on this plane for several centuries. I know when you ought not prod the dragon."

Dahl drew a long slow breath, trying to calm the temper that rose in him. "You want to know how we'd manage it? If I had to do it right now, I'd say in through the passage to the sorting courtyard. Up the wall and into the second floor—we're not nose-to-nose with shadar-kai there since we skip the cellars and the curtain wall—preferably in stolen Shadovar uniforms, but we can make do with the one we have. Then two floors up to the guest quarters as I understand it—she'll be there. The number of guards at that point isn't unacceptable, but we can work with that after a casting to peer ahead. After that, she's on our side."

Cereon smiled at Dahl as if he'd just suggested they ask

nicely to be let in. "Where do you intend to get the means to cast a ritual like that?"

Dahl pulled Farideh's ritual book from his sack and flipped to the ritual in question as if each turned page was a slap across Cereon's still face. "Gold salts, cerated sulfur, basilisk venom. Easily obtained from Rhand's stores." He hoped—Rhand's study was at the top of the fortress—either they'd go up blind and pray no one caught them, or Farideh would have to take the risk and smuggle out components. That made Dahl's nerves fray further still—he was supposed to be rescuing her, not putting her in worse danger.

Cereon tilted his head. "Wizard's sight," he said, naming the ritual, "cannot be cast without a focus. Do you have a very expensive mirror hiding in your pack? Or is the wizard going to provide you with that as well?"

Dahl shut the book. "We haven't pretended that this plan is complete, or that we're not still looking for solutions to make it work. All we want to know is if you and your people would be willing—under the right circumstances—to throw in with the rest of us. A provisional agreement—that's all."

"A provisional agreement to a hypothetical situation," Cereon said, "deserves careful consideration." He waved them from the makeshift chambers and back out into the street.

A wet snow fell, melting into the dirt paths and making them muddier still, and dampening all the sounds of the camp into stillness. Dahl wondered if the Harper mission was near. There was no way Tam would send the sort of army needed to retake the camp. He ran his fingers through his hair—there had to be an answer, and he had to find it. Before Rhand claimed too many more Chosen. Before the guards caught on or the possible traitor struck again.

Before something happened to Farideh.

"Well that was no good," Armas said. "We can try again in a day or so. Maybe don't talk so much next time."

Dahl blew out a breath."I don't know if we have a day," he

said. "If we leave Farideh in there, she'll have to keep sorting. If she stops . . ." He didn't want to finish.

"You don't need Cereon to rescue the warlock." Armas considered Dahl as they walked. "Why are we counting on a tiefling warlock?"

"Because," Dahl said firmly, "if we have to fight our way out, we're going to need casters, and so we're going to need someone to shatter those finger cages of yours. I'd rather count on a warlock than get cozy with a Shadovar wizard at this point, and those are your options. And she's not bad."

Armas grunted. "Neither's Phalar. And look at that."

Dahl shook his head. What had Phalar been thinking when he'd told the guards Dahl was in the armory? Probably nothing, Dahl thought. Probably just wanted to make some mischief, put Dahl in some danger. He had his dagger after all. Why worry about the rest?

Because to stop and tell the guards would give away his presence, Dahl thought. Risky. Too risky even for a Chosen of the drow gods. Phalar knew best how to survive, and opening himself to the guards just to strike back at Dahl . . . what had Phalar been thinking?

"Every time he comes out," Armas said, "carrying extra food or supplies or what have you, you think 'Maybe he's not so bad. Maybe he's not so different.' And then something like this happens."

Dahl walked along in silence. It was the sort of thing you expected from drow—like kicking a person through a roof, like knifing an ally in the dark—and yet it didn't fit. It was what you expected, and so the guards should have grabbed him. Made sure he wasn't lying, wasn't sending them on a wild hunt or into an ambush. Because *that* was what you expected from a drow. Phalar shouldn't have made it out of the fortress if he'd been foolish enough to stop and taunt the guards.

But Phalar wasn't the only one who knew that Dahl would be in the armory, Dahl realized. Nor the only one who came and went through the fortress.

"Does Tharra have a guard on her when she's in the tower?"

"Of course," Armas said. "Everyone does."

"Same one every time?"

"Since she started playing lady's maid for your warlock."

Dahl blew out a breath. Less likely than Phalar, he told himself. But then there was Tharra's insistence that he was making things worse by getting into the fortress, by trusting Farideh. By bringing weapons out. "She's not going to be happy about Cereon is she?"

"Happy about us talking to him? Or happy that he's exactly as difficult as he is with her?" Armas shrugged. "Either way, I doubt it."

They reached Oota's quarter as the sun began to set. The alleys around the makeshift court were packed with bodies—frantic, fearful bodies. The court inside was no better, except a circle in the center where Hamdir and Antama had held back the swarms of prisoners.

"This wouldn't have happened if you hadn't let Phalar and Dahl go in!" Tharra's stern tones cut through the crowd of voices. "They'd be alive—she'd be alive if they'd stayed out!"

Cold rushed over Dahl. *She'd be alive.* Oh gods . . .

"Watch your tongue," Oota said. "You don't know why things changed."

"Tharra?" Armas called, pressing through the prisoners, ducking past Hamdir. "Tharra what's—"

Dahl and Armas broke through the crowd, and Dahl saw what was truly holding back the other prisoners: a pile of bodies, at least a dozen, wrapped in blood-soaked cloths.

"Where have you been, fledgling?" Tharra demanded. "You were supposed to be watching the children."

"Gods," Armas said. "Gods, please, what's happened?"

Dahl's heart stopped and he couldn't look at the stack of bodies, couldn't bear to find a child-sized bundle among them. "He killed them in the sorting?" he asked.

"Surprised your warlock is no ally?" Tharra said. "From

what we can tell, she killed an entire courtyard of people. Took at least four. Including Vanri."

Shit, Dahl thought. Gods' broken books. "Where is Farideh?"

"With the *wizard*," Tharra said savagely. "We told you, and you didn't listen, and now Vanri's probably . . ." She faltered. "We were keeping them safe. And you've destroyed that."

"I got the boys through," Hamdir said, shouted in that way Dahl was uncomfortably familiar with. "I wasn't expecting the grays, I didn't lose hold of her on purpose."

Tharra fixed him with a hard stare. "Tell him what you heard."

"Screams. Definitely Vanri. And then . . ." Hamdir swallowed. "A roar. A terrible roar."

"She manifested." Tharra glared at Armas. "All those nightmares, all those worries about the ocean taking her . . . If she isn't dead, gods know what horrors are whispering in her ears now."

"If she isn't dead," Dahl said, "we can still save her."

Firm up, he thought, shaking. If Rhand was killing Chosen, it was because Rhand was angry. If he was angry, Farideh was in more danger than before. There was no time to wait for Cereon. There was no time to wait for the appointment he and Farideh had agreed upon. There wasn't even time to figure out whether he could trust Phalar. "We need to get in there, now. We need to get her out, get to the Chosen—"

"Get the rest of us killed?" Tharra said, as if *he* were her fledgling scout as well, as if Dahl were in need of censure. "What do you think you're going to do?"

"Save those of us who can still be saved," Dahl said. "Including Vanri."

"Do you have a plan?" Oota interrupted, calmer than any of them. "Or are you just expecting to walk in through the gates and come back out with all our lost following behind?"

Dahl faced her. He didn't have a plan—not as such. He didn't have a way to be sure no one else was going to die or be caught, or to prove to them once and for all that Farideh was someone to trust. But he could be certain it wasn't better to stay here, huddled together and waiting for the shadar-kai to come to them.

Nor was it better to leave Farideh in the tower when Rhand was slaughtering innocents.

"Do you?" he said calmly. "Or are you planning to just hope the tower collapses and the wizard drops dead? You were right before—you're going to have to make a stand, and the longer you wait . . ." He spread his hands. "This will keep happening."

"And a dozen daggers and a devil-child won't change that," Tharra said. "People's lives are at stake."

"Are they any less at stake right now?" Dahl demanded. "Right here?" He looked out into the crowd. "Can any one of you say you're better off holding your breath and hoping you're not the next one to be caught? You're the Chosen of the gods—are you going to spit so merrily in their eyes and lie down to die on Shar's altar?"

No one answered. It felt as if every eye were on him. Waiting for someone to do something. For something to change.

"This isn't a nursery tale," Tharra said. "The blessings we carry aren't weapons."

Dahl held her furious gaze. "How fortunate for me," he said. "Isn't that right?" She looked back, unblinking, no sign of the treachery he suspected save the sudden stillness of her features. He looked to Oota. "I'm in this alone, fine. Let's hope the gods still smile on those of us who give two nibs about the world. I'll find my own way in. I'll get Farideh out. And then we'll see what plans can come together." He leaned toward Tharra.

"And if you tell the guards that, fellow Harper," Dahl murmured, "I'll know." He turned without waiting for Tharra's reaction, and headed out into the darkening night. Reflexively he pulled the flask of Shadowfell liquor out of his pocket, passed it from hand to hand, then shoved it back again. If no one else was going to be the hero, then the Chosen were stuck with Dahl.

"Show me Lorcan again." Farideh doesn't care what it shows, or when, or why. She misses him and Sairché's words ring in her ears over and over. *He's done with you. She might never see him again, never get to explain herself,* and whatever Rhand's apprentices think about that, she doesn't care either. They haven't moved from their stations in nearly an hour—waiting, it seems, for some other development. There's no more blood, no more whispers, and no more hints about what might be, save for a pair of them fussing with the shelf of ancient scrolls, arguing over whether any of them could be useful. And Farideh wonders if all her plans are doomed to fail this badly.

A taproom in a waystation, sometime before Proskur. Farideh can't remember the name of the inn or the village. She remembers the night, though, and the taproom. There's a fiddler and a bard with a lute, another with a drum. The music is raucous and cheery. The dancers are wild and carefree, and the room feels like a hive of bees. Brin and Havilar are whirling, giggling, not caring that people are giving them looks. They crash into the table Farideh keeps between her and the mayhem and look abashed. Brin offers Farideh a hand. "Do you want to take a turn?"

"No thank you," she says. They whirl off.

"Don't you like dancing?" Lorcan drawls beside her. She hates it when he talks like that.

"Why would I like dancing?" she says irritably. "I don't like people staring at me. I don't like being crowded. I don't like strangers grabbing at me." She sips her ale. Farideh remembers wondering if he was going to ask her to, and if she'd say yes. And she remembers knowing he wouldn't. "Do you like dancing?"

Lorcan shrugs. "Why would I?"

Farideh sighs. "Right. You don't like anything."

"I like surviving," Lorcan says.

"Do you like anything that you don't need?"

Lorcan gives her such a puzzled look, and standing over the waters, Farideh is embarrassed all over again. How many times has he hinted at the terrors of Malbolge? Everything Lorcan does is, by necessity, to save his own neck—one way or another. Even when he saved her life, there was a payoff, a reward. Passage to the Hells, safety from his sisters, an alibi when he returned to his terrible mistress. Lorcan does nothing because it's just pleasant. She knows that now. She suspected it then. Enough she should have known better than to ask such a silly question.

"Never mind," she says and looks down into her ale. It's the first time, Farideh thinks now, she started to understand he would always be something alien, something inhuman.

But as the waters continue reflecting, she notices something she hadn't in the taproom that night: Lorcan's puzzlement fades into something bare and uncomfortable as he watches her. As if she wears him out. As if she vexes him. As if he's confused and frustrated. As if he knows all of this, and still, he wants her to stay there, beside him. He sighs, so quietly she never heard him.

"I like," he said finally, "this ale. I think I'll have another."

The vision fades, the waters stop, and there is only Farideh's reflection on the glassy surface. She wonders why the waters chose that moment, why they revealed it from that angle, why they let her see that strange look Lorcan gave her that makes her heart quicken. To teach her a lesson or to break her heart swiftest? To tease her or taunt her or none of it? The waters might be good or evil or neither.

Neither, she tells herself. The magic doesn't care one way or another. It's only her melancholy that makes it feel that way. It's only knowing that perhaps Lorcan wasn't as alien as she'd always thought that makes her feel as if she's failed him too.

CHAPTER SEVENTEEN

24 Ches, the Year of the Nether Mountain Scrolls (1486 DR)
The Lost Peaks

CONCENTRATE, FARIDEH ADMONISHED HERSELF, AS LORCAN climbed down from the windowsill, into the empty study. Between the embarrassing way Lorcan's embrace flooded her with want and the utter terror that gripped her when they took flight from the bedroom window, she had plenty to distract her from the Nameless One's powers nibbling at her thoughts.

"I hate that," she said, still trembling as she unwound her tail from his calf. "Gods, I *hate* that."

Lorcan shook a spatter of melting snow from one wing, then the other. "Didn't you *leap* from the window to get here before? You'll fall but not fly?"

"It's not the same," she said, crossing to the basin nearest the window. "You're *meant* to fall down, not up." The Chosen of Shar's effects slipped in through her thoughts and curled up like a dog at a fire. It was nowhere near as bad as it had been standing in front of the Nameless One, but still it made her thoughts sluggish, her heart heavy. She concentrated on slowing down her rattled breath, on the task at hand. Get in, get what you need, get out.

Lorcan came to stand behind her as she reached for a pinch of the blue petals in the bowl beside the vessel—close, too close.

"What about this Chosen of Shar?" he murmured close to her ear. "What am I meant to do if it takes you again?" She went still, her hand resting half in the pile of dried petals. He set a hand on her hip, and drew her ever so slightly closer, and she forgot the powers of Shar altogether.

"You could remind me," she said, eyes on the waters, "of all the things you said when you came here last. I think that would do it."

Lorcan straightened. "I *apologized* for that."

"You did," Farideh said, looking back over her shoulder. "Which is why we're still talking. But it isn't as if 'sorry' is a magic word that means none of that ever happened." She looked down at her reflection in the water, the gloominess of the Nameless One's presence across the hall unfolding in her thoughts. "It doesn't wipe the slate."

"Well, what *does*?" Lorcan demanded.

Farideh laughed once. If she knew the answer to that, she would do it herself and resolve her own sins once and for all. "I don't know. I suppose we'll have to wait and see."

Before he could respond, she cast a pinch of the flowers over the surface of the water.

"Show me the last time someone escaped from one of Rhand's camps."

The waters swirled and shivered, reflecting back another camp, with the same squat huts, the same obsidian tower, the same faint shimmer of a magical wall. Beyond, a desert stretched, red and frosted, the sun just creeping over a distant horizon. The guards on the wall were fewer—and human, yawning at the early hour, their eyes focusing on some half-remembered dream no one else could see. They certainly weren't expecting the prisoners who poured out of the graying shadows.

There hadn't been as many—perhaps a hundred, a hundred and fifty—but there weren't many among the people who rushed the stone wall who didn't scintillate with the blessings of the gods. A bolt of lightning struck the first guard who tried to sound an alarm, followed by an explosion of rubble as a stout dwarf woman planted her hands against the stone wall and brought it down beneath the guards' feet. The prisoners killed them swiftly, took their weapons, opened the gates, and filled the narrow courtyard. The guards regained their wits and struck back—cutting down anyone who came near. Blood soaked the sandy floor of the courtyard.

But the guards didn't seem to matter to the prisoners. Their efforts were turned against the tower.

There were Chosen who set flames against the building's base, hot enough to crack the crystal. There were Chosen, like the dwarf woman, who made the stone shatter into chips or stole the ground from beneath it. There were others who took a warlord's mantle, flush with the blessings of a martial god, who made their comrades into an army to bring the guards to their knees and to keep those destroying the tower from being attacked. Spells sizzled down from the tower's heights—balls of flame that clung to guard and prisoner alike, spheres of energy that seized whole groups of fighters. The commanders ordered the prisoners to break, to spread out, as another spell locked a dozen of them in place. It made the wizards' work harder, but it didn't stop the spells that rained down on the Chosen below.

But then the tower fell.

Some ran as the stone cracked. Some scattered to the edges of the courtyard, seeking shelter where they could. The Chosen who had stood right up on the tower's base didn't even try to flee—there was no fleeing as the structure fractured and split and fell apart in great, sharp pieces. The screaming blended together, a roar to match the pitch of the tower's constant vibrations.

The core of the tower split, and the shimmer of the wall ceased. The prisoners who were left fled into the red desert and vanished as the Fountains of Memory returned to their placid swirling.

"Shit and ashes," Lorcan said.

Farideh stared at the basin, shocked into silence. They had to bring the tower down to dispel the wall.

"The stone," she said, as much for herself as for Lorcan. "It looks like it breaks easily. If you attack it right, maybe . . ." She fell silent. That tower had been smaller. It hadn't been so well guarded—and still, half the prisoners had been killed bringing it down.

It's no use, that unwelcome voice in her thoughts seemed to say. *You can't save all of them. You can't save any of them without asking for a sacrifice.*

Farideh squeezed her eyes shut. "What do you think Magros intends to do?" she said. "What . . . what do we play off of?"

"Does it matter?" Lorcan said. "You can't seriously be considering bringing down—"

"What are our options?"

"He has a Red Wizard. Some undead. They're headed here with some magic in mind. I doubt," he added acidly, "that it has to do with freeing your prisoners. Maybe she wants an army of corpses? Maybe she wants to capture the camp for her own master?" He shuddered and pulled her nearer. "Darling, we don't *need* to be here. Please."

"I'm not coming back," Farideh said. "I don't want to find I missed something later on. Do you think the Red Wizard will be able to get through the wall?"

Lorcan shook his head. "Rhand has to make allowances from the sound of it. Even Sairché and I can't come through easily. Out though . . . It might be easier. I could get you away. Get us away. Let Magros and Sairché bungle things on their own."

"You know you can't," Farideh said. "You know I won't go." She ought to push him off. She ought to keep out of his reach. She ought to make sure she was absolutely clear about where they stood right now—and he was not in her good graces. But with the Nameless One's presence on the other side of the floor pressing on her like wave after wave of invisible soldiers . . . his arms around her made for pleasant enough armor. Regardless of why he offered it.

"Is she getting to you?" Farideh asked.

Lorcan cursed under his breath. "Yes."

"Keep fighting it," Farideh said. She tried to speak as carefully as he had earlier. "If the prisoners escaped—like in the vision—that wouldn't go well. You'd be at fault. You and Sairché and Glasya. It would be exactly the sort of thing this Magros might try to make happen." She dipped her hand into the water to feel the sharp jolt of pain the cold sent up her nerves. "It would be a good idea to see if that agent you mentioned knows about it. So you could be sure not to catch the blame." She pushed him gently away and turned to face him. "Or maybe they know about the Red Wizard."

"You'd have to find the agent," Lorcan said. "One soul in an ever-moving sea."

"I have connections. This completely ridiculous power." She shut her eyes and calmed herself. She had been doing a fine job of not thinking about being a Chosen of Asmodeus, of not considering what came next. If she could keep it out of mind, it was as good as not true—or as close as it could be.

But even brushing the edge of that knowledge stirred a panic in her heart.

"It's ridiculous as you're using it," Lorcan said. "Finding Chosen is a very odd little side effect Sairché decided to exploit."

She opened her eyes again and found him watching her with an uneasy expression. "What's it for then?"

"You see the state of mortal souls," Lorcan said. "How corrupted they are. How easily they would be claimed for the Hells."

"*Karshoj*," Farideh spat. She wrapped her arms around herself. "I'm never doing that."

"Never say never, darling," Lorcan said. "It may come in handy one day." He hesitated. "Is that all? The soul sight?"

"Yes."

His wings twitched in an agitated way. "It seems inadequate. Unlike His Majesty."

Farideh felt the Chosen of Shar's powers and her own worry twine around her chest. "So what comes next? I kill with a touch? I steal souls with a glance?"

Lorcan made a face. "Lords of the Nine, you're dramatic. No—I don't know what comes next. I only mean you should be on guard for more. Asmodeus only knows what will trigger it, after all. In the meantime, you need spells. Something to show Rhand and Magros what they ought to be afraid of."

"I'm nothing to fear."

"You are a Chosen of Asmodeus. The whole world will fear you, if you give them the opportunity. Here." He took her hands together and filled the bowl of them with a darkness that sloshed back and forth like ink. The magic seeped in between her fingers and ran up her arms.

Farideh swallowed. "What is it?"

"Another spell," Lorcan said grimly. "Face your foe. Hold the rod parallel to the ground and pull up. Say *chaanaris* as you do. You'll want to be some distance back. It doesn't . . . discriminate."

Farideh looked down at her hands, still cupped in his. "All right. Shall I practice?"

"No," Lorcan said quickly. "Not this one. Don't use it unless you have to."

"Why?"

He regarded her for a long moment. "There are spells I can give you," he said, "which might as well come from a wizard's study. There are spells that acknowledge their nature in subtler ways—the rain of brimstone, the word of corruption." He closed her hands in his. "And then," he finished, "there are those spells that are undeniably the gift of the Nine Hells. It is one of those. I don't want you to be afraid to use it when the time comes."

"Have I been such a coward before?"

"The pact has been gentle on you so far. There's no room for that anymore." He looked down at her hands in his. "Why didn't you listen?" he asked. "We would have been all right. I could have handled Sairché. I'm not worth this trouble."

Farideh pressed her mouth shut. It was the Nameless One's powers. It was just what happened to Lorcan when Shar's emptiness rushed over him. It didn't take away what he was, deep down. "She was going to kill you," she said after a moment. "And as you said, I can't do much with a corpse."

Lorcan let go of her hands.

Farideh turned back to the waters and scattered another pinch of petals over the surface. "Show me where Clanless Mehen was a quarter hour ago."

The waters took only a moment to show a group of people scaling the slopes of a densely wooded mountain. And among them, Mehen, hauling himself over a fallen tree, up onto the path where the others waited.

"Harpers," Lorcan said, coming to stand behind her once more. "Brin said they'd be following."

Farideh sighed and shut her eyes. "If I survive this, I think I'll never leave Mehen's side again."

"Don't make promises you can't keep. Is that . . . ? Gods be damned. The Thayans."

Mehen stopped beside a creature out of Farideh's nightmares—a corpselike thing with long, bony arms and talons like scythes. "What are they doing with Mehen?"

"A very good question," Lorcan said, leaning nearer to the water. The smell of him—musk and brimstone and strange spices—taunted Farideh, and the Chosen of Shar's powers seemed to catch hold of it, wielding it like a tool to dig into her heart.

"I need you to find Mehen," she said.

"He won't be happy to see me. You might end up with a corpse despite your best efforts."

She turned to face Lorcan. "Not if the first thing you say is that I'm all right. Give him some sign."

He didn't move back. His eyes flicked over her face as if he knew her anger had a chink in it, and he smiled. "What sign is that?"

Without breaking her gaze, she reached across and pulled the long blade from his scabbard. He stepped into her, so that the knife stopped halfway out, and Farideh stood pressed against the icy basin.

"Cut a plait of my hair," she said, remembering the vision in the pools. "Give it to Mehen. He'll know what it means."

"That's a lot of blade for a little lock."

And despite everything that had changed, Farideh blushed at that, and Lorcan's smile spread. She let go of the knife and separated out one of the small braids Tharra had left at the nape of her neck, hidden in her loose hair. "Here."

He drew the knife, and wound the plait around one finger and pulled it, hard enough to draw a gasp from her and force her head back. He hesitated, the sharp blade too close to the golden column of her throat. Farideh shut her eyes.

"Magros gave me this," he said. "He thought I might kill you with it."

"Would you?"

"I might have," he admitted. "But not anymore." He sliced through the lock of hair in one quick motion. "Remember?" he added silkily. "I have a slate to wipe."

Farideh rubbed the back of her skull and looked away. "You need to get the Harpers here as quickly as possible," she said. "I need to check on Havi." She reached for the petals.

"Don't bother," Lorcan said. "We should go and I can find her myself."

Farideh bit her lip. "If you can keep her away—"

"Don't even ask me to do that," Lorcan said, tucking the braid into a pocket. "You know I can't. Besides, she has a way into the wall—that necklace Sairché left you. The Harpers will need it."

Farideh looked back at the basin. "Then just one more." She tossed another pinch of petals over the water. "Show me Dahl Peredur, where he was a quarter hour ago."

The waters shivered and showed the camp, and the wet

splattering snow. Dahl leaving a crowd of prisoners, looking furious and hurrying down the road toward the south. Farideh bit her lip, hunting through the vision for clues.

"*Dahl*," Lorcan said icily, "is your friend in the camp?"

"Not now," Farideh said, marking a clothesline, a missing patch of thatching, a stone half-buried in the ground. The vision disappeared and she blew out a breath. "Yes, it's Dahl. If you're going to rage and moan over that, at least consider he's a *bit* better than Adolican Rhand."

"You didn't tell me about *him* either."

"Because I thought that trial was over," Farideh said. "I thought I didn't have to worry about him anymore." She met Lorcan's dark eyes. "I didn't want to worry about you getting into trouble, with some human's blood on your hands, trapped in the middle of Waterdeep—or what would become of me if that happened. Though I suppose you'll say it wouldn't have mattered. It's not as if Asmodeus would just let me go to waste, right?"

She left him standing beside the basin and collected the components Dahl had asked for—not caring if their absence showed. She went to the window and looked down—the snow had stopped, and the world beyond was dark and wet and moonless. Lorcan moved up beside her and brushed the hair from her cheek. She flinched.

"I am sorry," he said again. "And . . . not just because I wish you'd stop being angry. But you couldn't have stopped the king of the Hells from choosing you, and neither could I. You were born for this."

Farideh's throat closed around a fresh set of tears, but she only nodded, unwilling to cry again. "Come on," she said, hardly louder than a whisper. "We need to go."

Much as she hated the sensation of flying, and the mockery of an embrace that was holding on to Lorcan for dear life, the drop from the tower to the camp below wasn't nearly long enough, and when her feet touched down on the sticky mud beside the hut with the missing thatch, her pulse was racing and her throat still tight. Lorcan pulled her into an alleyway, peering out into the street.

"A quarter hour is a lot of time," he said. "Might be your paladin's found something else to do. Someone else to visit."

Farideh pushed past him, coming out into the street. "I think he knows about the massacre. So he's looking for me too." She started a little ways down the road. "A quarter hour is enough to get to where he's keeping his weapons and prepare, then leave again." She looked back at the fortress, looming over the camp. There was an awful lot of it to fall. "He ought to come back along this path, and—"

"Farideh?" Dahl's voice called. Farideh smiled as she turned to see the Harper sprinting up the road, dressed in a stolen Shadovar uniform and wearing a sword. "Gods books, Farideh?"

"I see he's still a quick one," Lorcan muttered.

"What *happened*?" Dahl cried as he reached them. "They're saying you murdered a dozen people and sent ten times that to the wizard's workshop." He looked her over once. "I was going to rescue you."

"I didn't kill them," she started.

"Well, I figured *that*," Dahl said irritably. He looked at Lorcan, but said to Farideh, "You're not hurt?"

Farideh rubbed her left hand, the healed finger. "Not much," she said gamely. She gestured at Lorcan. "I found us more allies. And a plan."

"A plan?" Dahl repeated. He shook his head and cursed softly. "Of course."

Farideh scowled at him. "You haven't even heard it yet."

"No, I—" Dahl stopped himself. "I haven't," he said diplomatically. "And it's probably better than the nonsense I'd cobbled together." He spread his hands. "Tell me what to do."

Farideh rolled her eyes. "Hear the plan first. And tell me yours. Likely they both need refining." She turned to Lorcan. "You're going to make sure the Harpers find Havilar and Brin, and point them here. Sairché's going to put Rhand off the scent."

"And we'll sort Magros," Lorcan added. "You handle the agent and . . ." He sighed. "Don't attempt this mad plan without telling me what exactly you're doing first."

"If it's too late—"

"I'll make sure it's not too late."

"Fine," Farideh said. "I'll see you then." She could only hope there were enough Chosen, enough powerful Chosen willing to attempt something so likely to end their lives—gods, she almost wished Lorcan were staying. It would take a devil to convince someone of something so dangerous.

She had so lost herself in puzzling out what came next that she didn't expect Lorcan to say another word.

She didn't expect Lorcan to grab her around the waist, to pull her right up against him. She didn't expect that when she started to tell him to leave off and stop acting out, that his mouth would close over hers and steal her breath.

Farideh's mind went blank as a fresh sheet, not even certain of what was happening. And then Lorcan's hands pulled her hips against his. His tongue slipped past her lips to brush against the roof of her mouth, and a branch of lust shot through her, as electric as a lightning storm.

I ought to kiss him back, she managed to think.

And then he released her, dark eyes dancing.

"Do be careful, darling," Lorcan murmured, and before Farideh could sort out what to say or even how to form the words, he plucked up the ring that made the whirlwind portal and was gone.

Farideh drew a sharp breath. Reflexively she pulled her cloak closer around her.

"Gods books," Dahl said. Then, "I thought you said he wasn't coming to save you."

That's why he did it, Farideh thought. He only kissed you because Dahl was standing there. He only did it to mark his territory, just like before. She touched her mouth without meaning to.

"He isn't saving me," she said firmly. "I think I'm saving him. I brought components. I found a way to take the wall down. Can we get inside?"

Dahl hesitated. "Yes." He looked up the road, toward the fortress. "But it may take some explaining. Come on."

It would have been too simple, Dahl thought grimly, if they'd been allowed to just see Oota like any other petitioner. He had meant to make Farideh hang back, out of sight, while he slipped back in and got them a little space. But as discreet as Lorcan might have thought he was being, someone had seen them flying out of the fortress, and Dahl ended up leading her straight to the mob of prisoners coming to see what had fallen among them.

After that, it was all he could do to hang onto her and keep the angry prisoners back.

"I told you already," Dahl all but shouted over the noise of the crowd. "She didn't kill them, and she's here to help us." But the prisoners recognized Farideh the moment they'd come close to the makeshift fortress, and no amount of Dahl's shouting or shoving prevented them from hauling Farideh up to stand before one-eyed Oota.

"Tharra has her doubts," Oota said. "As do I. Better to be sure of her."

"Better not to risk it at all," Tharra said. "Put her down or lock her up. If she's not with the wizard, he's going to come looking for her soon enough."

"I have three days," Farideh said. "We have an agreement." At that, Tharra shot Oota a knowing glance. Farideh flushed and wispy shadows edged her frame. "He thinks I'm . . . elsewhere. Serving another."

"Which of them are you murdering my people for?" Oota asked.

Farideh looked down at the piled bodies. "That was an accident. I told him I wouldn't identify the Chosen. I didn't know he would kill them," she said. "But I should have. I'm sorry. I will be sorry every day of my life."

"Might be able to shorten that for you," Tharra said, and Farideh's jaw tightened.

Oota glowered at Tharra. "Are you taking my place, *friend*? Making my orders?" To Farideh she asked, "Pretty clear you're no ardent follower. So why are you here?"

"Are you going to turn down a freed caster?" Dahl asked. He looked around the room, spotted Armas in the back and beckoned him closer. "You *can* still cast that spell?" he murmured to Farideh. "The one that shatters things?"

Armas held up his shackled hands. Farideh pointed her flat palm at the half-elf. "*Assulam.*"

The magic raced dark and virulent up her arms, shot across the room, and turned the cruel gauntlets into a burst of rust. Armas leaped back, surprised. He flexed his hands stiffly, and gave a nervous chuckle. "I'll be damned." He murmured a soft, sibilant word. A cloud of colored lights appeared at his fingertips, and he laughed again and looked over at Tharra, who kept her stern expression.

"Get Cereon and the elves," Dahl said.

Oota held up a hand. "Hold."

"I can tell which of you are Chosen, too," Farideh said. "I'll do it for you instead of him. You can separate those who are likely to gain powers, try and trigger them, and make an army of sorts. Or just keep them away from the wizard."

"Or get them all in one place?" Tharra said, still unconvinced. "Easy for your guards to scoop up?"

Farideh turned to her. "You'd be ready for that. You'd never let them stand around where they could be gathered up, and neither would I—not if I could help it." She looked to Oota. "Move me around the camp, if you'd rather."

Tharra pursed her lips. "We can't risk it. She could easily be a spy."

"Why would I bring you a spy?" Dahl demanded. "I vouch for her."

"How long have you known each other?" Tharra demanded.

Dahl hesitated. That wasn't a simple question. "Long enough."

Tharra reached over and yanked Farideh's sleeve up, showing her brand. "You two see the same skinscrivener?"

Farideh pulled her arm away. "Do you want my help or not?"

"It's not her you should be asking," Oota reminded her. The half-orc considered Farideh as if trying to force the tiefling woman to look away—gladly, Farideh stared right back.

"The wizard's finest," Oota finally said, "should sort this out."

Tharra stiffened, and Dahl said, "That's ridiculous. You'll lay her out for a day, and we don't have time for that."

"She said three days," Oota reminded him, not breaking her gaze. "Tharra is right—it's a mighty high risk. If she's what she says, we'll protect her. If not"—her crooked grin sent a chill down Farideh's back—"we'll appreciate the advantage."

"There has to be another way," Dahl said. "You don't need to put her through it."

"Oh, probably," Oota said. "But the wizard's finest is my offer. Take it or leave it."

"I'll do it," Farideh said. "I'm certain I've been through worse."

"We'll see," Tharra said. "I'll see all of it."

"No, Tharra," Oota said. "This one's mine."

"You can't afford to be laid out either."

"Hamdir and Antana can manage. And you." Oota spared Tharra another of her crooked grins. "You can manage without me, I'm plenty sure. But this one . . . I want to see this one."

Tharra pursed her mouth. "I'll get the flagon."

Farideh turned to Dahl, looking more than a little worried. "How bad is this?"

Dahl hesitated. "Not . . . good. She might see things

you'd rather not share. You might see things you'd rather not remember. And after . . ." He winced at the memory. "The next day is horrible. But it seems to be honest. So they'll see you're someone they can trust."

She looked up at him, that shadow-smoke growing thicker. "And if they don't?"

Dahl thought of asking her what they might find, but—no, not now. It was probably just the devil anyway, and he quickly shifted his thoughts away from *that*. "Then we'll think of something else," he said firmly.

Tharra brought the cup to Oota, the honey-sweet smell of the wicked brew's base overlaid this time by a murky, dirty scent that stirred Dahl's memories. He blew out a breath—how many hours had he carried the flask of shadar-kai liquor now? It felt like months.

"Bah!" Oota cried. "What is this?"

"Think it might have gone a bit off," Tharra said.

Dahl frowned. "Doesn't smell like old wine." What *did* it smell like? Something familiar.

"It's not wine," Tharra reminded him. "Not really. We can't wait until Phalar gets another batch."

"Is that a good idea?" Dahl said. "What if it . . . poisons as it goes bad?" He sniffed again—was it the base? Did the fruit turn that way? Had he eaten that, smelled *that*? "What do they make it out of?"

"Shadowfell things," Tharra said.

But things tainted by shadow always smelled musty to Dahl, old and cold and faint.

"Ready, devil-child?" Oota said.

"As I ever will be."

"Who do you serve?" Oota asked. She handed Farideh the cup and the tiefling drank deeply, coughing at the introduction of the heady brew.

This smell, Dahl thought, was wet and living and *virulent*.

"Feywild," he said. Ah shit. Shit.

Farideh handed the cup across to Oota, and Dahl saw the fine splinters floating on the scummy surface of the wizard's finest, looking like the remains of a bad cask, before the half-orc brought the cup to her lips.

Hamadryad's ash—that was the smell. Powdered roots of Feywild ash trees that the hamadryads let casters harvest when the ash trees threatened their oaks. Dahl used it in several rituals. Particularly one to amplify the effects of other rituals.

He looked over at Tharra, who was watching Oota, jaw tight. "Oh gods."

Oota flinched and glared at the cup, then at Tharra. "This . . . doesn't . . ."

Stop!" Dahl cried, even though it was too late. "Don't drink it!"

Farideh looked up at him, alarmed, and started to speak. But half a syllable out of her lips and she fell backward, the word becoming a grunt.

Oota stood, reaching for her cudgel. "Snake!" she said, her words starting to slur. "What have you done?"

Tharra took a step back. "What I needed to," she said.

If it worked like it did in rituals, Dahl thought, it would drive everything up. It would make the memories more than Farideh could handle—maybe more than Oota could handle—and it might well drive her mad. It might well *kill* them, Dahl thought, remembering how his heart had tried to pound its way out of his chest.

"Hamdir!" Oota shouted, weaving on her feet. "Antama! Grab . . . her. . ."

Dahl snatched the cup from Oota's limp hand a moment before she collapsed in a heap beside Farideh. A moment before her two heavies seized Tharra.

"What's the antidote?" Dahl demanded.

Tharra eyed him stonily. "No antidote. Are you going to listen to reason now?"

Farideh started shaking, and Dahl dropped down beside

her. There was nothing he could do, nothing he could change to stop this from happening. He could only watch.

He looked at the cup, the swallow and a half of wizard's finest left in the bottom. He could watch from here . . . or from there.

Please let this work, he thought to Oghma or whoever might be listening, and he tipped the rest back.

"Are you *mad*?" Tharra demanded.

"Not as mad as you," Dahl said. "Hold onto her. Oota's going to want answers at least half as much as I will. Try to wake us, however you can." By the end of the sentence his tongue had turned to clay, and before Hamdir, Antama, or Tharra could say a word, Dahl's vision turned black.

When Farideh could see again, she was standing in Arush Vayem, deep enough into winter that the snow was piled up to the top of her shins, the cold creeping through the leather. Wood smoke spiced the air, and the sing-song argument of children was the only noise.

There were two tiefling girls up ahead—both dressed in well-loved rabbit fur capes and mittens, their tiny horns just beginning to curl back over their dark hair. Farideh approached, her heart shivering: the girls were Havilar and herself, in their seventh winter, and she remembered this time, this place. She remembered what was about to happen.

It's not going to happen, she told herself. It isn't real. This was a memory, like the ones the waters showed.

The wind gusted, blowing open her cloak, as if the scene itself were laughing at her conviction. *What's memory? What's real? What's real enough?*

Oota came to stand beside her, watching the young twins stomping through the snow. "Shitting wizard's finest," she growled. "Never a simple answer. What are we looking at?"

"That's me," Farideh said pointing. "That's my sister Havi."

Havilar bounded over to the palisade. A tree had fallen, rotten and top-heavy with ice, at just the right angle to destroy this part of the wall. The tree had been chopped up and hauled away already—burning in a dozen hearths no doubt—and the replacement logs shaped and placed. But the weather was still cold enough that it would be longer still to get the stone and earth packed around the repairs. The man repairing the wall was off having his highsunfeast, and Havilar had a plan.

"She's going to break her arm," Farideh said, dread creeping in on her, as Havilar wedged the stick she was carrying in between two of the logs, working it back and forth.

"Godsdamned, Tharra," Oota said. "Probably ruined the damned question. You know she was going to do that?"

But Farideh only had eyes for Havilar. She didn't know a Tharra—there certainly wasn't one in the village. She shouldn't be talking to this half-orc either—Mehen wouldn't like it.

"Havi, I think we should go back," the younger Farideh said, and she felt herself mouth the words unconsciously. "I don't think this is a good idea."

"It's a fantastic idea," Havilar said. "And it's a fantastic idea right now—Zevar is going to be back to finish in a little, and then we'll never get out."

More footsteps crunched up behind Farideh, and she hoped it was Mehen, come to scold Havilar and make them both go back inside. She couldn't leave Havi, but she knew this would end badly.

"I don't want to get out," Farideh told her, and she wiped her tiny nose on the back of a mitten. "And you can't move it, anyway."

"I can so!"

"Hey," Dahl said, and Farideh startled, suddenly grown again and watching her memory of Havilar. His breath turned into steam on the air. "Are you all right?"

Farideh knew she should ask him how he was there, why he was there. She knew she should ask why Dahl had shouted at them to stop as the wizard's finest took effect. She should ask about the cold, and the footprints they made as they moved through the snow—that wasn't like what he'd told her.

But when she opened her mouth she said, "She's going to break her arm. The log falls and pins her. I have to stop her. Mehen will be so angry."

"You can't stop it," Dahl said. "It's already happened. This is just a memory, all right? You have to focus on that. You can't stop it. You just have to ride it out."

The top of the log wavered dangerously. Farideh shut her eyes. "Right. The wizard's finest."

"Exactly," Dahl said. "Only a bit worse. Tharra added something to the goblet. I think it's meant to amplify the effects, make it harder to come out of it."

"Bastard," Oota spat. "*Knew* she had a blade for my back."

"Worry about that later. Just stay alert and watch for the amplifications."

"They're already happening," Oota said. "You don't feel the cold or the heat in these things. You don't leave marks. Are we going to be wishing for weapons?"

"I suspect that will depend on how your question comes across."

A shriek, a heavy *whump*—Farideh's eyes snapped open as a scream tore out of her throat. Havilar lay half under the log, pinned in the snow. She started forward, even as her younger self did the same—ready to push the log with all her might, terrified to find Havi dead under there—

Dahl caught her arm and stopped her. "Hey! It's not real!"

Farideh kept pulling against him, watching her younger self snatch up the stick Havilar had held and lever up the log enough for Havilar to wriggle out. Overhead the pale clouds began to darken and billow, heralding a storm.

Dahl held her tight. "You were very . . . strong little girls."

"Swordswomen need to be strong. Mehen makes us lift

rocks," Farideh said flatly, as the little her wept and cradled her wailing sister.

"Made you lift rocks," Dahl said, turning her toward him again. "*Made.* This isn't real. You have to remember that."

Farideh shook her head. "Then what is it?"

Who do you serve? Oota's question echoed over the snowy village, dragging behind it a roll of thunder. The snow, the village, the girls clinging to each other bled together like ink on wet parchment. Only the wooden palisade remained. The sky darkened, swollen with clouds and blood-red lightning while the rest of the world faded.

And Farideh was suddenly very afraid.

"It's not real," Dahl reminded her. "Gods' books, you have to calm down." She looked over at him. His breath was coming hard and rattled. "Farideh, this is all coming from you—the visions, the sounds, all of it. You have to calm down."

But out of the palisade's shadows a figure unfolded: Havilar, all armed and armored, and eyeing the group of them with a very un-Havilarlike malevolence. She carried a glaive, but at its tip there was a crystal like the end of a warlock's rod instead of a metal spike.

Rohini, Farideh thought, trying to step back, to move away from Havilar. The succubus who had possessed her sister. Dahl was still holding onto her arm, and someone else was holding her by the hair.

"You'll be fine," Mehen said. "You'll have your sister with you. A blade at your side."

"They love her, don't they?" Lorcan was suddenly there, so close by her side that she could feel the heat of him. "But only so long as you keep after her, cleaning her messes and making sure no one realizes that she's causing so much trouble."

"Havi's not trouble," Farideh said, not taking her eyes off the devil nested in her sister's skin, even though her thoughts were all on Lorcan. The memory of him kissing her—when had that been? Not here, not now. He chuckled. Dahl squeezed her arm.

"Stop *that* too. It's not real," Dahl said, and it sounded as much like he was reminding himself as her. "Farideh, what . . . what are we looking at? Tell me what happened."

A stone wall erupted out of the ground on their left, followed by a crag of pale rock that looked like broken bone ahead. Havilar slipped into the shadows between them and vanished.

"I can help you, you know," Lorcan crooned. She shut her eyes. "Simple as it comes. No one will ever hurt you. No one will ever hurt her either."

"It's Lorcan from the day I took the pact," she said. "After Havi summoned him. He tells me all the ways I can use it to protect myself, protect her, and I say yes, even though I shouldn't. Mehen is from the day I went out on patrol for the first time. I don't want to go, I know it will end badly—it does. I nearly take the blacksmith's foot off, jumping at a marten. Havilar . . ." Her blood flooded with the powers of the Hells. She had to save Havilar, somehow, without hurting her too. "It's not Havilar, but it is. A devil in her skin. We have to be careful—she'll fight and not care if Havi—"

"It's not real," Dahl reminded her. "The only dangers are the feelings it stirs up."

"There is dangerous," Mehen said. "And there is *dangerous*."

Oota cried out suddenly. Farideh opened her eyes as Dahl pulled her behind him—she glimpsed Havilar darting past, her grin wicked and her glaive dripping blood. Oota held a hand to her upper arm.

"Gods' books," Dahl swore. He looked around and grabbed the dagger Mehen wore at his belt. It came away, solid as the real thing. The memory of her father made no sign he'd noticed or cared—after all, Dahl hadn't been there when Mehen had readied Farideh for patrol. Dahl tested it in his hand. "Remember someone with a sword," he told Farideh.

"It doesn't work like that," Oota said grimly. She checked her wound. " 'Course it doesn't usually work like this either."

"Think, Fari!" Dahl said. "Anyone with a sword."

Who do you serve?

"There's a very rare heir among the Toril Thirteen," a woman's voice said. The room sizzled and dissolved into a city in the heart of summer, and another cambion stood in front of them: Sairché, flanked by two erinyes. "The descendent of Bryseis Kakistos, the Brimstone Angel herself. Only three other devils have collected Kakistos heirs. Lorcan must have one. I think it's you."

Farideh's pulse started drumming again. Three, and herself—and Havilar, who was somewhere here, all too near. Sairché couldn't be allowed to find her.

Dahl moved toward the nearer erinyes, as if convinced she would strike. He pulled the sword and the devil didn't so much as flinch. But as soon as the weapon was free, Sairché and the erinyes vanished.

And Havilar's glaive swung out of the shadows once more, aimed straight for his neck. Farideh cried out, and Dahl turned in time to drop out of the polearm's path. He ducked under its swing and slashed at Havilar's face with the dagger. A line of blood appeared across her cheek. But she smiled.

And a line of pain seared over Farideh's cheek, right up to her silver eye. She touched her face, and met Dahl's gaze over her bloody fingers. Havilar laughed and vanished into the shadows again. Dahl cursed loudly, and both he and Oota moved to stand at Farideh's back. Red lightning raced over the sky and the roll of thunder echoed Farideh's runaway pulse.

"Are you all right?" he asked her.

"Fine," Farideh said mechanically, studying the shadows for Havilar again.

"Hamdir and Antama will be working at waking us up," Dahl said, passing the dagger to Oota and readying the sword. "We just have to stay alert until they do. Don't hit the tiefling. Just don't let her hit you."

"And if they can't?" Oota asked. "You know the best way to get out of this."

"Give them half a chance," Dahl said coldly.

Bodies erupted out of the ground two by two, fine lords and ladies turning with assassins and shadar-kai in a gently whirling dance that closed in around the three of them. Dahl reached out and grabbed hold of her wrist again. Adolican Rhand's revel.

"Your sister wants things well within her reach," Lorcan's voice said in her ear. "She never needed help. Though"—and the crowd parted to reveal Brin and Havilar, their arms wrapped around each other, and Sairché beyond them, watching—"that can always change."

A scream rang over the dancers, and all the gentility vanished as the assassins and shadar-kai drew weapons and attacked. The woman in front of Farideh swatted desperately with a fan at the grinning shadar-kai who'd slashed a deep rent through her bodice and down to her skirt. Farideh hardly thought, throwing up a hand, pulsing with the bruised and dancing magic of the Hells.

"*Adaestuo*!" But as the blast of energy hit the shadar-kai, he turned into Havilar once more, and it was her sister who took the brunt of the spell, and a heartbeat later, Farideh herself felt the concussion of power, the sharp electric crackle of the spell. It stole her breath and blanked her mind for a moment.

But she had to do it again, she thought panting, taking in the rampant carnage around her. She had to stop this. Stop all of this. Even if it was Havilar at the root. Even if it meant—

Dahl grabbed her and she nearly hit him with a second spell, before he wrapped his arms around her and tucked her head against his chest.

"Stop looking!" he said. "Stop. None of this is real, I promise. You have to remember that."

None of it was real, and yet all of it was real—Farideh's memories filtered through her very worst fears. That Havilar would be hurt. That Havilar would be lost. That Havilar would be turned into something terrible by sweet-voiced devils promising her easy answers.

"A favor," Sairché's voice said, over the screams and the sounds of fighting. "And I'll protect you and your sister from death and from devils, until you turn twenty-seven."

Just as they did to you, a little voice said. *Something terrible. Something that destroys everything it touches, thinking it knows best.*

"That's not true," she murmured. Dahl held her closer.

Who do you serve?

The landscape changed with a grinding sound, and Dahl gasped. She pulled away. All traces of the revel, of Arush Vayem, of Waterdeep had burned away, and they were standing at the edge of a hideous landscape—the suppurating ground sprouted tangles of wiry brush, sores of lava, and bony protrusions, watched over by a distant, enormous skull. A scream echoed across the plains, chased by another and another, a chorus of the tortured. Even the sky seemed to loom, ready to crash down on them. Oota was nowhere to be seen.

"Malbolge," Farideh said, feeling her very core start to shake. "It's not real. It's not real. It's not real."

Bars like thick insect legs burst out of the ground around Farideh, trapping her in place. Havilar eased out of the shadows, glaive still in hand. Dahl set the sword against the cage, reached through the bars, and took her face in his shaking hands. "Look at me," he said. "Look at me, gods damn it, not at her."

Farideh drew several long, slow breaths, trying to ignore the glimpses of Havilar she saw from the corner of her eye, and the spikes of panic that came with them—*you have to save her, have to save her.* The nightmare spun and spun around them, the Hells growing larger and more detailed beyond the terrible cage, hemming them in as surely as the bars.

"This is all my fault," Farideh said.

"*This* is that scheming Tharra's fault," Dahl said. "Unless you gave her the hamadryad's ash powder, you're just as much a victim as the rest of us are."

But Farideh had made this place, this terrible place—and she couldn't control it the way she needed to. If she hadn't taken Sairché's deal, if she hadn't ended up in the fortress, if she hadn't helped Rhand—

"What was yours like?" she asked, making herself look at Dahl. "You said you did this before. What was it like then?"

His eyes flicked to Havilar and back, almost as if he were weighing which was worse. "Embarrassing," he said. "But not deadly."

"What did they ask? What did you see?"

"It's not important."

"If I have to stay calm, to stop paying attention to all of this, then yes, it is important."

Dahl scowled at her, still holding her face. "They asked how I got here. And it started with my fall. Followed by every . . . shameful, awful moment of my life, and then you jumping in here." He averted his gaze. "I think I'd gladly trade you."

Farideh leaned closer, so that she couldn't see Havilar, her horn ridge resting against the bars. It was as close as she'd ever been to another person—save Lorcan. Dahl's gray eyes slid back to hers, and belatedly Farideh remembered the dreamscape echoed her reactions. She bit her lip. And Dahl looked down at her mouth.

"You would not trade," Farideh said quickly. "Watching your . . . what do you have? Brothers? I forget."

"Brothers," Dahl agreed, looking up again. "Older. But they're farmers, the both of them. I'm not really afraid they'll turn on me with blades in hand."

"I'm not afraid of that!" Dahl gave her a look, and she flushed. "I'm not," she said. "I'm afraid *they'll* turn her. They'll hurt her." Her heart squeezed and Havilar darted forward again. Dahl let go, scooping up the sword in time to block the weapon.

"I'd still trade," he said quickly, blocking a second strike. He glanced back at her. "It's not real."

Farideh started to retort, started to tell him it was *karshoji* real enough—but Havilar's glaive found an opening, slashing up through Dahl's belly, into his chest. He gasped . . . and vanished. Farideh cried out before she could stop herself. It's not real, it's not real—

Havilar turned and gave her a lazy smile. "Are you surprised?" she said, not at all in Havilar's voice. She stalked toward the cage. "It was always going to come down to the two of us."

Stay calm, she told herself. When she'd been able to keep herself from getting lost in the fear, things had slowed down. Havilar tossed her glaive from hand to hand, eyeing Farideh like a choice prize.

But it wasn't Havilar—those weren't Havilar's words, and those weren't Havilar's actions. What would Havilar really say? she asked herself. If you're doing all of this for Havilar, what would she actually do?

"Gods," her sister's voice said beside her. "You really think I'm a terror, don't you?" Havilar crouched atop a spur of bone, looking down at her devil-self with a wrinkled nose.

"It's not you," Farideh said.

"Right," Havilar said. "Then why do you care about saving it?" She shook her head. "That's definitely supposed to be me. Only you made me fight like I'm shoveling with that stupid thing. And you couldn't give me nicer armor? You wonder why I'm angry at you—it's 'cause you put me in ugly armor that makes me look like I have a ham for a backside."

"Oh for gods' sakes," Farideh said. "I did not."

"*Fine*," Havilar said. "Forget the *pothac* armor. You're still convinced you have to save me, and that I'm this big scary *something*. Do you see that?"

"I don't, though," Farideh said. "You're not."

"Then why do you have to be in charge of everything? Why is everything sitting on your shoulders?"

"I'm trying to *protect* you!"

The ground rumbled, shattering the bars of her cage and

raining pieces onto Farideh. A great, spiked beast—a dragon made wormlike and twisted by the Hells—burst out of the rock and shot skyward. The creature went stiff, clawed arms waving almost boneless and vinelike, before splitting neatly into three parts that fell away like the petals of a hideous blossom around a heart of stone.

Standing atop the heart was a devil—not merely a devil, Farideh knew down to her marrow. Where Lorcan was beautiful in a way that had made her listen when she shouldn't, the man on the stone, holding a ruby rod, was beautiful in a way that she wasn't sure she ought to be looking at. As if her eyes were going to turn inside out at the sight. He pointed the rod at her and spoke, in a voice like ground glass.

You have one task: Stay alive, tiefling. Give no ground. You may find we have more than one goal in common.

The core of the archdevil glowed suddenly blue and bright as a falling star, the light resolving into another of the strange glyphs that marked the Chosen.

"That's the secret," the devil-Havilar said.

For a terrible moment, Farideh couldn't breathe.

Then she shot up, out of the vision, gasping and wet. Dahl stood over her, similarly soaked, and holding a bucket. She sat, trying to make sense of the world. Trying to forget the threat of her possessed sister and the disappointment of her true one.

Trying to forget the glorious, terrifying devil standing on the stone heart.

Trying to pretend she wasn't sure with every fiber of her being that that had been the king of the Hells himself, Asmodeus.

She covered her face with her hands and fought the urge to wail, to scream, to be sick all over the floor.

"It's all right," Dahl said, easing her up to a seated position. "It's all right."

"Get her down to the shelter rooms," Oota said. She was sitting beside the big human man, drenched as well. "You've got 'til morning to recover, tiefling." As Dahl helped Farideh to her feet, Oota turned her furious gaze to Tharra, sitting bound and stern-faced between two more guards.

"Lock *her* up," Oota said. "I want to be at my best before I deal with this traitor."

CHAPTER EIGHTEEN

25 Ches, the Year of the Nether Mountain Scrolls (1486 DR)
The Lost Peaks

WHEN THE GUARD IN THE TOWER OPENED THE DOOR TO
Farideh's quarters, Sairché was waiting, along with four
erinyes. The shadar-kai woman's dark eyes flicked from Sairché
perched on the foot of the bed, to Faventia and Fidentia sulking
silently at the posts, to Nisibis standing beside the window
and leaning on a massive sword, and finally to one-eyed Sulci
standing all-too-close to the door. Sulci grinned.

"Fetch your master," Sairché ordered.

The guard did not, as Sairché had hoped, try to test her
steel against the erinyes, but turned and vanished down the
dark corridors.

"Pity," Nisibis said, as if she read Sairché's thoughts. "That
one seemed entertaining."

"The wizard will be entertaining," Sulci said. She grinned at
Sairché. "They always think they're so clever. But a clever mind
doesn't hold your skull together when my hoof comes down."

"You're not killing him," Sairché reminded her half sisters.
"Not yet."

"Nor are we to kill Lorcan," Faventia drawled. "Isn't that
strange?"

"There are complex deals in place," Sairché said. "Deals that will end one day." She smiled at her half-sister, easily one of the most reckless erinyes she commanded. "Which Lorcan surely knows. Savor his fear. You'll get your chance."

"And the wizard?" Fidentia asked.

"Is less aware," Sairché said, turning her eyes to the door once more. "Which is why I've brought you along. Now play your parts."

Rhand arrived, wand in hand and regarding her with that easy contempt she'd come to expect and loathe. But there was something worse there this time. His robes were tidily arranged but spattered with blood. A lot of blood, Sairché observed. She'd interrupted something.

"Well," he said. "You've returned. How fortunate." He looked around the room, his gaze hesitating momentarily on Nisibis and the twins and stopping altogether on Sulci. His expression shifted in a way Sairché had not been expecting. "And how intriguing. Where is my Chosen? She has much to make up for."

Sairché feigned surprise "My dear Saer Rhand—don't you read your agreements?"

"Always," Rhand said, icily.

"Then I shall remind you of the sixty-first section of our contract," she said sweetly. "And let you choose her proxy." She gestured at the erinyes, then leaned in, conspiratorially. "I would personally opt to waive the proxy option. They are none of them polite company. Particularly Sulci here. She has many impolite ideas about your skull, for example."

Rhand stared at Sairché, as if his gaze alone could make her quail, and despite herself, Sairché checked her shields. "They are none of them capable of the sort of magic I require," he said. "Bring me my tiefling."

Sairché feigned surprise. "The messenger hasn't reached you? My, my." She did not break her gaze but activated the little serpent ring she'd reclaimed, and reached into the pocket it created. In the cold void, her hand closed on Rhand's agreement.

She jerked her head to Faventia as the heavy scroll broke into the plane, and her much stronger sister took hold of it and held the voluminous parchment up for Sairché to read. "From the third section: 'They will be kept and maintained within the walls of the camp Adolican Rhand builds with assistance from the Nine Hells,' " she read. She waved Faventia away. "And I come to find that you have decided that means 'any camp you build with any assistance which might have once had its origins in the Hells.' Those are not, if you ask me, the same thing."

"Does your lord care?" Rhand said. "There are plenty of souls for his use left in this one."

"My lord cares about mere mortals assuming his preferences," Sairché said. "And I care about being made to seem a fool. So it would seem," she went on, as she'd rehearsed all the hours of the night, "I'm very fortunate to have that sixty-first section to fall back on. You'll find it very clear: in case of dispute, His Majesty, Asmodeus, Lord of the Ninth Layer and All the Hells Beyond, Ascended God of Evil, claims temporary ownership over all Hellish assets involved for three days, during which the dispute is decided. By him. You are entitled to a fiend to stand as proxy for said assets and your requirements are not in force during the deliberations—although I don't suggest you dawdle, you have quite a few souls outstanding—and your own soul is not in forfeit."

"Until it is," Rhand said.

"Now, now," Sairché said. "We have rules about this sort of thing. That's why they're in the contract."

Sairché kept smiling, wishing privately this had been Lorcan's problem to deal with. What she'd said was true—every word—but she hadn't claimed the contract in dispute, and she wouldn't. Even if there was no chance of Rhand being in the right, Sairché wouldn't run the risk of drawing Asmodeus's attention to what she had or hadn't been doing. Since Farideh hadn't left the camp, she remained—in the most technical of senses—in Rhand's possession and all the terms of their agreement were being met well enough to stand. Still, it made Sairché's nerves itch—too close to failing the agreement. To finding out what happened if she reneged.

"It does get a bit dull by the sixty-first section," Sairché said, to cover her nerves. "I don't blame you for skimming."

The dark rage lingering under Rhand's calm facade took over. "I don't have three days to spare. You call her back."

Sairché shrugged. "Alas, I cannot."

Rhand pointed the wand at her head. "*Yuetteviexquedot.*" The shielding spell dissolved with a dull whine. Sairché tensed, but in the same moment, the erinyes struck. Sulci's sword swung up like a club, setting off Adolican Rhand's own shield. He startled as it erupted, throwing Sulci back to the floor, and giving Nisibis a chance to dart in and clout him hard behind the head. The wizard fell to his hands and knees . . . and found Nisibis's sword held close under his chin.

"You can't kill me," he said.

"Really?" Sairché replied. "Where in our agreement does it say that?" She stepped down from her perch. "Did you really think you could twist an agreement better than a devil from the Hells?" Lords of the Nine, how satisfying would it be to give the signal, let Nisibis cut his throat, let Rhand clutch and the blood that fountained from the wound? She drew a breath—not now. Killing him now would mean she'd failed. She nodded to Nisibis instead, and the erinyes moved to stand beside her.

"You are still of a use to me, fortunately," Sairché said, opening the portal to Malbolge again. She looked down at Rhand, crouched on the carpet, and smiled. "Don't disappoint."

But she had no more than turned her back on him before he spoke once more.

"If those are the terms," he said, "then I select you as my proxy, Lady Sairché. If you'll come with me?"

Havilar woke, hazy and aching. When Brin had tried to brew the tea for her the night before, she'd put him off and climbed into her bedroll where she willed herself to sleep before he could say another word to her. She did not need caring for.

Brin dozed against a tree, on the other side of the fire. When she stood, he stirred and turned toward her, hand on his sword, and altogether she was still angry at him, and still so glad to see him.

"Good morning," she said.

He smiled crookedly and let go of the weapon. "Good morning. You sleep all right?"

Havilar shrugged. "I guess." She still wasn't happy about being told to sleep. "Did you stand watch all night?"

"Not exactly. I sleep lightly," he said. "You never know when some noble's going to get it into his or her head that offing me in the night is in their best interests." He rubbed his eyes. "Usually, though, my room's not full of owls and voles and things. I feel as if I woke a hundred times last night."

Havilar wondered what his rooms *were* full of, what noises he was used to. How many of them were someone else. It wasn't her business—not yet and maybe not ever. "You should have woken me."

"I'm all right." He stretched and tried to smother the yawn that escaped him. Havilar gave him a very pointed look. "All right," he admitted. "I should probably have woken you. You seemed like you needed the rest."

Havilar squatted down beside the fire. "You could sleep now. I'll pack things up. Or just rest your eyes at least, if I'm too noisy."

He gave her another crooked smile. "That would be perfect." He eyed her a moment. "Are we going to talk today, do you think?"

Terror sank its teeth into Havilar. "We're talking now," she said lightly.

"Havi," Brin sighed.

Havilar stood and went over to her bedroll. "Can we just get on our way before we worry about this?" He sighed again, but said nothing else, and when she glanced back, he was settling down to sleep.

She ought to be brave enough to hear him say that there was nothing between them. She ought to be sure enough to know if that was what she wanted or not. She ought to be more concerned with finding Farideh who—yet again—deserved the worry more than she did. It made her feel unseated and upset, like a plant pulled up by its roots and tossed onto the stones. She finished packing everything up, and considered waking Brin.

Havilar picked up her glaive instead and turned her attention to the pull of her muscles, the solidness of her bones. The weight of the glaive steadied in her hands. She didn't imagine opponents, this time, or make an enemy of a tree or a shrub. She moved the glaive through careful steps, patterns she knew by rote—a sweep, a slice, a carve, a chop. Step and slide and step and turn. Once upon a time, people had said her glaive was as good as her right hand. Once upon a time, Devilslayer had been the perfect anchor—as long as she had her glaive, Havilar knew who she was.

And now everything was different, but Havilar was the same. And she wasn't sure she ought to be.

Slash, sweep, pull the blade up.

Brin was certainly different—he was so *sure,* and so bossy, and she hated that *pothac* beard. Every time something dangerous came up, he tried to make her go home, back down, turn into someone else. Every time he sighed at her, she wanted to curl up and hide.

Chop, press forward, sweep low. Step forward. Turn.

And then he would laugh when she said something funny and everything was the same again. He would smile at her with that glint in his eye that made her think they were sharing a secret, and she was his again, and that was exactly right.

But then he'd sigh.

She lunged forward, barely holding on to the weapon's haft, the weight nearly pulling it out of her hands. She took an extra step trying to keep it, and stopped, panting. Again, she told herself, and she started over. She hadn't done these passes in years—*more* years she amended. She hadn't done all manner of things in years. It made her feel a little melancholy and a little giddy at the same time—like she was a girl again, learning for the first time.

She'd run through the passes once again and started a third time, when she realized Brin wasn't sleeping, but lay on his side watching her practice. She faltered, and pulled the glaive close. "Sorry. Was I loud?"

"No. I just wanted to watch. You're getting better."

She ran a hand over the end of her braid, and realized its shortened length wasn't surprising her anymore. "Thank you."

"It'll come back," he promised.

It had to, Havilar thought. Because otherwise she wasn't sure about a single other thing. Especially not Brin.

"What would you be doing today if you were at home?" she asked. "If you hadn't come with me? If I hadn't come back?"

Brin screwed up his face as if he were trying to remember his calendar. "I had a meeting planned about now, with one of my contacts, to talk about the state of things in the Dales."

"This early?"

"People assume if you're noble, you sleep in," Brin said. "Or, if you're a young noble, that you are finishing up a night of drinking and carousing." He shifted his position, as if trying to find a more comfortable bit of dirt. "They don't tend to look for you in back rooms with tinkers."

"Do you do a lot of that? Carousing?"

Brin laughed once. "No. People think there's something off about me," he admitted. "I don't carouse or whore or drink. I'm a terrible young noble."

Havilar looked away—she realized she was blushing. She wanted to know and she didn't want to know what he did in his free time. Whoring and carousing wasn't an answer she wanted, but then, did that mean he was off with sweethearts and brightbirds and romances? Did that mean he'd become someone who wanted none of those things? Or maybe—*maybe*—was he holding out for her to return?

You aren't going to know unless you ask, she told herself. She dug a little hole into the dirt with the butt of her glaive.

Before she could ask more, though, a line of bright light split the air and tore wide to reveal Lorcan stepping into the plane.

"Ye gods!" Brin shouted, suddenly on his feet.

"Well met to you too," Lorcan said.

"Where's Farideh?" Havilar said. "You said you were going to rescue her."

Lorcan looked at her with that irritatingly blank expression. "Safe," he said. "Out of the tower. But she won't leave the camp without first rescuing the people held prisoner there, so unfortunately your stubborn sister says this little adventure's not through."

"But she's safe?" Havilar asked. "She's all right?"

"Oh, safe as a ruby in Asmodeus's strong box," Lorcan drawled. "She's with *Dahl*, after all." Havilar gave him a knowing look, but Lorcan just glared at her. "As for Mehen, I'm finding him next, and I'll send him your way. Get around the mountain, toward the peak on the southeast slope. There's a plateau there where you can meet easily." He blew out a breath. "They're traveling with a Red Wizard and her attendant undead. Ghouls and such. Be forewarned."

Brin belted his sword. "Why are they traveling with undead?"

"I haven't the faintest idea, nor do I know how far off they are, but I assume you can find some way to occupy yourselves if there's a wait." He gave Havilar a significant look of his own, before he leaped into the air, flapped up through the gaps in the canopy, and disappeared from view.

Brin cursed, kicked the dirt, and cursed again. "Gods *damn* it."

"It's not so bad," Havilar said. "We'd have to climb anyway."

"That's not it." Brin heaved another sigh. "If that had been anyone else. If that had been another devil"—he shook his head—"I wouldn't have been able to do anything."

Havilar swallowed and turned back to the pile of gear. She tightened her grip on the glaive, the one thing no one could take from her, even if they knocked the weapon from her hands, burned the haft, and melted down the blade. I just have to get this right, she thought. Maybe nothing else could be fixed, but she'd die taking back the glaive.

"Well, at least we know where we're headed now," she said.

There was a limit, Mehen found, to how far the coursing of hot blood would carry a body. He was starved for food that wasn't Daranna's dry waybread, company that wasn't Khochen's ridiculous playacting, a bed that didn't lie beside a shambling mockery of a corpse, and most of all for his daughters. One would have guessed that after seven and a half years of their absence, he would bear it better. But when the group paused to send the scouts ahead, to stretch and eat their terrible waybread, Mehen turned to the woods to make water, and stayed alone in the trees to overcome his heavy heart.

Never again, he thought. I'll never let them out of my sight again.

It was a lie and he knew it, ugly as it was to realize it. He had no idea what having grown children meant. Except Brin, which wasn't the same. Or maybe it was? He had no notion anymore.

One thing at a time, he told himself, one thing—

He tapped his tongue against the roof of his mouth and tasted a stranger's scent. The Red Wizard's. Near enough to have stuck a dagger in his back.

Mehen spun on her, reaching for his own daggers. Zahnya only smiled.

"A nice private spot," she said.

"It was," Mehen said, releasing the weapons. "Did I take too long to piss?"

"I wouldn't know," Zahnya said. "I have something you should see." She pulled a small, clear crystal sphere from her sleeve and shook it once. An image formed around it, swallowing her hand and the ball together: Khochen and Vescaras on watch the night before. There was the fire, the shadows of the unsleeping ghouls, his own sleeping form in the distance.

"Do you have a plan for him?" Khochen asked.

Vescaras didn't look at her, peering out into the darkness. "I'm hoping we won't need one."

"It's his daughter," Khochen said, and Mehen narrowed his eyes. "We're not going to be that fortunate." She glanced swiftly back at the camp. "Daranna will just grab her, you know. Run him through if need be—or rather, try to."

"She's underestimating him less and less," Vescaras pointed out. "You're his latest friend, why don't you prepare him?"

"That's what I'm saying. I don't think we can."

"Then what is there to discuss? We can't let a possible Shadovar agent run free. You can't convince Mehen she needs to be caught. Where lies the middle ground?" He turned to Khochen. "Keep him apart when we get there. We'll get her in irons, and he'll have to stay calm once he sees we have her. Fair?"

Khochen nodded. "Fair."

The image disappeared with a pop, and Zahnya smirked at Mehen over her outstretched hand. "Imperfect allies," she said. "I thought you should know."

Mehen sighed. The Thayan was so young. "I know."

"If you like," Zahnya said, "I could . . . delay them. Allow you your access to the camp first."

"Do you know," Mehen said, "my daughters are tieflings? Foundlings? I suspect you must, with Khochen asking me every question under the sun, and you listening to every answer. If you think this is the first time someone has taken it into their minds to assume the worst about one of my girls, you are a fool indeed. They were always going to try and capture her. I was never going to stop them. But I will be one of your *karshoji* bone-puppets if that makes a damned bit of difference in the end."

Zahnya's mouth went small. "You're right. I've been listening. I would have thought you'd care enough to protect that girl."

"This is protecting her," Mehen said. Even if he was sure down to his marrow that Farideh had not gone off intending to aid the Shadovar, not been intending to play the traitor in wartime, there was still the small, unshakeable doubt that she'd given him for so long—so very long. There was always the pact. There was always the devil. He wouldn't let the Harpers have her—not easily—but he wouldn't let her fall either.

Zahnya pulled the crystal into her sleeve once more.

"But many thanks for the offer," Mehen said with a toothy grin. "And the warning that they're trying to 'handle' me. I'll make use of that." He considered her. "They won't turn on you, you know? Damned Harpers—don't like breaking their word, even when it seems a bad promise. Especially when it comes to stopping Shar."

"I'll believe that when it happens," Zahnya said. "Truth be told, I'm surprised we've come this far. I did expect the bite of your blade, goodman. Perhaps the infamous interrogations of the Waterdhavian Harpers."

"What do you want in the camp?" Mehen asked.

She looked at him and smiled with a wickedness that reminded Mehen she was not just a girl, and he wondered for a moment if he was in fact outmatched. "To take weapons from Shar."

"What weapons?"

"We'll have to see," Zahnya said. "What I hear is there is unconfirmed." She looked up the mountain path. "We shall have to see," she said again. "Take your time, by the way. I doubt you're the sort of man who needs to be told how long to piss." She climbed the slope back up to where the palanquin waited.

Mehen tapped the roof of his mouth again, trying to decide what to do next—confront the Harpers, or keep the secret for himself? He froze, the taste of some other human laying on his tongue between the ferns and the moss and the flavor of humus. The nurse log, he thought, turning toward the fern-covered mound of dead tree.

"Which of you is back there?" Mehen said.

Khochen eased around the fallen tree, an impish grin on her face. "I should have guessed you'd be so calm," she said. "Daranna's doubts are wearing off on me, I'm afraid." Her eyes flicked over him. "Are you upset?"

"Not yet," Mehen said plainly. "Don't you *karshoji* cut me out when we get there. I find her, I'll bring her to you. You find her, you find *me* and I don't leave her side. Understand?"

"Fair enough." Khochen eyed him. "You don't have a problem with the fact she might be a traitor?"

"She's my daughter," Mehen said. "And she can't betray *that*."

"Not even by dealing with devils?"

"Not even by dealing with gods," Mehen said. "Do you have children?"

"No."

"Then you have no idea what it would take for me to leave her—you cannot imagine. Don't ask me to, and I won't show you why those orphans of the Platinum Dragon want my training." He rolled his shoulders, as if he could shake the tension from them. His girls might have left him, but he would never leave them. Never.

No word from Dahl. No word from Brin since they'd reached Noanar's Hold—and broken planes, he was *not* happy about the boy taking Havilar through a portal as finicky as that one. But they were both safe at least.

"Well," Khochen said, "we'll have to see what happens. Incidentally, thank you for keeping her attention. It gave me a chance to peer into her inner sanctum, as it were." She stood on tiptoe and whispered, "She has a case hidden in there."

"Probably her wand's."

Khochen smiled and shook her head. "Too big for that. Too ornate. A scepter or a rod, I would say. Marked all over with very interesting runes. Nar, by their look."

Despite himself Mehen was curious. "Can you read them?"

"Not well," Khochen said. "The crafter seemed enamored of cinnabar and gold. If I had to make a guess, I'd say it makes fire. People are seldom imaginative," she added, "when it comes to gems."

Mehen snorted. "Well that's her business, then."

"I don't think so," Khochen said. "She hasn't touched it. Hasn't unlocked it, so far as I can see. I don't think it's for her—maybe it's for the camp, maybe it's for an ally, maybe it's part of her nefarious plans to kill us all." She said all of this so cheerfully that Mehen rolled his eyes. "But I doubt it's meant for starting campfires."

"Nothing is simple when I'm with you people."

"Never." Khochen hesitated. "By the by, I do apologize for the other day. For finishing your story and getting it wrong."

"I don't care. It's not your business—I don't want to make it your business—so it doesn't matter. I am who I am."

"Somebody," Khochen said, as if she were agreeing. "Though I still wish I knew the rest of your story."

Mehen heaved a sigh. "There's not much to tell. Pandjed told me to marry Kepeshkmolik Uadjit. I told him I wouldn't—if I had to marry, I wanted a bride who wouldn't force me to part from Arjhani." Saying his name still made Mehen's heart feel as if it were tearing, even after all these years. "Pandjed told me I could marry or be exiled. I chose exile. Arjhani did not."

Khochen's brows rose. "You ought to write a chapbook with that tale, goodman."

The roar of the boneclaw cut off Mehen's retort. Both Harper and dragonborn scrambled up the slope toward their waiting party and the sounds of a scuffle. Mehen drew his falchion as soon as he had room to, holding it ready to aid the Harper scouts . . .

Whose arrows were all trained on a familiar cambion, one arrow already dangling from his wing.

"Oh, Lords of the Nine pass me by," Lorcan said, sounding relieved. "Will you tell them to stand down?"

"Aim for his eyes," Mehen advised. The scouts adjusted their arrows. Zahnya held two wands, the air around both filled with thick, dark magic.

"Gods damn it!" Lorcan shouted, covering his head. "Farideh says to tell you she's safe! And if you kill me, you won't find Havilar."

"Stop!" Mehen bared his teeth in annoyance. "He's with me."

The Harpers lowered their weapons—all except Daranna, who stayed, still as a statue, her arrow trained on Lorcan's throat. Zahnya let the magic dancing around her wands fade and retreated to her palanquin.

"Curiouser and curiouser," Khochen murmured. Mehen ignored her, sheathed his falchion again, and crossed to Lorcan.

"If this is a trick," Mehen started.

"If this were a trick," Lorcan said, "do you think I'd be the sort of idiot who just drops out of the sky into the midst of a mass of weapons?" He glanced at Daranna over his shoulder. "Farideh sent me to find you. She wanted me—" He seemed to reconsider his words. "She wants me to send you toward Havilar." He told Mehen about the necklace Havilar carried, about the bead that would make it possible to cross through the magical wall encircling the camp.

"Take the bead to Farideh," Mehen said.

"She won't use it," Lorcan said. "It won't let more than a dozen of you pass before it closes. I sent Brin and Havi around the mountain and up a bit. There's a plateau there, a place where the mountaintop is sheared flat." He hesitated, then dropped his voice. "What are you doing with Thayans?"

Mehen didn't so much as blink. "Wartime makes strange allies."

Lorcan's eyes cut to the boneclaw, watching them with burning hatred in its eyes. "Indeed. Tell me you don't trust that thing more than me."

Mehen held up the amulet. "It comes with a leash."

Lorcan gave him a wicked grin. "Oh, so do I," he said. "But your daughter keeps a tight hold on it."

And whatever resolve Mehen had built up over the last few, terrible days, his rage overtopped it. He slammed his fist into Lorcan's face, hard enough to knock the cambion off his feet and bloody his nose. Stunned, Lorcan clutched his face and stared up at Mehen, looking too surprised to speak.

"Do you know why I don't kill you?" Mehen hissed. "Because you've proven to me—every time I am on the very *edge* of taking a blade to your throat, it seems—that you're better than useless and my daughter is wise enough to know that doesn't mean you're any good, even if she forgets to show it. This time, I have no proof, only suggestions, and if you think for a *heartbeat* I'm so grateful to you that I will sit and let you torment me like some old man sitting in the dust, stand up and let's see how many bones your pretty face has to break."

Lorcan daubed at the black blood streaming from his rapidly swelling nose. "Noted," he said, with a savage tone. Oh try it, Mehen thought, bunching his fists again. Give me another reason. "I meant the damned amulet, by the by, the one Havilar's carrying still."

"Of course you did," Mehen said.

Lorcan pulled himself to his feet once more, still wincing and pressing at his nose. "I wouldn't dawdle," he drawled. "The longer you take, the more opportunities to spot you. And I'm not the worst devil you have to contend with anymore." Before Mehen could make him say what he meant, Lorcan had opened a portal and stepped away, back to the Hells.

CHAPTER NINETEEN

25 Ches, the Year of the Nether Mountain Scrolls (1486 DR)
The Lost Peaks

FARIDEH'S DREAMS WERE A SOUP OF NIGHT AND FEAR, BARELY formed shapes rising out of the thick darkness and smothering her with pain and anger and terror. They were endless—I'll never wake, she thought, I have never woken. The feeling of being watched from every angle, the *wrongness* hiding where she couldn't see it . . . When she finally did open her eyes, her thoughts wouldn't accept it. She lay still, not daring to move for fear of what would bleed out of the dark next.

Then she felt the mat beneath her, the dirt below that. Her eyes adjusted to the shuttered lanternlight warming up the small, earthen-walled room, and picked out the shape of a man sitting against the wall.

"Lorcan?" His name hurt to speak, her throat was so parched.

The man stiffened. "No," Dahl said, and Farideh was fairly certain if she weren't so wrung out, she would have died of embarrassment. Dahl opened the lantern a little more, illuminating his face, and all the walls of the cellar she was lying in. She crawled over next to him, leaning against the wall. He handed her a waterskin, and he could have been Asmodeus himself, and Farideh would have been glad for him in that moment.

"You seem fair enough," he said as she gulped the stale water. He fiddled with a little metal flask as he spoke.

"Depends on what's fair," she said. Her head was pounding and her stomach unsettled, and she felt feverish. "Did I throw up on you again?"

"Again?"

Farideh felt her cheeks flush. Of course he didn't remember, why would he? "At the revel," she reminded him. "I was sick up your arm."

He looked embarrassed at that. "Oh. No. You . . . kept it to the gutters every time." He chuckled softly, nervously, eyes on the flask. "I hope it's not a recurring thing with you and I. Shady bastards putting things in your drinks."

"Once more and we'll have to part for good." Farideh took another long drink of the water, dimly recalling heaving oversweet and burning liquor onto the frozen ground several times. "Thank you," she said. "For getting me down here. And for coming in after us. I suppose I did need saving. This once."

He smiled. "I think that one should count double."

"Well good," she said, smiling herself. "You don't have so many to make up for then."

Dahl snorted. "Your count's off. The shadar-kai, the arcanist—"

"The arcanist was . . ." She hunted for the right word. "Mutual."

"The watercourse," Dahl said pointedly.

"The erinyes," she returned. "The Zhentarim."

"At the revel?" he said. "Where I was—" He stopped and turned from her, looking down at the flask again. Farideh could almost hear him thinking, *Where I was saving you, because I'd led you into danger.*

"The revel is a draw," she said lightly. "Mutual again."

Dahl was silent a long moment, still staring at the flask. "I wasn't in your visions."

Farideh had no sense of how she ought to reply to that.

"No," she said finally. "Should you have been?"

"You were in mine."

Farideh's felt the muscles at the small of her back tighten, her tail trying to twitch with nerves. Things had been so easy a moment ago—was he really going to criticize her for leaving him out of visions she had no control over?

"I'll try harder next time," she said a little tartly.

"Gods, that's *not* what I meant," Dahl said. "I just . . ." He hesitated a moment, staring at the lantern. "I haven't been all that fair to you over the years. You said something once that got under my skin, made me think I knew how to fix . . ." He trailed off again. "I thought maybe I could undo my fall."

"Oh," Farideh said when he had been silent another interminable moment. "Did it work out?"

"Do I look like a paladin?" Dahl asked. "It wasn't so. But so many things happened, made me think you'd said it to vex me or to help me or to doom me to searching for the wrong thing. I thought," he said with a bitter laugh, "that you might have literally been sent by Oghma in a more desperate moment."

Farideh thought of the vision of Dahl in Proskur, of the strange man with a voice like a prayer. She thought of the sight of Dahl's soul.

"And all that time," he went on, "I realize now, I made you into this . . . symbol of my fall. This symbol of the restoration I couldn't stlarning find." He dragged his hands through his hair. "And frankly, seeing your memories—even if Tharra twisted them—made it perfectly clear . . . I've made all that up. I was no one to you. You weren't an angel. You weren't a devil. You weren't an enemy or a source of answers. You were just some girl I knew once." He looked at her again, his gray eyes faintly bloodshot. "I'm sorry for that, even if it didn't make a damned bit of difference to you at the time. I think I might have been a scorchkettle the last few days because of it."

Farideh looked down at the waterskin in her lap. It was so uncharacteristic of the Dahl she remembered that she couldn't help but feel she was suddenly sitting in the dark with an absolute stranger.

"I haven't been all that gentle with you either." She wanted to ask what he'd seen of her, what the visions had shown him. What was important enough between them to answer the sort of question Oota and Tharra would have asked. "Please don't tell me you've been sitting down here waiting to tell me that instead of planning."

"No," Dahl said. "I didn't drink as much as you did, but I've had my own hangover to sleep off." He rubbed his forehead. "And I didn't want you to wake up alone in a hole in the ground, so I stayed. So what did you find?"

Farideh shut her eyes and leaned her head as far back against the wall as her horns would allow. "It's not good."

She told him about the other camps, about the tower and the wall. About the carnage it had taken to bring the tower down in the vision. "And there's another complication," she said, not wanting to say it, but not daring to leave it out, "the devil I mentioned? Sairché? She's not the only one involved."

"Lorcan?" Dahl said dryly.

That burning kiss momentarily rose up in her thoughts . . . chased by the odd moment pressed against the bars of the cage with Dahl. She pulled her knees a little closer. Better to never bring *that* up.

"I mean," she said firmly, "a devil set against us. Gods, it's complicated. It's like they're playing a game. Lorcan's sister and this other devil. They were supposed to make this camp and gather the powers of the Chosen for Asmodeus. Only they don't want to succeed, but they don't want to fail either." She shook her head. "The other devil has an agent in the camp. Whoever *that* is, they have the means to make the gathering happen—we need to find them and stop them before they manage." And do it in such a fashion that the other devil was blamed, not Lorcan, she thought.

"Gods' books," Dahl swore. "Do you have any idea of who the agent might be?"

"None," Farideh said. "Apparently the other devil's been coy. But they're almost certainly among the prisoners. They wouldn't be drawing a lot of attention to themselves. They're probably quiet, not trying to stir things up. If you've told people about our plans to escape, they might have stopped them."

Dahl's expression hardened. "Tharra."

Farideh's memories of the previous night cleared. "Oh gods. She's a Harper though."

"She says she is," Dahl said. He shook his head. "I never checked. I never even thought—" He broke off with another curse and turned the flask in his hands once more. "We need to talk to her. Before Oota decides to make an example."

"Tell me what you've planned while we walk." Farideh stood and her stomach threatened to invert itself again. She leaned against the packed earth wall. Dahl stood as well, frowning.

"If you need longer—"

"We don't have longer," Farideh reminded him. "Tharra's devil is going to tell her any day now to carry out the gathering—if he doesn't try to sabotage us first. Rhand only expects me to be gone three days. We need to move and a sour stomach doesn't change that."

Dahl's expression was grim, but at least he didn't insist on holding her up as she shouldered her bag and pulled her cloak on once more. He rolled the flask between his hands.

"Will you do something for me?" he blurted. He thrust the flask at her. "Take it? I can't . . ." He looked away. "I can't quite bring myself to throw it out. But I know better than to drink it. Not now."

"What is it?" Farideh started to open the flask, but Dahl clasped a hand over hers.

"Don't," he said. "It's the shadar-kai drink, the one they use in the wizard's finest. I took it on the way out of the fortress."

Farideh looked at him, puzzled, and he scowled under her scrutiny.

"I haven't drunk it," he said tersely. "I'm . . . just about fifty ales dry at this point, and I would really like *something* to dull this edge, and this is just about the only thing I've found. But we all know what it does on the way down."

"And you can't pour it out?" she asked.

Dahl looked away. "Will you just take it away? Please."

She tucked the flask into her pocket. She'd pour it out later, away from Dahl. "Tell me what you've planned," she said again.

They slipped through the dark tunnels and up pounded dirt stairs, while he numbered their assets—the weapons they'd stolen, the Chosen they'd retained. The potential aid of the enclave of elves on the farther end of the camp. "You break the cages on their fingers, they might just kiss you on the mouth," he said.

Farideh flushed deeply. "I'll settle for having the assistance of more wizards. It's not going to be easy getting the tower down."

"Right," Dahl said, nodding at a male dwarf who stood at the base of the stairs, and handing him the lantern. "Any news?"

"Nothing that new," the dwarf said. "Last I heard, they got Tharra locked up. Oota's still out. You got a damned garden of elves up there waiting for yon tiefling's blessings, and—" He broke off and pointed his sword back the way they'd come. "Hold, drow."

Farideh looked back over her shoulder and startled at the ebon-skinned man standing not a foot and a half behind her. He grinned at her. "Well met. I see the Harper's as good as his goals."

Something seemed to press on Farideh's thoughts, something small and alien and serious, that made her pulse speed. The drow tilted his head at her, still smiling.

"Knock it off, Phalar," Dahl snapped. "What do you want?"

"It sounds like you've got quite the little conspiracy going on," Phalar said. "I'm assuming you're planning to ask for my assistance at some point?"

"Not if I can help it," Dahl said.

Phalar clucked his tongue. "You wound me, *cahalil*. After all we've been through?"

"You shoved me through a roof!"

"And you told Oota I'd given you up to the guards," Phalar pointed out. "Well done."

Farideh squinted at the drow and focused on the thread of power that seemed to wind up her spine and clasp her brain. The lights flared into being—purple and silver and threads of deepest night, twining together to form a sinuous rune that seemed to slip in and out of the light. "Chosen," she said. She looked back at Dahl—and swiftly set her eyes instead on the dwarf, whose god's mark shimmered in shades of silver and steel gray. "Is that what these rooms are for?" she asked. "To hide Chosen."

"Aye," the dwarf said. "Anybody too obvious." He glared past her at Phalar. "Or too dangerous. Tharra's idea," he added grimly.

She let the lights fade and looked back, past Phalar and down the long, dark corridor, wondering what trick was caught up in the underground rooms. Would they collapse and consume the Chosen? Were there portals to the Hells nestled in the rooms? Or would they just mean that the prisoners were nowhere to be found when the gathering went off—would this flaw of the camp be laid on Sairché's lap? "How many are there down here?"

"Right now?" the dwarf asked. "A score, maybe. A fair number went up to see what Oota's about. Those as can pass," he amended.

"And how many can it hold?"

The dwarf waggled a hand. "Eh—few hundred if they pack in tight."

Not the whole camp, Farideh thought. So whatever Tharra's plans were, they couldn't take everyone. "Can you get those twenty somewhere else on short notice?" Farideh asked. "We need to make sure of something."

"Most of 'em," the dwarf said. "Not the drow."

"If you want my help," Phalar said, "it will cost."

"Never doubted it," Dahl said. "Go back to your room." He grabbed Farideh's hand again and started up the stairs. They were nearly to the door when she managed to yank her hand back.

"What are you doing?" she demanded.

He looked down at his own hand and cursed. "Sorry. It's . . . His powers get to me. I didn't mean anything." He closed his hands into fists, then pushed through the door, out into the low light of late afternoon.

There were, in fact, a great many spellcasters waiting for Farideh to return and grant them the same assistance she had given Armas. The half-elf sat off to the side of the crowded court, one arm around the long-legged Turami boy. Even at a distance, Farideh could see the tension that claimed the boy's frame when she walked in with Dahl.

"We talk to Tharra first," Dahl said, and she followed him past the spellcasters, and toward the rear of the space where the two big guards from the night before stood before a door hung in the space between two buildings.

"Oota's not handling the aftereffects well," the human man admitted. "She's been up once to question her, but had to lie back down again."

"Give me a chance?" Dahl asked.

The big man reached back and pulled the door open. "No secrets, Harper," he warned.

Tharra sat alone, her arms bound behind her back, her face drawn and puffy. She met Farideh's eyes as she entered. "I've got nothing more to say."

Dahl reached down and pulled a pin from the inside of her jacket, a round shield the size of a gold coin. "Were you ever a Harper?"

Tharra sighed, as if Dahl were asking all the wrong questions. "Yes. I'd say I still am, but I'm bound to hear you cite the code and call me a traitor, so why bother?"

"We can still set things right," Farideh said.

"Can we now? And how is that?" Tharra said. "Ask your brightbird—no clemency for Harpers, no matter the circumstances, when treachery comes up."

Farideh glanced at Dahl, at the cold anger etched on his features. "I'm glad," he said, "that I was no fledgling of yours. There's no clemency because the choices are clear."

Panic raced up Farideh's core—he didn't mean her, but he might as well have. And choices could get very murky, very quickly when devils got involved. She pulled him aside, back toward the door.

"Can you leave us alone?" Farideh asked. Dahl gave her a worried look. She rubbed her brand through the fabric of her sleeve. "You don't want me to peer at your soul," she said lightly, "I don't want to discuss my . . . entanglements in front of you." She looked down at Tharra. "I doubt she does either."

Dahl stared at her a moment, searching her face. "No secrets," he warned.

"None that matter," she clarified. Then added, "I'm not baring my soul or hers, because you don't trust me to know what's important and what's not." And she wasn't telling him about being the Chosen of Asmodeus, unless it meant life or death.

He studied her a moment more. "Fine," he said. "Remember I'm on your side though. She *isn't*." With a quick glance at Tharra, he turned and left the little room.

Tharra looked up at Farideh, warily, as she approached. "You might have figured me out," she said. "But I'm not like you."

"Aren't you?" Farideh asked. "I'm here because I accepted a deal to save two of the dearest people in the world to me, and the price was far more than I expected. What happened to you?"

Tharra's gaze flicked over Farideh once more. "Fine. We're

all unlucky ones." She fell into a silence, her eyes shining. "It wasn't supposed to be this way," she said after a moment. "I was figuring out a way to make it turn right. I'm not a monster."

Farideh's heart ached at her own words coming out of another.

"I always assumed," Farideh said gently, "that people ended up indebted to the Hells because they sought it out. But they come to you and there are no strings on their lures."

Tharra laughed once. "Until there are. They like those rumors, I think. Makes it seem like you can't be caught if you're clever."

Farideh settled herself beside the other woman on the cold ground. "Did he tell you what's happening? Magros?"

Tharra's lip curled. "As little as he could, of course. Just what I was supposed to do, but never why. He said there was another devil, another player. You."

"The both of them together were supposed to use this camp to collect Chosen for Asmodeus—to make Shar's followers collect them, really," Farideh said. "But Magros and Sairché are also under conflicting orders—they need to make the plan fall apart and lay the blame on the other one, so that Asmodeus doesn't get what he wants and the other archdevil gets faulted."

"So you want me to break my agreement?" Tharra asked. "Switch sides and lose my soul."

"No," Farideh said. "I want both of us to outsmart these *karshoji* fiends and find a way to save these people. What were you supposed to do? What were the powers they gave you—you made me want to agree with things."

Tharra shook her head. "That was the pin. Magros enspelled it, so I could pass for a Chosen and do my job. Keep everyone in line. Keep them calm. Keep as many as I could out of the wizard's laboratories. That was easier than you'd think until you came along. And then—" Her eyes flooded. "He gave me a ritual—a scroll and components. I knew it would be bad. He told me as much, without saying it. 'Make sure you dig yourself a hidey-hole and make enough time to get down to it.' You don't say that about anything subtle."

"He never said what it would do?"

"The agreement did. 'Gather the Chosen,' as you said. He means to kill them, maybe all of us." Tears started falling. "But I owed him."

"How did he catch you?"

Tharra wiped her face, hesitating. "Seven years ago, a warm Eleint night, a fellow came up to me, out of nowhere. Said there were two folks being held by cultists for a sacrifice near to the village we were standing in, and they'd be dead by morning. Gave me a single clue—'cowslips'—and vanished. I'd just been given a pin of my own and was looking for my own troubles to right. I knew the meadow he meant, the hollow hill—so I headed in and played the hero. Magros found me the next night—he didn't bother hiding his horns that time. Thanked me for the assistance—those cultists worshiped someone he didn't want gaining any power, and wasn't it nice how we could help each other? I asked why he didn't just tell me, and he smiled. 'Where's the fun in that?'

"So that's how we were for years after. He'd turn up, give me a clue, and I'd save some innocents and end some evils. I'm sure someone better than I would say that helping Magros was tilting the balance—weakening his enemies only meant he got stronger—but I saved a lot of people. I got to be the hero.

"And then, the better part of a year ago, Magros came to me and said there was a Sembian force moving through the Dales. That they were going to sack one of three farmsteads—three families I knew and loved and counted on. And this time, no clue. He would tell me which it was, for a price—my soul. I told him no, made for the nearest farm, and got them packing—down to the little ones. Out of harm's way.

"I rode hard for the next, but there wasn't time. Magros came and made me another offer—he'd throw off the Sembians, force them from their path and save my friends. But I'd have to do something for him. I'd have to run his half of this camp scheme. I'd have to trigger the gathering ritual. And if I didn't, my soul would be his. I thought I could handle it. I thought it was fine. And then it wasn't. The only thing I could do was agree to this awful deal."

"But you saved those people," Farideh said.

"Those, yes. But Magros turned the army into the path of the ones I sent fleeing. Because I'd said no the first time." Tharra looked up. "I wouldn't have gathered the children, I swear. I made sure I never promised to catch everyone. I read that agreement, every word." She chuckled through her tears. "Made that devil spitting mad. And in the end, it didn't matter."

"It matters," Farideh said. "If you don't break your agreement, you keep your soul. We can make this turn out—"

"That ritual has to go off," Tharra said. "Even if Oota let me out of here to do that . . . People are going to die. Will you tell me that you'll let that happen?"

Farideh squinted at Tharra. "Where's the ritual now?"

Tharra shrugged awkwardly. "The scroll's buried under my bed. The components are hidden in the thatching. Rotate a poison or two out of them and keep it on me, for safety."

"That's where you got the hamadryad's ash," Farideh said. "Have you got any more?"

"What's left is in a pouch in my sleeve," she said. She met Farideh's gaze as the warlock fished the pouch out. "What are you going to do now?"

"See if these are secrets Dahl can use," she said. She bit her lip, not wanting to ask, but knowing she had to. "You read your agreement, and you agreed anyway?"

Tharra lifted her head. "In the moment, there were no other options."

Farideh left the former Harper in the makeshift cell, not sure whether she was more culpable than Tharra or less, or if it mattered in the end. A soul was a soul, after all, however it landed in Asmodeus's basket.

She found Dahl just beyond the dais, talking to a haggard-looking Oota. "What did she say?" Dahl asked. Farideh told him about the ritual, about the components hidden in Tharra's hut.

Dahl frowned. "That's strange. Destructive magic doesn't make for very stable rituals."

"Well, you can tell what it is if you read it, so that's your task. The devil also told her to dig herself a hidey-hole and get there quick. She was pretty sure that meant the spell wouldn't penetrate the ground. That's why she was encouraging the shelter rooms—she was hoping she could save at least some people." Farideh turned to Oota. "That still might be our best bet. We have to destroy the tower to break the wall. Either the ritual will do it for us, or the ritual will kill the guards and Rhand, and we'll have a chance to take the tower down ourselves, without being attacked all the while."

Oota frowned. "You want to carry out this devil's plans?"

"We need to find a way to destroy the tower," Dahl said. "That's the only way we know of to shut the wall's magic off. This ritual might be the simplest way to carry that out."

The half-orc didn't seem convinced. "The shelter rooms only hold a hundred or so."

"We have to make them bigger," Farideh said. "Maybe deeper. How many do you have who can move earth?"

"Torden," Oota said. "A few of the dwarves might come out of the middle ground for this. Maybe others—but we'd have to free the captured ones to get a decent count."

"Start with who we have out here," Farideh said. "We need to break in to rescue the rest—even if they can't dig, they won't be safe if the tower collapses—but the very breath we do, Rhand's going to know something's happening. Then we're all in danger."

"Tonight," Dahl promised. "As soon as it's dark enough to get Phalar's help."

There was a commotion near the doors, and the crowd of

caged spellcasters stood aside for a very regal-looking sun elf in rags just as tattered as the rest of them. "We come to parley," he said in thickly accented Common. He held out his hands. "And to let you prove, tiefling, that you are what the Harper says."

Oota stiffened and turned to face the elf with her cunning smile. "Well met, Saer Cereon," she said. "And welcome to my court."

"Please," the elf said. "The cages first. Then we talk."

Farideh drew up the soul lights. Greens and golds and umbers dappled the sun elf, but nothing shaped into the strange glyphs that marked the prize of a faraway god. "You aren't Chosen," she observed. The elf tilted his head.

"Will I become so?"

She shook her head. There was no rune, not even disguised in the light and shade of his soul. "I don't think so."

"A relief," Cereon said. "Honoring the gods is difficulty enough. Pleasing a particular in times of trouble, this one wouldn't wish it." He held his hands higher. "Can you? Or was that not so?"

Farideh raised her palm. "*Assulam.*" The cages shattered into dust and Cereon flexed his long hands with a curious smile. "Many thanks, tiefling." He looked to Oota and inclined his head the barest amount. "Now, we must see how to lay down old anger and aid our people."

Oota raised an eyebrow and gestured to the dais. "My home is yours, then, eladrin." Cereon gave her a cold look, but walked ahead.

Farideh looked back at Oota and spied the crimson and green swirl of lights that overtook her, the traces of gold. The lack, again, of any sort of rune. "Are none of their leaders actually Chosen?" she asked Dahl quietly, keeping her eyes off of him.

"Oota is. They call her Obould's Shieldmaiden . . ." Dahl trailed off. "Are you saying she's not?"

Farideh looked again, but no—there was nothing there. "Nothing I can see." She let the powers recede before she turned to

Dahl, who was goggling at Oota's back. "Maybe she can hide them?"

"Maybe she's just good at what she does," Dahl said. "Maybe she doesn't need a god to aid her." He shook his head. "Don't tell anyone, all right? I think a fair number of them are fine following a half-orc when they think they have no choice. We have plenty of chaos as it is."

"Someone's been this way," Brin said, examining the brush on the side of the path. A broken fringe of dried fern fronds lay against his palm.

"Might be deer," Havilar said. "Or an owlbear woken up early?"

"It's too wide a path. This is people, stomping along the trail. Too wide to stick to it."

Still could be deer, Havilar thought, but didn't say. "Maybe it's the Harpers?"

He shook his head. "Could be." He looked up at her. "Or maybe it's from the camp."

Havilar looked up the slope of the mountain, into the thick trees. It might only go up another dozen feet. It might be thousands, right up high enough for the sun to trip over. "I think we ought to start climbing. We're never going to get there winding around like this. Especially not before something bad happens."

"It's not safe," Brin said, standing and dusting off his breeches. "We haven't got the tools to climb."

"We'll have to eventually."

"We'll wait for Lorcan," Brin said. "If it gets too steep, he can fly us."

"How about," Havilar tried again, "we climb until we *can't* and then we wait for Lorcan. Otherwise we're going to be exhausted by the time we even get there."

"Havi," he said sternly, "you need to trust—"

"How about you trust me?" Havilar interrupted, her cheeks burning. "I get it—I'm the fool for storming into Farideh's room without knowing what was in there. But I *do* know *something* about tracking and traveling in the woods." She looked up the mountain's slope. "Whatever Mehen taught you, he taught me first."

Brin stood, looking as if he'd been caught between steps, as if the core of him hung off-balance. "I know," he said.

"Then act like it," Havilar replied. She started up the slope without him.

Farideh was right, she thought. Whatever hopes she had that she might take back what Farideh's deal had stolen from her, they were shriveling into nothing. Her glaive might as well be a hoe for all the skill she had wielding it. She couldn't stop having nightmares that splintered her sleep into spans so short she might as well have been blinking. And Brin thought she was a stupid little girl—a millstone, a nuisance.

She heard him start up the steep path behind her, but she didn't dare look back.

"I don't . . ." he started. He fell silent for a moment. "I don't think you were a fool for going into Farideh's room that night. I just . . . I just wish you hadn't. Or maybe that you'd waited for me."

Havilar hauled herself over a short wall of rock, up to another plateau. "Then you would have been trapped in the Hells too."

Brin gave a short, bitter laugh. "Do you think I haven't been?"

"I think the court of Suzail is a far cry from the Hells."

"It's not as far as you think."

Havilar looked back at him. "Are there devils and lava fields and things?"

"No, but there are assassins and stupid rules and noblewomen who spend their days trying to trick you into marriage so they can be queen, even though that's *not* an option."

Havilar flushed. "Armies of princesses," she said, ignoring the twist in her stomach. "Got it." She scrambled up the next bit of slope, crushing moss and sending little stones tumbling down.

"Ye gods," she heard Brin sigh behind her. "I'm not bragging."

"Didn't think you were," Havilar said, her eyes on her hands and her face on fire.

"Havi," he called. "Havi, stlarn it, wait!"

She kept climbing, up over another rock wall slick with melt and moss. When she hauled herself up onto the wide ledge beyond, her throat felt as if it would close around her panting breath. You knew this would happen, she thought. Why wouldn't it? You're no one.

Brin's hand grasped the edge of the rock. "Help me up?" he asked. Reluctantly, she grasped his hand, pulling him up the cliff. For a moment, they stood so close, Havilar fancied she could taste the grassy smell of waybread on his breath. She stepped backward. He held onto her hand.

"I know you don't want to talk about this," Brin said. "But we're going to have to. Please—whatever you're going to say, I've imagined it, I promise." He looked down at her hand in his. "It's not armies. It's not bragging. It's not even pleasant. I could quite frankly be a sparring dummy in fancy clothes, and I'd be just as much of an interest to them. There's one—this noblewoman—who has actually taken to telling people we have a secret understanding, because once—*once* mind you—I walked with her. I said four words altogether, and she's well convinced we're in love. But you—"

"Have you told her to heave off?" Havilar interrupted, taking her hand back. She walked across the rocky ledge, considering the slope above. It was gentler, and the trees were thinner. She could see, high above between the trees, the edge of the mountain's peak.

"I've been told not to," Brin said bitterly. "She ought to know, so no need to make a scene." He turned back the way they came, and Havilar followed his gaze out over the thick forest, the setting sun reflecting off low clouds and staining the sky pink and crimson.

"This must be where he meant," Brin said. "Or at least, it's a good spot to make camp. Do you want—"

"You should just say you're not in love with her," Havilar said. "That's not something it's fair to sit on."

"I know that."

"You shouldn't leave her wondering."

Brin stared at her for an uncomfortable moment. "Are we talking about Arietta?"

Havilar's cheeks burned and she turned toward the slope again. "Let's just make the fire."

He shook his head, still staring. "Havi, you are *killing* me—"

A shadow crossed the sun, more than a cloud. Wrong, out of place—old instinct made Havilar leap back, out of reach, under the tree branches. Yank her glaive free of its harness and get it between her and whatever shouldn't be there. Whatever was making the wind shift as it dived.

"Brin! Duck!" she shouted. At the same moment, a ring of teeth flashed across her field of view, a lamprey with a mouth made for sucking the lifeblood out of dragons. Havilar jumped toward it and slashed with the glaive, catching the fine membrane of its wings. She shoved upward, the skin breaking with a pop that shook her weapon. The monster screeched.

Brin had hit the ground flat and rolled back to his feet as the creature, hissing and spitting, swung its eyeless head toward Havilar. Brin shouted her name, but Havilar only had eyes for the monster.

The wing, the wound—she hit it again, tearing the hole larger, knocking the beast to the ground. The mouth—catch it on the blade, the heavy shaft, twist the head down. Black blood poured out through that ring of teeth. Its whole wing slapped her, hard enough to shake her focus a moment. The mouth flexed, grasping at the space near her.

It screamed. Brin's sword pinned the narrow point of its

triangular body to the ground. The creature lashed and squalled, still trying to find Havilar even as it struggled to pull itself free. Its wing slapped Brin and knocked him off his feet.

Havilar brought the end of her glaive up under its head, driving it up, ready for her next strike to plunge up into its throat. It rolled and slammed her into the rocky ground, driving the air out of her and sending a lightning bolt of pain through her ribs.

Brin cursed a steady stream. Havilar gasped, as the creature loomed over her, mouth grasping toward her. But even as it descended, Havilar pulled her weapon up, tearing into the soft underside of the creature and spraying her with blood and slippery viscera. It jerked back, as if to escape, rolling onto its wounded wing. Havilar swept the glaive toward it, across its belly, spilling more blood out on the frozen ground. The thing screamed and flopped like a fish in the bottom of a boat, and died.

The woods were silent but for the sound of Brin and Havilar's panting breaths.

Havilar eased herself up onto her feet, surveying the monster—well and truly dead. Well and truly dead by her hand. "Gods," she said. "Gods! That was *fantastic*!" She thrust her glaive skyward. "Ha!—*oof*!"

Brin caught her around the middle and squeezed her tight enough that her ribs spasmed. "Never, never do that again!" he shouted. "Watching Gods—you could have been hurt!"

"What? Why?"

"You're not invincible!"

Havilar didn't want to push him away, but that was too much. "I *killed* it. I'm invincible enough for a flying lamprey monster."

"Veserab," Brin said. He shook his head. "Don't. Please. I can't just *stand* there and . . . I lost you once already, I can't do it again."

Havilar felt her face grow hot, unsure of what to say—it was more, so much more, than he'd uttered the entire trip, but none of it was right. "I'm fine," she said, and tentatively brushed a chunk of veserab off his shoulder. "I know you're thinking—"

"You *don't* know, all right?" he said fiercely. "You don't know what it's like. You had your share of horrors, but you didn't get this one—you didn't have to face the fact that I was gone and you couldn't get me back. Maybe you would have dealt with it better, or been braver, or got to a place where you didn't care, but I didn't. And if you're going to start barreling around, throwing yourself into the clutches of monsters . . ." He shook his head again, as if he were trying to shake away the sudden emotion that grabbed at his voice. "You can't ask me to just duck."

"Well," Havilar said, "you didn't just duck. You pinned the tail—that was really quick and clever."

Brin gave her half a smile. "You hardly needed it, I suppose."

"I needed it," Havilar admitted. "But you needed me too." She smiled—and she felt a little more like herself again. "And I *killed* it."

He looked over the creature's corpse. "We must be near. Only Shadovar ride them. Unless there's some Shadowfell portal around here, it must belong to the Netherese camp." He turned to Havilar again. "Are you sure you're all right?"

"Wonderful," she said, unable to suppress her grin. "Except for the rib."

"Broken?"

She shook her head. "Maybe." She stretched up and winced as the twang of pain hit her again. "Or just sprained."

"Bad enough."

She shut her eyes and smiled. "It was worth it."

Brin shook his head. "Here." He set his hands around her battered ribs, one just under her breast and the other in the middle of her back. He murmured the prayer to Torm, but Havilar didn't hear a word of it. When the sound of a whetstone ringing came and the injury faded, there was still only the feeling of Brin's hands encircling her. He wouldn't look at her. But then, he didn't let her go.

You killed it, she thought. You took the glaive back.

You're out of excuses.

"Brin, I love you," she said, feeling as torn open as the veserab. There was no hiding the declaration, no smothering it anymore with "wait until" and "not yet." It wasn't something you sat on, after all. "I love you," she said again. "Still. And that's . . . Maybe that's not all right, maybe you have all those princesses, and maybe you don't want me. But you should know. I love you."

He didn't say a word, for so long. But he didn't let her go either.

"There is not a thing in my life," he finally said, "that I regret like I do not telling you how much I loved you then. I was scared, and I was stupid, and if I'd known she was going to take you from me . . ." He swallowed hard. "I loved you, Havi. I should have said it." He pulled her nearer. "I love you still."

He kissed her and kissed her and kissed her. And it didn't matter that her hands were still clumsy or that they were both covered in gore or that the ground was cold and hard: he still loved her.

CHAPTER TWENTY

26 Ches, the Year of the Nether Mountain Scrolls (1486 DR)
The Lost Peaks

HAVILAR WOKE TO THE SUN STREAMING THROUGH A LOW break in the clouds, through the gap in the trees. Every bit of her was sore, but that, too, was worth it. She smiled to herself. She reached for Brin, but found him already dressed and stirring up the fire under a cook pot. Her clothes were thrown over a nearby tree's low branches. The smell of the veserab was a faint mustiness on the cold air, almost hidden in the woodsmoke.

Brin stared into the empty air, still looking sad and distant. Like there was a cloud over him, keeping out the sun and turning everything dark again.

"Good morning," Havilar said after another moment. He turned to her, and the cloud over him lifted. He smiled, and something similarly cloudy lifted off Havilar.

"Good morning," he said. "Did you sleep all right?"

"Well enough." Havilar smiled, feeling suddenly shy. She nodded at the pot. "What's for morningfeast?"

Brin grinned. "Bathwater. There's a little waterfall near here, but it's basically flowing ice. I figured this would be nicer for you."

Havilar wrapped her cloak around herself and went to sit

beside him, not saying that she was pretty used to washing in cold streams. It was too nice of him. She leaned against him.

"How long do you think we have before they find us?"

"Hopefully, we get a little more time," Brin said. He slipped an arm around her, over the cloak, and drew her close, nuzzling her behind the ear. "If a godsbedamned devil shows up now, I swear to every Watching God . . ."

Havilar giggled. "Which is worse right now? A devil or Mehen?"

"A fair point," Brin said, but he didn't stop. "I suppose you ought to put some clothes on."

"I suppose. When I'm ready," Havilar said, arranging her cloak over her knees. "You've had a lot more . . . practice, haven't you?"

Brin chuckled softly. "A little less clumsy, yes?"

Havilar wet her mouth. "How . . . much practice?"

He pulled back, far enough to look her in the eyes. "I don't know. I didn't really keep track of the times."

"More than one girl?"

He seemed to search her face. "Yes," he said.

A weight lifted off her chest. If it had just been one girl for all those years, then he was surely in love with someone else and Lorcan was right, it was all going to end badly. But it wasn't. "More than a hundred?" she asked.

Brin burst out laughing. "Do you think I became a heart-warder while you were gone? Quit eating and sleeping? Gods."

Havilar crossed her legs over, pulling herself tighter in. "I don't know."

His expression softened and he pulled her close again. "Hey, sorry. It's three," he said. "Just three."

Three—why was that worse than "more than one, less than a hundred"? Havilar shifted. "Do you . . . Did you love them?"

Brin hesitated. "I tried to. I thought I could let go of you. I thought I had to."

"Did you?"

He rested his chin on her shoulder and sighed. "What do *you* think?"

Havilar bit her lip. She thought it was still too lucky to believe. She thought it was still too wonderful for there not to be some secret trap nestled in the middle of it that she hadn't found yet. She still wondered why he looked so troubled when he thought she wasn't looking.

Havilar considered the water, still working toward steaming. "What were you thinking of before?" she asked. "While I was sleeping? You looked awfully unhappy."

"Court things," he said, brushing her hair back. "Cormyr's mired, badly." He kissed her jaw. "As I said, I probably shouldn't have left. And before . . . all I wanted was to be sure you were all right. Not send you running because you were already completely overwhelmed by everything under the sun, and suddenly here I am, asking you how you feel about me." A smile quirked the corner of his mouth. "For all I knew, you wanted to be away from everyone. I couldn't make that harder."

"That's good of you," Havilar managed. She leaned into him again. "What would you have done if that was the case?" *Marry the crazy noblewoman,* she thought. *Fall in love with one of those other three.*

"Kept waiting?" Brin said. "I could love you from any distance closer than the Hells, and my life would be happier for it. But this . . . I like this best." He was silent a moment, before adding, "I would fight an army of devils to keep this."

Havilar smiled. "Me too."

She could have gladly stayed there, beside the fire, curled so close to her love. She could have sat on the cold stone for seven and a half years, for twenty-five, for an eternity. And then her thoughts started drifting—the Harpers were coming, Farideh was in trouble, there were still devils afoot.

"Water's ready," Brin said.

Reluctantly, Havilar left him there, so she could scrub the last of the veserab from her skin and dress in her still-damp clothes. She had mastered the glaive again, Brin was hers once more, and now they were going to save Farideh. Everything was going right again.

Unless . . .

She stopped, midway through lacing her blouse, struck by a sudden fear. What if Farideh was the thing that would go wrong? What if Havilar got back everything she'd lost, except Farideh? She was still furious with her twin, but she didn't want that.

It doesn't work that way, she told herself. But her fingers suddenly felt stiff and shaking, and the sense that she'd somehow ruined things lurked in the back of her thoughts.

It wouldn't go wrong, she told herself. She put the amulet of Selûne on once more, and slipped the ruby necklace into her pocket. It wouldn't go wrong because she wouldn't let it.

She'd finished braiding her wet hair and begun cleaning the corners and crevices of her glaive she'd missed the night before, when the sound of another group approaching from the north end of the ledge reached them. Havilar stood, peering out into the distance for some hint of who it was.

At the lead were the Harpers from Tam's office that awful night, trailed by robed wizards and shambling ghouls. Elves, carrying bows and arrows. A litter hauled by horrible-looking beasts, and something straight out of one of Havilar's worst nightmares. But she hardly noticed any of them, because Mehen himself broke from the group and ran toward her.

He caught her up in a fierce embrace, and Havilar found a part of herself wanting to weep all over again. She hadn't realized just how badly she missed Mehen, how awful it had been to leave, until then.

"What were you *thinking*?" he muttered.

Shame bloomed in Havilar's heart. "Sorry," she said, but only for making Mehen worry, for leaving so abruptly. She would have done the same thing over again a second time, she felt sure—waiting in Waterdeep even a breath longer would have killed her. "But you found me," she offered. "And now we can find Farideh."

Mehen held her a moment longer. "If I could send you safely back, I would."

"I promise to be careful."

He gave a short laugh. "How long has it been since I heard that?" He let her go finally. She saw Mehen's gaze sweep the camp, lingering on the bedrolls that were packed and set together, then finding Brin beside the fire. He narrowed his eyes. "How long were you waiting?"

"Just a night and the morning," Brin said, not quite meeting Mehen's gaze.

Mehen made a low growling sound in his throat. He looked down at Havilar—she grinned back.

"I killed a veserab," she told him. "It's a flying lamprey thing."

"Well done," he said, setting an enormous hand on the back of her head. Mehen looked back as the Harpers came to stand beside them. They introduced themselves to Havilar.

"Zahnya says the camp is at the top," Vescaras said. "Unless we're waiting for further instructions? From a demon prince perhaps?"

Mehen scowled at him, then looked up the last slope of the mountain. "Is there a path?"

"Don't know," Brin said.

"You didn't scout for one? You had the time."

"In the dark?" Brin demanded.

"It's not steep," Havilar pointed out. "Not *that* steep. And the trees aren't nearly as thick. We can just climb until we reach it."

"Daranna seems to have had the same thought," Khochen said dryly. They looked back at the rest of the party, at the scouts disappearing up the slope.

"Watching Gods," Vescaras swore. "*This* is why no one wants to work with Daranna."

Lorcan examined his face in the still scrying mirror. Such a waste of a healing potion, and the cure had been worse than the broken nose, by far. But he'd weighed turning up bruised and battered, considered what Farideh would do when she saw, when she asked what had happened.

No, he thought. No sympathy from that quarter. Not yet. She'd take Mehen's side right off, and everything he'd done to coax her back would be worth far less—the apology, the rescue, the kiss . . . He hadn't considered the consequences of that as carefully as he should have—but the memory of her shifting toward him in those last fractured seconds, changing from a body to a participant, boded very well indeed.

He looked around the room—still no Sairché. She was supposed to lock down the situation with Rhand, then sort out Magros, while Lorcan saw to their more heroic tools. They'd agreed to meet back here once they'd both discharged their duties.

Lorcan took the dark braid of hair from the pouch on his belt and rubbed his thumb over the ridges of purplish-black hair. He considered his reflection in the scrying mirror a moment longer, then sifted through the rings he still wore to find a familiar iron band. This one he pulled off the chain and placed on his left hand—Sairché wasn't getting his scrying mirror back.

He waved the trigger ring over the mirror's surface, one hand on the leather scourge necklace he wore—the necklace imbued with Farideh's blood. The surface of the mirror shimmered like a slick of oil, before resolving into Farideh, looking as though she had never slept a day in her life and never intended to remedy that. A line of people moved past her, and she studied each with a pinched expression, waving them to one side of the space or the other.

Lorcan narrowed his eyes. She hadn't said she planned to sort the prisoners—why? And what other surprises were going to crop up in his absence?

He looked around the room again—still no Sairché, and Lorcan needed to get to Farideh as soon as possible. He walked back to the room with the portal, but found no sign that Sairché had returned. He waved his ring before the scrying mirror again and got . . . nothing. He cursed. Sairché would—of course—find a way to block her own scrying.

Or she might be in trouble.

"Shit and ashes," Lorcan cursed again. Whether this fell under the terms of their agreement or not, he'd have to go after her. Acting without being sure of Rhand or Magros would be suicide. He opened the portal to the primordial forest, the same little grove where he'd spied Magros the first time. He took from his pocket the iron cube, and unfolded the cloth wrapped around it. Frost still etched its surface.

Despite his agreements in the interim, Lorcan found himself tempted.

Lorcan had never lived anywhere but Malbolge, never sworn allegiance to any archdevil but Glasya, and that only by virtue of his birthplace. He was not angry enough or foolish enough to think that Stygia would be a paradise, or really anything except a different sort of game, a different battle for survival. A different Hell.

But Stygia would not have Glasya—and how could he not want that? For himself, for his warlocks . . . .

Warlock, he corrected himself. The rest were gone. And whatever dangers fickle Glasya brought to Farideh, Levistus and his legendary appetites would be another world of danger.

He picked up the cube, focusing on a star peeking through the branches of the oak beside him, so that when the violet portal opened and Magros stepped out, the agony of clutching the frozen cube was nowhere for the other devil to see.

"Ah, good," Magros said. "You've come around."

Lorcan regarded him coolly. "Where is Sairché?"

Magros raised an eyebrow. "Have you lost her?"

"Don't be coy," Lorcan said. "You must have heard by now."

"I did hear something about Lady Sairché prowling the halls of Osseia once more. Though, I don't generally countenance the gossip of imps. I take it she's escaped."

"As if you don't know," Lorcan replied. But perhaps he didn't—ah Lords of the Nine, keep it balanced, he told himself. Remember he thinks you're an idiot half-devil with an erinyes's temper. "She came straight to you, didn't she? What did you tell her?"

Magros's smile flickered, as if he might laugh. "Dear boy, why would she ever come to me?"

"To ruin me?" Lorcan said. "To make certain I failed? What did you tell her?"

"I told you," Magros said. "She hasn't come to me." He tilted his head. "It seems she's given you ever more reasons to flee Malbolge, though. Have you seen to my agent?"

"It would help if you told me who it was," Lorcan said.

Magros smiled. "Oh, but where's the fun in that?"

Lorcan fell quiet, considering the misfortune devil. He'd assumed that Magros had wanted Lorcan to act—swiftly, rashly—and ruin Asmodeus's plans by simply killing the Stygian agent or Rhand or Farideh. It had been a slapdash maneuver, one Lorcan assumed grew from the devil's disdain for the cambion siblings.

But Magros had never told Lorcan *who* to kill.

"Well, you're a sly one, aren't you?" Lorcan said. "Let me think you don't expect much at all from me, let me think you think I'm stupid enough to kill your agent and upset the plan so plainly. And all the while—what? What were you doing right under our noses?"

Magros shrugged, smiling all the while. "The world will never know. I notice you say 'our.' I take it Sairché is not escaped so much as freed? And still, you cannot find her. How interesting."

"Not as interesting as the puzzle of your Thayans," Lorcan tossed back. Magros's smile flattened. "Didn't think I knew about those, did you?"

"I hadn't," Magros admitted. "Until dear Zahnya alerted me to your intrusions. Whyever are you trucking with Harpers?"

Lorcan smiled wickedly. "The world may never know."

"Well your Chosen won't," Magros said. "At least, not unless you get her free of that place in the next few hours."

Lorcan froze again. "What happens in the next few hours?"

Magros spread his hands. "What do you think we're doing here? Asmodeus's plan must continue apace. The gathering must happen. If she's within its reach . . . well, you can guess, and we'll see how His Majesty feels about that."

Every drop of his mother's blood urged Lorcan to seize hold of Magros, to shake the answers from him—Where was the agent? What was the gathering? Where in the Hells was Sairché?—but he fought it. Magros would have his due, but that wasn't as important as getting Farideh away from that camp, nor as important as protecting his own skin.

"I think we can consider Prince Levistus's offer rescinded," Magros said, opening his own portal. "We have no need of the second-best leavings of discredited erinyes in Stygia."

Lorcan watched the violet swirl of the portal surge and then fade, the wind of a frozen layer sending goosebumps across his red skin. Not an ally he wanted, Lorcan reminded himself, and he hoped Harpers and tieflings and the Chosen of Asmodeus made a better army than what powers Prince Levistus could muster from the heart of his glacier prison.

He pulled the portal to Malbolge open again. A few hours was not enough time to find out. Especially when he couldn't find Sairché.

But he could find the erinyes she'd taken with her, he realized as he stepped through the portal. He crossed to the balcony and peered out over the suppurating landscape of Malbolge. Near Glasya's garden walls, a group of erinyes loitered. Even at a distance he could spot Sulci's shock of yellow hair. He glided down to land among them.

"Well, well," Nisibis said, "are you in charge again?"

"Think we might want Her Highness's input on that," Noreia said lazily from her perch to the side.

"Where's Sairché?" The erinyes all chuckled.

Sulci swung her blade up onto one shoulder. "We left her with the wizard."

"What?" Lorcan cried.

"She invoked the disputation clause," Nisibis said, "and offered a proxy. I thought he'd take Sulci there—gave her quite a look—but he chose Sairché instead. You'll get her back in three days."

Lorcan shut his eyes and silently cursed his sister's damnable hubris. Sairché would not be back in three days, because she had not invoked the disputation clause of her contract with Rhand—she had only bluffed him, and Asmodeus would hand down no judgment on a contract that was still in force.

And worse, Lorcan knew Sairché was in danger. "I wish you had not told me that," he said to Nisibis.

Havilar frowned at the space in front of her. It looked as if the mountain continued up, the trees blocking much of her view of the peak. But there was a faint distortion to the air, a not-quite-shimmer that made her eyes ache. She blinked hard a few times, then reached to touch it as the scout who'd found it had prompted. There was something smooth and hard there where there seemed to be nothing. With her other hand, Havilar squeezed the ruby necklace in her pocket.

"Beyond," the Red Wizard declared, "is the camp. And here is where my aid is of no more use to you: I cannot pass the barrier."

Vescaras considered Zahnya. "How is it you plan to claim Shar's weapons if you can't get inside?"

"I have a confederate," she replied. "My spells will center on her. After . . ." She shrugged. "I've been told I can access the camp then. But I can't make promises for anyone left inside."

"You expect that we're going to stand here and let you kill a camp full of people?" Vescaras demanded. "We outnumber you as of yet, goodwoman. By still more than when we began."

"Don't be dramatic, saer," Zahnya said. "You and I both know that a weapon in Shar's hands is far more dangerous. The number of lives at stake should she raise herself any higher, gain any more kingdoms, or worse, rebuild her Shadow Weave, pale in comparison to the number of souls inside these walls. So yes, I will act. And you will have time—if, of course, you can enter—to stage a rescue. My spell will take hours to cast, after all."

Havilar watched the Harpers, but none of them seemed to react to that. Good or bad? she wondered. Zahnya talked too much like Lorcan—made too much sense of things that shouldn't make sense at all—and it set Havilar's tail lashing. Beside her, Brin slipped his hand into hers and squeezed it furtively.

"How long?" Mehen asked.

Zahnya smiled. "Ten hours. It is complex."

Vescaras narrowed his eyes. "Very well." He looked at Havilar. "Have you still got the bead your father mentioned?"

She pulled the necklace from her pocket and held it up. "Bomb, charm, beacon, passwall," she recited.

Vescaras crossed to her and plucked the passwall bead from the necklace. He held the red gem up to the growing light. "How certain are you?"

Havilar glanced over to Zahnya and her apprentices, who were clearing a square off the forest floor and taking various items out of their packs. Preparing for the casting.

"Sure enough for this," Havilar said.

"I suppose we haven't another option." He gave Khochen a grim look and beckoned the others closer. Then the half-elf stepped forward and slapped the bead against the invisible wall. A ripple spread out through the seemingly empty air, then another, then a third that came with a crackle of rock. The air seemed to part like a pair of drapes, and there beyond was a valley—a crater, Havilar corrected herself—filled with small, close together huts and dominated by a shining black tower. The Harpers and Mehen hurried through, and Havilar followed. The spell faded quickly after, sealing the wall once more.

Behind them, the slope appeared just as they'd left it, with Zahnya and her minions working hard at the spell. She was smiling to herself in a way Havilar didn't like.

"Do you trust her?" she asked Vescaras.

"Not a bit," he spat. " 'Ten hours,' my broken chamber pot. We have six at the outside." He turned to his colleagues. "So we're out of here in three."

"I haven't got another bead," Havilar reminded him.

"Which is why we'll have to be clever," Khochen told her. "But first, we find Dahl and your sister."

"We need to fan out," Daranna said. "Khochen, take the dragonborn and his friends—"

"No," Mehen said. He bared his teeth, tapping his tongue against the roof of his mouth repeatedly before saying. "You want to capture her, I want it to be safe and easy. So you put one friendly face in each of your groups."

Vescaras and Khochen exchanged glances. "We'll be cautious, goodman," Vescaras said. "There's no need to worry."

"There is no need to worry because I or Havi or Brin will find her and make *sure* you keep your word," Mehen snapped. He turned to Havilar. "Much as I don't want to leave your side."

Havilar hugged him awkwardly. "I know. Be careful."

"*Everyone,* be careful," Mehen said, looking past her to Brin. "I'll go with Daranna." The elf didn't look pleased at that, but she nodded at one of her scouts and the three of them moved east and along the wall, down into the camp below.

"Very well," Vescaras said. "Lord Crownsilver, you are with me." He gestured to one of the scouts, an elf woman with reddish hair, as well. "Come on."

"Do you think," Havilar murmured, as Brin hugged her tight, "that this could be the last time we do this for a long while? I'm getting sick of it." He laughed softly.

"Let's try. I'll see you soon, I promise." Havilar watched him head along the northern edge of the invisible wall's curve, tailing Vescaras and the elf. If this were a chapbook, she thought, he would definitely be getting hit by an arrow soon. She shook the thought from her head and turned back to her assigned allies.

"Come on, Ebros," Khochen said to the remaining scout, her laughing eyes on Havilar. "This will be fun."

"Your ladyships," Rhand said as he crept over the threshold. For all the deference he showed the girl with no name, there was only cruelty in his smile. Sairché's pulse became a voice shouting in her ears. "How are you getting on?"

The girl sitting beside the window looked up at Sairché with luminous eyes and smiled slightly. Panic rose up in Sairché, and there was no trick, no clever turn, no magic ring that could save her.

My doom, Sairché thought. Lords of the Nine, damn you, Lorcan.

The girl's gaze inched its way over Sairché. "She is less amusing than I would have expected for a devil."

"A cambion," Rhand corrected, "my lady."

She sniffed and Sairché's pulse became a voice shouting in her ears, *Run, run, run.* "Where's the other one?" she said. "The tiefling you mangled."

Rhand's expression tightened. "Still absent. But she'll return, I'm assured, the day after tomorrow. Isn't that right, Lady Sairché?" Sairché couldn't speak, couldn't find the clever words to string together. Damn Lorcan, damn Rhand, damn Farideh and Glasya and Asmodeus too. Every muscle of her body felt flooded with fear and adrenalin. She was a deer in the wood, too startled to move, and after a full day of the Chosen of Shar's company, she felt as if she were dying.

"It sounds as if your experiment has failed, Saer Rhand," the girl said.

Rhand cleared his throat, nerves Sairché had never managed to inspire in him clear even at a distance. "Not failed. Delayed."

"I was told," the girl said loftily, as the world threatened to roll over Sairché and smother her, "to assess the usefulness of keeping your camps going."

"Yes, my lady."

You have lived this every day, Sairché reminded herself, gazing down at the floor. She thought of each of her surviving half sisters in turn, the terrible tortures they'd gladly heap on her, one by one. It kept her sane, it kept her in the little room and not drowning in the void that threatened her mind. But still she could not bear to speak.

"You are not a very popular man within the Church. No one powerful left to speak for you."

"Save you," Rhand said. "My lady."

"I don't speak for *you*," the girl said. "In fact, I think it is plain that this experiment is not worth the resources of Shade. I am ordering you to destroy it and return to the city."

Sairché spared a glance for Rhand. His rage was enough to push aside the plain discomfort he'd worn since he'd entered the room.

"You don't have the right," he said.

"Don't I?" the girl said. "I believe you'll find you owe me your obedience, just as Shar intends." The feeling of looking into an unending maw intensified. Sairché squeezed her hands into fists. Megara would spit me like a lamb, she thought. Oenaphtya would just cleave me in twain. Tanagra would stake me to the ground and let Malbolge deal with me . . .

Beside Sairché, Rhand gave her the uncomfortable impression of one of her worse sisters about to snap. The girl smirked at him. "Order my veserab saddled."

"It hasn't been recovered," Rhand said. "And if you think I'm ending this on the whim of a—"

"Saddle yours, then," the girl said. "And call for carriers. I intend to leave. Take care of your experiment, or you will find yourself answering to people much more powerful than you."

Rhand started forward, all inchoate violence, but he stopped just past Sairché, his eyes locked on something over the nameless girl's dark head.

Sairché dared to look up—feeling the girl's eyes still on her, still shrinking her down into something small and unnecessary—and followed Rhand's gaze to the winking bluish light that hung in the air over the center of the camp.

Magic, Sairché thought. And not his.

Rhand swallowed, but the rage in him didn't fade. "Excuse me," he said. "I'll let you know when the carriers have arrived."

The girl watched him leave, a smug smile playing on her mouth. Her luminous eyes fell on Sairché once more. "How droll you assumed a mere archdevil could stand against the might of the Lady of Loss," she said. "If you find your tongue. devil, perhaps you can tell me another funny tale."

The scroll lay in a box, buried only a few inches under the packed earth floor of the tiny hut. Dahl levered it out of the hole with the blade of the stone spade Armas had found him. The half-elf stood silent and watching in the doorway.

"Half-done," Dahl called. Armas said nothing. "You can start looking for the components in the thatch any time," Dahl added. The fledgling Harper stood silent. "Armas?"

Armas jerked at the sound. "What?"

"Components."

"Sorry." Armas stepped into the hut and sighed, reaching up for the roof. "Your friend . . . do you think she knows what she's doing?"

Dahl opened the scroll to find a very detailed spell and smiled—gods, he loved this. "Which part? The sorting?"

"Aye."

Dahl shrugged, his eyes on the lines of runes before him, the diagrams, the list of components. "Seems so. Tharra and Oota made it sound as if she picked people they knew had been Chosen. Though with any luck, it won't matter to us." He glanced up at Armas, realization dawning on him. "Oh . . . You're one of them?"

Armas kept his eyes on the thatch. "She stopped me as we left."

"Oh." Dahl looked back down at his scroll. "Well, many blessings."

"I suppose."

Dahl had read the first few lines several times over when Armas cleared his throat.

"She says she can't tell what will come of it or when. And all I can think of is how many gods there are . . . It's a fearful thing."

"Yes," Dahl said dryly. "The gods smiling on you is terribly frightening." He heard the venom in his own voice and cursed himself. *You're not seventeen and newly fallen,* he told himself. *Armas has taken nothing from you, and he doesn't deserve your pique.* "I suppose," he said, more kindly, "it probably is frightening. You do have my sympathies." He wondered how many of the Chosen Farideh named might be favored by Oghma, and realized he was reading the same line on the scroll again.

Armas sighed again. "She said she thinks it will be soon. Says the mark is sharp. I suppose that's a small blessing on its own. Not long to wait and wonder." He stepped to the left, rifling through the straw and twigs. "If it's something wicked, I don't know what I'll do. Maybe walk into the lake with my pockets full of stones."

"Why would a wicked god choose you?" Dahl murmured. "Are *you* wicked?"

"I was helping Tharra."

"That hardly counts."

"According to who? Who can claim to know the will of the gods, right? Ah!" He pulled a small jar and then another out of the thatch, like plucking apples from a tree. Dahl took them: oils of sacred juniper and distilled troll saliva. He frowned and looked back at the ritual scroll—both were mentioned. The latter was a very expensive component and there was quite a lot of the former—but neither was used to achieve the sort of effect Tharra had described.

He unrolled several more inches of the scroll—familiar phrases, familiar directions, intermixed with unfamiliar forms. This line was reused from pre-Spellplague castings of destructive magic out of Lost Halruaa; that one borrowed the structure of protective spells the Turmishan wizards crafted during the Wailing Years; that focusing diagram was absolutely crafted by Oghmanyte casters in Procampur. Very complex, Dahl thought. Very confusing.

Armas pulled down still more components. Powdered silver and salts of copper, resins of obscure flora and ground teeth of strange beasts. A packet of dragon scales, a pouch of iron filings, a purse of dried purple blossoms that smelled strongly of mildew. A delicate crystal bottle of residuum. Bottles of specially imbued inks and paints.

"That's all," Armas said, rubbing his uncaged hands as if they ached.

"That's more than enough," Dahl said, at a loss in regards to the sheer quantity of components. Eleven different items. Easily thousands of coins worth, especially when you added in the hamadryad's ash. He wondered if Tharra had used it all or if Farideh had reclaimed the rest. He'd have to check.

Each component was included in the ritual—which made no sense at all to Dahl. The various ingredients had their own attributes, their own abilities to draw or repel or create patches of magic. But together . . . Together these made a mess.

"What do you think the chances are I end up being able

to dig the shelters faster?" Armas said abruptly. "Maybe it's someone who's seen what trouble we're in."

Dahl shook his head, still studying the ritual. "Would be nice."

"Torden's got people carrying dirt out of the shelters, dumping it in secret places. They're moving quickly, but they've got only enough room for eight hundred or so—no more. Would be nice to make earth turn to air or some such."

Dahl kept his tongue, all too aware that his envy was misplaced and unflattering. Armas had no idea why Dahl should even *be* envious. He read on, through several more utterly tortuous steps, half his mind on the puzzle before him and half on the never-ending puzzle of Oghma.

Dahl sighed and rolled the scroll back up. "We can go. I'll need to look at this some more. It doesn't make sense."

"What does these days?"

Indeed, Dahl thought, as they collected the multitude of components into a cloth and bound it shut. Preparing to fight Adolican Rhand and some crafty devil at the side of a drow, a cunning half-orc, an arrogant sun elf, a girl you thought was dead, Lorcan, and scores of people the gods have given the powers to make daisies and see souls.

And all you have is a ritual that makes no sense, he thought glumly. He looked up at Armas, who was studying the space outside the hut with a similar glumness. A pang of guilt went through Dahl's stomach—the day after his mentor turned out to be a traitor, the half-elf turned out to be the Chosen of an unknown god. It wasn't worth ranking hardships.

"My former teacher told me something very wise once," Dahl said. "The sort of wisdom you don't believe at first, at least not for yourself. But maybe you're not as pig-headed as me."

Armas regarded him. "I've never been called stubborn."

"There are times when what you want doesn't matter. Things are already in motion and the gods have already made their wills plain. So the very best thing you can do is to just remember who you are and take things as they come—one at a time."

Armas smirked. " 'Shut your mouth and accept it'?"

"You don't have to shut your mouth," Dahl said. "But there's something to be said for recognizing you'd best let a god have their full say before you decide to retort." They walked back through the camp to Oota's court. The paths and alleys were all but empty, faces peering out of windows as they passed. Off in the distance, he heard the jangle of guards patrolling.

"They're going to notice sooner or later," Armas muttered. "Then what?"

"Then we hope your god's a fighting sort," Dahl said, "and your gift happens to be punching those bastards back into the Shadow Plane."

They made it back without incident to find the makeshift hall still busy with people—all standing a good distance from Farideh, who sat on the edge of Oota's dais, her head in her hands. Dahl went over to her.

"You all right?"

"Headache," she said, her voice muffled. "This is exhausting. I just need a breath."

Dahl sat down beside her and unrolled the scroll once more, to the line he'd read twice. "Have they gotten any farther with the rooms underground?"

"Torden thinks they'll be able to get a thousand in, if they don't have to be there long. If they squeeze."

Two-thirds, Dahl thought. Five hundred souls left behind to be wiped off the plane.

Farideh lifted her head. "Do you know the worst part? There's a scroll in Rhand's study that would solve all of this. A spell to make a cavern in the earth. And I didn't take it."

"How were you to know?"

Farideh shook her head, as if she ought to have, somehow. "I could go back. I could steal it—"

"No," Dahl said firmly. "We have time still. We have the

ritual—" He stopped, a sudden stillness in his heart. He unrolled the length of the scroll, skimming down the parchment, hunting for the completion of the spell-piece he'd just read, knowing it would have to be there.

It wasn't.

"Stlarn and hrast," he swore. He threw the scroll to the ground and clutched his own head. "It's broken. It's *shitting* broken."

"What?" Farideh said. "Can you fix it?"

Dahl shook his head. "That's why it makes no sense—that devil must have made it senseless."

"Can you fix it?" Farideh said again.

"No," Dahl said, considering the pieces that he'd found, the ways they seemed to just miss each other's effects. "The problems are too big, too . . . *insidious*. It looks like a proper ritual, all together. It feels like it should make sense and I'm just missing something. There's bits here that have the sort of hints and markers that suggest some very recognizable wizards' handiwork. See"—he picked up the parchment and pointed to a line of runes—"that's absolutely one of the Blackstaffs from around the turn of the century. Really common element in their spells, starting around—"

"Dahl," Farideh interrupted.

He pulled his hand back. "Right. So if you're just looking, there's no reason to think this isn't built off of some powerful old spells that have been repaired and strung together. But if you trace the effects, you get nothing. That Blackstaff magic? It's missing the completing line—that part won't do a damned thing. The magic's just going to fade as you cast it. Other parts, they actively cancel each other out.

"And," he added, "if that weren't bad enough, these components—while they're all very potent and high quality—are the wrong sorts of things." He sighed. "I should have guessed. Godsbedamned devils."

Farideh shook her head. "Why would he sabotage his own

end of the plan? If she doesn't carry out the gathering, he's the one who gets blamed. And I don't see how he could turn this around—he's the one who gave Tharra the ritual and the components."

"Gods' books, he's a devil," Dahl said. "Who knows what they're thinking?" Farideh looked away and Dahl wished he'd kept his tongue that time too. "Sorry," he said. "We have a hole in the ground and another day before Rhand expects you back. And I sold them on a worthless ritual—I'm not in the best of moods."

"We'll have to attack the tower," Farideh said.

"How's our army coming?"

"I have no idea," Farideh said. "There are still Chosen among them, and Cereon and the others are trying to find gentle ways to spur their powers. But so far? We have numbers, not strength." She rubbed her neck. "We have to rescue the ones he's captured. Soon."

"Tonight," Dahl said, well aware that the delay was killing every one of them. But they needed Phalar, and the drow wouldn't go out in the daylight. And the moment they breached the tower, Rhand would know he had a rebellion on his hands. Everything would have to happen right after.

And they had nothing to throw at the black glass tower but their own selves.

He closed his eyes. Lord of Knowledge, he prayed, Binder of What Is Known, for the love of all that is good and right and true, help me figure out what in the Hells I'm supposed to do here. You may have given me the means to seek the truth, but I am well out of options and now would be an excellent time to stop being so—

He stopped himself and blew out a breath. "You don't still have that flask do you?"

She stiffened. "No."

"Liar," Dahl said.

"I'm not giving it to you," she said. "It just doesn't seem

like the kind of thing you pour out where someone might stumble into it."

"It's not some sort of dragon acid—"

Armas pushed through the remaining prisoners, looking blanched and out of breath.

"You need to see this," Armas said.

They followed him down several roadways, out through a growing crowd of prisoners waiting for the underground shelter to widen enough for them too. They were all staring up at the same spot, thirty feet above the middle of the camp: a ball of energy the size of a fist hung in the air over the camp, sizzling blue and black.

"It started," Cereon said in heavily accented Common, "as a mote. That was a quarter hour ago. It's magic—strange magic. Destructive and something else. Something—" He turned and spoke Elvish to Armas.

Armas frowned. "It's going to collect something."

Dahl said a silent apology to Oghma, because here indeed were the means to solve the unsolvable: Magros hadn't given Tharra the proper tools to perform the gathering, because someone else was going to do it.

"Get everyone underground," Dahl said. "Let's hope this spell works the same way."

"My lady," the apprentice says, "have you nothing to do but muddy the Fountains?"

Farideh doesn't—at least she tells herself that. She cannot act without knowing where her enemies are, she cannot strike without being sure of who stands in the way. At least here she has a view of what's happening—as slim and mendacious as a sliver through a cracked door. But it's better than walking blind.

And if she wants to see clearly, the next vision has to be called. She's been avoiding it, almost-asking more times than she cares to admit. But as she's crawled back and back and back through the past, until the waters grow cloudy with the detritus of the petals, it's hunkered there in the back of her thoughts, waiting like a dragon in a cavern, knowing that eventually it will be time to come out.

"Show me," she says, trying for solemnity, "the Toril Thirteen and the day they cursed the tiefling race."

The waters shimmer and shiver, and a faint mist seems to rise up off their surface, followed by the image of a grove at night, the ground burnt bare up to the roots of winter-dead trees. There are thirteen tieflings arrayed around the grove. Hooved and horned and winged and tailed and some who might as well be human, for all their fiendish blood shows—but Farideh knows they are tieflings all the same. Six men, six women, and the Brimstone Angel herself.

Bryseis Kakistos stands on polished black hooves, facing a statue shaped like what must be the king of the Hells: a man with the great horns of a ram, broad-shouldered and beautiful even hewn out of bedrock. Blood paints the stone, as if tides of it have lapped Asmodeus's feet.

Farideh peers into the waters, waits, but Bryseis Kakistos doesn't look away from the statue, her confederates arrayed around her. Farideh can see that Lorcan was right—some do not seem to wish to be there. A man with snow-white hair and antlers sprouting from his brow. A woman with serpent's eyes and a jungle of red curls around her long horns. A boy on the edge of manhood, whose fretful hands seem to have been attached the wrong way around.

And others watch the Brimstone Angel as if she is the source of all riches. An ancient man with ram's horns and a beard to his knees. A fox-faced woman with a smile that sets Farideh's nerves on edge, even through the waters. A handsome man who wafts shadow and darkness with every move.

But Bryseis Kakistos doesn't turn. Farideh finds herself edging to this side and that as the chanting rises and the magic gathers, as if she can move around the surface of the water and see her wicked ancestor's face. The magic around the basin snaps and fizzes as if Bryseis Kakistos is calling on it, too.

"What are you doing?" one of the apprentices demands. Farideh looks up, just as the chanting reaches a terrible peak, just as it turns into screams. The apprentice pushes her back, away from the waters, and she doesn't see the end or whether Bryseis Kakistos ever turned to face her coven. She can only see the reflection of a terrible light—a fire to rival a crashing star—that reflects so brightly off the waters that it dapples the ceiling as if it were truly there in the room with them all.

"That is enough!" the apprentice all but shouts. And Farideh realizes, it will never be enough. She cannot stop Rhand's experiments by spying. She cannot change the past by watching it. She cannot change where she stands, not now. No matter what features she recognizes in her ancestor's face, she is not the Brimstone Angel, she never will be.

She cannot save them all. They are already damned.

CHAPTER TWENTY-ONE

26 Ches, the Year of the Nether Mountain Scrolls (1486 DR)
The Lost Peaks

Dahl fought the urge to bury Cereon and Oota in details that made it clear this was the only viable option. But the longer the two of them watched Dahl, waiting for the other to speak first, the harder it was.

"You were willing before," Farideh pointed out quietly, "when Dahl was the one casting the scroll."

" 'Willing's not the word I'd use," Oota said. " 'Back against the cave wall,' on the other hand—"

"You are quite a madman, Harper," Cereon interrupted. "We shall die."

"You said yourself the spell is destructive, that it gathers," Dahl said. "If that's not a replacement for the ritual scroll Tharra thought she was given, what else is it?"

Cereon raised a slim, pale eyebrow. "There is no way to know."

"Just as there's no way to know who's casting it," Oota said. "Or what they want from us."

"Their motives don't matter," Dahl said. "They want you all dead so that they can claim the Chosen's powers—whether that's to raise up a new god or armor an old one or just sacrifice us in the name of stopping Shar is *irrelevant*. The spell is already

436

happening and our best bet is to ride it out."

"What do you intend to do instead?" Farideh asked them. "Can you disrupt that thing? Can you stop the casting?" Oota's eye slid to Cereon. The sun elf's impassive expression tightened ever so slightly.

"No," Cereon said. "We may be able to deflect some of it. A shield, perhaps. I can make such a casting. I suspect some of the others can assist me, make it stronger." He shook his head. "It will not be enough to protect all the *tel'Quessir*."

Oota gave Dahl a knowing look. "Thank you, Harper, for bringing me such valued allies."

Dahl scowled. "Look, there are three basic possibilities. First, I'm right. That spell does exactly what I've said and we need to be ready. Second, it's not what I've said and it's not going to kill us. In that case, we end up exactly where we are now: convincing people to attack the tower and try to bring it down. Third, it's not what I've said, it's far more powerful, and it's going to harm us all no matter where we hide." He spread his hands. "And if that's the case, so far as I can see, there is nothing we can do about it."

"Except a shield for the favored of the elves," Oota said.

"Rhand must have taken notice," Farideh went on. "We should be prepared for him to try and stall things."

"A force near the shelters," Oota agreed. "Spread out to catch the guards coming at us if need be. And a second," she added significantly, "to free the prisoners in the fortress."

"Now," Dahl said. "We don't have the time to spare waiting for nightfall. Though Phalar—"

"Can hide beneath a cloak," Oota said. "I'll deal with Phalar. We'll take Hamdir, him, and you as well, Harper. Get everyone armed and back here as quick as you can." She strode from the court, leaving Dahl and Farideh.

"She declines my spells," Cereon said, "as well as my followers."

"We'll take Armas," Dahl said. "She trusts him." Cereon

sniffed, as if to say that wasn't enough, and left without another word. Farideh watched him go.

"You want to come with us, don't you?" Dahl said as soon as Cereon was out of earshot. Farideh sighed.

"Wouldn't you? But I'm not a fool—I owe them, but none of the Chosen is going to be cheered to see me. And then there's Rhand." She rubbed her left arm. "I'm a liability."

"Don't fish," Dahl said lightly. "You've already been a help."

"And a hindrance." She sighed again and shook her head. "Don't mind me. I'm not feeling well."

"Fight some shadar-kai," Dahl said. "That seems to perk you up."

And at least that coaxed a smile from her. "Be careful," she told him.

"You too," Dahl said. He looked at the thinning crowd of prisoners, feeling sure he ought to say something more, but not knowing what it was. "Do you expect Lorcan to come back?"

"Gods only know," she said. "I almost hope he stays away." She considered Dahl a moment. "*He* could go in for that scroll. The one to make the cavern."

"Better him than you," Dahl said. "Promise me you won't try and get back in."

She nodded, in an absent sort of way. "How will we decide who has to . . ."

"Not now," Dahl said. It wasn't a question Dahl wanted to answer, especially when he knew he'd be the last one into the shelter rooms. "Maybe they'll manage it."

"Maybe," she said. Then, "Did you tell Tharra about the ritual?"

"No," Dahl said. "Why would I?"

Farideh rubbed her arm again. "Because she ought to know. Maybe she'd be back on our side if she knew the other devil had tricked her. Maybe her deal's undone if he didn't follow through."

Dahl regarded her a long moment. "Tharra's not you, you know."

"What is that supposed to mean?"

"It means she's not coming back over to our side. She broke her oath."

"She made a bad decision. She did the same thing I did."

Dahl's temper rose. "Yes, well, you're not a Harper. So it's different. You . . ." He struggled for the right words. Because he knew she was right. Even if he was also sure she was wrong. "You've never betrayed anyone. You're very . . . dependable."

She stared at him, unblinking, and Dahl fought the urge to guess what she was thinking—that *was* a compliment.

"I can think of more than a few people who would disagree with you," Farideh finally said. "Starting with the Chosen in the wizard's workshop."

The woman guarding Tharra looked as if she would have liked to stop Farideh from entering, but she only fixed a suspicious scowl on the bowl of thin gruel the tiefling carried with her and let her pass.

Tharra watched Farideh stonily as she shut the door. "I'm not hungry."

Farideh sat down on the mat that lined the floor and set the bowl beside her. "Did you know that the ritual wouldn't work?"

"What are you talking about?"

"Dahl studied it. He's pretty knowledgeable about these things. The components are all wrong. The spell's not constructed right. So," she said, "did you know?"

Tharra searched Farideh's face. "It has to work," she said. "If it doesn't work, what's the point of my deal?"

"I think you're a decoy," Farideh said. "When the spell collected nothing, he could blame it on me, and you'd be too dead to argue. But now someone else is casting a similar spell."

"And you can't stop it," Tharra finished. She looked away. "We have to get them down into the shelter rooms. As many as will fit."

"We're only up to a thousand," Farideh said. "And we only have a few hours."

Tharra pursed her mouth. "I'm not the one who brought them here. I'm not the one who'll kill them. If Magros hadn't caught me, he would have caught some other. If you want to lock me in here and recite my crimes—"

"No," Farideh said. "I've come to ask for your help."

Tharra stopped. "What sort of help?"

"In the wizard's study, there's a scroll," Farideh said. "A very old, very rare scroll. It will open a chamber in the ground—big enough to make the difference."

Tharra raised an eyebrow. "Why does he have that?"

"Windfall. He found it and he hasn't come up with a use for it yet."

"But you didn't take it?"

Farideh's chest squeezed. "I didn't know we needed it. And now if I go into the fortress, Rhand will know he's being played."

"So you expect me to traipse into the Abyss in your place."

"You know the fortress," Farideh said, "and the guards know you. If someone spots you, they're not going to assume right off something's wrong. You know how to slip in and out—I don't know much about Harpers, but I know that. You're our best chance for saving them all."

Tharra's expression grew serious. "It's in his study. The one at the top of the tower."

"On the rack against the right-hand wall," Farideh said. "Second shelf down. There's scorch marks along the end, and a chip missing from the roller. If you open it, you'll see the drawing of the cavern it makes."

"If I can get to it," Tharra murmured. "I can't go in the gates. Not without a guard."

"Dahl and Oota are planning to free the Chosen in the wizard's workshop very soon."

Tharra laughed once. "I think I'll stand a better chance charming the grays." She paused. "You have to get my pin back. I won't survive without it."

"How long will it work for?"

"Half a bell. Long enough, if I don't trigger it until I have to." She chewed her lip. "This is a little mad, you know?"

"Mad times call for mad plans," Farideh said. "I'll get the pin. But you don't use it on me, or anyone else on our side. And after, you have to answer to the Harpers all the same."

"If I'm alive," Tharra said. Farideh kneeled and untied her bindings. "Doesn't work well on you anyway. People tell you you're stubborn?"

"Constantly," Farideh said. She grasped the other woman's hand and stood. "Come on."

"What are you planning to tell Antama out there?" Tharra asked.

"Nothing. We're in a hurry," Farideh said, and she pulled enough Hells magic through her brand to make a slit in the fabric of the planes, and stepped through the slat-board wall to reappear in the alley beyond.

"Did you choose the least concealable weapon available on purpose?" Khochen teased Havilar as they crept through the alleys between huts.

"No," Havilar said irritably. "I chose it because I'm good at it."

"You were good at it before you chose it?" Khochen asked cheekily. "There's a tale I long to hear." Beside her, the scout, Ebros, chuckled softly.

Havilar scowled. "Do you have any idea of where we're headed?"

"The same way everyone else is headed," Khochen said. "Where there are people, there are answers."

"Where there are people," Havilar said, "there's usually someone who wants to start a fight."

Khochen looked back and smiled. "Don't worry, little tiefling. You have me."

Havilar gripped Devilslayer and started to retort that she did *not* need some puny thief with her blades in her boots to rescue her, and *anyway* Havilar had a solid half foot on Khochen. But her reply was cut off by sudden shouting from behind them.

"Well, well—not in the Hells after all." Havilar turned and caught the chain of a shadar-kai guard on the haft of her glaive, the bladed end slicing inches from her face.

The guard's companions—a woman with enormous arms and a heavy broadsword strapped to her back and a wiry fellow with a pair of curved knives—shouted after the chainmaster. "He doesn't want you ruined," the man said to Havilar. "Even though he won't be happy to find you again. Come quietly, and we'll kill your companions quick."

The woman grinned. "No watching for you this time."

Havilar didn't stop to wonder what that meant—whoever *he* was, he could go to the Abyss before she'd follow *karshoji* shadar-kai *anywhere*. As the chainmaster yanked the chain free of her weapon, she followed the pull, swinging the weight of the glaive toward his face. As he pulled back, she shifted and pulled the butt of the glaive up and into his right wrist. He pulled back farther, eyes dancing, favoring his injury. The chain snaked along the ground, catching in the sticky mud. Havilar stomped onto the weapon, grinding the blades down into the muck, before leaping back off. The chainmaster hauled hard on the lodged chain and caught the point of Havilar's glaive in his gut for the hesitation.

Ebros's arrow hit the swordswoman in the chest and pierced her leather armor. She grinned horribly and pulled the arrow free, barbs and all. A second arrow hit the smaller man as he tried to maneuver around his allies in the narrow passage. Khochen darted past in the corner of Havilar's eye and with a flash of steel blocked the swordswoman's dagger on her own blade, then jabbed her dagger up under the woman's arm.

The chainmaster gave Havilar a terrible grin as he straightened. Havilar matched it—daughter of Clanless Mehen, wielder of Devilslayer. The glaive as good as her right hand.

The chain flashed up and encircled her right forearm, biting into her bracer. She let go of half her grip and moved with the tug to punch the shadar-kai in the base of the throat. That stunned him and she yanked hard on the chain, pulling it from his grip.

Step, shift, turn the blade—she sliced the glaive deeply across the shadar-kai's belly, ripping under the leather jack. His eyes widened and he lunged at her. Havilar moved with him, turning to hook the glaive behind him as he passed, and pulling him forward hard enough to trip him. She planted the blade of her weapon in his back and the air went out of the shadar-kai in a horrible, wet gasp.

Khochen scrambled back from the shadar-kai with the broadsword on her back, the alley still too narrow to draw such a weapon. But Khochen was keen enough with her daggers that it hardly mattered. Bleeding from many cuts, the shadar-kai advanced, taking her own blood from the Harper as she did.

Havilar narrowed her eyes and brought the butt of the glaive up into the guard's bare wrist, smacking it hard enough to make her grip loose. Slide the haft up and nick the blade—the dagger flew from the shadar-kai's grasp. The startled guard looked to Havilar, then froze.

Ebros's arrow protruded from the shadar-kai's left eye. She dropped to her knees and tripped over on the fallen chain. "Well shot!" Khochen gasped.

Ebros nodded, shaking, and trained his next arrow on the man between Havilar and Khochen's blades. But the wiry shadar-kai took quick stock of the situation fell backward, into the shadows, and disappeared.

"Running for reinforcements," Khochen panted. "Damn." She rubbed her wounded shoulder and looked back at Havilar. "What was that shadar-kai talking about?"

"He thought I was Fari," Havilar said, feeling her stomach twist into knots. "We have to go."

"*Ilharess-iblithin* sun," Phalar cursed for at least the fifth time. A heavy sheen of sweat stood out on his ebony skin, even in the cool air—low as the sun was, it still irritated the drow. Dahl hadn't discovered what Oota had traded him. When he'd asked, Phalar had chuckled in an unpleasant manner and cleaned his nails with the tip of Dahl's dagger.

He wasn't so relaxed now. "Let's go already."

"Go ahead," Hamdir said, standing over the drow with a cloak as a shield against the sun. "Run out into the daylight and knock on the gates."

"I could hit them from here," Armas said, with a familiar eagerness. He flexed his hands and blew out a nervous breath. "I could definitely hit them from here." Phalar chuckled.

"Wait," Dahl said. The force of Phalar's god seemed to grip Dahl even more firmly this time, and dressed once more in the stolen uniform, Dahl had a hard time waiting for the guards to pass by before he rushed out to unlock the gate with a ritual. They needed to time it perfectly—there was no speeding the ritual, after all, no matter how sure Dahl felt in that moment that he could make it happen.

If the same effect took hold of Oota, it wasn't obvious—she rocked on her feet, tense and ready, but she counted the beats of the guards' footsteps under her breath and kept her hands on her belt and off the stolen sword she wore tied there. She did not look at Tharra, crouched beside her and wearing the black kerchief and apron—but then no one did. Farideh had turned up with Tharra as they were easing Phalar out of the shelters, past the crowds heading in, and even if Dahl had to admit he greatly preferred this plan to Farideh's last one, he wasn't going to pretend he liked it.

One more pass, Dahl thought, when the guards reached their farthest stations . . . Dahl drummed his fingers against the blue silk cover of Farideh's ritual book, the pouches of components dangling from his wrist. He was so consumed by the plan, by forcing himself to run through the ritual instead of falling prey to Phalar's powers, that he completely missed the fact that they were being approached until Oota turned, axe high, and nearly took Lord Vescaras Ammakyl's head off.

"Hold!" Dahl hissed to Vescaras as much as Oota. He stepped around the half-orc and saw Brin and a red-haired elf behind Vescaras. "Gods' books, where did you come from?"

Vescaras raised an eyebrow, but lowered his rapier. "Good to see you're well. Your sendings were clear enough—no need to follow up and waste resources."

Brin looked around. "What in the Hells is this place?"

"Internment camp," Dahl said. "He's collecting people with divine powers, and—" He stopped himself. "And we're in a bit of a rush."

Vescaras peered around the corner. "Infiltration?"

"Rescue," Dahl said. "Forty or fifty. No idea about their state. No idea about guards."

"No time for reconnaissance," Vescaras said.

"I'll get the first door unlocked. After we have . . ." He glanced at Phalar. "Resources."

Brin and Vescaras seemed to notice Phalar for the first time, and for a moment, Dahl was sure they were going to flee.

"Don't provoke them," Dahl said to Phalar.

The drow spread his hands. "Haven't I been good?"

Vescaras recovered and looked very deliberately over at Dahl. "Well, Goodman Peredur, I suppose you have the lead."

"Oota," Dahl started, intending to acquaint her with the Harpers. But the guards had reached their farthest stations.

"Now," Oota ordered, as she shoved Dahl forward along the reaching shadow of the building they'd crouched behind. Without stopping, Dahl sprinted up and pressed himself flat against the great door, where a passing guard would have a difficult time spotting him. He slipped the components into a pile beside him and flipped the book open to the ritual he needed.

He worked quickly, his hands remembering the passes and actions—the streak of powdered silver worked into the grain of the wood, the line of bright blue salts along the base of the door, the charcoal-marked keyhole he added to the center. The stream of words that finished the ritual seemed to collect great fistfuls of the Weave and pull them close like a cloth over a conjurer's table. When it released, the door swung open a crack, its bar dangling on the ground.

At the next opportunity, the others darted across and into the passageway. Dahl hurried to the fore. The tunnel was unguarded, as was the open courtyard. The smell of blood still tainted the cold air.

"What happened here?" Brin breathed. Dahl didn't answer. He could imagine Farideh standing on the ledge above, being made to watch the slaughter below and realizing how far Rhand was willing to go.

"Our hand was forced," Tharra answered after a moment of quiet.

Dahl turned to retort, but the expression of grief on Tharra's face stopped him. He might not count her as his fellow, but she counted the dead prisoners among hers. The living ones too, he thought.

"Here," he said, interlacing his fingers. "You don't have long."

"Good thing I'm quick," she said, her voice too light.

"Go out over the wall," he advised. "Just past the veserab stables."

Tharra nodded and stepped onto his hands, reaching high to grasp the sharp, polished edge of the black stone above. She peered back down once she'd pulled herself up. "Best of luck, Harper."

Before Dahl could reply, she was gone, slipping alone into the forbidding fortress.

"Come on." Oota went to the smaller door and forced the lock—another narrow hallway, empty and lightless. She edged inside, followed by the rest.

At the end was a second door—a portcullis, and this one guarded. Dahl gestured for the others to stop and crept forward, near enough to see what lay beyond.

Two guards waited by the door, distracted by at least three wizards—two younger-looking fellows and Rhand—considering a young elf man in a cage, whose skin radiated soft light. One of the novices prodded at him with a thin, sharp-looking rod. The man made no noise.

Rhand sighed heavily. "We haven't time for the hot irons," he said. "Make them ready to depart. If that little witch thinks I'm leaving behind such resources, we will have to disabuse her of such fancies." He turned to two of the wizards. "Come along. We haven't much time to prepare before—"

Another guard, a shadar-kai woman with pierced cheeks, came in through the far door and called out to Rhand. "Your devil is a liar, master."

Rhand spun on her. "What?"

Dahl gripped his sword. The room was larger than the stables outside, and lined with cells and cages—holding more prisoners, fifty at least, many with the glitter of strange magic worked on them. And more guards—another four. As he reached the edge of the light, he nearly stumbled, and leaned heavily against the tunnel wall. His eyes crossed, the lids almost too heavy to lift.

"I'll return in an hour," he heard Rhand say as he started to drift off. "I expect everything to be prepared. The same goes for you two—get upstairs and work quickly. I need to deal with something out . . ."

Someone grabbed hold of Dahl and pulled him sharply back into the tunnel. "All right?" Vescaras whispered.

"Yes," Dahl said, extricating himself. "There's . . . There's something magic happening in there." He peered back through the portcullis. None of the wizards seemed to feel the strange sleepiness, and all six of the guards he'd spotted stood around the space, lazy and unconcerned.

"Six guards," he said. "Two wizards. A lot of bystanders." He shook his head. "The Chosen aren't affecting the wizards, either, I don't think. And there's—"

"They're sleeping too," Armas said. "There's something about halfway across the room giving off a magical field. I'll wager that's it."

"How are the guards awake?" Vescaras asked.

"Amulets," Armas supplied. "The gold ones are making some sort of dispelling field. Weak, but enough to keep them on their feet."

"So without those amulets we fall asleep, too," Brin said.

"Well we shouldn't wait," Vescaras said. "Shadar-kai can't take that kind of thing draining on them long. I would suspect they cycle through the guards regularly. Better we take on someone who's been on their feet a while than someone fresh."

"Why are they keeping them sleeping?" the elf asked.

"It probably keeps their powers from affecting everyone else," Dahl said. "Otherwise, you'd have to worry about . . ." He stopped. "Oh. Oh, that is *perfect*. What's your name?"

"Sheera," she said, sounding puzzled.

"Well met, Sheera." He nodded at her crossbow. "How accurately can you shoot?"

❦

Farideh pulled the dancing eldritch light into her hands and shook it out again as she waited at a crossroads for Tharra and the others to return. It didn't rid her of the feeling that the Nine Hells themselves were about to boil out of her. She did it again, not daring to cast fully, but needing to expend that power.

Lorcan's words kept coming back to her: *Asmodeus only knows what will trigger it, after all.* What if all this worrying just brought on worse powers? What if it made their rescue plan unworkable? What if it made Asmodeus notice what was happening in the prison camp?

She rolled the rod between her fingers, all too aware of the flags of shadow smoke that had started curling around her again, and tried to slow her pulse. If there were anything to make people *more* nervous about her, leaking shadows like some Shar-blessed creature was probably it. She looked down at her bone-white finger and shivered. She pulled her sleeve down over it again and scanned the crossroads once more. Still no guards, and that worried her—hopefully they weren't out among the stragglers, keeping people from reaching the shelters. Hopefully they weren't all defending the wizard's workshop. Hopefully they wouldn't stop Tharra from reaching the study and meeting Farideh back here.

Movement—the flames leaped to Farideh's fingers again. A little boy—the same towheaded boy she'd spared in the courtyard the day before—marched across the crossroads, not seeming to care that Farideh stood guard.

"Well met?" she called, shaking the flames out.

The little boy looked up. "Well met." And he started off again.

Farideh hurried after him. "Wait. You have to go back into the shelters. It's not safe."

"I know," he said. "They don't say why, but I know. That's why I have to get Samayan." He stopped at the next alleyway, studying the muddy ground. "He got nervous—he doesn't like being underground. So he ran away." He gave Farideh a very serious look. "I don't think he knows how dangerous it is."

"You need to go back to the shelters," Farideh told him again, unsure of what to do. He wasn't afraid of her. "Would you like me to walk you back?"

"No," he said, continuing to the next crossroads. "I have to find Samayan." He peered down the alleyway and froze. Farideh leaped ahead of him, ready to cast flames into—

"Havi?" Farideh said. There in the alley opposite, her twin

and two others—the Harper Khochen from Waterdeep and a half-elf fellow—were hurrying toward them. Havilar glanced quickly at the crossroads and darted to her sister's arms. Farideh nearly wept.

"Oh, you're safe," Havilar said. "You're safe, you're safe." She held Farideh tight. "Lorcan said, but he's *such* a liar and I wasn't sure."

"You shouldn't have come," Farideh said. "Gods, Havi, you—"

"Oh shut up," Havilar said. "What was I going to do? Let you have all the adventure? Besides, you needed saving." She let Farideh go, but her eyes were worried. "Mehen's here. Brin too. They're looking for you in other spots. But, Fari, there's guards looking for you too. They thought I was you and—"

"You should go to the shelters," the little boy said. "It's dangerous." He trotted up to the next crossroads and gasped. He darted out of sight, and all four adult sprinted after him. A line of snowstars, tiny white flowers on tiny dark leaves, headed down toward the lake.

"Stop, poppet," Khochen said, setting a firm hand on the little boy's shoulder. He looked up at the Harper as if he might scold her.

"That's Samayan's trail," he said. "He went this way."

"If we follow it, we'll find him?" Farideh asked. The little boy nodded. "Then you go back," she told him, "and quickly. We'll go find Samayan and bring him to you."

The little boy eyed her skeptically. "All right," he finally said. "But you have to tell him you won't make him go past the bottom stair. And that I'll stay with him."

"I promise," Farideh said. "Go." The little boy ran off, back toward the shelters.

The Harper woman eyed her oddly. Farideh stared right back, not caring what she saw. "Samayan's only a little older than his friend," she said. Khochen's gaze flicked over her once more.

"Then we ought to find him."

Farideh ripped the flowers up as they passed, removing any trace the shadar-kai might follow. They went on, twisting through the camp, heading for the lake. When the four of them passed the edge of the buildings and came out onto the broad shores of the icy waters, Farideh saw the trail of flowers, in distant patches as if the boy had bounded over the pebbly beach, ending in the water.

"Gods be damned." Khochen breathed. They had found Samayan.

The boy stood up to his ankles in the water, shivering as half a dozen shadar-kai closed in, another dozen crowding the shore. Samayan backed away, deeper into the water. The shadar-kai's voices shouting, taunting.

"Come out of there, or we come in for you!"

Samayan stood up to his thighs now, struggling against the pull of the water's strange flow. His lips were turning pale. He kept shaking his head, kept moving backward.

Khochen caught Farideh's arm as she started forward. "They'll catch you, and then we're all done for," Khochen said. "We just need a distraction."

"Chase him in," one of the guards called. There were more of them now, at least a dozen, gathering out of the alleyways to watch the sport of drowning a young boy. Farideh's temper rose.

"All right," Khochen said, "Farideh, set one of these huts on fire. Havi and Ebros—"

The nearest guard slashed at Samayan with her blade, scoring a line of blood across his chest. He flinched, curling away from the weapon as she made another slice across his shoulder, cackling as she did. Samayan stumbled backward, as if over an unseen rock, the choppy waters closing over his dark head.

And Khochen's plan didn't matter anymore.

Khochen cursed and she and the twins raced toward the fight, balls of dark energy peeling off Farideh's fingertips, Ebros's arrows sailing over their heads.

"Keep them back," Farideh shouted at her sister. "I'll get Samayan."

"What?" Havilar cried, as she stopped a shadar-kai's sword on her glaive.

Ahead of Farideh, Samayan's face broke the lake's surface, gasped too little air, and dipped under again.

Farideh ran through the lapping water, toward the bobbing shape of the boy, heedless of the threat of the shadar-kai. The water was cold enough her bones ached—colder than the tarn she'd grown up swimming in, colder than the waters of the Fountains of Memory. She dodged the lash of a spiked chain, and—as Samayan's head dipped below a wave—she leaped through the fabric of the planes to close the distance. She stepped free, catching hold of the lanky boy in her arms and realizing that the lake bed had dropped off precipitously under her feet.

The icy water closed all around her.

There was no swimming through this—so much cold her every nerve was screaming and fading into numbness already. She could hardly move her arms, locked around Samayan, and each kick of her legs felt as if she were dragging them through concrete. The cold seemed to still her lungs, making it harder to draw breath when she did break the surface. She was turned around, unable to find the shore. Her heart hammered in her chest, and it did no good. She couldn't warm herself, couldn't draw her magic, couldn't keep Samayan above the water. The lake would kill her.

No . . .

She tightened her arms around Samayan as they sank into the freezing water.

No . . .

Air bubbled out of her mouth, water flooded in.

No . . .

. . . there are thirteen tieflings arrayed around the grove— hooved and horned and winged and tailed and some who might

as well be human for all their blood shows—but they are tieflings all the same. Six men, six woman, and the Brimstone Angel herself who stands facing the symbol of the king of the Hells, painted in blood on the spire of stone that they have dragged out of the bedrock with will and the frayed scraps of the Weave, the engines of the Nine Hells and the tortured howls of souls long-lost. This is how it starts, where it begins. Where Farideh and Havilar and every tiefling walking the plane begin. This is how they damn us all . . .

Farideh opened her eyes in the freezing water, the water that once filled the Fountains of Memory—*and sees the vision as real as it was in her head, as real as it would have been if she stood there; the blue-black fall of her ancestress's hair where the surface of the lake should be*—before her sight began fading. She blinked once, and suddenly she saw the ghost woman's face, inches from her own, her teeth bared in a grin that was more animal than human . . .

Relax, Farideh heard her say. *Let go . . . Let me help you . . .*

NO—Farideh's wordless scream made the ghost woman recoil. The last of her air spilled out.

And fire rolled from the core of her out.

She clung tightly to Samayan as everything around them was suddenly bright as a sun and hissing with the furious sound of boiling water. Her thoughts reeled, wordless and scrambling, but her lungs were screaming for air and her legs knew well enough to answer the need. She broke the surface, flames still filling her sight, and pulled Samayan up with her. A spill of water poured out of his nose and mouth. She could hear people shouting and weapons clashing on the shore. A burst of Hells magic pulled her nearer, near enough to regain all her weight as air replaced the water around her. Through the flames she could see the shadar-kai watching her warily. She could see Havilar and Khochen frozen where they'd stood holding off shadar-kai. Samayan coughed, gagged, and she set him shivering on the shore. Khochen sprinted forward and dragged the boy back, away from the fire. Away from Farideh.

Away from the Chosen of Asmodeus.

Farideh turned to the shadar-kai, and she felt her fury, her certainty that she would not let them take another soul, burst out of her like a wave. The flames burned hotter still. She would do anything, in that moment, to keep them from torturing the boy.

"Leave them to me," Farideh said to the others. She drew the rod from her sleeve and held it out in front of her, parallel to the ground. "*Chaanaris.*"

CHAPTER TWENTY-TWO

26 Ches, the Year of the Nether Mountain Scrolls (1486 DR)
The Lost Peaks

LORD OF KNOWLEDGE, BINDER OF WHAT IS KNOWN, DAHL chanted to himself, *Make my eye clear, my mind open, my heart true. Give me the wisdom to separate the lie from the truth . . .*

Dahl had not been a paladin for ten years now, but still he remembered the feeling of the god of knowledge's presence—the sure, tranquil truth of Oghma that lit his mind afire. It bore little resemblance to the oddly strangled calm that seemed to surround and hold tight to his nerves, foreign as some Chosen's power on his thoughts.

You can do this, he reminded himself. You have done it plenty of times before. He turned his sword in his hand, adjusting the grip. And if you can't, he added, then all these people are going to die for your stupid plan, and Vescaras will be there to see you—

He nodded to Sheera, before he lost the calm.

The Harper raised her crossbow and stepped quickly to the portcullis, firing off a bolt before the guards turned at the sound, before the orb in the center of the room could ensnare her. True to her promise, the bolt flew across the room and struck the sphere on the pillar, knocking it to the ground.

The glass shattered.

And the Chosen woke.

The sudden cacophony of powers vying for his attention made Dahl's stomach plunge and his heart race. The man in the cage beside the wizards opened his eyes and started to scream.

Lord of Knowledge, he chanted to himself, *Binder of What Is Known* . . .

As soon as the bolt flew, Sheera threw herself flat against the wall as Phalar summoned the globe of darkness around himself once more and let the blessings of his god wash over them all. Dahl gripped his sword more tightly as the urge to reach through the grate and cut the guards' throats raced through him. Phalar chuckled softly within his bubble of night, and then ran at the portcullis.

The iron grating sizzled as Phalar's magic let him phase through it. The guards startled, reaching for their weapons. Dahl hit the grate and saw their dark eyes deepen as Phalar's god stripped off any caution they had left.

"Hey!" Dahl shouted. "Hey! Shadow-kisser!" He banged his sword against the grating, drawing the door guards' attention, as Phalar streaked across the room. The globe passed over the surprised wizards, swallowing them both for a moment. The darkness vanished—but Phalar was already past, running for the far door and dropping the crossbar before turning to defend against the near guard who'd shaken off her shock and realized the drow racing through the room didn't belong.

The clanking of the portcullis seized Dahl's attention, as a shadar-kai ducked under the rising gate in front of him. Idiot, he thought, and he brought the pommel of his sword down hard on the exposed back of the man's head. Still, it took all his effort not to duck under the portcullis himself to get to the second guard faster.

Make my eye clear, my mind open, my heart true, he chanted, a hymn to hold onto his real self.

The shadar-kai finished hauling the gate open, his eyes dancing as if he were relishing the idea of running Dahl through, as his fellows closed on the entrance. But he wasn't expecting Oota to come screaming out of the tunnel, sword first. She forced him back, slashing wildly. Dahl followed, trailed by Vescaras, Armas, and Hamdir.

"*Hrast*," Armas cursed, searching the cages that lined the shadowy edges of the room. "She pulled a lot of people."

"We need a key," Dahl said. He glanced back at Brin and Sheera. "You, keep shooting. You, keep the guards off her. Hamdir—"

Oota's bellow filled the room, drowning out the building shouts of the prisoners. Dahl saw her shove the dead door guard off her blade.

"Which of you is next?" she roared. "Which of you thought you could capture my people and survive my wrath? Which of you cowards thinks you can best the Chosen of Oboulds?"

Two streaks of burning air whizzed past Dahl. Behind him, the air went out of Armas in an ugly gasp. Something else set the air behind him humming. Dahl didn't dare turn—his sword caught the blade of a rangy shadar-kai man with his pale hair in tight braids. Slight as he seemed, the man forced Dahl back and off-balance. Something behind Dahl rumbled as the man pulled his blade up to cut Dahl down—

And stiffened as a blast of greenish light slammed into him. A deranged grin spread across the shadar-kai's face as one dagger punched into his lung, then another. A second bolt of magic screamed past them.

Dahl looked up—it wasn't Armas who stood there, but his likeness in dirt, looking impassively down at Dahl. Beyond, Armas clutched one hand to his burned and bleeding chest, staring shocked at the quartet of protectors who'd risen up out of the ground around him. The faintest halo of silver seemed to shimmer over the half-elf.

"So she was right," he said numbly.

Bad wound, Dahl thought. He needed healing—but Brin was busy, fending off another guard. The four defenders arranged themselves silently around Armas. The new-made Chosen straightened, still bleeding, still wounded, and raised a hand. A burst of light streaked from his palm, and with the guardians around him, he forged a path toward the cages on the right end of the room, where Phalar still battled the guards. Dahl saw the drow duck into an open cell and slam the door behind him.

The wizards were still on their feet, sending burst after burst of magic streaking out into the fight. Too many overshot the attackers and burst against the cages—or maybe they aimed their strikes there . . .

Give me the wisdom to separate the lie from the truth, Dahl chanted as he and Armas forced their way past a guard harried by Vescaras's swift rapier, past Hamdir struggling to hold back another two, toward the two wizards and the man in the cage. The young man's frantic screams and the Chosen's blending powers threatened to make Dahl break. *Give me the strength to accept what is so . . .*

Armas's defenders reached the wizard by the cage. Eyes on Oota and Vescaras, attention on the spell he was casting, the wizard didn't notice the golem until it slammed a solid fist into the side of his head.

"You idiot!" the other cried as his spell shot off to envelop Phalar in a fog of poisonous-looking gas. "Pay attention." He cast another spell and vanished, reappearing nearer to Phalar. Sheera's arrows chased him. Armas reached up and shook the cage with the panicking young man in it.

"Mreldor!" Armas yelled, as the wizard reeled. "Stop screaming!"

My word is my steel, my reason my shield, Dahl chanted as he searched the walls. *And I shall fear no deception, for the truth remains—*

A crackling orb of energy burst into being between the Armas, Dahl, and the wizard. Dahl's muscles all went stiff, and for a moment there was only the searing pain that drove all else—even the powers of the gods—from his thoughts. The energy dissipated, but Dahl's mind still reeled and—

"Dahl!" Armas shouted, and suddenly two of the golems stood between him and the wizard he'd struck. There was a sizzle, a spatter, like fat in a fire. And the golems collapsed into piles of dirt and acid. Armas stood panting over them.

"Gods," Dahl cried. The wizard gathered another spell.

The screaming man reached through the bars and grasped the wizard's shoulders. A pulse of energy rushed outward, and Dahl could have sworn the young man seemed larger, broader, his eyes in shadows. Lightning leaped from Mreldor's hands, crackling over the wizard's form, small and spindly but as powerful as the orb, and with a thunderclap loud enough to make Dahl's ears ring. Flames burst out of the wizard's robes. He yelped, and before Dahl could do anything, he cast again, this time at the young man. Three bolts of magical energy hit the Chosen, one after the other, and he collapsed against the cage.

The wizard looked up, still burning, saw Dahl, and reached out to cast. One of Sheera's bolts caught him in the shoulder. Dahl swung his sword, hardly thinking, and cut the man's hand at the wrist, severing the veins. His next spell flew wide, giving Dahl a chance to run the wizard through and stop his casting.

"The . . . wall . . ." Armas panted behind him. His wounds were worse—the acid had caught his arm. "It's . . . by the exit."

"Hamdir!" Dahl shouted. "Get him to Brin!" A rune-scribed gem throbbed in the stone near to the door. An arcane lock.

And Oghma has made me a lantern in the gloom, he chanted to himself, *a compass in the wilds . . .*

Another guard came at him, chain wheeling. The heavy weapon smacked against Dahl's upper arm, hard enough to make him feel the bone, and more than enough to grab his attention. He heard Vescaras's shouts, Hamdir's shouts, Oota's bellows, and he could not track a one of them as he dodged the heavy spiked chain. He backed away, leading the chainmaster away from his fellows . . . and toward the rune-scribed gem glowing in the center of the wall.

"Come on, little mouse," the shadar-kai crooned. "Come and play."

The chain darted out, nearly catching Dahl's shoulder, but he dropped beneath it. The chain crashed into the gem. A stream of ice burst out, encasing the guard. The shimmer of magic dropped from the cages. Dahl finished off the guard and started prying open doors. On the other side of the room, he saw Vescaras do the same. Oota roared as the last of the guards fell to her sword.

It is my duty to find what is hidden, Dahl chanted through the noise of the Chosen, *and my gift to know what is unknown.*

He heard a strangled sound. The last wizard was pulled against the bars of the cell beside the one Phalar had ducked into, the chain of his amulet stretched between two ebony hands and pulled taut against the wizard's throat. Against the back wall of the cell, an old woman watched in horror.

The wizard's last strangled gasps were cut off by the *twang* of Sheera's crossbow. The bolt lodged in the wizard's chest, and he fell still. Phalar dropped him with a look of disgust.

"*None* of you," he announced, "are any fun."

"The sands are running," Dahl said. "We have to move."

Those prisoners who had not broken out into the fight on their own were easily recovered. Many of them were wounded, all of them were shocked and shaken. Dahl had to coax little Vanri out of the corner of the cage she'd been thrown in.

"I don't want to," Vanri sobbed. "Tell her I don't want to."

Dahl picked the girl up and held her close. He looked over her shoulder at Armas, at Brin straightening, woozy and off-balance from trying to heal the half-elf's ruined chest. The wound had healed over, a shiny patch of pink skin where the bloody mess had been. But Armas still looked drawn and sallow. Vanri's grip on Dahl's neck tightened and the sound of the roaring ocean filled his ears.

"Hush," Dahl said, and he rubbed her back. "It will be all right."

As they came to the door, however, a sudden sense of utter dread clenched around Dahl's heart, so strange and sudden that it only took a moment to realize it wasn't natural.

"What in the Hells was that?" Oota demanded.

Lord of Knowledge, Dahl thought, don't let that be from the Hells.

Havilar watched, horrified, as flames leaped across Farideh's skin when she stepped from the water. A whirlwind of fire shifted, collecting, haloing her form, but building, building, up her back until . . .

Wings of fire unfolded around Farideh, shielding her like two massive hands. Pure dread gripped Havilar in the very base of her belly, and for a moment she couldn't quite feel her knees or her glaive in her hands. Samayan clung to Ebros, shivering. Among the shadar-kai, even, some stepped back, away from this nightmare creature Farideh had become.

No, Havilar thought, gripping her weapon. She's still Farideh. She's still Farideh.

Farideh held her rod out in front of her. "*Chaanaris,*" she said, almost a hiss. She pulled the rod up.

In concert, a dozen hands made of shadow and flame broke out of the ground. The shadar-kai who noticed yelped and cursed and backed into still more hands, still more bodies pulling themselves up out of the ground and snatching at the guards with hands more claw than finger. Hungry hands, Havilar thought, edging toward her sister.

Farideh dropped the rod with a soft cry. The flames sputtered and failed. Havilar grabbed her arm.

"What are those things?"

"Get back!" Farideh cried, snatching up her fallen rod.

"They're not on our side."

The creatures grabbed hold of several guards, hooting and howling like wild apes, like things all empty of all but the simplest needs. Their shadow-and-flame hands sank into the shadar-kai, who screamed as the creatures tore flesh and something deeper from their forms.

"Ebros, keep shooting!" Khochen cried, pulling throwing knives from her boots. Farideh recovered herself and sent a rain of brimstone after them, and Havilar kept her glaive moving, keeping the frantic guards away from her sister and trying hard not to watch the clawing, Hellish souls.

Farideh's terrible spell faded, and the shadar-kai who weren't lying dead or dying came at them with renewed fury. Fifteen still, Havilar guessed. And five of us. Not pleasant odds, but she adjusted her stance and held her glaive low and ready.

A flash of light seared Havilar's eyes.

"Hold," Adolican Rhand said to his guards. And as welcome as the order was, it sent a trill of panic through Havilar. The wizard's creepy gaze was fixed on Farideh.

"Well, well," Rhand said, his voice like a razor, "I see you are *not* in the keeping of the Hells, after all. I shall assume that this was just Lady Sairché's attempt to enjoy my company." He smiled at Farideh, and Havilar shuddered. Twelve steps, she estimated. Just far enough she couldn't be sure that she'd hit him before he cast another spell. She edged toward her sister.

Farideh was as still as an oak in the forest. "You didn't come here to ask after Sairché's motives. What do you want?"

"My patron's interest has diminished," Rhand said, "and we seem to be under attack. We are departing for Shade, and so you have a choice to make." His gaze bored into her. "You can depart with me, and I will leave these people to their own devices. Perhaps they will manage where others have failed and escape before the remaining stores run out.

"Or you can refuse," he went on, "and be swept from the face of Faerûn with the rest of these unwashed pretenders, knowing you could have saved them."

Farideh glanced at Havilar, her terror plain to her twin. Havilar shook her head, ever so slightly. She couldn't. She wouldn't. Rhand couldn't destroy the camp faster than they could finish getting people underground, right?

Farideh swallowed and gave Havilar a look that said volumes: There wasn't another way. There wasn't a way to be sure. And she was sorry, again. So sorry.

"Don't!" Havilar said.

"I love you, Havi," Farideh said. "Tell Mehen and Dahl and the others I'm sorry, and . . ." She gave her twin a significant look. "Don't follow this time."

"Fari!" Havilar shouted, running toward her. "Fari, *karshoj*, don't—"

But Farideh took hold of Adolican Rhand's proffered hand and vanished before Havilar could grab hold of her and make her stop. The shadar-kai glanced at each other, as if none of them wanted to follow orders, but each stepped through the nearest patch of shadow and disappeared, back to the fortress.

Silence hung over the bloody beach. Then, Havilar screamed.

Lorcan knew he ought to ask the mirror to show him Adolican Rhand—if it couldn't find Sairché, it could at least find her captor and narrow Lorcan's search. But instead he caught the scourge pendant in his hand and asked to see Farideh.

Asmodeus's demands outweighed his agreements with Sairché, he told himself. The mirror shivered and shifted to reflect Farideh tearing down a slope toward a score of armed shadar-kai, and Lorcan cursed.

Lorcan sprinted back to the portal, holding in his thoughts the image of Farideh, the edge of a frozen lake.

The portal to the fortress didn't behave any better for Lorcan than it had for Sairché. He stepped out, not into the middle of the battle with the shadar-kai, but into empty streets between ragged huts. He heard the shouts and scrambling of a handful of people running from his entrance to the plane. Good riddance, he thought, trying to orient himself. The lake would be to the south and west—

Out of nothing, an all-too-familiar horror clutched at Lorcan's throat—

Calm, he told himself. Calm. It might be something else. It might be some Chosen's trick, some other god's sleight of hand. He leaped into the air, gaining enough height to spy the lake, the beach, the shadar-kai scurrying back as wings of fire unfolded from Farideh's back. There was no hoping this was some trick of the wizard, some errant Chosen fallen into the wrong fight.

The rest of Asmodeus's blessings had fallen on Farideh.

An arrow whizzed past Lorcan. He looked down to spot Mehen, the sour-faced elf with her longbow out and aimed at Lorcan, and the straggling scout besides.

"Save the arrows!" Lorcan said. "Farideh's in trouble. Get to the lake." Screams rose from that direction, and he said a little thanks to the Lords of the Nine that Mehen didn't protest, didn't ask what was happening. There would be plenty of time to think of ways to explain without explaining—now, they had to get Farideh out of there, first and foremost. Whatever she thought she was doing, it was obviously dangerous and not necessary to stopping Magros. He'd pull her out of there, convince her—

He crested the last row of buildings in time to see Farideh take hold of Adolican Rhand's outstretched hand, and vanish.

No, Lorcan thought, hitting the ground. No, no, no . . .

Havilar let loose a keening scream, part war cry, part anguish. Some part of Lorcan—the sensible part—tried to stop his feet, to turn him anywhere but where he was headed. But he ran straight to Havilar, cursing. "You let her go?"

She turned, eyes alight with fury, and shoved him hard "*You* said she was safe. I told you not to leave her with him, and you said it was fine! Now she's *gone,* back into that *karshoji* fortress."

"What?" a gruff voice cried, and Lorcan cursed again. Mehen and the Harpers had caught up to him. Havilar took one look at her father and burst into tears.

"Rhand took her," Havilar said. "Back to the fortress, then back to *Shade.* And Zahnya's spell is going to finish, and we all have to be underground. She's going to *die!*"

Mehen swung his head to Lorcan. "You're popping in and out of this place. Get me to that fortress."

"You're not leaving me," Havilar said, and Lorcan felt sure that even sending her to the stasis cage in Malbolge would not stop Havilar from following. "If you go, Mehen, I'm going too."

"Havi, go back with the Harpers. Get to shelter." Mehen hesitated. "Find Brin. Make sure he gets somewhere safe."

"Brin is perfectly capable of taking care of himself," Havilar said—though she had no luck in hiding the fear and the doubt in her voice, not from Lorcan. "I'm coming." She looked back at the odd assortment of Harpers, at the short, dark-haired woman. "Will you tell Brin what's happened, and that we'll be back?"

The dark-haired woman shook her head in disbelief. "I'll say those words," she said. "But do you really think—"

"Yes," Havilar said fiercely. "Promise. I will find him after." She turned back to Mehen. "But first, we take care of Fari."

Lorcan hesitated, his eyes darting between them. "You two understand that means passing through the Nine Hells? It means crossing the planes—twice. I can't simply leap into the fortress."

Mehen took hold of Havilar's hand. "Then start crossing."

Lorcan spared a glance for the two Harpers and the shivering boy who looked as if he'd fallen into a nightmare. He took the trigger ring from the chain around his neck, held it over the tip of his index finger, and held his other hand out to Mehen. "Don't let go of me *or* Havilar. And shut your eyes," he advised.

Mehen took hold of Lorcan's hand, eyes resolutely opened as the portal to the Hells opened around them.

CHAPTER TWENTY-THREE

26 Ches, the Year of the Nether Mountain Scrolls (1486 DR)
The Lost Peaks

DAHL LED THE FIRST GROUP OF CHOSEN THROUGH THE CAMP, sword out, eyes sharp. Armas, carrying Vanri and surrounded by his god's earthen guardians, came close behind, followed by another ten Chosen and Oota at the rear, the strongest of them arrayed throughout the group to give cover to the weakest. Surely, he thought, the guards have noticed something's wrong by now. Surely the shadar-kai will be everywhere. Surely the small force of Shadovar guards would be sent out as well. They'd selected four paths through the camp to keep the guards from positioning themselves to catch everyone.

But either Dahl had drawn the luckiest route or the guards were nowhere to be seen.

Overhead, the gathering spell had grown large enough to rival the orb of the midday sun in size. They didn't have long.

They reached the shelters at the same time as Vescaras's group, halting at the edge of the milling crowd of prisoners. "Looks as if it's getting tight," Vescaras said, eyeing the stalled lines of Chosen descending into the earth, the basket carriers who shoved past, shouting to keep back, to keep the tunnel open. "We may have a problem."

Tharra hadn't returned yet, and neither had Farideh. Dahl

wondered if the Harper agent would return at all, if Farideh would give up and turn back. It had been at least half an hour, hadn't it? "Tell them all to inhale," he said. "Did you cross any guards?"

Vescaras shook his head. "Not a one. That worries me too."

Hamdir and Sheera's group of Chosen arrived, then Brin's. Tharra and Farideh were with neither. "We found a few guards," Brin said. "They were retreating, though—their leader wasn't happy about them scuffling with us."

"You'll have to call the course," Vescaras said to Dahl. "If she doesn't come back—"

"Then we stand out here and die," Dahl said. "I'm happy to hear another plan."

Tharra came running full tilt through the alleys, her auburn hair unbound and blood streaming from a wound on her forehead. Her blouse was soaked in blood and the daggers she'd carried were gone. In her hand, she gripped the ancient scroll hard enough that Dahl had to stop himself from snatching it away as well. Farideh wasn't with her.

"Got it," she panted. "They're pulling back, but—"

"Get down and cast it!" Dahl shouted. "We haven't got time." She darted past, weaving her way between the prisoners, down into the tunnels below, Vescaras following her.

Khochen came running up from the direction of the lake, tailed by a man with a bow carrying Samayan pickaback, another fellow, and Daranna. Brin searched the road behind them, and Dahl's stomach dropped.

"Where's Havi?" Brin demanded. "Where's Mehen?"

Khochen gave Dahl a grim look. "Your friend the wizard took Farideh hostage. The other two went with the cambion to rescue her."

Dahl cursed and cursed and cursed, as if his breath couldn't come any other way. "We have to go after them."

"There is no time," Cereon said.

"There's all the godsbedamned time we have, if we can't

all fit down there!" Dahl shouted. Which meant it wouldn't matter. They were all doomed—on the ground, in the tower, at the bottom of the lake.

A deep boom shook the ground beneath their feet, and for a terrifying moment, Dahl was sure Torden's warnings about the stability of the mountainside had caught up with them. Shouts came from the shelters, and a moment later the prisoners began to flow down through the main entrance, down into the room that the ancient scroll had crafted.

A weight came off Dahl's shoulders, but he found he couldn't follow them, not yet.

Dahl turned back to the tower and saw smoke pouring out of the highest windows. His pulse beat harder, and if he could have done anything in that moment, he would have run for the fortress again, just to try and do *something*.

But Dahl knew he could not save her this time. If Mehen and Havilar and Lorcan couldn't manage it, none of them would have been able to. He looked over at Brin—the Cormyrean watched the tower too, looking faintly gray.

"I'm sure she didn't want to leave you behind," Dahl started.

"It doesn't matter," Brin said quietly. "She'll always choose her sister. I know that." He gave Dahl a wan smile. "She comes back, and then she's gone again. I thought it was bad before. If I lose her *and* Mehen—"

"She's not gone," Dahl said firmly. "None of them are. Not yet."

"Not yet," Brin agreed.

High up on the tower's farthest edge, something exploded, scattering shards of black stone.

Rhand's teleportation felt nothing like Farideh's own spell, the one that seemed to make a slit in the planes and move her through something like the edge of the Hells, hot and close and whispering. This was bloodless and cold—just a gray, airless place, and then she was standing in the study, once more beside the Fountains of Memory.

Rhand smiled at her, and Farideh thought, there was no devil in the Hells she feared like she feared that smile. Cast, Farideh thought—a burst of energy, a vent of lava, a rain of brimstone. Call the grasping souls back and let them tear him apart—

She closed her eyes and fought back a shudder. That is where you'll end up, she thought. Begging for a little life from the living . . .

Not yet. For now, Rhand was enough to focus on. And she couldn't count on him not having the same sort of shield Sairché had borne, something to stop her spells if she tried the wrong way to remind him she wasn't a lamb brought to slaughter.

But without her spells, without the gifts of the Nine Hells—without her friends, her family—she was little better.

"You should know," he said conspiratorially, "your mistress has already fallen. Her deal with me, as it were, is not an issue." He crossed to the sideboard, poured two goblets of a dark red wine, and brought one over to Farideh. "The devils planned to unseat me, didn't they?"

Farideh nearly laughed. "You shouldn't assume they care about you at all."

His eyes darkened. "Well they certainly don't care about you, do they?" He handed her the glass.

"I'd rather not."

Rhand laughed. "Oh please, it's not drugged." He shoved the glass into her numb hands and leaned in. "I don't have any need to drug you this time."

It wouldn't matter how conscious she was in a short time. Magros's spell would complete and they would be dead without a layer of earth shielding them. She wondered if the blast would kill them, or if they'd be crushed when the black rock shattered.

Still, if Rhand tried anything between now and then . . . she could still feel the powers of Asmodeus, like something deep inside her had snapped and bled awful ichor into her. It dripped, it drizzled, but she knew it could rush forth again.

"You have no idea who you're dealing with," she murmured.

"Nor do I care," Rhand returned. He toasted her and took a stiff swallow of the wine. "I believe I told you once, you are not unique." He strode to the open windows, setting the glass down beside him on the sill and looking out at the growing ball of magical energy. "Neither are your devils' allies. Whoever it is, they will have a surprise shortly."

"It's going to explode."

"No, it's not," Rhand replied. "My two best apprentices are preparing to dispel that nonsense. Just as it reaches its full strength. With luck," he added, reaching for the goblet once more, "it will reverse the spell and blow the bones of whatever pretender is casting it back to his master." He took a sip. "But I will settle for ensuring his failure."

Farideh's stomach dropped. If the spell were stopped, then their plan was pointless. The prisoners and Harpers and Havi and Mehen would just stay here until they died of hunger or thirst. Or risked destroying the tower themselves. Her sacrifice had meant nothing.

Rhand gave her another unpleasant smile. "Drink up."

Farideh stared back at him, wishing she was foolish enough to. Even the suggestion made her stomach protest, after the wizard's finest—

Farideh's breath caught.

Dahl's flask of the shadar-kai liquor was still in her pocket, Farideh realized. And Tharra's strange herbs were tucked into her sleeve. A shield wouldn't stop the wizard's finest. Rhand's expression hardened, and she took a careful sip of the wine, her eyes on the swirling basin of water beside her.

"How long before the spell completes?" she asked.

Rhand turned back to the window, as if gauging his apprentices' progress. "As I said: it won't. The dispelling is already underway."

As he spoke, Farideh drained the wine from her own goblet, swallowing a cough and praying he hadn't lied about the drugs. She dipped the empty goblet into the basin beside her, filling it halfway with the cold waters of the Fountains of Memory. She pulled Dahl's flask from her pocket, still sloshing with the shadar-kai's brutal brew.

"What if it doesn't work?" she asked, her eyes locked on his back as she tugged the little pouch from her sleeve. Her stomach churned as the fetid smell of the splintered roots hit her nose.

"Whatever you think you know from slinging lumps of forsaken souls at weak enemies, it is a trifle compared to what we do. This is magic of a higher order. It won't fail." Rhand set the goblet down again, off to his left, still watching the dancing light that could be seen off to the right.

Farideh made herself keep breathing as she crossed the room on feet so swift and silent, even Mehen would have praised her stealth. Her hands were steady as she reached for his goblet and replaced it with her own.

Rhand turned at the sound of the metal against the stone, but there was Farideh, leaning out over the sill. He picked up the tainted goblet, and Farideh's heart threatened to beat its way out of her throat. There only remained the question—the best question to keep him laid low.

"I think you're wrong," she said.

He raised an eyebrow. "A wager, then?"

She held the goblet with the untainted wine in it close. "When it explodes," she said "we'll be dead."

"And when it doesn't, what will you forfeit?" he asked. He brought the goblet toward his lips again. "I know—do you still have your ritual book? You never did let me show you how those first few work. Perhaps we'll start there." He tipped the goblet back.

All the anger, all the horror, all the hate in Farideh's heart poured into her next words: "What have you done?"

She wanted to make him watch it, live it, have every crime

torment him in the nightmarish fashion the potion had. That broken part inside her felt as if it gushed with righteous anger.

Rhand did not seem to hear her at first. He stopped mid-sip, swallowing what was in his mouth already, as if in reflex. A mouthful was all it took, she thought, remembering her own trials.

Staring into the cup, his face curled in a sneer. "What have *I* done? You little . . . What is this?"

"The wizard's finest," Farideh said, balling her hands into fists to stop the urge to cast and strike him. Adolican Rhand lunged at her, a spell flickering in his own hands, but the drink was already slowing him down.

Farideh took a step back and felt the powers of Asmodeus flood her like an aqueduct after a rain. The flames poured through her and out her skin, and the great wings of fire unfolded from her back once more, setting the curtains ablaze. She saw terror cross his features and she savored it.

"Drink up," the Chosen of Asmodeus said.

For a moment, Rhand's eyes widened with horror, aware, suddenly of what he was facing, and then the wizard's finest claimed him. Rhand's eyes rolled back in his head, and he collapsed to the floor.

Farideh bolted—Rhand would keep, and the wizards on the other side of the tower would be ready to stop the explosion any moment now. As she passed, she heard the *whoosh* of flames catching the wall hangings, the rug beneath her feet. The polished black stone reflected the dancing orange light.

The tiefling woman's ghost appeared in her path. The woman gestured sternly for Farideh to retrieve the comb, to talk to her, but the memory of the ghost in the water, telling Farideh to let go, rose up again.

"Do I even *need* the comb?" Farideh said, still burning. "I don't know who you really are. I don't know what you think to use me for, but while I'm obviously plenty of people's pawn, I won't be yours."

The ghost's form peeled back to reveal glowing bones and the dark chains of magic that seemed to hold them together, the pulse at her core . . . and a glyph of sharp, broken lines that hid there. She was Chosen.

She was dead. And she was Chosen. A chill ran through Farideh, and nearly made her falter. That shouldn't happen—a dead Chosen lost their spark. That was the key, after all, to all of Asmodeus's plans.

But whyever the tiefling woman had held onto her powers, there were a thousand other Chosen out there who were still living, who would die if Farideh stood here wondering. She sprinted through the ghost's chilly form and across the hallway, into the opposite room.

The two wizards stood in front of the window, looking ill and distracted, but armed with wands and watching the growing ball of magic as if taking their eyes from it for a moment would mean the death of them.

Farideh stepped into the room, and the wings of fire spread as wide as the space would allow, setting the wall hangings ablaze. The wizards turned to her, and Farideh cast a rain of brimstone at them.

In the same moment, she realized the Nameless One was still there. She was huddled against the right-hand wall, looking for a moment as small and fearful as a child in a room full of monsters should. Beside her, Sairché sat, her wings curled limply around her, her golden eyes on Farideh as if she weren't certain in that moment which of them was worse—the Nameless One or the Chosen of Asmodeus.

Then whatever restraint the Nameless One had shown, whatever she had done to make the wizards' jobs easier, fled, and the smothering sense of the void of Shar swept through the room. Farideh gritted her teeth and found the anger in her rose to meet the sadness of Shar.

"You're back," the Nameless One said, a mocking edge to her voice, "and *so* changed. Have you given up your soul to him, then? Have you lost your sweet sympathy?"

Farideh tore her eyes from the Nameless One. She had lost nothing, but the pity she felt for the girl Shar had stolen was caught in the heart of a maelstrom, overtopped by the waves of anger and power. She focused on the two wizards, who were no longer watching the spell but standing fearful and overwhelmed, their eyes on Farideh.

As it should be, she thought. The whole world fears you—and finally to your benefit. She pointed the rod at the wizards. "*Laesurach.*"

The ground beneath them opened, as if somehow a vent of lava reached up through the tower itself, as the plane peeled back to let the Fourth Layer of the Hells pour through. Molten rock and leaping flames surrounded the stunned apprentices, lighting their robes afire and setting off what protective spells they'd carried. One of them seemed to shake off the Chosens' effects and leaped out of the fire and pointed his wand at Farideh. "*Ziastayix!*"

Farideh smiled as the fireball struck her, the flames surrounding her absorbing the spell and sending a sharp prickle of pain over her skin. She cast another spell, a cloud of burning gases—the still-startled wizard tried to run, and toppled over the windowsill. She heard him shouting spells as he fell.

Beyond the window, the ball of magic had grown as large as a human curled into a ball.

The second wizard's missiles hit Farideh in the shoulder, rocking her off her feet. But another blast of flames was enough to make him reconsider his ally's escape. Burned and bleeding, he climbed onto the windowsill.

Farideh's bolt of energy struck him squarely in the middle of his back. The air went out of him in a grunt, and the wizard fell. Beyond the window, the spell kept growing, unimpeded.

Farideh turned to face the Nameless One, and for a moment, she was nothing more than a frightened girl, staring after the fallen wizards. "That spell will explode—that's what they said."

"We can still escape," Farideh told her. She felt the flames start to fade. "If we hurry."

The Nameless One shook her head. "The carriers are coming. They'll take me back to Shade. And you will come with me—both of you." She held herself up, the arrogance of Shar overwhelming whatever fear she'd shown as surely as it overwhelmed all in her presence. "Tell the guards."

"The guards will not come for you," Farideh said. She looked out the window—the spell had grown larger still, the size of Mehen. "You'll be dead, if you don't come now."

"Then we will *all* be dead," the Nameless One said, her voice shaking. The emptiness of Shar surged forth, washing over the room. Sairché squeezed her eyes shut again, murmuring something under her breath. "Everything comes to nothing," the Nameless One said.

Farideh felt the powers of Asmodeus fill her again, the flames leaping higher, the dizzying power filling her hands. Behind the dancing fire of her skin, her veins were black as the obsidian tower. There wouldn't be time to get down to the shelters.

Then through the turmoil of fear and sadness, a sudden calm, cool as a beam of moonlight washed over her. Think, her own voice seemed to say. Remember. Stay alive. This is not the only way.

"The fountains," she said. "The fountains make portals." She held out a hand. "Come on."

The Nameless One narrowed her eyes, fear flickering through her expression. "I will not." The sense of loss and loneliness wrapped around Farideh's heart, threatening to snuff out the flames. "And neither will you."

Magros of the Fifth Layer watched from a comfortable distance as the Red Wizard and her assistants poured ever more magic into the spell. Magros was not himself fond of that sort of magic—spells were tedious, particularly spells on this boiling plane. But casters made good tools and crafted such clever little things. He knew better than to interrupt.

Zahnya looked up at him as the runes at her feet flared with a peculiarly dark light. It made even Magros's eyes ache. "We are nearly finished," she said.

"Please," he said. "Take what time you need. What happened to the Harpers?"

"In the camp," she said. "They don't have much longer."

"A pity," Magros said. "I suspect they are distracted by a traitor in their midst."

Zahnya didn't ask what he meant, and Magros pretended he wasn't a little disappointed at that. "I'll take the scepter while you're free," he said.

"Our deal's not complete," she said.

"Do you think I intend to be caught standing here when you succeed?" Magros demanded. "I stand to lose a great deal if anyone finds out how I've helped your master."

"His Omnipotence doesn't look kindly on foolish actions," Zahnya said.

"His Omnipotence, I understand, doesn't look kindly on anything," Magros said. "There is nothing more for me to do—you cast the spell, you collect the powers. I've set everything up, and now I would like my payment." He held out a hand. "Please."

Zahnya hesitated a moment, but she went to the palanquin and retrieved a case, all covered in Nar runes, cinnabar and gold. "As promised," she said, "the scepter of Alzrius."

Magros opened the case and fought not to flinch at the heat that radiated from the heavy implement that rested inside. Even lying still and inactive, the scepter could melt the remains of the snow that clung to the buildings just beyond the barrier and the High Forest's magic. And in the right hands, it might melt a great deal more. He closed the case and took Zahnya's hand, bowing low over it.

"A pleasure doing business with you, dear lady. Our agreement is complete. Tell His Omnipotence to enjoy the godhood while he can."

Before Zahnya could reply, Magros activated his portal and returned to the chilly Fifth layer. It didn't matter what she had to say, after all, when the deal was complete.

CHAPTER TWENTY-FOUR

26 Ches, the Year of the Nether Mountain Scrolls (1486 DR)
The Lost Peaks

MEHEN HELPED HAVILAR OUT OF THE PORTAL AND INTO A bedroom hidden under dustcloths. "You can open your eyes again," he said. Havilar looked around once, holding tight to her weapon.

"Where is she?"

"Near," Lorcan said. He unlatched the door and peered out. "Before we find her, though, you need to know two things. First, there's a Chosen of Shar somewhere in here. She's exceedingly powerful—you'll feel it."

"How do we fight her?" Havilar asked, as she moved ahead, out into the hallway beyond, scanning for guards.

"Strong feelings seem to get you a little space," Lorcan said. "But not much. And you may not need to worry about that," he added, "because Sairché is in here somewhere, too, and I know you both have *very* strong opinions about *her*."

Good, Mehen thought, tasting the air. The devil who'd tricked Farideh. The devil who'd stolen his daughters.

"But that's the second thing," Lorcan said. "She and I have a pact of our own. I'm bound to protect her, and she has to protect me." Mehen started to tell Lorcan he could try however he liked to stop Mehen from hurting Sairché, but Lorcan held up a hand.

"It doesn't come into play," Lorcan said significantly, "if I don't know what's going to happen. Understand? I have to make sure Farideh's safe—that agreement is"—he shuddered—"more pressing. But then I'm obliged to save Sairché, and if I know that she's, say, in the way of your falchion, I have to stop it."

Mehen bared his teeth. "I'll keep my thoughts to myself."

Havilar cried out as a pair of human soldiers came up the stairs. Their swords were out, and as they spotted Havi, they turned and called back to someone out of sight.

Mehen pulled his falchion, ready for a fight. But Havilar yanked the remains of the ruby necklace from her pocket and threw the whole thing over the guards' heads.

The explosion threw the guards from their feet and sent a rattle of stones sailing through the hall. Havilar ducked, shielding her head from the flying rock.

"Well done," Mehen said. The flight of stairs below was a crater, the outer wall blown wide to the cold daylight. The guards below who'd survived shouted conflicting orders.

Mehen looked back to see Lorcan straightening over the guard's body, his blade wet with blood. "Start climbing," he said.

The broken rock extended half the flight. Mehen climbed to the next landing and found his heart suddenly racing, as though he were in the heat of battle, his thoughts sinking as they had on the lowest nights, the times he was sure his girls were gone forever.

Lorcan stopped dead. "There," he said. "That's it. That's the Nameless One. And . . . shit and ashes. That's not just the Nameless One."

Mehen looked down the empty hallway. Smoke clung to the ceiling, and the crackle of flames echoed through the space. He looked back at Havilar and saw the pinched look of her features.

"Brin won't know what happened," she said. Mehen took hold of her shoulder and steered her down several steps, past the point where the unwelcome feeling took hold.

"Stay here," Mehen said. "Make sure no more guards come up the stairs. I'll get Fari." Lorcan trailed him as he stormed toward the farthest room, each step driving his pulse faster, each breath a little harder to draw.

Mehen squared his shoulders and pressed on.

In the middle of the room, a flaming angel faced off against a child of shadow, a battle of wills, a battle of proxies for the powers that filled the black stone room, the only sign of their presence the maelstrom of fear and loss that stirred in Clanless Mehen.

"Farideh," Mehen said. The flaming angel didn't move. He stepped into the room, focusing on his daughter in the middle of that fire. "Farideh."

Dread gripped his chest. He'd been ready for a wizard, a devil, a pack of guards. Whatever this was . . .

Whatever it is, he told himself firmly, she's still Farideh.

"Farideh," he said, coming to stand beside her, just out of reach of the wings of flame.

"Go," she hissed. "If I stop, she'll overwhelm you."

He glanced at the shadowy girl, at her manic grin. Briefly he imagined his girls at that age, and thanked the gods no one had given them such strength. He could feel the girl's powers pulling his soul open, making a hollowness he was all too familiar with.

"Let her go, Fari," he said. "Come back."

Farideh shook her head. "Go, please. It's not safe."

"Trust me," he said. "Put the flames out and trust me."

Farideh swallowed, and for a terrible moment, with the growing light of Zahnya's spell flashing on their faces, Mehen feared she would refuse once more. Then she let out a gasping cry, and the flames, the wings, and the terror all vanished. At once the Nameless One's gift rolled over them both, and Farideh's knees buckled. Mehen caught hold of her, and she let out an explosive breath.

Sairché remained, shaking against the wall.

Mehen gritted his teeth and looked to Lorcan, standing frozen in the doorway.

"Your sister," Mehen called. "Your problem." He hooked an arm under Farideh and helped her toward the door, holding her close as the waves of aching emptiness crashed against them.

"Stop!" the girl cried. Her whole frame seemed to tremble with the powers that poured out of her, as she glared at Mehen. "You can't leave. You can't *bear* it." The force of her powers intensified and Mehen's heart felt as if it were shattering all over again.

But beside exile, beside Arjhani, beside losing his daughters, and losing them again, the powers of the Nameless One were nothing. For all the sadness and emptiness tried to tangle him up to drag him down, Mehen had lived long years with that feeling—and he'd learned how to ignore it.

Mehen looked down his snout at the girl. "You have scant time before this camp is destroyed. Find your way out."

The Nameless One looked up at him, shocked and horror-struck. The powers ebbed and Lorcan rushed past Mehen and scooped Sairché ungently from the ground.

"Get that portal open," Mehen growled as Lorcan passed.

"We need to go down," Dahl said, looking nervously at the crackling ball of magic. It had doubled in size since Brin and he had started watching for the twins. "We need to get the doors shut." Brin didn't move.

"Brin!" Dahl shouted. He didn't want to go down any more than Brin did, didn't want to assume the worst. But the longer they waited, the thinner their chances grew. "Gods books, Brin, come on!"

"I should have stayed with her," Brin said.

When he didn't turn, Dahl ran from the open door to the Cormyrean's side and grabbed hold of his arm. "She gets out, and you're going to be looking back from the afterlife a great fool," he said.

Brin looked at him, as haunted as Dahl had ever seen a man. "And if she doesn't?"

"Then I think she'll forgive you waiting a few days," Dahl said, "if you're going to be a great fool and join her. Come on."

He shoved Brin toward the door, ignoring his own racing fears. They were nothing beside Brin's—and it was an insult to the other man, he thought, to make the comparison. But as Dahl pulled the wooden door shut and followed Brin down into the dark, he said a little prayer to Oghma.

If you don't let her figure out a way to escape, he said, *then I really am through with you.*

The girl who had long since offered her name up to Shar watched the field of magic that had grown to the size of a cart, sizzling and flashing in the air beyond the study's open windows. As she slipped into the room, her eyes fell on the wizard, twitching uneasily in his sleep, but they didn't linger. She came to stand instead over the basins with their ice-cold waters. She didn't ask her goddess for deliverance—no one thought she understood what she had pledged herself to, but she knew down in her bones that Shar would not save her, not a second time.

She took a pinch of the powdery blue blossoms and scattered them over the surface of the water, closing her eyes for a moment and cursing her want. "Show me Sakkors . . ."

Zahnya looked over the shimmering runes that burned into the forest floor, the lines of power that strengthened and directed the spell. Her two remaining apprentices lay dead on the ground, their blood spilled—quickly and quietly—to bolster the magic. Nothing in the grove breathed but Zahnya.

In the camp beyond the dancing light of her spell shone down on the huts like a second, sickly sun and reflected off the polished tower, green and orange and gold.

Zahnya held her wand before her chest and spoke the last words of the spell. They struck the air like the rattle of grave dirt on a casket lid, and turned into motes of darkness that swirled together over the runes, collecting into a mass that suddenly evaporated into the ether.

And beyond the wall, everything became sound and light.

CHAPTER TWENTY-FIVE

26 Ches, the Year of the Nether Mountain Scrolls (1486 DR)
The Lost Peaks

THE SILENCE AFTER THE EXPLOSION FELT LIKE A LIVING THING to Dahl, something tense and ready to pounce. He climbed the crumbling stairs and pushed the remains of the wooden hut off the exit, scrambling out through the dirt. Beyond, there was nothing left but rubble and the faint, winking remains of the Thayan wizard's spell.

Dahl's breath turned heavy in his lungs. The tower was gone. The wall was gone.

Farideh was gone.

Others came up out of the ground, surveying the damage. Dahl found he couldn't look at any of them.

Oota clapped him on the shoulder. "Well done, son. I won't lie. I was half-expecting to come out and find nothing changed."

And instead, Dahl thought numbly, everything's changed.

He turned to see Brin step out of the shelters, squinting at the light unimpeded by the many buildings. Brin shaded his eyes, looking toward the spot where the tower had stood, ignoring the people pushing past him. Staring as if every part of his mind refused to accept what lay before him. There was nothing Dahl could say.

A line of red light split the air beside them, followed by the scent of brimstone, the sizzle of the moisture burning out of the air. Dahl leaped back, the instinctive parts of his brain sure there was another explosion happening—and then Havilar stepped carefully down onto the ground, pulled Mehen after her, and then Mehen led Farideh down, still holding onto a scarlet hand. She looked back into the portal, as if she weren't sure she ought to leave. But then Lorcan's hand released her, and the portal sealed itself shut.

Havilar shuddered violently, looking through the crowd. "I can't believe you *looked*," Dahl heard her say, moments before Brin threw his arms around her. "Oh!" she cried. "Oh, you're all right!"

Farideh looked out at the place where the tower had been, marveling at the empty crater. A chilly breeze stirred the air and lifted her dark hair. "*Karshoj*." She looked back over her shoulder at Dahl. "We were lucky."

"Very," he said, smiling.

"Goodwoman?" Vescaras stood beside Farideh, holding a pair of shackles. "Your hands, please."

"What?" Dahl cried. "No—don't be ridiculous. She's not a spy."

"We have to be sure," Vescaras said. Farideh looked past him, up at Mehen who stood over Vescaras like an unwelcome shadow.

"It's just until we reach Waterdeep," Mehen said. "We'll be with you every step."

"And you'll not be harmed," Vescaras said.

Dahl couldn't believe what he was hearing. "You don't have to do this. You have nothing to prove."

"Yes, I do," Farideh said with a sigh. She held out her hands. "I always will."

The prisoners wasted no time leaving the destroyed camp behind. Beyond the wall, down on a lower plateau, they made a makeshift camp, even as groups of them vanished into the forest, heading for faraway homes. Dahl considered the sheer numbers of people milling around—there was no surveying them, no keeping track of who'd been lost and who had left, who had which powers and whether they were safe. But at least, he could make sure that folks heading for Waterdeep or Everlund waited for the Harpers who would be returning that way. Oota and her most loyal were heading north. Cereon and the elves, south. Armas, Vanri, and Samayan would go with them for a ways.

"Turmish," Armas said. "Then Airspur."

Dahl frowned. "What about the other little boy?"

"Stedd has things to do," Samayan said quietly, poppies unfolding around his feet.

"And the Harpers?" Dahl asked. Armas turned away angrily.

"Be gentle with Tharra," he finally said. "She wasn't all bad."

Daranna had found a solid tree root, arching out of the ground, and slipped Farideh and Tharra's shackles through it. Farideh quietly dealt Wroth cards in a tight square atop the rocky ground. Khochen, standing guard, looked up as Dahl approached.

"I've found a score who want to head to Waterdeep," she said. "We're going to be ages walking."

"Better than not making it back," he said. "I need to make a sending to Tam. Have you seen Vescaras?"

"He's bothering Daranna. Don't tell him I gave her the cards," she said, nodding at Farideh. "He'll think she's sending messages to a confederate in the trees." She grinned at Dahl. "And then you'll have to admit you gave her them."

Farideh looked up, puzzled. "Were you not supposed to?"

"Ignore her." Dahl scowled at Khochen. "Do you have a cover of some sort?"

Khochen shook her head. "How many of them already

figured you out?—there's no pretending at a cover. Better to just get them where they're going. Collect a few to our cause."

Dahl considered all the clever folk he'd met in the past tenday. "I can think of a few."

But the sending came first. He found Vescaras standing off at the edge of the rocky plateau, leaning against a tree and talking to Sheera, Daranna's fledgling with the crossbow.

Flirting with Sheera, Dahl realized. He glanced back across the camp to where he'd left Khochen. She hadn't seen—thank the gods. The long trek back to Waterdeep would only feel longer if Khochen were angry.

"Vescaras!" Dahl called. "I need to talk to you." The half-elf scowled down at him. He gave his excuses to Sheera and skidded down the rock toward Dahl. "What is it?"

"I need to make a sending for Tam—have you got your kit still?"

"I have a spare," Vescaras said, taking it off his belt and handing it over. "Is that all?"

"Thanks," Dahl said. Then, "Look, I don't want to get into your business, but Khochen doesn't deserve you flirting like that behind her back, where *everyone* can see."

Vescaras frowned. "What in the world are you talking about?"

"She told me, all right?" Dahl said. "I know it's a secret, and believe me I wish it had stayed that way, but it didn't, so . . . treat her right. Or I have to tell her, and I don't think she's someone you want to wrong."

Vescaras narrowed his eyes. "She told you we're lovers?"

Dahl nodded. "I've kept it to myself."

The other agent studied Dahl for a moment longer. "I know you're friends with Khochen," Vescaras said, "so please believe me I say this with the utmost respect: Khochen is a snake. She's a good agent, but there is no way in all the layers of all the Hells that I would let her get close enough to my vital organs or my coin purse to become anything remotely like her lover."

Dahl colored. "Gods damn it——I *knew* she would lie."

"It happens to the best of us," Vescaras offered. "She did say you wouldn't need rescuing, and she was more than right about that. So perhaps your friendship isn't ended?"

Dahl regarded Vescaras warily—it was as complimentary as he'd ever heard the other man be. "Thank you."

"Not at all. I presume this means you'll be rejoining the rest of us in the field?"

"We'll see what Tam thinks," Dahl said. They started toward the center of the camp again. "Khochen also said you don't like me because you think I snubbed your sister."

"Did she?"

"Is that it?"

Vescaras squinted as if considering his words. "It would be unmannerly to get into," he finally said. "But no. However, should one of my sisters give you another invitation to attend on her? I suggest you politely make your excuses, quickly and clearly."

"No room in the Ammakyl's manor for a farmer's son?" Dahl retorted.

"No room for a smug hardjack who trails trouble," Vescaras corrected. "But as I said, it would be unmannerly to get into."

Farideh woke to someone shaking her shoulder. A hand clapped over her mouth as she stirred, and she saw Tharra leaning close over her, a finger to her lips.

"Don't scream." The Harper took her hand carefully from Farideh's mouth. "I owe you," Tharra said. "For saving Samayan. For trusting me. Despite the wizard's finest." She held up a bent piece of metal. "I'll break you out too. There's a lot of world to escape to."

Farideh blinked at her. "Isn't that against your code?"

"Lot of ways to read the code," Tharra said. "I'd argue I

didn't betray the Harpers, so it's not treason and not a hanging offense. But will the Shepherd?" She shrugged. "I'm not taking that risk. Neither should you."

"No," Farideh said. "I'm not leaving." Mehen slept on beside her. Havilar lay beyond with her head in Brin's lap. Dahl was somewhere out on the edge, standing guard. "My family's here. My friends."

"Do you think that's going to last? A devil's deal—that leaves you tainted. Not something that love and wishes will wash away."

"It hasn't stopped them yet."

"And the Harpers? They didn't listen to Dahl about the shackles, why would they take your word? What's to say they're not just going to make your family face your execution?" Tharra looked down at Farideh's chained ankles. "You come with me, and you can tell them at least that you kept on living."

"I do think they'll care what happened," Farideh said. "And maybe they'll care for you too—if you're right, if you didn't betray the Harpers, why not say so? If you're innocent—"

"Innocent and guilty all depend on the judge," Tharra said. "And I'm a lot better for the world if I keep running free. You would be too."

Farideh considered that. There remained the fear that she was wrong about Tam, that she was wrong about everyone. That whatever she told them, the truth would be too much.

But beside her, Mehen stirred in his sleep, and her heart squeezed. "I won't leave them."

"Suit yourself," Tharra said. "They'll stop trusting you eventually."

"And they'll hunt you down."

Tharra smiled. "Then I'll have to lead them on a merry chase in the meantime."

Farideh shut her eyes and laid her head against the tree once more. She heard Tharra stand and pick her way through the sleeping guards. She heard the alarm called out, and people running through the underbrush. Mehen woke at their shouts, and Farideh opened her eyes again to see him, blade in hand, eyes on Dahl coming to stand beside her. Dahl took in the unlocked shackles beside Farideh.

"Good," he said, sounding relieved. "Good. You're still here."

Mehen reached over and took her hand. Farideh squeezed his back. "I'm not going anywhere," she said.

The night after the explosion, when the prisoners had finally cleared out enough to make it safe to approach and the Shadovar carriers had long since circled the battered mountain and fled back to Netheril, Zahnya moved across the charred field of rubble that had once been Adolican Rhand's internment camp. The spell had leveled the fortress and burned the hundreds of huts into ash. Not a living soul remained—only Zahnya, moving like a ghost in the moonlight toward the wisp of colored light hanging over the middle of the field.

The boneclaw and the zombies that had been her apprentices followed after, but there was no need. Nothing on the surface had survived the ritual—not a mortal, not a mouse. Only the lake, shimmering under the stern light of Selûne, remained the same, somehow untouched. Zahnya eyed it in the distance. A curiosity—but not one she could worry about now.

No, the spark dancing just higher than her head took all of her concern. It looked like nothing so much as a half-soaked firework, a sputtering pinwheel losing intensity by the second as it weaved over the ground. Magros had promised her a divine spark great enough to raise a mortal to the heights of demigodhood. He hadn't counted on the Harpers, true, but who could have known better than a devil that a handful of meddling spies would throw their plans into disarray?

His Omnipotence would not be pleased.

Zahnya took a box made of enameled bone from her sleeve

and held it open. The spark flew into it, as if it were coming home to roost. Not enough, she thought. Not nearly enough.

"Do we return now?" the boneclaw rasped.

"In a moment," Zahnya said. She climbed up onto a chunk of sharp black stone and faced the field. "We cannot return empty-handed," she said. "We cannot leave anything for Netheril."

Selûne watched over her dark rituals, impassive as Zahnya had always seen the moon goddess. Perhaps she knew, much as her Harpers had, that there were darker enemies on the field. It may take all who would stand against Shar to thwart her.

Zahnya smiled to herself as one by one, corpses recombined and rose from the destruction. Perhaps Selûne doesn't know yet, Zahnya thought, what Thay is capable of.

At her feet the rubble stirred and rained off first a pair of shadar-kai—still missing pieces from their faces, but unmistakable in their studded armor—and then a bearded human man whose eyes glowed eerie blue.

"Mistress," the wight growled.

CHAPTER TWENTY-SIX

8 Tarsakh, the Year of the Nether Mountain Scrolls (1486 DR)
Waterdeep

DAHL SCRATCHED THE LAST LINE OF RUNES ACROSS THE parchment, completing Farideh's account of the internment camps, Adolican Rhand, and the Nine Hells acting out on Toril.

"I'm assuming," Tam said to Farideh, "that you're leaving things out."

Farideh colored a little. "Nothing that matters."

Tam sighed heavily. "You remember I have artifacts in hand that can make you share."

"I remember." She rubbed her still-shackled hands together. "Although I wish you wouldn't. It's just private things."

Tam regarded her for a long moment. Dahl wondered what she was talking about. Lorcan, he decided, dropping his eyes to the page. Probably Lorcan. He caught Tam's eye and shook his head surreptitiously. It wasn't worth heavier methods to make her admit she'd kissed the devil.

"Since this is a great deal of information we had no knowledge of," Tam said, "since there are coordinating accounts, and since you will have at least two sets of eyes I trust on you—"

"And since I'm not a Shadovar spy?" Farideh interrupted.

"Even if you were, at this point you're more useful to us than to them." Tam smiled. "I won't keep you. But should anything further come to light, we may ask you to return. And I hope if those private matters turn out to matter to the rest of us—"

"They won't."

"Six internment camps filled with god-blessed prisoners," Tam said, "and not a soul noticed." He cursed and propped his hands behind his head. "This is going to be a nightmare of an undertaking."

"You're going to have to contact the other networks," Dahl pointed out.

Tam shot him a dark look. "Later." Farideh was not, after all, a Harper, even if she was exonerated. He stood. "Get those chains off her and get her back to Mehen. I want a list of available agents. Be back here in two bells."

"Where are you headed?" Dahl asked.

"Barber," Tam said, as he passed out the door.

Dahl kneeled and unlocked Farideh's shackles. "That was painless."

"Relatively," Farideh said, a small smile tugging at her mouth. She spread her fingers, the pale third finger standing out like a ghost among the darker ones. An unwelcome reminder of Adolican Rhand. Dahl took her hand in his.

"There's probably a way to change it," Dahl said, examining her finger. "I don't know it off the top of my head, but people do it all the time for cosmetic reasons. Fancy revels and things." He smiled at her. "I am completely certain someone can turn it dryad-green."

"Better than this." Farideh looked away.

Dahl squeezed her hand. "Worst comes to worst, we'll find you some nice gloves."

Farideh took her hand back, and Dahl stood and found something else to look at. "I suppose," she said, standing, "there are plenty of places that sell gloves in Suzail."

"Probably," Dahl said. "Probably Lord Crownsilver can find a merchant who'd be delighted to fit his dear friend with gloves."

"So long as no one knows that dear friend is me."

Dahl didn't argue. He didn't have the faintest idea how Brin and Mehen thought returning to Suzail with tieflings in tow would work. He half hoped it didn't and he wouldn't have to trek to Cormyr when Tam decided he needed more information from Farideh. "What *did* you leave out?" Dahl asked. "Is it just—"

She met his gaze. "Please don't ask me. I won't lie to you, but . . . please, if you and I are friends at all, don't ask. I promise it's not anything the Harpers need to know."

"All right," Dahl said. "But you'll tell me if you're in trouble?"

"I'll tell you if there's anything you can do about it." She pulled her sleeve down over her ruined hand. "Dahl . . . I know you don't want to know about your soul and . . . things."

"I don't," Dahl said firmly. If she was going to bring this up again, there were a hundred other things he could slip away to do. "I won't keep you from Mehen," he started.

Farideh wet her lips. "It's only . . . You should know, Dahl. I don't think Oghma's finished with you yet."

Dahl felt his chest squeeze tight. "What makes you say that?" he asked, as nonchalantly as he could.

"The others," she said, "the Chosen, they all have runes—symbols—that I can't read, as if the gods have marked their souls."

"And I have one?" Dahl said. "I doubt that."

"You don't," Farideh agreed, and Dahl was embarrassed at how suddenly his heart seemed to collapse at that—even though he knew better. He struggled to think of some glib thing to say, but then she went on, "Yours are . . . in other tongues."

Dahl went still. "What . . . what do they say?"

Farideh still wouldn't meet his eyes. "You asked me not to look again. I haven't . . . I only managed to read one line of it—in Draconic. It might be that it's the same all through—it's a lot of writing, as if someone made the light into ink—"

"Fari," he said sharply. He felt dizzy, as if none of the blood were reaching his head. "Please. What does it say?"

And finally she looked up and met his eyes. *"Vur ghent veth-sunathear renthisj."*

" 'And after,' " Dahl translated, " 'my priest speaks.' "

"You're all right?" Mehen asked Havilar again. "You don't need anything?"

"I'm *fine*," Havilar said, grinning. All Mehen's worrying—everything that had made her feel smothered and annoyed before—just felt like home. "And I will be here in the morning, I promise."

Mehen studied her for a long moment, as if he thought she might be lying, as if he knew she was hiding something. "All right," he said finally. He stroked her hair once with his great hand and smiled halfheartedly. "If you change your mind, you can wake me."

Havilar rolled her eyes, but still she smiled. Everything was falling back to the way it should be. Everything was almost normal again.

She dawdled with the hand mirror she'd been left, trying to decide if she ought to take her braids out or pin them up or something altogether different. The face that stared back was strange, but happy—and Havilar was less and less surprised each time she saw herself.

The knock at the door half a bell later made Havilar leap from her seat, all but throwing the mirror down. She yanked the door open to reveal Brin.

"Havi," he started.

"Well met," she said, pulling him into the room. They'd hardly had a decent moment alone on the way back, always crowded by strangers and Harpers and Mehen—and even though Havilar was pretty sure Mehen knew by now what was going on, she'd rather keep things quiet until they sat down and told him properly.

Brin went a little stiff as she drew him in, and Havilar frowned. She shut the door behind him, but he didn't relax. "What's wrong?"

"Havi," he said again, "I have to tell you something and . . ." He swallowed. "It's not an easy thing—to hear or to say—but I need you to listen to the whole of it before you make up your mind, all right? Can you promise me that?"

All the blood seemed to drop out of Havilar's head. "Brin, you're scaring me."

He looked as if he were scaring himself as well. He guided her back to sit on the edge of the bed. "Just promise me? Please?"

"All right," she said, too afraid to say otherwise. She watched his mouth as he wet his lips again, the moment stretching out, taut and sharp and horrible before he spoke:

"I'm engaged."

"En . . . engaged with what?"

"Engaged to be married," he said hesitantly. "Come summer."

Havilar pulled her hand back, the blood somehow sinking farther away from her head. She felt as if she were going to faint. She felt as if she were someone else, somewhere else, watching this happen. "But . . . you said you loved me."

"I *do*," he said. He reached for her face, but she slipped away. "I do," he said again. "I love you—"

"But you love her too," Havilar finished.

"No," Brin said. "It's not a love match. It's a political marriage. Raedra and I are . . ." He seemed to hunt for the right word. "Allies."

"She's a princess, isn't she?" Havilar realized. Tears welled in her eyes, and she looked away. "How can you not love a princess?"

"Because she's *not you*," Brin said fiercely. He pulled her nearer, as near as she could get. There were tears in his eyes too. "I will fix this," he promised. "I will find a way out, because *this* is all I want. Not a princess. Not a throne. Just you. Here."

He fell silent a moment. "But it's going to take a little caution, a little time. Please—give me a chance. I . . . I have to unravel some things that won't take well to being unraveled."

Havilar nodded mutely. He hadn't said anything. He hadn't even hinted. "You said you never gave up," she finally managed.

Brin looked at her sadly. "I didn't. But I tried to."

It was all more than she could manage. Havilar pushed him back. "You . . . You can't stay here tonight," she said. "I want to be alone. I have to be alone." Brin stood, folded his hands, and for a brief terrible moment, Havilar wasn't sure if she was glad or not that he wasn't arguing.

"That's fair," he said. "I hope it's not always true. I mean it: I love you, and I will fix this if it destroys me." He bent to kiss her on the cheek, and she let him, even though she didn't know what it meant anymore. Even though when he shut the door behind him, Havilar curled her knees up tight, feeling lonelier than she could ever remember.

The little room in the Harper hall seemed even quieter the second time around. Farideh stood, waiting for the faint creaks and pops of the building, the soft vibrations of the warding magic, to break the silence.

As much as she ached for company, she wasn't sure she was ready for it. Evenfeast with Mehen and Havilar, with all the many guests of the Harpers watching her surreptitiously, had grated against her nerves. She'd hardly spoken—glad for the too-many things Mehen had to tell them about Cormyr and Suzail.

"Don't worry," he said, long after Farideh had stopped counting the number of times he had said it. "It's a lovely city. And we have a home there. And people will get used to you—just as they've gotten used to me."

"And if they don't?" Farideh asked.

"If they don't," Mehen said mildly, "I will remind them

what the Crownsilvers employ me for."

"You can't thrash an entire city," Farideh said.

"*Don't* tempt him," Havilar had said. And despite the fact that she had no doubt Cormyr had no place for twin tieflings with unfortunate ties to the Nine Hells, Farideh had to chuckle at that.

She still had not explained to Mehen what had happened in the tower room, what it was he had pulled her back from the brink of, and he had not pressed. Not yet. She wondered if Tharra would prove to be right—if this would be the fault that Mehen could not forgive.

She looked down at her bleached white finger. For so long she'd thought Mehen had a hard time loving her—she was stubborn and clumsy and strange beside Havilar. She wanted things Mehen couldn't fathom the reasons for. They argued and she felt as if she'd never be enough to make him proud. And then she stole Havi—his peerless heir—from him for seven and a half years.

But he had come to the black glass tower and faced the Nameless One, and helped her back from the edge of losing herself. And she realized maybe she'd been a little blind all that time. She thought of the vision of Mehen, braiding her hair. Maybe she'd been lost in her own guilt and grief.

She was sure she would tell Mehen. But not before she told Havilar—not before she was sure she knew how bad things were—and that would have to wait for tomorrow. Farideh took off her boots and her leathers. She braided her hair and fished through her haversack for a thong to tie it off. Her hand brushed the ruby comb, tucked into the bottom of the bag, and she pulled it out.

The wind of the portal opening was hot against her neck. She shoved the comb back into the bag before turning to face Lorcan, standing in the middle of her room, not saying a word.

"What do you want?" she asked.

"Nothing," he said. "Only to check in on you. Make certain

you're happy with how things fell out."

"I wasn't executed," she said dryly. "Fortunately."

"I saw."

She rubbed her brand. "I *know*. Does it have to hurt like that?"

"What do you *want* it to feel like?" he asked with a smirk.

Farideh turned back to the dressing table, hoping she wasn't blushing as hard as it felt. "If you're just here to tease me, you can go, many thanks. I don't like you spying on me."

"Watching out for you," he corrected. "I would have stepped in."

Farideh watched her hands as she tied the haversack shut. "Are you settled, then?"

Lorcan heaved a sigh—sounding so tired, so *human* that she looked up at his reflection in the mirror. "Hardly," he said. "Sairché is not recovered—or at least, she's insisting she is not recovered. Her Highness is unhappy without *saying* she is unhappy. His Majesty is . . ." Farideh dropped her eyes at the mention of Asmodeus, and Lorcan didn't finish the thought, but slipped his arms around her.

"I was thinking," he said, "you might let me borrow your protection once more. Until things do settle."

Farideh turned, as surprised as she would have been to hear him ask if she might consider handing her soul over for a moment. She pushed him off. "I cannot believe you'd ask me that."

"Why not?" Lorcan smiled wolfishly. "I could make it worth your while."

Farideh blushed hard enough her cheeks ached. "Shall I go get Dahl, then? Or will any jack do?"

Lorcan's dark, dark eyes fixed her for a moment, his mouth shifting into his familiar smirk. "Is *that* what you think? How interesting."

She folded her arms. "Please—you wouldn't have . . . if he hadn't been standing there, you would have just left."

"He's not here now," Lorcan noted, easing toward her. "It would be a simple theory to test."

Farideh didn't move. She felt tired and worn through as an old sleeve—threadbare and ready to tear right through. If he asked, if he pressed, she wasn't sure she could put him off, or that she wanted to. All she could think of was how he'd kissed her, how much she wanted him to kiss her again. How easy it would be to just put everything else out of mind, if he pulled her close against him again—

How much she would hate herself if she let him make her forget that easily. *You cannot save him,* she thought, as his hands found her hips. *You cannot make him safe. You are losing all the ground you gained in Proskur, in the fortress.* It was as if she was in the frozen lake once more, at the edge of her air. *I know I have to let go of him,* she thought, *and I can't.*

"This is all a game to you," she said. "You're trying to trick me."

"A little," he admitted. "But you enjoy it. And who says I don't?"

"And when I say no again?" Farideh looked into his dark eyes. "How quickly will you start railing and threatening and pouting? How long will you make me pay for *that*?"

Lorcan hesitated. "What if I promise not to?"

"If you can manage it?" Farideh said. "Then I might think about forgiving you." He leaned close, one hand sliding up her back to pull her nearer. "But you won't," she added, hardly able to think of the words. "I know you."

His lips brushed her cheek, her jaw, her mouth. This time it wasn't sudden, it didn't surprise her. He kissed her slowly, thoroughly, enough to make her forget the reasons this was a very bad idea.

Almost.

She pushed him away, shaking. "Gods. You're dangerous," she said to him, to herself.

He hesitated. "Not so dangerous as you."

Someone knocked at the door, and Farideh let out a breath she didn't realize she was holding. Neither of them moved. The knocking came again.

"Tell them to leave," he said.

Yes, she thought, tell them to leave so you can make another impulsive, stupid decision.

"Hold on a breath," she called. Farideh shut her eyes. "Go home, Lorcan."

Lorcan let her go, and when she opened her eyes again, he was several paces away, sorting through his magic rings. "Fine. That's what you want, that's what I'll do." He held the silver ring up and looked over at her with a wicked smile. "That's what you *say* you want. And let's be clear, I *do* get credit for *this*."

Farideh found herself wishing someone would give *her* a little credit for putting him off. "All the praise due to someone for having basic morals."

Lorcan clucked his tongue. "Good night, darling." He blew through the ring and the whirlwind drew him back to the Nine Hells.

Farideh pressed her hands to her face and cursed a few times before opening the door to find her sister waiting there, looking as if someone had told her they'd lost seven and a half more years, and thrown her glaive into the bonfire besides.

"Oh gods," Farideh said, "what's happened?"

Havilar heaved a gusty sigh, her eyes shining. "Brin's engaged. To a princess."

"Oh, Havi." Farideh pulled her into the room and into an embrace. "Oh. Oh gods."

"He says it's just *political*. But he can't just chuck her to the cleric since it's political." She buried her face against Farideh's shoulder. "He says he loves me."

Of course he says that, Farideh thought savagely. "What are you going to do?"

Havilar pulled away and wiped her eyes. "Wait, I guess. For a little. I mean, we have to go to Cormyr anyway." She hugged her arms to her chest. "And I do love him, and I believe him that he loves me. I just wish he'd said something before . . ." She trailed off and looked away, into the room.

"Before what?"

Havilar's golden gaze held Farideh's for a moment. "You said you don't want to know," she said delicately. "Can I stay with you tonight?"

"Of course," Farideh said, shutting the door behind her sister. Havilar sat down in the chair beside the table and unlaced her boots. Farideh hesitated a moment.

"You can tell me," she offered, "if you need to."

"And then you'll say you told me so." Havilar pulled off her boot and chucked it against the door. "In the woods," she said, once it had landed. "I . . . Things happened. I was *still* worried about you, only . . ." She sighed again. "I *do* love him."

"So you wait," Farideh said. "And see if he's as good as his word. Does Mehen know?"

Havilar made a face and started on her other boot. "Oh, he must. I don't think you have secret political marriages. What would be the point?"

"I mean about you and Brin."

"Oh. Right." Havilar sighed. "I think he knows about the first time, and he suspects about this one. A better reason to sleep in here." She looked down at her toes. "I'm still angry at you, you know."

"I know," Farideh said. "I'm just glad you don't hate me."

"I never really *hated* you. And . . . I get it. You were stuck between a wyvern and the Abyss. It was still a *pothac* thing to do, but it was a *pothac* situation." She met her sister's eyes again. "No more secrets, though."

"None," Farideh promised. She swallowed against the tightness in her throat and sat down on the foot of the bed. "Starting with this one." But the words felt as if they wouldn't pass her lips. She blew out a breath.

"I can handle it," Havilar said. "I could have handled that

stuff about devils and warlocks." She shucked off her brigandine and hung it on the back of the chair, over Farideh's. "And *you* could have handled it better if you'd just let me help."

"I know."

"*Now* you know," Havilar corrected, changing her filthy shirt for a linen nightdress. "So what is it now? More devils? More Shadovar?"

She was so sure of herself, Farideh thought. So light, so hopeful. Farideh was going to crush that again, with two little sentences.

But it wouldn't change the truth. It wouldn't help Havilar to be left in the dark any longer. Or so she hoped. Farideh sighed.

"I'm a Chosen of Asmodeus," Farideh said. "And I think you are too."

EPILOGUE

THE GHOST HUNG UNNOTICED OVER THE GUEST ROOM IN THE
Harper hall, waiting, watching. Trying to focus her tattered,
scattered mind on the task at hand.

For so long, she had wandered—it wasn't supposed to be
like this. The spells had gone awry, the vessel had been broken,
and her own soul shattered. A lesser creature—a less *determined*
creature—would have relented then, and let herself fall away
into oblivion. Or perhaps crawled back to Asmodeus, admit
that he'd won, and give up the game, beg for a meager place
in the Hells, far beneath what she was promised.

But even dead, she was nothing if not determined. Those
fragments of soul, those pieces of self found each other, stole
bits and scraps of desperate magic to stitch herself back together.
Every day she was closer to being whole, closer to becoming
someone to fear once more.

Except for the vessel. Except for the fragments still lodged
therein.

The unfinished ghost of Bryseis Kakistos looked over her
sleeping great-great-granddaughters, the broken vessel that was
meant to hold her. The protection spell still swaddled them both,
still kept her at arm's reach from what was rightfully hers.

Twenty-five years on, and she still wasn't sure who the traitor
had been—had Adrasteia softened at motherhood, unwilling to
do what must be done and amend the problem her disloyal body
had wrought? Had Chiridion found some fondness for the little
errors—or more likely, had he been jealous that his purpose was
not theirs? Was it Nasmos who always held a dagger to her back?
Threnody? Lachs?

And which of her followers had crept in, a sheep in wolf's
clothing, to channel the sort of miracle from the sort of god

504

that could be guilted into protecting two weakling babes from rightful death?

There was no knowing. The few who remained loyal and present were quick to blame the rest. They had scattered since, died some of them, and so she set that aside.

There would be time for retribution.

Ironically, it was Asmodeus who led her back to the girls—not intentionally, of course. He might pretend that this was all a mistake, all an unfortunate result of Bryseis's impatience, but she knew him as well as any mortal could, and this was nothing but a clever play to get around their deal in one swift move.

When Asmodeus had imbued his Chosen with divine power, Bryseis Kakistos was ashamed to admit she had felt it and come running, like a dog seeking scraps. Some measure of that strength still hid within her, incomplete and untappable. The rest, the parts that mattered and made the magic work, rested in the vessels that still trapped the last pieces of her soul.

She stared at the young women, sleeping peacefully side by side. Not the powers she'd been promised for aiding Asmodeus in the first place, but *something*—a step toward her rightful place—and they were unreachable, locked in a vessel that Beshaba's meddling touch had split in the womb.

The Brimstone Angel willed herself nearer and reached out to touch the edge of the protection—it sizzled as she brushed against it, again, and she curled her essence tighter. The dead shouldn't feel such pain.

What officious god had laid that magic, barging in where they didn't belong? She still didn't know, no one seemed to know, and not for the first time, she wondered if it were Asmodeus's doing, if the god of sin had simply changed his tactics more than she'd thought possible. What other deity would waste a miracle on tieflings?

One who knew to ward against Bryseis Kakistos, she thought, still smarting from the protection's effects, and that suggested Asmodeus too. Who else knew what she was capable of now? But the Brimstone Angel had felt that sting before: this was divine magic from a much more beneficent source.

She drifted close enough to Farideh to feel the protection's crackling, close enough to see the young woman's eyes twitch and shiver beneath her lids as the ghost's presence drew nightmares up out of the well of her mind. How much had that divine source steered the tiefling as she grew? How much was it reining her in? She had been born—both of them had been, damn it all—to resurrect Bryseis Kakistos. Yet the ghost had watched as Farideh had nearly killed herself a dozen times over trying to right a wrong that was none of her doing and gained her little for the effort.

Such stupidity must fall along the sire's line, she thought. But stupid or wise, there was no escaping the fact she needed to get past that protection in order to gather the rest of her soul.

And if she wanted to defeat Asmodeus, she needed a body.

There was time still. If Asmodeus could be patient, then so could Bryseis Kakistos.

ACKNOWLEDGMENTS

This book would not be possible without the keen insight and calming influence of my editor, Nina Hess. I am a much better writer for having had the chance to work with her. Many thanks as well to James Wyatt, Matt Sernett, and everyone else at Wizards of the Coast who made this book possible, and my fellow Sundering authors who have been full of good advice and better stories. And Susan J. Morris, who listened to me ramble about quite a lot of plot problem—I think I still owe you coffee.

Many thanks to my family, especially Andriea Moss, Julia Evans, and Vicki Goodier, whose invaluable help with the kiddo meant I had plenty of time to write. And thank you to the baristas at my local Starbucks, who let me camp out in the back and who always asked after the book.

ABOUT THE AUTHOR

Erin M. Evans got a degree in Anthropology from Washington University in St. Louis—and promptly stuck it in a box. Nowadays she uses that knowledge of bones, mythology, and social constructions to flesh out fantasy worlds. She lives in Washington State.

More from the
SCRIBE award-winning author,
ERIN M. EVANS

BRIMSTONE ANGELS

BRIMSTONE ANGELS
LESSER EVILS

If you loved *The Adversary*, read Farideh's
adventures from the beginning in *Brimstone Angels*
and *Brimstone Angels: Lesser Evils*.

Available as audiobooks, ebooks and in print.

Discover more on
DungeonsandDragons.com

THE TOP AUTHORS IN EPIC FANTASY

COME TOGETHER AS ABEIR AND TORIL TEAR APART

THE COMPANIONS
R. A. Salvatore

THE GODBORN
Paul S. Kemp

THE ADVERSARY
Erin M. Evans

THE REAVER
Richard Lee Byers

THE SENTINEL
Troy Denning

THE HERALD
Ed Greenwood

Enjoy the entire series now!
Available as audiobooks, ebooks and in print.

Discover more on
DungeonsandDragons.com

SPACE IS NOW UNLIMITED

Hundreds of your favorite D&D novels—even hard to find
and out of print titles by your favorite fantasy authors—
are now also available as ebooks and audiobooks.

Pick the format you prefer
and continue to expand your collection at

DungeonsandDragons.com

Dungeons & Dragons, D&D, Wizards of the Coast, and their
respective logos are trademarks of Wizards of the Coast LLC
in the U.S.A. and other countries. © 2014 Wizards.